# SIEN

Vincent van Gogh & Clasina Maria Hoornik
The greatest love story NEVER told

# SIEN

## LAUREN FRANCES

First published June 2021
Gatecrasher Books, London, England


www.gatecrasherbooks.co.uk


Copyright © 2021 Gatecrasher Books

This is a work of fiction, based on the life of Clasina Maria Hoornik.
Although the characters in it are real, some of the events and places
are dramatised for effect and are an interpretation of events.

Hardback ISBN 978-0-9957515-8-3
Paperback ISBN 978-1-9168998-1-0
eBook ISBN 978-1-9168998-0-3


Cover image by Lauren Frances in the style of Van Gogh's
early drawings – www.instagram.com/labhrai


Design and typesetting www.ShakspeareEditorial.org

To my beautiful daughter
JESSICA

# CONTENTS

# PROLOGUE

$C$lasina Maria Hoornik was born in The Hague on 22nd February 1850, the eldest of eleven children. Her father was Pieter Hoornik, a porter in the poor district of the Geest, and her mother was Maria Wilhelmina Pellers. When they were young, the Hoornik children often relied upon assistance from the public soup kitchen and church charities and, for a time, Sien and some of her brothers lived at a Catholic orphanage. After Pieter died in 1875, Sien was forced to turn to prostitution to help support the family.

Before meeting Vincent van Gogh, Sien had two illegitimate children who died in infancy. She also had a daughter who was born in 1877 and who survived. She first encountered Vincent van Gogh when she was a prostitute in November 1881 – then, about a month later, van Gogh found her wandering the streets with four-year-old Maria Wilhelmina. She was destitute and starving, with addictions to alcohol and tobacco. Van Gogh was on the edge of a nervous breakdown himself: "I must immediately find a woman – or I will freeze and turn into stone." She was ill and in danger of losing her life, due to the post-operative effects of earlier gynaecological surgeries.

In a letter to his brother, Theo, van Gogh describes his second meeting with Sien:

> Last winter I met a woman who walked the
> streets – she had her bread to earn, you'll know
> how. I took that woman on as a model and have
> worked with her all winter. I couldn't pay her
> a model's full daily wages, but I paid her rent

*all the same, and thus far, thank God, I have*
*been able to save her and her child from hunger*
*and cold by sharing my own bread with her.*

Sien posed for a huge number of van Gogh's drawings and paintings, these mostly reflected the difficult life of the working poor. As payment for modelling, van Gogh provided Sien and her daughter with a place to stay and food to eat. He referred to her as "the woman", then "Christien" and finally "Sien". In June 1882, he spent three weeks in hospital with a bout of gonorrhoea which has been attributed by historians to Sien – but it was not her who infected van Gogh, an assumption which this book will set right.

Sien had led an extremely difficult life which, in some ways, made her an ideal match for van Gogh. In July 1882 van Gogh left hospital early, against his doctor's wishes, to take Sien to a free clinic where she gave birth to a son, Willem. This child was van Gogh's, though never confirmed as such, because of Sien's lowly status in life. Looking at the cradle in the poor part of the maternity hospital in Leiden, van Gogh revealed his true feelings for Sien: "I cannot look at this without emotion, for it is a strong and powerful emotion which grips a man when he sits beside the woman he loves with a baby in a cradle near them."

After the birth Sien and van Gogh moved into a larger apartment. He bought a yellow blanket for the baby boy's cradle – yellow became his favourite colour.

Sien required an extended period of recovery from the difficult pregnancy and delivery, but by September she was ready to pose again. The baby boy seemed to bring a lot of happiness to van Gogh. He explained that, while he endeavoured to go deeper as an artist, he was also looking to do so as a man. He lived with Sien in The Hague for nearly two years. The couple survived in abject poverty and their relationship was hot-tempered and volatile, marked by physical and emotional instability. But they loved each other deeply and Sien made the prophesy to van Gogh that would come true when she eventually drowned herself: "Yes, I'm a whore … it's bound to end up with me jumping into the water."

During the two years van Gogh lived in The Hague, he produced more than 50 drawings of Sien. This relationship was the only true domestic life van Gogh ever experienced. Van Gogh longed for a family of his own and, despite his often-volatile relationship with Sien, his letters clearly show the happiness he derived from his time spent with her. Van Gogh decided to marry Sien, as he considered it to be the best way to take care of her and keep her off the streets. However, there was no country in Europe more class-conscious than Holland in the 19th century. It was impossible to break out of the class to which you were consigned by the accident of birth. Vincent came from a religious middle-class family who were deeply scandalised by his association with Sien. They could not allow it to continue.

> People suspect me of something … it's in the
> air … I must be hiding something … Vincent
> is keeping something back that may not be
> divulged. Well, gentlemen, I'll tell you, you who
> set great store by manners and culture, and
> rightly so … provided it's the real thing. What
> is more cultured, more sensitive, more manly, to
> forsake a woman or to take on a forsaken one?

His family and associates, including his brother and supporter, Theo, pressured van Gogh to abandon Sien and her children with the threat of discontinuing their financial support, but he resisted. Finally, at the end of 1883 and following Theo's urging, Sien left van Gogh so as not to have deprived him of his lifeline.

He was devastated and went to paint in Drenthe, then Paris and finally Arles. After her lover's departure, Sien gave her daughter to her mother and gave the baby boy to her brother. She moved to Delft and drifted around to many places and fell back into prostitution. After The Hague, Sien again met up with van Gogh in Paris, at Theo's request, because he couldn't cope with his wayward brother, and again in Arles. The break-up troubled van Gogh so much that he sliced off his left ear in remorse and took it to a brothel, looking for Sien – but she wasn't there. Theo could see that nobody else could bring peace of mind to his wild brother and that it was a mistake to separate the lovers.

Finally, in Auvers-du-Oise, Vincent died of a gunshot wound. It has been recorded that he killed himself, but what actually happened was, both he and Sien were being threatened by a youth with a gun. Sien tried to defend them and the gun went off, wounding van Gogh. The youth fled and van Gogh told Sien to do the same, or she would be charged with murder and sent to the guillotine. He made his way into town and told people he'd shot himself. He died two days later.

After van Gogh's death, Sien told her son that he was the boy's father. She wanted to kill herself, but had to continue living for her two children. She married a seaman, Arnoldús van Wijk, in 1901, to give her son a respectable name, as the van Goghs would have nothing to do with him. The marriage was one defined more by convenience than by love, however, and Sien found that married life provided her with no means of release from her own personal despair and anguish.

Once her children were grown she threw herself into a canal in Rotterdam's harbour on November 12th 1904, aged 54 – ending a life filled with tragedy and profound unhappiness, apart from the times she spent with van Gogh. It fulfilled the prophecy she made to him when they were together.

Van Gogh's relationship with Sien made a huge impact on his way of drawing, and it served to build his character and influence his later, now famous, oil paintings. He helped her when he himself was in need of help and lacking the luxury of money. Van Gogh despaired of her rejection by "respectable society" and the loss of his little family.

*Sien* gives the reader an insight into the life of one of the most enigmatic characters in history. It's her story, told by her, in her own voice. It's a love story in the true sense of the word, between a woman and a man who just wanted to be together, but who weren't allowed that simple desire.

*I love you as certain dark things are loved,*
*secretly, between the shadow and the soul.*

Pablo Neruda

# Note

Ed Hoornik (1910-1970) Dutch poet and nephew of Sien
Mies Hoornik-Bouhuys (1927-2008) Dutch writer and broadcaster (Ed Hoornik's wife)

# CHAPTER 1

# VINCENT

The dogs along Schoolstraat were barking at Maria Wilhelmina and I as we trudged through the cold. Our clogs made soft scraping noises on the snow-covered cobbles and our breath came in steamy jets, forming little clouds in the freezing air. Maria Wilhelmina coughed – I knew she was hungry, but I had nothing to feed her with, nowhere for her to rest her head, no shelter from the cold.

I had to bring my daughter with me when I walked the streets, because my mother had thrown us both out. My daughter was five then, thin and pale and delicate. I hoped she wouldn't die like the others. It was December in the year of 1881 – just after Kerstmis* and not as cold as previous years, but enough to make someone with threadbare clothes shiver. The clock above Grote Sint-Jacobskerk struck ten and we tried to quicken our step. Foxes barked in the distant fields and hawk-owls hooted their frowning disapproval at us from the trees along Visbanken. The wind hid round corners and drove its dagger into us when we turned towards it, and a mist from the Hofvijer crept up along the Riveriervismarkt, enveloping the dim street lighting and making outlines obscure.

Every shadow seemed surreal and threatening.

The smell of poffertjes from a stall made me feel faint and I had to stand for a while, leaning against the wall of a noisy kroeg. Maria Wilhelmina stood with me, shivering in the half-light. Yes, I was a hoer, streetwalking in the Zuidwal – looking for a client or two. Trying to make enough stuivers for a loaf of bread and maybe a room for the night. But today there were no takers and I'd have to find some shelter on the streets for myself and my daughter. I thought about going to my mother's house on Noordstraat with empty pockets. She would be angry – she'd wring her hands and ask how were we going to live. She would shout at me for being so useless – for being abandoned by the men who made me pregnant.

For being a careless fool.

We worked as seamstresses and cleaners, my mother and I, but wages were meagre and never enough to keep the hunger away. So I had to use the only other asset I had – my body – to keep us alive and out of the dreadful poorhouse. Now my body was failing, from bearing three children and an excess of alcohol and tobacco. I looked older than my thirty-two years – I was thin, my bosoms sagged and my skin was grey and marked from malnutrition. Men would not pay much to lie with me anymore and I had to sell myself to the poor unskilled labourers who drank cheap akavit or jenever in the workingmen's tavernes, for whatever they would offer.

We trudged on, Maria Wilhelmina and I, down along Schoolstraat and into Vlamingstraat. I was getting weaker and weaker with each step. I would never be able to make it to a soup kitchen shelter and for sure I would sink down and die on the streets. What would become of my young daughter then? She'd be alone and fall prey to the Wittewijven.

I forced myself to move forward, but the effort made my legs tremble and it was just a matter of time before they gave up altogether. Maria Wilhelmina was tired too. I hated having to bring her with me, but I had no permanent home and my mother couldn't or wouldn't look after her without money. If I got a client, he'd pay for the hire of a room in a bordeel and she'd wait on the stairs for him to leave. Then we'd eat and sleep together until morning. I'd bring what money was left back to my mother and work either sewing or cleaning during the day, then walk the streets again in the evening.

Everything was quiet in the Zuidwal. People were making their way home – getting in out of the cold. The only ones left were the drunks and stray dogs and the streetwalkers like me. A few horse-drawn drays trotted their way through the streets, delivering barrels of bier or crates of vegetables for the next day's trading. Gruff voices of maréchaussée carried on the night air, the flames from their torches glowing like red ghosts in the gloom of the mist. We moved away from them, because they would shout at us and kick us if they came close, maybe even arrest us. Shadows moved past us in the dark, silent and sinister – maybe swarthy gypsies or heidens or zigeuners. I couldn't say for sure, because my vision was becoming blurred and it was difficult to see. I had to sit on the step of a tailor shop. Maria Wilhelmina sat with me.

I don't know how long we stayed there – maybe a minute, maybe an hour. I closed my eyes and allowed my soul to escape my body, to fly away to the warm summer fields that I'd never seen, but only imagined. I could feel the sun on my skin. I could smell the hills and taste the air and I held on to Maria Wilhelmina's hand as we soared together across the cornflower sky.

My mind was dragged back to reality when I heard a male voice. It wasn't harsh and it wasn't soft, it was somewhere in between, and it smelled of absinthe and pipe smoke.

'Hallo.'

I opened my eyes to see a man of medium stature standing over myself and Maria Wilhelmina. He looked younger than me – not more than thirty and he had gember hair and the beginnings of a gember beard.

'Are you alright?'

I nodded my head and stood up, in case he tried to grab Maria Wilhelmina and run off with her. He seemed unsure of himself, fidgety and self-conscious. It was obvious he wanted intimacy of some kind, but was shy about asking for it. I took the initiative.

'Are you looking for company?'

'Yes … yes I am.'

There was a small late-night café across the street and I looked towards it suggestively. He understood.

'Are you hungry?'

'My daughter is.'

'Come with me.'

We crossed the street and into the warmth of the café. The heat and the smell of food overwhelmed me and I almost fainted. The gember man held my arm and guided me to a secluded table in the corner of the room, close to an open fireplace. A serveerster came across and looked at us with a disdainful eye. The man ordered klapstuk, with hutspot and winterpeen, and a bottle of absinthe.

Maria Wilhelmina and I ate quickly and without speaking, while the man smoked his pipe and watched us, occasionally sipping a glass of absinthe. He stood up before we finished eating and left the café. The serveerster watched us suspiciously and I was afraid he would not come back. They would call the maréchaussée and we'd be arrested and thrown into jail. I poured some absinthe and drank it nervously while we waited. He came back about twenty minutes later, sat down and filled both glasses again.

'What's your name?'

'Clasina.'

'Mine is Vincent. We've met before.'

That was men all over, they always thought there was something special about them – different to all the other men. I'd lain with so many of them they blended into one. But he was paying, so I didn't want to hurt his ego. I lied.

'Yes, I remember.'

He held out his hand and I shook it, quite formally. It seemed strange to me and a little ridiculous, considering what we were going to do. I almost laughed, but decided it would be disrespectful to do so.

'About a month ago, in November.'

'Where was that now … ?'

'Close to the canal, I'd been to my cousin's studio. You took me to a little room with a simple bed. You had the child with you, remember?'

'Of course.'

4

I did not. I'd used many little rooms with simple beds in the tavernes by the canal. They were all the same to me. He told me he'd had a bad experience with a woman from Amsterdam during the late summer and had come to The Hague in November in search of a real woman.

'She was perhaps your age, with a silly notion about mystical love.'

'Mystical love?'

'Yes … a frigid devotion to her dead husband.'

They all had their own story, these men, and I listened to them, not really wanting to know. I had my own problems. But it seemed that the gember man had been badly hurt through his encounter with this woman and now he was looking for a kind of solace from me – or had been when we first lay together back in November. Once he mentioned it, I recalled a very vague memory of that occasion. I was stronger and in better health then, even though life had already left its mark on me. He was carrying pencils and chalk and paper which he'd drawn on – that's what I remembered. He must have picked me up by one of the tavernes I used, ones that had rooms for rent by the hour. I don't remember which one, or how long we spent together – not long, I think. Now he was in no hurry and neither was I.

The café did not have rooms like the tavernes, so we would have to find some place for me to perform my part of the bargain.

When the bottle was empty, he ordered another, paid the bill of five stuivers and we left the café. We walked a short distance down Vlamingstraat until we came to a modest herberg. Vincent took us inside and up a flight of narrow stairs. The room was small and bare, but warm, with a little fire. There was a single bed and a wooden table and one chair. An alcove was curtained off and, behind the curtain, was a small cot for Maria Wilhelmina. She was very tired and, after the meal in the café, sleep came quickly to her.

Vincent smoked his pipe and drank from the absinthe bottle he'd taken from the café. There were no glasses in the room and he offered it to me to drink from as well, which I did. He was still unsure of how to approach me and, with the alcohol taking effect, he began to sing a peasant song. It reminded me of the egg dance that I'd seen when I was younger – the peasants would jig wildly around an egg in a chalk circle. He told me that, as a boy, he sang with a clear voice in church and round the parlour piano.

I could not remember how it had been in November but, on that night, when he came to me with my daughter asleep behind the curtain, he was indeed different to the other men. He was a man full of mystery – full of some strange force he didn't even understand himself.

We danced together, slowly at first – so close I could feel his breath on my neck. I was happy to be in out of the winter cold, happy to have eaten for the first time that day. We moved round and round the small room – him singing, humming, to the music in his mind. The absinthe music. My lips accidentally brushed against his. He pulled away slightly. Embarrassed. Almost apologetic.

We began to dance faster. And faster. Round and round. I was weak from malnutrition and exposure, but I didn't try to resist. I allowed my mind to whirl inside my head as the alcohol took hold of my blood – and warmed it. His voice had a velvet sound, humming words from another world I'd never heard before, but knew I'd hear again – inside my head. He held me closer so I wouldn't fly away and it felt as if our bodies were now one, within the wild peasant dance. Joined. Dark and light – or dark and darker. The merging of shadow and silhouette. Two halves of the same hallucination. Part of some inevitable primal force. And I felt an ecstasy I'd not known – but with it came a deep sinking of the soul, as if my very heart would be ripped out and lie bleeding on the poor, bareboard floor.

When we finally lay together, it took him a while to do the deed. Maybe it was the absinthe and maybe it was his lack of experience with real women – maybe both. He was extraordinarily gentle, compared to the men I'd been with in my life. I'd known many men, but I'd never known love. Vincent was full of love, for life and nature and everything around him, but it was a troubled love – like the beating heart of a small bird. It could be easily damaged. Hurt. Crushed. Yet it caressed an essential part of my inner being that believed intrinsically in the old ways of earth and essence.

There wasn't much light in the small room, except for that coming from the flitting red shadows of the fire. An unseasonal scent of celandine hung in the air and the sound of violin music came from somewhere far off – outside in the deserted streets. He had a boyishness about him, even though he was a man – something endearing and indefinable. For once, it seemed perfectly right to be there, with this man. Splendid and surreal and sensuous and sublime all at once. In accordance with the poetry of nature – blending with the shadows and dusky colours and strangely hued chiaroscuros and dancing phantoms in the room.

It was as it was.

And there were three ways of knowing a flame – to be told of it – to see it – and to be burned by it.

I slept well that night, expecting Vincent to be gone in the morning. But he wasn't. He'd brought up some bread and erwtensoep from the herberg downstairs before Maria Wilhelmina and I woke. Now he served breakfast to us as we lay in bed. How wonderful! How could I ask this man for the money I charged for my services?

'What's your name?'

'I told you, Clasina.'

'I mean your full name.'

'Clasina Maria Hoornik.'

But it seemed as if he wasn't listening. He picked at the food, in between puffing on his pipe. He seemed thoughtful, wanting to say something but not knowing how to say it – like he was the previous night.

'My name is Vincent.'

'You told me.'

'Vincent van Gogh.'

When we finished eating, he asked where I lived. How could I tell him I was homeless? So I said I sometimes stayed at my mother's house in Noordstraat, where I helped her to sew clothes and clean kelders. He asked how much he owed me and I said nothing, the cost of the food and room were enough to cover my services. He put his hand in his pocket and gave me a guilder – more than I charged. I didn't want to take the money, but he insisted – and it would be enough to stop my mother's melodrama.

We went back down the narrow stairs and out into the pale morning. The cold made us shiver after the closeness of the room. I shook his hand again and thanked him and was about to walk away.

'Would you model for me?'

'Model?'

'I'm an artist.'

He told me he was about to rent a small studio on the Schenkweg, at the edge of town, and he was looking for people he could draw. He was interested in the working poor and wanted reality in his art. He could not afford to pay me a modelling fee, but he'd give me food and a place to stay whenever I wanted. I told him I knew nothing about posing for an artist, but he didn't mind that – it was part of the authenticity he wanted for his pictures. The natural reality, as he called it. I knew as time went on, I would be able to earn less and less from streetwalking, and his offer of food and a roof when I needed it was good – for just sitting there doing nothing. So I agreed.

'Excellent! Where did you say your mother lived?'

'Noordstraat 16.'

'I'll come for you soon.'

And so began my relationship with Vincent van Gogh. True to his word, he came for me at Noordstraat the following week. My mother was not too pleased about the arrangement. It would take me away from my work as a seamstress and cleaner, and it would interfere with my streetwalking – and there was no profit in it for her. How would she feed herself?

I told her it was time my brother Pieter helped out, he was a grown man now and able to make chairs.

Vincent said he would sketch my mother's house and sell the drawing and she could have the money. He made several sketches, but was unable to sell any of them.

During the winter at the end of 1881, I went with Maria Wilhelmina to Vincent's studio on the Schenkweg and he drew me on paper while I posed. In time, it became more than an artist–model relationship. We became lovers and were, indeed, in love. Vincent was poor as an empty pocket, almost as poor as me, but that didn't matter – in the beginning. He received support from his brother who was an art dealer – money and materials, and that kept us going as best it could.

He first drew me with an umbrella and prayer book, using a pencil and black mountain chalk. Then he drew me sitting on the floor by the fireplace, smoking a cigar – he used pencil and pen and brush and sepia, heightened with white. Then sitting on a chair, wearing a dress like the one the woman from Amsterdam used to wear, before she rejected his proposal of marriage and humiliated him. He also drew my mother, wearing a cap and shawl.

Though we were always poor and hungry, those were happy times for me – getting to know the gember man, falling in love for the first time, like a young girl. I could already read and write, as I'd learned to do so while in the Catholic orphanage. But Vincent made me see and understand other things – he showed me things. Did things to me – to what was inside me. Not just carnal things, more than that. He made me a woman inside. Treated me like a woman – not like a dog. I wanted to be treated like a woman, I could take it, the challenge of our closeness – the equality of our relationship.

Sometimes he sang to me in different languages – songs like the English "Greensleeves" that made me want to weep, or the French "Alouette" that made me feel like dancing, or the Dutch "Alleluja Den Blijden Toon" which made me believe I was in an older time long ago. His singing made me feel so alive. More than alive. Eternal. Part of everything.

With him. I soared up into the sky and knew what I was, what I really was. Without him the songs were not the same. I tried singing them on my own and they weren't the same. Something was missing.

Vincent was very well educated and he spoke to me about many things – sometimes when we were naked on the bed in the studio. And his voice was velvet, like when I heard it on the steps of the tailor shop, looking down at me in my dream. His words were little kisses on my ears. And he laughed at things other people didn't laugh at – didn't think about. Things I didn't think about – until he told me. Then I thought about them all the time. He was more than a man. Or maybe he wasn't and it was just that the others were less than men. He showed me things I had not seen before. Taught me things. How to live. How to love. How to listen.

And laugh.

Would he teach me how to cry, even though I had cried many times in the past? Really cry – the lament that comes from within a broken heart. Was that the next lesson? Was it something I had to learn, to be a real woman, not a false, sterile phantom – someone I might have been without him? To be a woman with a deeper light – a more profound identity. With a soul that any man could float away on. A woman who needed no man to make her whole but who could accommodate men if she felt like it – if it was something she wanted. Vincent would make me that kind of woman.

With time.

# CHAPTER 2

# BRECHTJE

Even now, as I stand on the side of the wide canal in Rotterdam's harbour and look down into the black, swirling maelstrom of water, it feels as if I'm back there, dancing with the gember man, feeling his breath on my neck, hearing his humming in my ear. Memories are real things, they can be seen and touched and felt – like diamonds. Or pain. They remind us of who we once were – who we will never be again.

They say life is sacred, but some lives are not sacred at all, they are ignominious and brutal and misunderstood. Yet they have to be lived until they end or until we decide to end them. They are part of what we call being, for want of a better definition. Part of everything. And everything that lives moves – or seems to. Nothing is constant. Nothing can be depended upon to remain. Some things I would have liked to remain and others I would have liked to change.

Yes, everything is transient. At one time the fear of death was just as real as the fear of life for me. Now the dark water calls. It is the only alternative. Vincent is dead and I must follow him. I hear him calling from the water. Crying. For me to come to him. My choices and the circumstances of my birth have moved me to this moment – through the infinite worlds of a future that already exists and a past that has always been there.

But to truly know the story of me and Vincent, it is necessary to first know something of the story of me.

I was born Clasina Maria Hoornik on 22nd February 1850. I was the eldest of eleven children – nine brothers and one sister – born on a night when rain came falling down in sheets from the dark low-lying, crow-flying sky. I didn't want to be here, in this world. I wanted to stay where I was, in the womb where it was warm and safe. But I couldn't keep in there, my mother did not want me to, so I was sent tumbling out into the poverty-stricken life that God had given me.

As the industrial revolution in Europe began attracting workers to the cities, the rich people left to live in residential areas on the outskirts and their big houses became slums. Rooms were divided up, making way for more and more families – floors were added with low ceilings and stairs were nothing more than ladders. Water was only available from handpumps in the streets and there was always a long queue, this contributed to frequent outbreaks of cholera and tuberculosis.

My father was Pieter Hoornik, a blacksmith and railway porter who lived in the poor district of the Geest, which was a deprived area of The Hague then, and my mother was Maria Wilhelmina Pellers. They lived in a house in Noordstraat – a house that was large and shared by many families. It was damp and candlelit and we had two rooms to begin with, when I was born. Later, when the others came along, we had three rooms – one for cooking and eating and two for sleeping.

Rain came through the roof and the floor was wooden and broken, so the soil underneath was often wet and oozed through the boards. We had few beds and, when my brothers and sister were born, it became very crowded. My father slept on a cot and I slept with my mother and my young sister. Four of the boys slept in two bunks and two more in hammocks, with the other three on the floor, when they were not in the orphanage, wrapped up in rough hessian. The rooms were flea- and rat-ridden and we lay on mattresses made from sacking filled with straw. There was a brick fireplace for cooking and a bench for sitting on.

Nothing else.

They had no furniture, my parents, so they made a table out of one of the doors and supported it on one end with crude batten legs with the other end fixed to the wall. They collected other bits and pieces of furniture over a period, until the place was at least liveable in for a fast-growing family.

If you could afford it, you could buy from water-sellers, otherwise collect rain, or bucket it from the canals, where the people threw their excrement and sometimes dumped dead bodies. No matter where it came from, the water was never clean – it was very dangerous and full of disease and infection.

The privy was a small hut with no door and a seat with a circular hole in the middle, which led down into a pit to hold the excrement. It was common to the whole street and located outside in a courtyard. The waste wasn't washed away, it fell into the pit underneath and stayed there until it was collected by the night-soil men, who were paid by the landlords. Some landlords did not want to pay for this service and the cesspits overflowed. Rubbish was dumped in the streets and collected infrequently by horse-drawn tipcarts.

The city was frequently plagued by fatal diseases like tuberculosis, typhoid, scarlet fever and cholera, caused by contaminated drinking water and poor hygiëne and they killed many people in the time when I was young. The doctors thought the germs were spread through bad air that they called "miasma". Pigs, cattle, horses, chickens and geese soiled the streets and it was said that sailors could smell the city twenty kilometres out to sea. Because of such poor living conditions and lack of light, air and healthy food, there were many orphaned children on the streets.

I remember seeing one such child dying from cholera when I was a girl. The youngster began to vomit, then got diarrhoea, its skin turned a blue-black colour and its eyes sank into its face. Its skin went cold. All the people in the neighbourhood could do was watch in pity as the young girl slowly expired and be thankful it wasn't them or their child. And it's strange and elusive how some far-off things never fade from memory and other more recent events disappear quickly, like evaporating mist over a river.

Vincent was born twice – the first time on 30th March 1852, when I was two years and one month old. But he was dead and they buried him. He was born for the second time exactly a year later, on 30th March 1853, when I was three years and one month old. Both times in the town of Groot-Zundert in the Brabant region, ninety kilometres from The Hague and close to the border with Belgium. Zundert was a country village, inhabited by simple folk – his father was a minister in the Dutch Reform Church and some of his uncles dealt in art. Even though I was only three years and one month old, I remember the night he was born again – it was full of stars. I don't remember the first time, either because I was too young or because he was dead and didn't light up the night. On 30th March 1853 I looked up at the sky and knew that something rare and strange was happening, but I didn't know what it was. My child's mind was not capable of understanding what I understand now, it just seemed for a moment or two that the hunger in my belly had gone away and been replaced by a feeling of warm fullness.

Pieter Hoornik worked long hours, while he was able, before he became sick – sometimes from early morning to late evening, first as a blacksmith and then as a railway porter. Even so, his wages were meagre and barely enough to survive on. My mother was a seamstress, when she wasn't having children – I came first, in the year 1850, then one every year after that until 1860. There was no state support for us poor people back then – no safety net to slip through. Myself and my younger brothers and sister often relied upon the public soup kitchens to prevent us from starving. There were church charities as well, that were contributed to by the better off, to ease their consciences for taking more than they needed and leaving so little for us.

Vincent drew pictures of the public soup kitchen when we were living together. I was talking about them and he asked me what they were like, so I described the scene to him.

Maria Wilhelmina and I posed there while he painted and drew on several different occasions. I don't know where those pictures are now – probably lost forever.

As well as sewing and cleaning kelders, my mother washed clothes for money. She used homemade soap that was constructed from the guts of pigs, mixed with ash and soda crystals and boiled up, then left to go solid. It smelled bad, but washed well. I had to collect firewood from the streets and the woods on the outskirts of town and fetch water from the shallow parts of the grachten and boil it as best I could so it wouldn't kill us when we drank it. When the family grew larger, I would help my mother to cook what little food we could afford. The larger the family grew, the harder it became.

My mother was not a soft woman, life was too hard for her to be sentimental – and love was not a word that was ever said or even understood by her. Pieter Hoornik, on the other hand, was a soft man. He was light-hearted and felt things inside his soul. Maybe my mother did too, but she never showed it. My father liked to laugh and dance with me and he told me stories that came from another world, perhaps a world he caught glimpses of in his job as a porter. As the family grew larger and life grew more laborious, which was mainly his fault, the laughter grew less – until it stopped altogether and lead replaced the lightness inside his head.

When I was six, my mother taught me to sew and I helped her to earn a few stuivers. At other times I would beg in the streets with the younger ones at my side, to keep them away from my mother while she worked. There was a girl called Brechtje Vos who came by with food for us when she was able to. She was a beautiful person and I was in love with her – even though I didn't know what love was at the time. She wore nice clothes and her hair was cut fashionably and her skin was soft and white. My clothes were ragged and I cut my own hair and my skin was rough from work and weather. I had neten on my head and rashes on my skin and I was always filthy dirty. But we found that closeness children develop, Brechtje and me, whether they are poor or rich, clean or dirty – that connection of childhood, before the prides and prejudices are learned from the adults. It wasn't as if she felt sorry for me or I felt reverence for her – it was just a gentle affection for each other that two innocents experienced when our small hands reached out across the dissolute chasm that divided us.

We begged in the marketplace, where the traders welcomed the farmers and they bartered together. But we weren't welcome there – they treated us like outcasts – little zigeuners – inferior – and would chase us away. If we stole, we had to be stealthy, like animals. If they caught us, they would beat us. Or we would sometimes break into the local school and take whatever food had been discarded by the teacher and the children who could afford to go there.

Brechtje was about my age, but she had an older brother called Christoffel Martinus who tried to make me take off my clothes, which was very embarrassing for a six-year-old like me. He tried to do things to me I knew were not right. He said his father was an officer in the maréchaussée and he'd have my parents thrown into gevangenis if I didn't do what he wanted me to. Christoffel and his friends would sometimes surround me on the street and push me from one to the other and stick their hands up my grey skirt. I felt contaminated inside and believed I'd slowly rot away and the sin would show itself on the outside and everyone would know how bad I was and I'd surely go to hell. Being an ignorant child back then, I believed this treatment was normal and a part of my life for being so poor. I accepted it because it was what happened to wretched girls like me.

I did not know then that Christoffel would marry a woman called Cornelia Stricker, who Vincent would fall in love with after she became a widow. She would spurn the gember man's affections and drive him to The Hague, where he would meet me. So, in a strange and indirect way, Christoffel would become an instrument of fate in my future.

Time passed so slowly in that far-off life – weeks like months and days like weeks and hours like days. Everything was moving, but it didn't seem so – to me at least. I believed time to be inanimate, so it couldn't move, and I was only moving within my own limited concept of what time should be. By the year 1860, my friendship with Brechtje had grown into something that was more than mere sisterhood. It was special. We kept company when she wasn't at school and we planned for our future together. We would go away and buy a house and live happily ever after. One day Christoffel and his friends came upon us. They beat me and dragged Brechtje away.

I never saw my friend alive again.

I knew nothing about anything back then – except looking after my brothers and the hardships of hand to mouth. But I'm not complaining. I knew no better and believed it was my own fault for being born poor, so I just got on with it. Surviving from day to day was the only reality in my little life. I was an urchin, blown like thistledown hither and thither, spilled like water from an open hand, a thing with no face, frightened by the bat and the rat and the club-footed ghoul. But it made me hard and able to survive on the streets – to give as good as I got. For a while. Until, over the years, the constant struggle drove me down into desolation – where I was when the gember man found me.

When I first met him, I thought that Vincent had been an artist all his life, that he dreamed about being a painter when he was a boy. Not so. He had little interest in art as a child, no more than any other boy, that is. He told me, when we lay together at the house in Schenkweg, that he was a very serious and sensitive jongen who preferred solitude to the companionship of others. Of course, he always loved nature – flowers and birds and bees and things like that, things you find in the fields, things I knew not much about, being a city girl. He liked to take walks through the countryside with his mother Anna and his nanny, Leentje Veerman. He loved his mother, but Anna never really understood her eldest son. To her, he was filled with starry-eyed notions and, as time went on, she liked him less and less.

Vincent was a village child, playing among the beds of marigolds, mignonette and red geraniums in his parents' garden, watching the colours change from sunrise to sunset. Snow-white linen was stretched across the bleaching field to dry, enclosed by berry bushes and a beech hedge and separated from the fields of wheat and rye that stretched away into the distance. Fruit farms populated the adjacent countryside and the Grote Beek flowed under a white bridge.

How idyllic, how so much different from my own childhood. He told me himself that he was a strange boy, despite the apparent enchantment of this upbringing. He looked like his mother and shared her fretful view of life. He was obstinate, self-willed and difficult to deal with. His father punished him more often and more severely than any of the other van Gogh children, and so, he felt increasingly alone and rejected.

When he was outside, he walked with a bent back and his head hanging, his gember hair hidden under a straw hat, his face older than its years, his eyes sometimes blue and sometimes green. But I'm sure that, despite his early awkwardness and gloomy appearance, he held inside himself the beginnings of the deep inner emotions that made him so complicated in later years, but which were also destined to destroy him.

He could read and write by the age of seven and he consumed books with breathless speed. When he wasn't reading, he spent his time watching and thinking. He would go to places where no one else of his bourgeois class went – where peasants cut peat and shepherds pastured their sheep and where smugglers roamed.

He preferred always to be alone and shunned the company of his younger brothers and sisters – except for Theodorus. He was always close to Theo and the younger boy worshipped his older brother more than was imaginable. But Theo was a sickly child and not nearly as robust as Vincent. They differed too in disposition – Vincent was dark and suspicious, while Theo was bright and outgoing. While

Vincent brooded, Theo was cheerful. But all that was before art, which the gember man didn't think about at all, except at rare intervals – like when he modelled an elephant from sculptor's clay that someone gave him, or when he drew a cat for his mother. Spontaneous expressions that were few and far between. Forgotten now. Dead as the man to whom such memories belonged.

In those days, Vincent was more interested in going down to the stream with a bottle and a net to catch water insects, beetles especially, and things with spindly legs and compound eyes and shiny metal colouring. They all had Latin names, which Vincent knew, and he pinned them into a little box which was lined with white paper, with the name of each carefully pasted above it. He also knew the places where the rarest flowers grew, forget-me-nots and pink water lilies – and the birds, he knew all the birds and the sound of their song. He knew their nests and how they lived and he could get close enough to watch them without making a sound. Nature spoke to him with a thousand voices and a million colours – and he listened.

And saw.

How do I know all this? Because he told me, over and over – many times. It was in such stark contrast to the place where I grew up, with its hungry streets and crowded houses – the constant threat of violence and even death. When Vincent spoke of his wonderland, I listened and saw it in my mind's eye. I went back there with him in my imagination and I was a girl again, climbing the stacks of dried pea-vines and sliding back down, laughing. Tripping along the stream, feeling the coolness of the sand beneath my bare feet and dipping my hands into the delicious water. Picking the flowers, braiding them in my hair. Lying in the high grass in summertime, while the little donkeys grazed round my ears, with elderflowers laced in their bridles to keep the flies away. And the bees buzzing and the butterflies flitting and my eyelids heavy in the heady air.

That's how Vincent spoke to me, with words that formed pictures, even more beautiful than the ones he drew. Later, I came to know that life was not quite as wonderful as he made it seem. Zundert was, in fact, a wasteland of swamp and heath, windswept and treeless. He was never a full part of the happy family group, his awkwardness compelling him to shy away from people and always seek solitude. This aloofness, as some considered it to be, was not being sullen or morose, but simply an inability to give himself, even to those he loved. He would not learn how to do that, how to give himself completely, until he met me. His memories of Zundert conjured, as is sometimes the case when we are distant from a place or a period, rosier colours than they actually were. Conceptions are often clouded by time or distance or both. Nevertheless, Vincent's nostalgia for the life of his early youth was real, even if the fact of it was not.

But that life was not to last for him. He was sent away to boarding school at the age of eleven and it ceased to exist.

Just as it had never existed for me.

I couldn't bear not seeing Brechtje, so I had to go to the Calvinist Quarter where she lived. I didn't know which house was hers, but I asked some people and they sent me towards a medium-sized building near to the Statenkwartier. I waited under a lamp post every morning for two days – but she did not emerge. I was afraid to go to the house in case someone there might beat me. Maybe her parents sent her away somewhere. I knew she had an aunt in Amsterdam and maybe they'd sent her there to get her away from me. Maybe she would never be allowed to come back, until we were both too old to go away together and buy a house and live happily ever after.

It made me cry.

Finally, after two days of waiting, I decided I had to go to find out what happened to her, even if it meant risking a beating. When I got there, I saw a lot of unusual activity outside. Carriages were pulling up and people were going into the house. I stayed some distance away and waited, hoping

Brechtje would come out and I could wave to her and she'd come to me. I waited for a long time, but there was no sign of her. People were coming and going and I assumed there must be an occasion – maybe a birthday or an anniversary or something. Then Christoffel appeared at the door. I moved round the corner in case he saw me. I watched him for a while and noticed he looked sad. His head hung down and he stared at the ground. Then I realised he was crying. I decided to approach him. Cautiously.

'Christoffel … '

He didn't answer. He didn't even seem to notice me.

'Why are you crying?'

When he looked at me, it was as if he didn't see me – as if he was looking through me. His voice was hoarse when he spoke.

'It's Brechtje … '

'What? What about Brechtje?'

'She's dead.'

What he said did not actually register itself in my brain for a moment or two. I thought I had misheard him – that he'd said "cheese bread" or "she's fled" or something like that. But it slowly sank in that he was telling me Brechtje had died. I screamed and sank to my knees. Christoffel just turned and walked back into the house. I stayed on the ground, sobbing, feeling a pain inside like a hot knife was burning my heart. If Brechtje was dead, I would have to die too. But first I had to see her, in case Christoffel was playing a cruel joke on me.

I got to my feet and followed some people in through the front door. I tried to make myself invisible, so her family wouldn't see me and throw me back out on the street. I followed the flow of visitors to a room and saw Brechtje lying on a bed. She was dressed in a white blouse and a black skirt. She looked different. Older. More grown up. Not the young girl who had made friends with me and brought me food when she could. Her eyes were closed and there was a kind of half smile on her face. She didn't look dead, just pretending. I wanted to go over and shake her and tell her to get up because she was upsetting me.

Her family were all there and people kept coming and going all the time, paying their respects. Then a man saw me and pushed me out and closed the door. I found myself in another room with a long wooden table. The table was laden with food and people were helping themselves to bread and meat. But, for the first time in my life, I wasn't hungry. At any other time this would have been like Kerstmis and I would have gorged myself until I threw up, but now that food meant nothing to me – it was revolting. And it was equally revolting to see people stuffing it into their mouths without caring.

Just then, some men came through, carrying a long white box. They went into the room where Brechtje was lying and I watched from the open doorway as they placed her in the box. She did not wake up. She was really dead.

I left the house.

Outside, I was thinking about how I would kill myself and follow Brechtje to heaven. But I didn't have the courage to do it and I was afraid of the pain. Later, I visited her grave and knelt and said a prayer that I made up myself.

> *Als tranen een trap konden bouwen*
> *En herinneringen een weg*
> *Ik zou regelrecht naar de hemel lopen*
> *En bring je weer terug*

Someone told me she died of cholera from drinking contaminated water – I thought only poor people like me died of that. Obviously not. I lost track of time and just wandered aimlessly about. There was no hope of a better life now – all the simple plans I'd made with Brechtje would never come true. I didn't have the courage to kill myself and I knew if I tried, I would only fail. But then I realised there was no need to – I possessed Brechtje in death, her memory. The remembrance of our small friendship was mine alone. To keep. No one could take it away from me.

Ever.

# CHAPTER 3

# THE ORPHANAGE

Of course, back then, neither Vincent nor I knew that our lives were on a converging course – moving closer and closer until they finally collided.

Loneliness grew to define his childhood. He later said that his youth was gloomy and cold and sterile, far from the idyll of younger years. Despite his earlier connection with his mother, just like me with mine, he grew apart from his parents as he got older. He retreated into nature and books, just as I would, once I learned how to read at the orphanage. Back then he was still religious, as I was – him Protestant and me Catholic. At school he was uncooperative and often had his ears boxed by the master, which led to him staying away a great deal. His mother blamed the proximity with peasant boys at the school and withdrew him, saying it had made him coarse. She hired a governess who taught Vincent at home, but that got on his father's nerves.

By contrast, school was not an option for me, I had to work and take care of my younger brothers. Yet I knew, or at least sensed, that something was being denied me – something I had a right to. It was being denied me because I was weak, in order to keep me weak. They said I would be rewarded for my innocence and superstition in the next life. It was a lie, perpetrated by the powerful. A little knowledge is a dangerous thing – but complete ignorance is a crime. Knowledge is necessary to know truth. And truth is not absolute, it is multiple and contradictory, either known or not known. And a thought, once created, is as real as a stone. It is indestructible. I think like that now, but not then, not before I met Vincent. He taught me how to think like that. He taught me many things, things even he himself didn't really understand.

At the time I was visiting Brechtje's grave, Vincent was passing by his own grave, every time he went to church in Zundert. By the time he was ten, he had a brother and three sisters, with another brother yet to come. Vincent's closeness to Theo, who was four years younger than him, was a closeness that would last all their lives. He always spoke about Zundert and his young life there. He talked about it with a wistful voice and a faraway look in his eye. Sometimes a tear would roll down his cheek and he'd wipe it away quickly, before it was followed by others. I loved to listen, because his childhood seemed so picturesque compared to mine. For me, poverty overwhelmed everything else. It lay on me like a shroud and tried to smother me.

It was common for poor children to be sent to the orphanage when things became too difficult at home, to give the parents a breathing space. This happened to me and my brothers from time to time. The orphanage in The Hague was run by the Catholics. Girls and boys were kept separate and were supervised by a House Father and a House Mother. We had to wear orphanage clothes while there and, when we went out for walks, everybody knew where we came from. When we were together, just like the soup kitchens, Vincent drew a herd of orphans with their spiritual shepherds – girls with their white smocks and caps and boys in their coarse grey suits. It reminded me of my own time there.

The orphanage itself was a huge building, much bigger than anything I'd ever seen and the rules inside it were strict. But it was where I learned to read and write and for that I am thankful. The older girls had to take care of the younger ones, which wasn't a hardship for me, as I was used to taking care of my younger brothers. We would also be taken to local farms and put to work doing whatever seasonal jobs needed to be undertaken. It was cheap labour for the farmers, but we were fed better than when we lived at home.

The Catholics were dismayed when they learned I had never been to school, so it was arranged that I would go to lessons in the mornings and work in the afternoons and evenings. The school was a small room with a little kitchen and a wooden floor that us children had to wash after lessons. There was one classroom with a blackboard and not enough desks for the dozen or so pupils that went there at any one time. The teacher's name was Lotte and she came from outside to teach us and sometimes she slept in the kitchen. In winter, it became too cold for us to hold our pencils, because we had no gloves. So Lotte would send us out into the sun, whenever it shone, to warm our hands. And I would daydream, like my father, in the golden glow, and try to think about all the things there must be in the big world. I wanted to know about it all – everything. I wanted to drink from the pierian spring of knowledge that had been denied to me. And my wishes flew up into the air and stayed there, like silver moths.

I liked the orphanage school and I was a quick and eager learner. Life wasn't so bad there, while it lasted. I had two meals a day and as much milk as I could drink when I worked on the farms. Lotte was a very kind and pretty woman and she treated me as if I was her daughter, I don't know why – maybe she saw some potential in me? If so, it was potential that was never realised. But I learned to read, to write, to know about things I'd never known about before. Later, when I met Vincent, I'd learn how to think for myself, to agree and to argue, to say what I thought, even if it was wrong. And, if it was wrong, to have the ability to realise that and to put it right.

Lotte bought ointment to get rid of my rashes and picked the nits from my hair, but she couldn't do anything for the worms that distended my stomach and wriggled out, sometimes through my nose. On Sundays, I would go to Mass with the other girls and listen to the priest tell us about hell and damnation, things that were waiting for us when we grew up. Little did he realise that some of us did not have to wait until we were grown to experience such monstrosities. I never liked the Catholic religion, even though it afforded me a basic education. It was unfriendly and guilt-ridden, always threatening, and it put less value on a girl than it did on a boy. Which angered me sometimes.

Lotte made me a green skirt out of some leftover material, to replace my tattered grey one, but I didn't like it because it was too tight and my distended belly made me look as if I was carrying a child. She also gave me a pair of clogs and it was the first time I had ever worn anything on my feet. They felt strange and took me a while to get used to. It was as if my feet had suddenly turned to wood and they made my skin sore, even though it was rough and hard from being barefoot.

Our stays at the orphanage were always short. My father would come and get us when things improved at home and we'd have to go back to Noordstraat. You would imagine I'd want to stay, that I wouldn't want to go back to the slum, but no, it wasn't like that. When I was in the orphanage, I suffered from nightmares that my mother had either died or been killed. Despite my love for my father, I also missed my mother. You see, I felt guilty for being happy – guilty about the food I was eating when my mother had nothing. It's hard to believe that I would want to go back to the hunger and dirt and violence of Noordstraat when I was happy in the little wooden school with Lotte. But I did. I wanted to go back to my mother. Something deeper than the small happiness I experienced was pulling me – that ancient thing which is ingrained in all of us – written into our creatureness.

Our blood.

I was always very popular with the other street children when I came back the orphanage. Everyone wanted to know all about it – what I'd learned about reading and writing. They wanted to know what it was like to drink milk – to wash every day – to use a proper privy – not to be hungry. Gradually, I began to feel different somehow, not like them anymore. I'd experienced something that had changed me, even if I didn't know it. I told them lots of stories – some were true and others were made up, to enhance my new status. But I was worried about meeting Christoffel Vos in my green skirt, the one that made me look fat. Maybe he liked green more than grey – maybe he envied green more than grey – maybe he would want to hurt green more than he wanted to hurt grey. I hadn't seen him since that day outside Brechtje's house when he was crying. When I did see Christoffel Martinus again, from a distance. He seemed distracted and didn't bother with me. Maybe he was afraid to, because anyone who had learned about reading and writing was respected.

Or maybe he just didn't like green.

Our house was cramped and dirty and everyone smoked, even my younger brothers. We smoked rough tobacco in clay pipes and my mother drank cheap jenever when she could afford it. All this seemed perfectly normal before I went to the orphanage but, after being there a few times, I realised there was something better. Maybe not better, but different. I learned that there should be choices in life, not just unrelenting fate. I didn't want to have to live as my mother lived, from hand to mouth, from one day to the next, without any hope of improvement. During the time I was with Lotte at the orphanage, I felt guilty for experiencing a small piece of happiness. But gradually I came to believe it was something I was entitled to – waking up each morning and not having to fight over a crust of bread – having a woollen trui to put on when it was cold – to wash before bedtime. As time went by, a dissatisfaction with my life began to envelope me.

Once I grew to be eleven years old, I didn't go to the orphanage again, just my brothers. I'd already learned to sew, but now it was time to be a seamstress and to put that as my occupation on census forms. The work was hard and the hours were long. The wages were meagre, barely enough to survive on. My father was often ill and, when he was out of work, things became even harder for the family.

And so the young years went on, until I was thirteen.

When Vincent was eleven, on a dull, overcast day in October 1864, his mother and father took him to the town of

Zevenbergen. They left him on the steps of a boarding school and drove away. He later wrote to his brother Theo about it, saying how he watched the yellow carriage moving further into the distance, wet with rain, and the bare trees on either side of the road waving goodbye. He felt cast off – set adrift and forsaken.

Zevenbergen was twenty-five kilometres to the north of Zundert and Vincent was distressed to leave the family parsonage, even though he was never really a fully participating member of it. He was homesick for what was familiar to him, what was the normality of his introspection. Exactly the opposite to me. The Provily School was an expensive place, populated by the sons and daughters of government officials and wealthy merchants. Vincent's father was not rich, so he expected his son to study hard and achieve greatness. But Vincent just felt unhappy and abandoned and was overwhelmed by even more loneliness.

His days at the Provily School were dark and paralysing for such a sensitive boy with a strange temperament. He was the youngest student there and he felt totally out of place – a gember-haired country boy with a short temper. When his father came to visit, Vincent flung his arms round the man's neck and pleaded to be brought home, but the father refused. Vincent wrote many homesick letters over the next two years, and his father finally agreed to allow him to leave Zevenbergen – but not to come home. Instead, he was sent to the Rijksschool Willem II in Tilburg, even further away from Zundert.

Neither of us had any idea of the extraordinary circumstances that would throw us together later on. Our lives continued, with me sewing and cleaning and Vincent learning. The Hague I grew up in was a place unknown to Vincent until he came to live and work there. Even then, he would not see it through my eyes – the bleak side of the city, a side which was a vivid narrative of infant mortality, illegitimacy, poverty and exploitation. Vincent would see it through his artist's eyes – see redemption in the darkness.

The kind of sewing my mother and I did at home was unreliable, underpaid and underlit and often led to blindness in women. Unregulated workshops paid a pittance for long hours in bad conditions because women's work was considered to be secondary to men's. It was always undervalued, even by benevolent employers. My mother and I were classified as seamstresses and cleaners by the officials to cover the shame of destitution and its inevitable consequences. Church charity and public assistance provided only the thinnest insulation from catastrophe. For anything more, it was prostitution.

Prostitution offered money when it could not be found elsewhere. But competition was fierce – a profession that needed no qualifications, apart from a reasonable body, drew women from all over Holland, and even other countries, to the bier halls and tavernes and brothels of cities like The Hague and Amsterdam and Rotterdam and Utrecht. Campaigns for public health and decency, popular with the puritans and the pulpiteers, only pushed prostitution into larger enclaves and created an underworld of nocturnal sweatshops, which were just as crushing and inescapable as the women's day time workshops.

It was what lay ahead of me, but I did not know it.

Even though I was streetwise and hardened, I was still a girl and untouched, apart from the times when Christoffel and his friends tried to assault me. But that was over, I never saw Christoffel Vos much after Brechtje died and, even if I caught an odd glimpse of him now and then, he always ignored me.

From the age of eleven I grew quickly and, by the age of thirteen, I looked like a woman. I developed bosoms, which was a source of annoyance to me because I wasn't emotionally mature enough to deal with the attention from men in the street. Then I began to bleed with the menses and the onset brought doubts and delusions about my future. It was constantly implied that I was "my mother's daughter" and that seemed to be proof enough of my natural progression to a life of sin.

At least, that was the poisonous perception some people held, engendering a feeling of shame in me for becoming a young woman. I did not know what they meant as, to me, my mother was a hard-working woman. She could be unforgiving, but surely that was nothing to be ashamed of? The constant insinuations left me with a fear that I might be contaminated with whatever was wrong with my mother, even though I didn't know what that could be. I had already built up a reputation as a headstrong and spirited girl, but it was only because I asked questions and had an enquiring brain that was trying to know more than they wanted me to.

Once, when I was with my father, he left me outside a taverne on Vondelstraat and warned me not to talk to strangers. I was sitting on a long bench and a drunken man emerged and blew a kiss at me, then he came closer and lunged at me. My father heard me shouting for him and he came and pushed the man away.

'I told you not to encourage strangers, Clasina.'

'I did not encourage him.'

He just shook his head and we went home. After that, I stopped talking to men, even ones I knew, and avoided any situation that might be interpreted as encouraging.

Any money I earned from sewing or cleaning had to be given straight to my mother. On one occasion, I drank from her bottle of jenever, but vomited afterwards. This brought more wrath down upon me and, that night, I found myself locked out and alone on the dark, cold street. I went to the orphanage and asked if they could let me live there permanently. They allowed me to sleep there that night, but informed my father where I was the next day. He came and took me home. I was finding that I didn't really fit in anywhere – not at home on Noordstraat or in the orphanage or with other street people. So I kept to myself and was shunned by the other girls of my age in the area.

I remember once a group of them were whispering and laughing behind their hands and speaking in some kind of code they had devised. I couldn't take any more of it, so I just exploded and started fighting and punching. I was grabbed by a politieagent and taken to the maréchaussée station. They kept me there for five hours before telling my father, and they made me feel so ashamed, even though I had done nothing to be ashamed of. But the others left me alone after the attack. I became fiery and argumentative and people kept away from me. I said I didn't care about any of them, even though I was crumbling inside from the lack of love or a sense of belonging in life. I became disruptive and used to set fires and steal from the markets and go into the woods and eat poison mushrooms that made me see visions and the family threatened to have me put into an asylum.

Just as Vincent's later did with him.

I was an urchin, with dirt under my fingernails and unruly hair and my brother's britches rolled up to my knees and people I passed in the street scowled at me. My clothes were always hand-me-downs from the church jumble and my mother did not seem to care much what I had to put up with on the street – then, I never said much to her as she had enough to worry about. I only knew one way to deal with people my age and that was with my fists. Once, I had a fight with one of the unruly boys. He was always picking on me like Christoffel used to and I wasn't going to take any more. He hit me with a stick, so I hit him back. It escalated and I ended up giving him a nosebleed. I got a reputation after that, which I did not want. I just wanted so much to be like Brechtje and not grotesque. Not deviant or shapeless or grey. I wanted to learn – to add to what had been given to me at the orphanage and be a good person. But I knew that would never be the case, so I just had to be who I was.

I used to plait my hair at night so next morning it would fall about my face in ringlets. I was the only girl on Noordstraat to have such long hair – it was right down my back – and I had dark eyes and straight teeth that I inherited from my mother. I also loved music and would go to a small church on some wasteground in the evenings to hear a choir singing. I didn't know if it was Catholic or Protestant or any other religious denomination and I didn't care. I just went there for the music.

On this night it was chilly when the sun fell behind the horizon and I wished I had a coat to keep me warm. Spectres played hide and seek along the narrow, bush-lined lane – ghostly hands, touching me with cold fingers. Ghostly sounds and smells and fleeting shadows that disappeared when I turned my head. I wasn't frightened. I knew they weren't real, just figments of my wild imagination.

I shivered as I walked. The ghosts screamed at me from the trees, they ran around me and away across the fields to some place I didn't know. To wherever they lived. It was dark now and no moon or stars were visible in the night sky. A strange wind played among the branches of the trees and whispered their terms of endearment in my ear – words I didn't want to hear. When I got to the church, there was no singing. The lights were dim, but I could see candles flickering up near the altar. They cast an eerie light over a coffin, standing motionless in the gloom on a wooden frame. The sight startled me and I wanted to leave, but I told myself I didn't have to be frightened – the choir would come soon.

I moved slowly forward and came level with the coffin. It was closed, with wreaths of flowers resting on the lid. Nobody came, so I decided it was time to leave. I moved quickly to the main door, where I had come in, but I was unable to open it. I moved forward again, towards the chancel door. I turned the metal handle but the door didn't open. I tried again, but it was locked from the other side. I took a candle from the altar and went back to the main door to try again, but it still would not open. There was no way out.

I lit more candles, placing them in a ring so I was encircled by the flickering light. I didn't know why, but it seemed to me that I would be safe within the circle. Outside was darkness, but I was protected within the ring of light – protected from what, I didn't know. Time meant nothing in that place, so it stood still. Every time a candle started to burn down, I replaced it with a fresh one. After a while, as the temperature fell, I began to sob – inside the circle of light.

The ring of candles flickered violently as a breeze came from somewhere and blew at the flames. I rocked myself to and fro and hummed a tune that I remembered from long ago. All the darkness outside the circle was filled with ghosts. They moved round the ring of light and asked to be let in. I told them to go away, but they wouldn't. I shouted at them and they disappeared for a time, but came back again and again. I kept the candles lit and rocked and hummed.

As the night wore on, there were no more candles on the altar to keep the circle intact. The ghosts were getting in! I sank to my knees, rocking to and fro, to and fro. Then I collapsed on to the floor and started to convulse, as if I was having a fit. More candles were burning out and more ghosts were getting in.

But then I heard a musical note – not a melody or a tune, just a single note – and an inner peace glowed through the darkness of the old church until the first streaks of morning light came through the stained glass of the small high windows.

Ravens circled outside, searching for an early breakfast. Their harsh cawing woke me and I sat up, rubbing sleep from my eyes, trying to remember where I was and how I got there. Rainbow light shone down from the stained glass and struck the coffin, surrounding it with a sort of bluish luminescence, just for a few seconds. Then it passed on.

I heard a heavy bolt being drawn back and a key turning in a lock. An old priest emerged from the sacristy. He stared in disbelief at me for a moment, his mouth opening, but the words not emerging immediately.

'I got locked in.'

'I am so sorry … how could this have happened?'

'The wind jammed the door.'

The old priest rushed to the main door and pulled at it. It swung open without any effort.

Outside, I shivered in the early morning chill. I thought I heard a sound behind me as I walked away from the old church and I looked around quickly. But it was nothing – just my imagination.

# CHAPTER 4

# THE HORROR

Life is breaking down a person to their most basic level and putting them back together again. What comes back is not always what went in. Bits are missing or added or changed about. The same ingredients, but a different person, looking for a place that was once known, in the remote past.

Part of my job as an apprentice seamstress to my mother was to go out looking for work. I would go from door to door, asking people if they had garments to be mended. Early in the year 1864, when I had just become fourteen, I was in the affluent Koninginnegracht area of the city, wheeling my handcart, on which I carried the work home, and wearing the clogs Lotte had given to me, even though they were almost worn out and too small for my feet by now. The green skirt had long been turned into a hat for one of my brothers. I climbed the steps to the front door of a three-storied house and knocked. Nobody answered. I knocked again. Still no answer. I was walking away, back down the steps, when the door creaked open.

'Hallo.'

'Hallo.'

'My name is Jacobus. You look sad.'

'I am sad.'

'Why?'

He was a big man – old, maybe fifty. He had greying whiskers and large hands. His eyes looked black in the light from the street, but they were probably brown or green. I told him I was sad because I'd been looking for work all day, but hadn't found any. Also that my father was ill again and my brothers were hungry. He was sympathetic. He said I was too young and pretty to be so sad and he said he could cheer me up.

'How?'

'With a genièvre brûlé.'

I did not know what a genièvre brûlé was, but it sounded enticing. He asked me to come inside, which I did, cautiously. He showed me into a large, well-furnished room and mixed some liquids in a glass container. Then he poured the liquid into two glasses and gave one to me.

'Drink.'

I wasn't used to people giving me exotic drinks and I hesitated.

'What is your name?'

'Clasina Maria Hoornik.'

He drank what was in his glass.

'See, Clasina Maria Hoornik … it won't poison you.'

I wasn't sure, but I took a sip anyway.

'What do you think?'

'It's lovely.'

'Just like you.'

'Where is the lady of the house?'

'I'll go and get her.'

He was gone a long time. While he was away, I drank the rest of the liquid in the glass. It tasted strange, sweet and bitter at the same time. I'd never tasted anything like it before. Then my head began to feel strange and the room swam before my eyes. I tried to stay on my feet, but could not.

Then everything went black.

I don't know how long I was unconscious but, when I woke, I was on a bed in a room with no windows. My head was hurting and I felt unsteady, but I managed to get to my feet. I could hear music coming from the next room – it was music I'd never heard before. I stumbled towards it and found myself in a small kitchen. There was a window in the wall, but it was boarded up. Jacobus was there, playing a violin. He must have sensed me, because he spoke without turning.

'Do you like the music?'

I didn't answer. I was too afraid.

'It's a sonata, by Willem van Wassenaer.'

He turned and looked at me with a leer. His eyes were wide and protruding. He became strangely excited and his voice sounded low, like an animal's.

'I want to go home.'

'You are home, Clasina … for now.'

He stopped playing the violin and began cutting some meat with a large knife. I was very frightened now. He slid his hand along the edge of the knife, while smiling at me in a wild kind of way. I decided it was best to humour him. I wanted to die when Brechtje left this life, but not now. It's strange, is it not – people think they want to die, but when death is staring them in the face, when it's so close they can smell its stinking breath, then it doesn't seem like such an appealing option anymore.

I wondered how he could be so interested in a skinny fourteen-year-old like me. I was too young and naive to know that some men had a longing inside them that was left over from before – tolerated somewhere in history – in remote genophyla where carnality was nothing but a restless internal energy and physical desire had no connection with merit as a civilised human being. A primal thing that was still alive in the world, an animal instinct which was beginning to be seen as perverted, but still tolerated out of compliance with patriarchy.

I decided to humour Jacobus until I could find a way out of the house. I went to the table and ate some of the meat, even though it almost choked me. He smiled at me when I finished, as if I had been a good girl.

'You should wash now.'

'I don't want to.'

His mood changed immediately.

He grabbed me by the hair and dragged me to a water pail and shoved my head into it.

He was still holding the knife.

'Take off your clothes!'

I did and he took them away with him. When he came back, he was naked as well.

He pushed me back into the room with the bed and began to bite me – on my arms and shoulders and neck and back. All over. I was terrified, but I did not try to fight him because I had the feeling that would have excited him even more. He was a big man, much bigger than me, and I would have been no match for him. Then he was on top of me and pushing his erect organ up into me. It was really painful and I started to bleed, but that didn't put him off. I wanted to cry, but I stopped myself. I just lay there, looking at a little clock on the wall and waiting for it to be over. It was as if I went completely dead inside – with no feeling and no emotion.

'I can tell you're a virgin, nice and tight.'

It seemed I was underneath him for a lifetime, while he grunted like a hog. He kept licking me and I could smell his breath, almost taste it. The bed was creaking and my head was banging against the wall and he was making noises like an animal. Finally, he let out a groan and I could feel something coming inside me. It stank. He stank. I jumped up and ran from him when he rolled off me. He did not follow.

I ran round the house, trying to find a way out, but the heavy front door was locked and the windows were all covered by wooden shutters that kept out the light of the day.

I started to scream – somebody passing by might hear me and come to my rescue. But nobody did and my screams echoed back, as if they were trying to escape on their own, but couldn't. I tried to open many doors, but they were all locked and I could not budge them. I wondered if there were other people in the house – what about Jacobus' wife? Where was she? Did he have a wife at all? I ran to the kitchen to look for the knife he was cutting the meat with but, the next thing

I knew, I was grabbed from behind and dragged back into the room with the bed.

For what seemed like many hours, I was repeatedly violated by Jacobus. I was crying now and bleeding and it was like a scene from hell. He made unnatural noises while he was ravishing me, the like of which I had never heard before. I think I must have been fainting, because I'd be in the middle of this maniacal abuse and then everything would go dark and quiet. Then I'd revive and see his obscene face and hear the horrific sounds and feel the pain, and I'd cry and scream and he'd laugh and shove himself up inside me again. I don't know how long this went on for but, when I finally woke from the horror, it was over and he was asleep on the rank and bloody bed beside me.

I gathered my clothes from where he'd put them and crept to the front door and tried it again, forgetting that I had already found it locked. I searched for a key – it was on a small wooden table in the hallway. I heard a sound behind me as I turned it in the lock and, when I looked round, Jacobus was coming towards me. Then a bell rang somewhere in the house. He turned, as if summoned, and I pulled the door open and ran out into the street. It was dark and deserted, which was just as well, as I was naked and carrying my clothes. My handcart was still outside, which I dared not lose or my mother would be furious. So I pushed it as quickly and as far as I could before getting dressed, then made my way slowly and painfully back to Noordstraat.

It was very late when I got home and everybody was sleeping – except my mother. She looked cross and I was afraid to tell her what had happened to me.

'Where have you been, Clasina?'

'I lost my way, mother.'

'How can you lose your way, you know the city very well.'

She saw the marks where Jacobus had held me down and bitten me. I started to cry.

'Tell me!'

'A man … he … '

She pulled my dress from me and saw the blood and bruises on my legs.

'Clasina … you are ruined!'

'I'm sorry.'

'No man will have you now.'

She was wrong.

My mother never asked for the name or address of the man who violated me. She knew it would be futile to try to do anything about it. Poor children were abused all the time and nobody ever brought the guilty to justice – not the maréchaussée nor the priests. Poor children were nothing, less than the value of a pig or a goat. But I did not forget the man who behaved like an animal – I remembered him and where he lived. I didn't know it then, but we would meet again.

That was my first horror.

Vincent had his own, though less physical and more mentally critical. The Rijksschool Willem II in Tilburg was the stuff of nightmares. It looked more like a prison than a college, where close-order military drill when shouldering a cadet gun was required – something which was totally alien to the reclusive boy who dreamed of being home with his beetles and larks' nests and his attic sanctuary. It wasn't something Vincent liked to talk much about, but I gathered that the cost of the Provily School had proved too much for the preacher father, especially as his son was not achieving the greatness demanded of him. Tilburg was state-sponsored and affordable and Vincent filled his lonely hours there by reading French, English and German poetry. When he reached the second level, he was introduced to the art class and its colourful teacher, Constantin Huymans, who rejected the tricks the other art schools taught and encouraged his students to seek the power of expression.

'Sketch the impression the object makes, not the object itself.'

They went outside the college walls to draw what he called the source of all beauty – nature. And he encouraged the students to see, in more ways than one.

Although this was a welcome diversion from the soul-destroying emptiness inside him, Vincent still showed no interest in becoming an artist and he continued to keep to himself, hunched up in his solitude, allowing no one in. He was viewed as eccentric, but those eccentricities did not manifest themselves in a creative or artistic manner. It would only be later in life that what he learned in Huymans' art class would come back from being buried in his unconscious.

All the students went home after the last lesson bell, except for Vincent. Only he trudged through the rain and snow to his lonely lodgings. Then, in March 1868, weeks before his fifteenth birthday and two months before the end of term, he walked out of the Rijksschool Willem II in Tilburg. Vincent's school days were over. It took him ten hours to get back to Zundert on foot, where he stayed for almost a year and a half, despite the bewailing of his father over the money that had been wasted on his education. But he knew, sooner or later, he would have to leave again.

'I had to choose a profession.'

After spending all that time at home in Zundert, Vincent was sent at sixteen to The Hague to work as a junior clerk with the firm of Goupil & Cie, which was founded by his art dealer uncle, Cent. So, here we were, in the same town, getting closer to each other but not yet knowing it. It was considered a tradition, for the young man who was now earmarked to become an art dealer like his uncle, to receive his training from Goupil. They had houses in Brussels, Paris and London as well as The Hague. Vincent packed and unpacked paintings and did a lot of humble jobs, which might have been considered beneath a youth of his learning, but he was content in the doing. He never considered himself to be too good for anything – even me.

Vincent's gérant at Goupil in The Hague was a man called Hermanus Tersteeg, who Vincent came to admire. He was one of the people who would later try to come between the gember man and me when we lived and loved together. In his new job, Vincent worked from daybreak till after dark and he was in close contact with art from all over the world. And, just as he had been engrossed with nature at an earlier age, now he became engrossed with art. But some of the pictures didn't represent nature as he knew it. It troubled him. When he made his feelings known, he was told that the pictures were fashionable. So, it was fashion that was leading art around by the nose, like a prize cow, and Vincent hated fashion as a precedent, he scorned what the world called "form".

Of course, I knew nothing about art then, and fashion and form were a foreign language to me. It was only when I became Vincent's model did it make some kind of sense. I could see, though still not fully understand, that Vincent was struggling with the revolution in art which he encountered back then – paintings with vague forms, loose brushwork, muted colours and gauzy light. They looked unfinished to Vincent, but Tersteeg began to buy them and the gember man met the artists who painted them when they came into the emporium. One of them was Anton Mauve, Vincent's cousin, another man who would try to force us apart. Both Tersteeg and Mauve were of a class to whom the servants who cleaned for them, like myself and my mother, were invisible. Consequently, they considered me to be something less than a human being.

Vincent lived in The Hague for three years and our paths may have crossed in that time. It was a smaller city then than it is now, in 1904. Perhaps we stood next to each other at the trotting races, during the Nationale en Internationale Tentoonstelling, on the Malieveld, on the anniversary of the Hollandesche Maatschappij van Landbouw. Perhaps we glanced at each other, maybe even smiled, then moved on, not staying long enough to know each other, as we would ten years later. What a cruel joke fate played on us. Had we met then, when I was young and unscarred by sorrow, when he still had the courage of his convictions – who knows how it would have turned out.

When we were young, Vincent and I both longed for understanding – to understand and be understood. We were confused by the doubts inside us. We needed answers to our many questions – an explanation of our emotions. The answers we received weren't the ones we wanted, they were the ones people thought we needed. We may have confused love with longing. Longing is desire and desire can destroy. There is always a price to be paid for longing. In my life, love was something that belonged to other people and they loaned it to me because they liked the way I looked or the way I fucked. But they always wanted it back in the end. One way or another. And it turned sour and left the bad taste of regret in my mouth – like a lie.

Real understanding came when we escaped from that small world of the moral and opinionated and assertive. For me, it was when I met Vincent and realised how small the ego was against the backdrop of everything. For him, it was finding the meaning of real love – which is giving, not taking. Of course, that day was a long way off and he would have to discover himself before then.

And so, we waited –

For tomorrow to come.

# CHAPTER 5

# MEHDI

My father was often sick and couldn't work at blacksmithing or portering. At times like that, my mother and I had to take on more cleaning and seamstress jobs. My oldest bother Pieter began to make and sell chairs to help out, but it was still not enough to support such a large family.

'You must make more money, Clasina.'

'How, mother? I'm working as hard as I can.'

'You must use what God has given you.'

I didn't understand. Even though I was almost nineteen, I wasn't familiar, at that time, with the world of strumpets and straatmadeliefies and I had not had knowledge of men, apart from Jacobus, because I'd always remembered my father's advice and avoided situations that might be considered encouraging to them. My mother prevailed.

'You have lost your purity, Clasina, it is gone. No man will marry you, so you must use what you have already given away for nothing to feed the family.'

'And how will I do that?'

'Go along to Poeldijkstraat and watch.'

And so I did.

The Poeldijkstraat district was a rough, dirty place, even worse than Noordstraat, but I couldn't tell who were straatmadeliefies and who were not. Most seemed to be ordinary people going about their business – buying and selling food, delivering coal, driving drays and catching stray dogs. I didn't know what to do, so I did nothing. It was late when I arrived and, as day turned to night and the candle-lamps were lit over the doorways, the streets emptied of the gewone people, who were replaced by the hoers, who sat on chairs outside the buildings and beckoned to the soldiers, sailors, opium eaters and absinthe drinkers passing by. The maréchaussée patrolled, showing their authority and collecting bribes and the souteneurs hulked about in the shadows like hump-backed hounds, watching over their women.

Poeldijkstraat may have been a safe place during the day, but at night it was hostile and angry and threatening. Brothels shimmered red from the gas lights, while homeless people shivered down narrow alleyways, wrapped in dirty blankets or sprawled on sacks of straw. The opium eaters looked dazed, shuffling along in their strange world with glazed eyes, their grotesque faces illuminated by flashes as they lit their pipes. Some drunks were fighting and screaming at each other, more were weeping and wailing. It was difficult to tell the age of an individual, because most of them looked a lot older than they probably were. People vomited and defecated and urinated openly and the smell was overpowering. It was the worst place I had ever been, with streets of filth and piles of waste everywhere. Rats and dogs scavenged, along with children who searched through the rubbish for scraps of food, or gathered up the discarded fruit and vegetables from the street markets. Others begged from those passing, who tried to ignore them.

The maréchaussée moved people on – the children and those who were homeless and those who had no money to pay for opium or absinthe or a straatmadelief or a bribe, just to prove to the authorities that they were doing something about the place. They beat people for fun, kicked them and sometimes killed them. Who was going to complain if a worthless drugsverslaafde got crippled? Nobody. Bourgeois men wearing velvet hats sauntered with swarthy bodyguards at their sides – knowing that nobody would try to rob them because they had the law on their side. A law that protected them and their laced-up ladies, but not us poor creatures.

I stood back in a doorway, out of sight, afraid of being arrested or beaten or ravished by another Jacobus. That's when I saw a girl giving birth on a pile of sacking, with dirt and decay all around her and no one would help. I was going to go to her, but a hand on my shoulder stopped me. It was the maréchaussée.

'Do you know her?'

'No.'

'Are you a hoer?'

'No.'

'What are you doing here?'

'I'm on my way home … from work.'

'Then go.'

'What about her?'

'It would be a mistake to get involved.'

'Why?'

'You must not get involved. If you get involved, you will be overcome by it.'

I walked around the streets, pretending to leave, until they were gone. When I returned to my doorway, the girl was gone also. I waited, fretfully, not knowing for what, constantly frightened by the sounds of distress and dark spectres leering past me in the red gaslight. I don't know how long I was waiting there, until I was approached by a man. He was younger than Jacobus, maybe thirty, I thought.

'How much?'

I didn't know how much. He asked again.

'How much?'

He was becoming impatient.

'A guilder?'

He looked me up and down, as if he was buying a sow.

'Alright. Do you have a room?'

'No.'

'Come with me.'

He took me to a taverne, where he paid for a room and a bottle of absinthe. I didn't drink alcohol then, as I do now. I was not seeking my window in the wall – yet.

There are many windows in the wall. Some see love and some see hate and some see life and some see death. Everybody chases their own dragon. Everybody wants heaven – Eden – Elysium. To transcend the world for even a few minutes is a longing of the soul. People do not chase their dragon because they want to be bad – they do it because they want to escape. Sanity and sobriety will only go so far – after that it has to be religion – or death.

To me, the way to consciousness was through unconsciousness and the way to unconsciousness was through the chemistry of the mind. I was made up of those chemicals – I am those chemicals still. It was just a matter of control and understanding. Some may have said bad was not good no matter how I phrased it. Perhaps not. But to become good – I had to admit that I was bad.

The man took off his coat and poured two glasses of absinthe. He offered me a long, thin cigar and I took it, although I didn't smoke. When he lit it for me I coughed – and he laughed.

'What's your name?'

'Clasina. What's yours?'

'My name doesn't matter, just my money.'

A chill entered my bloodstream and I almost panicked. I wanted to run from the room, just as I tried to run from the house of Jacobus, and fall along the dark, shadowy streets of Poeldijkstraat until I was completely free and there was not a sinner in sight. But I did not.

I stayed.

The room was gloomy, with just a little light from a candle in the corner – and this strange-looking man with light grey eyes watching me, blowing smoke from his cigar into the unconsecrated air. Who was he? Why did he come to this part of the city looking for a girl like me to molest? I would never know, because it didn't matter – it was just his money that mattered.

He laughed again, as if he knew what I was thinking, and the sound of his laughter mocked at me – it said I was something to be used for lust, but not for love. Maybe he was making a pilgrimage to the memory of a moribund life that was, at one time, filled with a kinder friendship. But now was gone forever.

'I'm a widower, Clasina.'

He offered this information, again as if he was reading my thoughts.

'And now you're a ghost?'

He laughed again.

'Do you want to know what happened to my wife?'

'No … '

'I killed her.'

'Jezus Christus!'

'Many years ago.'

Why was he telling me this? To frighten me? I was already frightened. Was he going to kill me also? I'd heard of such men, who can only derive pleasure from pain. Perhaps he often performed this macabre ritual and I was his next victim.

'Do you believe in heaven, Clasina?'

'No.'

But I was not so sure about hell.

He came closer to me, as if he was gliding on a cushion of air, with no movement from his body, except for his lips, which drew back across his teeth in a threatening smile. Was he a vampire – I'd heard of them also. Creatures who sucked blood to live in an eternal niflheim. He rubbed himself against me, as if his whole body was assaulting mine. Catching my hand quickly, he held it with surprising strength as he drew me reluctantly towards the bed. The candle flame in the corner grew larger, until it became a blaze – they say Judas hanged himself from an elder tree and the burning of that wood unleashed the devil.

We fell onto the bed in the chill twilight of the unholy room. I felt hypnotised with fear and didn't resist, as he began to strip off my clothes, until I was completely naked. Then he stripped himself, the candle flame blazing at me from his eyes, his lips blood red and pressing against mine. My mind was melting and I thought I was on some monstrous carousel machine which began to swirl, slowly at first, but with increasing speed. The man mounted me and, somewhere in the distance, I heard a door slam, to lock out all logic from the strange and savage scene.

His voice was hoarse and gravelly when he spoke. I didn't understand the words and maybe I wasn't meant to. Maybe they weren't meant for me, but for his long-dead wife who was haunting him. He began to suck at my tongue, while his thighs writhed above me and his manhood seemed to consume me. Because of Jacobus, I was no longer a virgin and I experienced no pain, as I did when he ravished me five years since. But this man was different to Jacobus, there was no violence to his lust, no danger in his desire. His fingers ran through my hair and his eyes rolled in his head. I felt his frame grow rigid and he laughed a dark laugh when the climax came upon him and seemed to erupt from his very soul. We lay together in a rolling ball of soft sweat and sighs.

He lit up another cheap cigar and offered me one. I took it. This time I did not cough when I smoked it. He rose from the bed and put on his clothes and walked towards the door.

'What about my money?'

'Oh, yes … '

He placed a guilder on the table and looked at me. It was as if he was sizing me up again – weighing my potential.

'You know you're underselling yourself, Clasina.'

'Am I?'

'Yes. You're young and fresh, not like most of the hoers in this district. You're too clean for this place, you should be working in Doublestraat or Geleenstraat.'

'I'm new to this … not sure what I'm doing.'

'I'll help you … if you want me to.'

And so began my relationship with Mehdi, which was what he wanted to be called and what I called him. I don't know if it was his real name, or if it was a nom de guerre, to make him seem more mysterious and ill-disposed. He said he was Algerian, born of a French father and Tuareg mother.

I do not know if this was true either. He bought me a new dress and shoes and a fanchon to perch on my head, and he educated me about the oldest trade in the world, as he called it, which I was about to enter.

When Napoleon occupied The Netherlands, sixty years earlier, he lifted the ban on prostitution that had been imposed by the sanctimonious and self-righteous. But he also wanted his soldiers to be safe from disease, so he introduced compulsory health checks for the straatmadeliefies. They had to register with the maréchaussée and were given a red card, which was like a permit to work. If they were found to be infected, the card was taken away until they could prove they were safe. Unfortunately, there was no reliable treatment for the more serious diseases. Except for the inhalation of heated quicksilver in steam baths, so many prostitutes died while trying to get clean.

The red cards were gone in 1869, but straatmadeliefies were still regulated so, as long as I was discreet and kept myself disease free, I was in no danger of being arrested. Mehdi found a space for me on Geleenstraat, not far from a taverne where rooms could be hired cheaply. He became my souteneur and, for his generosity, he took half of what I earned and helped himself to free service whenever he felt like it.

'One guilder is too cheap for a girl your age, Clasina.'

'How much should I charge?'

'It depends. If a customer looks rich or if he wants something different, then charge five guilders. If he's not so well off and is a man with normal tastes, then perhaps two or three.'

Mehdi handled aggressive customers and protected me from the maréchaussée and the psalm-singers. I considered myself lucky to have found him, otherwise I might have been bound to a madam and kept prisoner in a brothel, or sold to slavers and taken to Arabia.

'It is a proven scientific fact, Clasina, that sexual abstinence for men is unhealthy.'

'Really?'

'That's why prostitution is an honourable profession. You offer yourself to protect the rest of your gender from depravity.'

'I never saw it that way.'

Neither did the orthodox Christians or the crusading women. And my clients were not the young unmarried men prostitution was meant for, but more often were well off, middle-aged married men. But I was oblivious to understanding at the time. My family needed money and my souteneur gave me a safe means to make that money. That's all I needed to know. Later, Vincent would expand my consciousness to accommodate much more but, in 1869, I was still who I was.

Even being in the city and lodging in a crowded house, Vincent kept to himself, as he had at school. Then, in February 1871, he was told his family was leaving Zundert. His father had taken a position in Helvoirt and the things he loved from his childhood were gone forever. It was like me losing my innocence. Vincent lost that indefinable essence of his youth. It was when he began to use prostitutes for company – something he never denied to me, no more than I ever tried to hide my life from him.

'If I couldn't get a good woman, I'd take a bad one. I'd sooner be with a bad hoer than be alone.'

He was driven more by loneliness than desire.

'My physical passions were very weak.'

Sometimes he went to them just to sit, share a drink, play cards or to talk about his lonely life. As a substitute for genuine affection, he sought the intimacy that was available and he only finally knew true closeness when he met me.

He began to fall out of favour with Tersteeg, who moralised about his activities and made complaints to the family. Vincent resented him for not minding his own business – what he did outside of work was nothing to do with the gérant. Tersteeg did not see it like that. Vincent was bringing into disrepute his Uncle Cent's name and the firm of Goupil and Cie. Between them, Uncle Cent and Tersteeg decided it was time for Vincent to leave The Hague. So, you can see how scandalised they all must have been when the gember man announced, many years later, that he would be marrying me.

Before we could meet in one way or another, Goupil sent Vincent away to Brussels and then to Paris, where he disturbed the fine ladies of the art world by contradicting their conceptions of what art should be. They didn't care to be criticised by a "Dutch boor", as they called him. So Goupil sent him to London, where they considered the English sensibility to be less fragile than the French. He lodged with a family called Loyer in the south of that city and he would walk every morning with jerky steps over Westminster Bridge to Goupil's gallery in Southampton Street, off The Strand. He dressed in a top hat – because he said you couldn't live in London without one – with a rolled-up umbrella and a stiff collar, and now and then he made little drawings of the places he passed. His landlady was a widow called Ursula, who had a close relationship with her daughter. Vincent fell in love with the daughter and wrote to his sisters that he was happier than he'd ever been. Her name was Eugénie and she was the same age as Vincent.

She had a straight, hard mouth, dark hair, parted in the centre and hanging in long curls down the sides. She was a bourgeoise, whose father had been a professor of languages. She dressed primly and had a stern disposition. Ursula was very hospitable, but Eugénie was severe and stand-offish and carried herself more like a man than a woman – it was just as well, for Vincent's sake, that he didn't marry her. In any event, she rejected his advances and proposals of marriage, saying she was secretly engaged to someone else. This made him more lonely than he'd ever been. He began to smoke a pipe as a remedy for melancholy and he left the Loyers.

Soon after, Goupil brought him back to Paris.

# CHAPTER 6

# LUCAS AND FLEUR

Only knowledge can recognise truth – real truth. And truth creates more knowledge. As I stand here, looking towards the black water, do I see the glow of realisation – the purity of perception? Or just the glare of confusion, without shadow or relief – ubiquitous and implacable? If meaning is menacing, if it is hell, then it's a hell of my own making. Life itself is daunting – short and indiscriminate. I've been wandering in the desert – shunned by society – misunderstood – despised – discriminated against. I went from god to god until they cried from me in me – O thou I! The bread I ate was only mine when no one else wanted it.

Those words were mostly Vincent's, but I didn't understand them – until now. And now is too late. Now I must look at the swirling water, even if I cannot bear it – the glare from it. I must look until I understand. Look at it until it blinds me – until I'm so blind I can see.

It was Kerstmis of 1873, almost four years since I became a prostitute. During that time, I had learned the oldest profession and was much sought after in the Geleenstraat district. I was earning good money for my family and also for Mehdi, who took care of me and we got along very well. Everybody was happy. I was having an on-and-off relationship with my mother – sometimes I would go home for a while and continue my work as a seamstress, but we would always end up quarrelling. Then she would tell me it was time I was on the streets again as the money was running short. So I'd go back to Mehdi and live from room to room and from man to man.

I'd grown from a girl of nineteen to a woman of almost twenty-four. I had changed a lot – I considered myself to be a woman of the world, having been in the company of men ranging from sailors and traders to rich businessmen and even aristocrats. I had earned a lot of guilders, even if I didn't have any to show for it, and I was better educated than I had ever been. I bought as many books as I could and, when I wasn't working, I was always reading. I lost myself in books. I'd sit outside the taverne, smoking cheap cigars and reading – the plays of Joost van den Vondel and the poems of Anna Bijns, along with a translation of stories by Charles Dickens and Victor Hugo. And Mehdi gave me an illustrated copy of Alice's Adventures, which cost him a lot of money, as a token of his appreciation.

I absorbed myself in the imaginations of those writers and lived their adventures in my head. Reading took me to other places, away from Geleenstraat and the straatmadeliefies – to London and Paris and Wonderland and Camelot and wild forests where dark princes roamed and magical castles where princesses were held captive by wicked witches. Mehdi was able to get books for me from the public library on the Spui, because he had a contact there. As long as I took them back, I could get more. I would take six at a time and could finish three in one night if business was slow.

I'd had breathing problems all my life and difficulty speaking without getting breathless. I don't know why – maybe it was something to do with my poor diet, or the worms that crawled inside me when I was a child. Mehdi taught me to speak and breathe properly and to walk with my head up and my back straight. He was always correcting my diction and commenting when I did something that was not within his sense of etiquette. To begin with, I thought he was picking on me.

'You never correct any of the other girls.'

'I don't care about them, Clasina. You're pretty and clever, but you could be much better.'

'Why do you care about me?'

'Because I believe you can do well in life.'

I found out that Catharina van Rees, who wrote her novels under the name Celéstine, was in The Hague for a period and Mehdi managed to get me an audience with her, I don't know how – Mehdi knew a lot of people and was a man of surprising resourcefulness. She was interested in educating women and we got on very well. I visited her several times and we talked about comets and violins and clouds and seabirds and life and loneliness. It was another world for me, where I could be someone else, not Clasina Hoornik, the hoer.

I hoped my mother would be happy with what I had achieved and we could have a pleasant Kerstmis. I arrived at the house in Noordstraat at the ringing of the angelus bell. The apartment we lived in grew smaller as we grew bigger and there was scarcely enough room for us to fit in when we were all at home together, as we were for Kerstmis that year. I couldn't tell if my mother was pleased to see me or not, her hair had gone grey prematurely and her face was wrinkled. She was slightly bent over and she walked with difficulty from the back problems she got from her cleaning work. Come to think of it, my mother had never looked young, not that I could remember, at least – her hair was always straggly and she had very few teeth. But this year she looked older than usual, and she could only have been in her forties, or so I estimated.

My younger brothers and sister treated me like a stranger. I wanted to show myself off – my clothes and my make-up and my hair and my learning of the world. But they were not impressed.

'We used to pull the worms from your nose, Clasina. Have you forgotten that?'

I discovered that my younger brother Carolus was now living with the sister of Brechtje and Christoffel Vos. She'd had a baby for an older man when she was thirteen and she would have been treated very badly if it hadn't been for my brother. The match would never have been tolerated under normal circumstances, especially with me working as a straatmadelief, but Carolus looked after her and gave her a version of respectability that was not ideal but was acceptable, and so he was allowed into a class that was deemed to be on a higher level than his. When I met Christoffel again, he did not seem to remember doing anything bad to me, so I said nothing about it – for my brother's sake.

My father was fifty now and he was very ill. He was not able to walk at all and he couldn't eat properly because the food hurt his throat. Everyone thought it was just some kind of infection, but I knew it was more than that. I got Mehdi to take him to the hospital in Voorburg, where they did some tests. A few days later he was diagnosed with consumption.

I loved my father more than I loved my mother, if I ever loved my mother at all. I'm not sure – maybe I did, but it didn't seem like love to me. My father was different, he was an easy-going man and he danced with me and made me laugh when I was little. He told me stories and jokes and I called him pappje.

'Who is this pappje Clasina? I know no pappje.'

'You are.'

'Am I?'

And he'd laugh. Now he wasn't laughing anymore. He wasn't dancing or telling jokes, and I missed the years I hadn't spent with him. I couldn't stand seeing him so fragile – knowing there was nothing I could do about it.

We ate rabbit with potatoes and kerstbrood and sang "hoe leit dit kindeke". Sinterklass did not visit our house, but Zwarte Piet was seen in the street and the younger children were able to collect some of the snoep he threw about. Then Kerstmis was over and it was time for me to go back to work.

Up until then, I was still considered young enough to ask a reasonable fee for my services. Then, in the year of 1874, I discovered I was carrying a child.

'How do you know, Clasina?'

'My menses … '

'How long?'

'Three months … I think.'

'Has quickening occurred?'

'Not yet.'

My mother was angry and told me I had to get rid of it, but I did not want to.

'How could you let this happen, Clasina … after five years of being careful?'

'Careful, or lucky, mother?'

'Whichever.'

I had to tell Mehdi, who said the same thing.

'You'll have to get rid of it, Clasina.'

'Why?'

'What kind of a question is that? How do you propose to continue as a reine des trottoirs with a baby on your back?'

'Some do.'

'Yes, the poor trollops who patrol the Poeldijkstraat and offer their services for a couple of stuivers, because that's all they're worth.'

And so, Mehdi arranged for me to go to a woman in Spoorwijk, close to the railway lines. We went there at night, when it was dark and there weren't many people around. The woman examined me and gave me a female potion, which Mehdi told me later was a mixture of tansy oil, pennyroyal, rue, ergot and opium.

'Is it safe, Mehdi?'

'As safe as having a baby, Clasina.'

After taking the potion, I descended into seizures, but it did not cause a miscarriage. So, Mehdi brought me back again.

This time the woman produced a female syringe and filled it with a mixture of hot carbolic soap. She gave me a glass of absinthe to drink, then inserted the syringe. It was very painful and I almost fainted – I can't imagine what it would have been like without the absinthe. I was in great agony all that night and, in the morning, I took a great flooding. But the piercing of the bag of waters caused blood poisoning within me and I suffered for a week with chills and fevers, my breathing was laboured and my heart beat faster. Mehdi said I was lucky to survive.

My father died the following year. There was a wake, like with Brechtje, all those long years before. My father's coffin was placed on the table with a veil covering him inside it. Worse than losing my father was seeing my mother's stoicism. She never knew her parents, because she was orphaned as a baby. She was brought up as a servant by another family, who treated her like a slave from the time she was very young. My father took her away from that when she was thirteen and they had been together ever since. He was the kindest person she had ever known – the most easy-going person she had ever known. But it seemed to me that she did not love him. And now he was gone.

I stayed by his side, constantly crying, until they came to take him to the church. I'd never cried like that before and I wanted so very badly to hug him – maybe if I hugged him enough, he would come back to life. They put my father's coffin onto a carriage and many people followed it to the church. I was just hanging on to the side – crying, crying, crying. There were blisters on my face from the tears. Then they took him to the cemetery and buried him, while the people around the grave prayed and my mother stood emotionless. I cried louder with every shovelful of earth that thudded on the coffin lid. In the end, I had to be led away by my brothers.

I went back to Mehdi in Geleenstraat straight after the funeral. The first thing I did was go to a taverne to have a drink, trying to forget the terrible pain in my heart and feeling utterly alone. I was coming to be in love with alcohol – absinthe and jenever. I also smoked incessantly, the thin cigars my souteneur had introduced me to when I was nineteen.

Shortly after my father died, I discovered that I was with child again. This time I was determined to have it and refused to go back to the woman by the railway lines. It ended my relationship with Mehdi – the day after I told him of my decision, he disappeared from my life. Without a souteneur to look after me, I was forced to go home to Noordstraat to live with my mother, which wasn't easy, even though some of my brothers were in the orphanage and my sister Maria was only three. I tried to stay off the streets and work again as a seamstress, but the alcohol had taken hold of me and I needed money to satisfy my craving, so I worked with my mother during the day and streetwalked the Poeldijkstraat district at night. By now, at twenty-five, my youthfulness was fading and I could not charge as much for my services as before. I was growing thin and my health was not good. I coughed from smoking cheap cigars and my clothes began to hang on my bones.

I grew large on the baby through the second half of 1875 and I developed cravings for stamppot and the smell of coal. Labour started with back pain that went on all through that cold night, with whistling wind and snow flurries. I did not have a doctor, just a local midwife from Noordstraat, who stuck a knitting needle up me to break the waters. In the end, I gave an almighty push and my daughter was born on 23rd December. She was small and I could not feed her because my bosoms were hot and painful, with blisters forming around my paps. I called the baby Fleur and she lived for three days, until December 26th. They told me my womb had been damaged by the abortion the year before and I would never be able to carry a baby again.

They were wrong.

I became with child again after only a month back in Poeldijkstraat. I was surprised, because they'd told me it wouldn't happen. But, again, I didn't seek the services of the woman who lived in Spoorwijk. My little son Lucas was born in September 1876 – he survived for four days, one day longer than Fleur.

Loss is a sad colour – the colour of melancholy. The loss of something once loved. Someone once loved. There is always a residue – a redolence – an essence that will never go away.

Non-existent. Ghostlike. Hypothetical. I knew I would never be free of it – truly free. Light and laughter were the flowers and dreamscapes of others and mine were of unbearable sorrow – and the understanding that there would never be any escape from the sadness. And it was never enough to say the earth went round the sun – I had to ask why it mattered.

And the more of life I knew, the less I understood.

Later, a tone would bring me back towards Mehdi, who I would see only one more brief time in my life – not to him, but in his direction. A musical modulation, the same note I heard when I was locked in the old church at thirteen. All music was inherent in that one tone – like religion. I followed the sound until it faded into the distance. Just the vibration was left. Maybe it was the sound of my soul, trying to break free and fulfil itself in an eternal present – not in a past that never was or a future that never would be.

Meanwhile, Vincent's family had moved to Etten, a little town only six kilometres from Zundert and he was delighted to be able to visit the places of his youth again. He took unauthorised leave from Goupil and went there for Kerstmis 1875. Goupil dismissed him when he returned to Paris in January 1876, giving him until the end of March to be gone. There was an argument – a scene – very unpleasant, as the gérant at Goupil put it. Vincent told the man that he was nothing better than a thief for bargaining over the price of paintings, but it was the culmination of a series of customer complaints, disciplinary actions and punishment transfers back and forth from London to Paris.

After visiting his parents in Etten, Vincent decided to go back to England. He wasn't welcome in Etten – his father mourned as if his son had died and his mother scolded him for not living according to the family's station in society. Without that, he could not be a normal person. He began responding to advertisements in English newspapers seeking teachers and private tutors, but they were all rejected or unanswered. Then, on his twenty-third birthday, a letter arrived offering him a position at a small boys' school in Ramsgate, a resort community on the English coast. It paid no wages, just room and board and Vincent made a pencil drawing of the church at Etten before he left, just to remind him of home.

When I married Arnoldús and tried to portray myself as a respectable woman, in order to retrieve my son Willem from my brother, I met Vincent's sister Elizabeth Duquesne in The Hague and we spoke about him. She showed me some letters he had written to the family while he was away in England. He wrote well and without any trace of shyness, though halting and abrupt, as if the subject of his words had to find its true expression in his heart before he could relate it. He wrote about the things he saw with exquisite insight – landscapes, sunny corners, street scenes, people, small things that were great to him, but might have been passed unnoticed by someone with less perception. Sometimes he'd draw little sketches to illustrate his thoughts. In fact, he sketched frequently in England, but they were mostly clumsy in composition, as he had not yet developed his style and the pictures were mostly done to give his family an impression of where he was.

At the end of June, the boys' school moved to Isleworth, fifteen kilometres west of London. But Vincent didn't want to stay there, so he found a position with another school, within the city, run by the Reverend Thomas Slade-Jones.

'The vicar is a long, lean man, bent with care of his large family. His clothes just hang on him and his face is heavily lined, the colour of some wooden saint in an old picture. His wife is a quiet, delicate little woman, with eyes as blue as the early March violets.'

That's how he described Slade-Jones to his sister.

There were twenty boarders, more or less, in the vicarage boarding school, which was overgrown with clematis and roses and the boys looked like they had stepped out of a Charles Dickens novel, in their short jackets, long trousers and high hats. Boys between eleven and sixteen, lean and pale, caricatures of themselves. But Vincent didn't want to be a tutor, no more than he wanted to be a painter at that time.

He felt trapped, his intellect unused by the repetitive duties. The pupils came from lower middle-class families and if the fees weren't paid at the end of the term, Vincent would be sent out to collect them. It was something he hated doing, trudging around the lesser-known precincts of London, visiting the small shopkeepers and butchers and cobblers who'd sent their sons to boarding school, without considering if they could afford it, because there were too many other children at home. They weren't the poorest in that city, but they still left an impression on Vincent and probably planted the first seeds of a desire to put paint to canvas, to capture something that created a sense of sympathy inside him. If the people didn't have the fees, Vincent wouldn't press them and often returned to the boarding school empty handed, eventually getting fired for his empathy. So that was the end of that.

But, before he could become a painter, he had to become a preacher.

Six years later, in a moment of reflection, Vincent told me that, in many situations, there was something infinitely futile and presumptuous about speech and only silence was appropriate. That was not always true, however. Sometimes words were all that was left. Sometimes there was no other warmth – no other cold. No other right or wrong. No action. No conflict. Just consequences. Of what is. What was. What would never be again. Between one thing and another. Neither one thing nor another. And life was like that – word-like. Wraith-like. An illusion. Sometimes. Most times. A mirage. A vision. There but not there.

Like now.

Looking down at the water.

# CHAPTER 7

# THE BORINAGE

**B**ack in The Netherlands, Vincent got a job with Blussé and Van Braam Booksellers on the market square in Dordrecht. He was a great reader and had a wonderful knowledge of literature in many languages. The old town of Dordrecht was quaint, with beautiful scenery – the silver edges of clouds; the last rays of the sun; dark reflections in some mysterious pool, mirroring back a glint of blue sky. Only Vincent could describe things like that, only he could make me see them without drawing them. But the reality of Dordrecht was picturesque poverty, its former glory preserved in the amber of neglect and nostalgia.

Like all clerks, Vincent worked standing at his desk, from eight in the morning till midnight. Much of that time was spent "puttering", as his employer called it, or falling asleep from the drowsiness caused by short, restless nights. They said he couldn't be trusted with customers and was only allowed to sell cheap prints to children. His employer complained that he was next to useless because he had no knowledge of the book trade and made no effort to learn.

At that time, Vincent was much more interested in preaching religion, which he'd begun to do in England. He shared a room with a young teacher called Görlitz, who commented that Vincent said lengthy prayers and ate sparingly like a penitent friar. His spent his nights translating the Bible into French, German, English and Dutch and writing sermons. On one occasion, he gave half his last crust of bread to a hungry dog.

I suppose it was inevitable that Vincent's loneliness and longing would take a religious shape. He'd been surrounded by religion all his young life and it was familiar to him, like a friend in a forlorn world. So, strict piety became the core of his being and he dedicated himself to the Bible.

'The Bible is my salve, my support in life. It's the most beautiful book I know.'

And Vincent knew many books. He drew and hung religious sketches on the walls of his lodgings and on each image he wrote the same inscription; "sorrowful yet always rejoicing". He would use the word "sorrow" again, when he came to sketch me naked in the year of 1882.

Pieter Braat, the bookshop owner, was becoming irritated by Vincent's lack of attention to business and he made his feelings known.

'That boy is standing there translating the Bible again!'

Dismissal was coming, so Vincent's father tried to arrange a position for him in Amsterdam, in a bookstore that belonged to his Uncle Cor. But, by then, the gember man was thinking strongly about becoming a pastor, like his father and grandfather. Anyone would think that Dorus, as the father was known, would have been pleased, but not so. Vincent's strange behaviour over the years and his failure at everything he tried, convinced Dorus that he would also fail as a pastor. Nevertheless, Vincent left Dordrecht early in 1877 and travelled to Amsterdam, not to work in a bookshop, but to live with another uncle, Admiral Johannes van Gogh.

Earlier, his brother Theo had accepted a position as an apprentice art dealer at Goupil and he was succeeding where Vincent had failed.

To become a pastor, Vincent would have to be admitted to university – a formidable task for someone without Latin, which was the language of instruction for admittance to the clergy. It would take at least two years, but Vincent was determined to do it in less. He stretched the day at both ends, from before dawn until deep into the night. He studied under the tutorship of Johannes Stricker, a clergyman who was married to his mother's sister Mina, and the father of Cornelia Stricker, who Vincent would fall in love with and be rejected by. Herein lay my unknown connection to Vincent, even before we met – my brother Carolus had married Christoffel Martinus' sister and Christoffel married Cornelia. Vincent would come to me when Cornelia rejected him, after Christoffel died.

Was it fate – was it kismet – was it always meant to be?

The gember man also studied theology under a professor called Mendes da Costa, who said Vincent would go out in cold weather without a coat, with an expression of indescribable sadness and despair and he spoke with a profoundly melancholic voice. All he wanted to do was to give peace to poor creatures and reconcile them to their existence on earth and he didn't think he needed Latin or Greek to do that.

At this time, after my father's death two years earlier, the large Hoornik family in Noordstraat had been greatly reduced. Three of my brothers had died, the oldest three were gone out into the world – Pieter, who made chairs; Carolus, who married the sister of Brechtje; and Hendrik, who drifted around thatching roofs and earning just enough to pay for his alcohol and tobacco. My mother had put the younger ones back in the orphanage, so all who were left were my mother, myself, and my little sister Maria.

It was also at this time that I discovered I was pregnant again. My mother told me to get rid of it, but I was not sure if my health would be able to stand such a trauma, so I carried the baby to term, expecting it to die, just as Lucas and Fleur had. But the little girl, born on 21st December 1877, survived and I called her Maria Wilhelmina, after my mother.

You will see by now that Vincent's life was far more interesting than mine and I should like to just talk about him and not me for another moment or two. However, apart from the times we spent together, my knowledge of that earlier life is limited and I only know what was told to me by other people, including Theo van Gogh. Vincent wrote many letters in his time, mostly to his brother, and I hope that, at some point in the future, a publisher might find them interesting enough to put into print, so that everyone will know him, just as I did. If that happens, I hope people will also know the worth of his paintings and maybe even buy one or two of them. What a great tragedy it would be if they were all lost forever and there was no trace left of the gember man and his extraordinary soul.

Both he and Theo are dead now, as I look down into the winter water and prepare to follow them. I'm not as important, but maybe some day I might be remembered too.

Anyway, the strain of his study became too much for Vincent and he had a mental breakdown – he burned the flame at both ends and it consumed him. He took to wandering the streets at all hours of the day and night, going to all the churches and synagogues, throwing his silver watch into the collection plate at one time and his gloves at another. Until he wandered into a French church in Amsterdam and heard a sermon about how the industrial revolution, which had made some very rich, had thrown hundreds of thousands of others into unimaginable poverty. He heard about the inhuman working and living conditions, the child labour and the widespread disease, and the plague of exploitation and suffering.

Of course, it wasn't new to me, but it had been a hidden world to Vincent, until the French evangelist preacher described it. The gember man immediately saw the images in his mind's eye and he suffered along with the suffering. Distress had a profound effect on Vincent, it made him sensitive to the pain of others and intolerant of greed and grabbing. Instead of learning Latin and theology and preaching bourgeois sermons, he decided he would go and do good works among the wretched people. In his eyes, they were the true Christians, bearing their labour with patience and dignity until they died. He wanted to become like them – it was a calling higher than piety or aesthetic sanctimony.

By now, Vincent was discovering that art could bring life to his thoughts and imaginings and chronicle the many places where he was and would be. Things that would otherwise be lost in the turmoil of his life. In July 1878, he gave up his formal studies and went instead for three months' study at a school for missionaries in Belgium. Because of his erratic behaviour, he failed the course, but they agreed to give him a trial term as an evangelist in a poor village called Petit Wasmes in the French-speaking Belgian black country – the Borinage.

On one of his walks along the Charleroi canal in Brussels, he found the Au Charbonnage Café. The café was attached to a large shed where coal was brought by canal barge from the mines in the south of the country. With the coal came the people who mined it, driven from their homes by unemployment and hoping to find work in the foundries and factories that lined the canal. They came from the Borinage and congregated in the little café, which Vincent drew in pencil and ink on paper. He put the drawing in a letter to Theo and announced that he too was headed au charbonnage – to the coal fields.

Vincent lived with Jean-Baptiste Denis, a baker who made the best baguettes in the Borinage, and his wife Esther at 22 Rue de Wilson. On my way to Antwerp in the year of 1886, I called at the village of Petit Wasmes and spoke for a long time to Esther Denis. She told me the story of the "Christ of the Coalmines".

The people there worked in satanic mines under a yellow-grey sky, perpetually foul with fumes and coal gas. Dead trees blackened by smoke stood like permanent scars on the earth and the only vegetation was thorn hedges. Ash dumps and heaps of coal littered the landscape. Hob-nailed boots clattered on cobblestones, drowning out the subdued conversations of the miners on their way to work. The people were squat, with thin unhealthy faces – the women, particularly, were skinny and emaciated and faded before their time – even worse than me. Their posture bore all the marks of long hard work under the earth and their voices sounded as if their throats were clogged with coal dust.

Vincent found that men, women and children were working like slaves for twelve hours each day. There was no church and no salary and he went down the deep shaft of the notorious Marcasse mine to preach to them. He insisted on sleeping in a little shack at the end of the baker's narrow garden that tapered away into the mine-ravaged land. He rushed out every morning to visit the poor, without stopping to wash or do up his laces – such details as that didn't matter in heaven. In the end, he gave away his shirts and socks and had to make clothes out of sacking. He held improvised services for the miners down the shaft, in the hut, and even in the street, dressed in nothing but an old sack – he even helped the local women, doing washing for them if they were tired.

To Vincent, the source of all true art was real human love, a love that had to express itself over and over, in case it wasn't understood the first time. He was always filled with generous human sympathy and sometimes the unanswerable questions of life consumed him.

'I wonder if there's anything more truly artistic than to love people?'

The faces of the miners were lined and withered – their children never knowing the meaning of youth, but coming into the world with the features of age. The women wrapped their heads in black shawls to protect them from the coal dust – they were thin, unattractive and old before their time. He found time to draw them plodding their weary way to and from the pit and he wrote to Theo, saying that drawing liberated him. Every new work was a sacrifice to his love. He even began to make copies after Millet, the French painter of labourers.

Vincent drew the baker at work, but his wife threw the drawings out when he left. He'd pick up caterpillars and put them back on branches and even put cheese and milk out for the mice, while he was living on bread and water himself. Esther Denis told me he called one mouse Vincent and the other Christien, for some reason. People in the village thought he was mad, but they respected him just the same.

The gember man set up a makeshift church in the baker's workshop, with its red brick flooring and blackened beams. It was heated by the warmth from the bread ovens and it was attended by a small group of miners who came irregularly. There were always accidents in the mine – there was a series of firedamp explosions and, in the absence of a doctor, Vincent elected to see to the wounds. He worked frantically for days and nights to help the injured miners – tearing his remaining clothes into bandages and steeping them in olive oil and wax to treat the miners' burns. Many could not be saved and the funeral processions wound through the shrouded landscape by the score in black trains. Vincent would cry all night in his hut and the miners gave him that name – the Christ of the Coalmines.

Then an epidemic of typhoid broke out. No one was spared, old and young, the community was decimated. He gave them his clothes, his money, his boots. Day and night he nursed them, regardless of his own welfare. Vincent gave them everything he had to try to relieve their suffering, to an extent that the baker's wife wrote to Dorus about his strange son and his even stranger activities in the Borinage: "le jeune monsieur qui n'était pas comme toutes autres".

Vincent's father came for him after receiving the letter from the baker's wife. He found his son lying on a straw sack, with his jacket for a cover. Still, Vincent wouldn't leave until the baker promised to continue looking after the sick and, even then, he did not go back to Etten. A farewell service was held, attended by a handful of miners, ravaged by hunger and illness. The hanging lamps cast grotesque shadows on the whitewashed walls and threw bizarre shapes across the ceiling, where they danced, as if in mockery.

Vincent went to the Borinage to expel the darkness that was in his soul. Through religion, he tried to bring light into the lives of the poor miners. Instead, he plunged himself into the deeper darkness of disillusionment.

This was the time when Vincent began to draw in a serious manner and when he first saw himself as an artist. It was a faltering start, as a child learning to walk. He brought some sketches of the miners back with him – a miner in front of his hut; a miner with his haggard wife, whose arms and legs seemed too long because of the thinness; worn clothing and faces, carrying heavy sacks of coal on their backs, walking home along a path made of coal dust; everything poor, cold and dirty.

The evangelical committee terminated Vincent's ministry for poor speaking, but it was really because he lived with and like the miners he preached to. They didn't like it and thought he was lowering the standards of the ministry. All he did was follow the words of Jesus Christ, "open wide your hands to the needy and the poor".

After leaving Petit Wasmes, he lived through that winter in the nearby village of Cuesmes. He walked there, half starved, and lived with a miner called Decrucq and his family. Vincent went to the mine bosses to complain about the conditions and demanded a fairer share of the profits for the miners. In return, he received insults and the threat of being locked up in an asylum. He left the house of Decrucq and lived wild, in barns or just in the open. He survived on crusts of bread and frostbitten potatoes. He was seen by locals with his face blackened, barefoot and clothed in rags, wandering the bleak landscape through snow and thunderstorms. People heard him weeping and I'm sure dark thoughts of suicide must have threaded through his mind during those months of self-torment.

I myself would wander this land and others in similar fashion some years later.

It was at that point when Vincent gave up on religion and decided his true calling was as an artist. Before the winter was over, he set out on a punishing journey, whipped by freezing rain and wind, with no money for food or lodgings. He wandered like a tramp. He slept in abandoned wagons, woodpiles and haystacks and woke covered in frost. He limped on crippled feet back to his parents' house in Etten, but there was more friction and his father decided to commit him to a lunatic asylum.

The town of Gheel lay sixty kilometres south of Etten, just across the Belgian border. It was called the "City of the Simple", where a thousand lunatics lived among the inhabitants. Insanity was an unspeakable stigma for a family such as the van Goghs, with their pride and pretensions – so Vincent needed to be hidden away somewhere. They called a family council and declared him deranged, because of his inability to take care of himself. But, before they could have him locked away as a madman, Vincent left Etten and arrived in Brussels in October 1880.

Before and after Maria Wilhelmina was born, I was not able to work the streets. I spent some time with my brother Hendrik, who lived in a barn on the outskirts of The Hague, close to the farmhouses he thatched. It was here that I began to drink more heavily – cheap jenever mostly and absinthe when we could afford it. Maria Wilhelmina stayed with my mother and sister until she was three years old and could walk. Then she came with me.

I had a young child and I felt unattractive to the men who were keeping us both alive with their stuivers, so I kept away from the fancy tavernes where I knew there would be a lot of swanky women. On this night, Maria Wilhelmina and I went to a place on the Papestraat, on the eastern flank of Geest and an unfamiliar area to me. My body humours were not good and I felt vulnerable and did not want to be out on that night, but I had no choice. I felt tired and worn down. I was stuck in this life – trapped. And I had to try to make the best of the hand I had been dealt by fate.

That night I was dressed as well as I could and my hair was put up and, even though I really did not want to be there, I put on a show of enjoying myself. I ordered jenever for me and apple juice for Maria Wilhelmina with the little money I had and I could see I was attracting the attention of some of the men in the taverne – one in particular, who was dressed in black and wearing a wide-brimmed hat. As time wore on, nobody approached me – I had spent my money for nothing.

Outside afterwards, I began to get severe stomach cramps and needed to urinate, so I had to crouch behind a bush while my daughter kept watch. Just then, the man in the black clothes came upon me and gave me a fright.

'What are you doing?'

'What do you think?'

'In a public place, like a teef? Get up!'

His voice was gruff and Maria Wilhelmina was frightened. My first instinct was to protect my child so I put myself between her and the dark man.

'I saw you inside, flirting with those men.'

'Who are you?'

'I am a Lutheran abolitionist.'

'And what is that?'

'We're cleaning The Hague of low, dirty lechers and the women who serve them. What you do is degrading and spreads unspeakable disease.'

'I need to live, sir, and to feed my child.'

'Then do it some other way.'

With that, he dragged me from the bush, out on to the street. I tried to fight him away, but he brought his knee up into my face. Blood erupted from my nose. I was screaming, and Maria Wilhelmina was screaming, as he dragged me further along the road. I scratched at his eyes and his hands went round my neck. He was trying to strangle me and my face was turning blue.

Then I heard a voice coming from close by, 'Don't you think you have hit her enough?'

'What has it got to do with you?'

It was Mehdi. He put his face close to the man in black.

'I can make it to do with me if you want.'

Mehdi took me and my daughter to a nearby infirmary, close to the Papestraat. As we were going into the hospital, the man in black jumped out from behind some bushes and tried to attack me again. Mehdi struck him a blow to the head and he ran off. By now, both my eyes were turning black and my nose was broken in several places. The nurse there straightened my nose and Mehdi escorted me and Maria Wilhelmina safely back to my mother's house in Noordstraat, then he disappeared into the night.

'Au revoir, Clasina.'

It was the last time I ever saw him.

# CHAPTER 8

# SLAVERY

'Everyone I know will go and I'll be left with the hostile strangers. I'm losing touch with language. And love. And logic. And life. No more change. No more choice. I'm aware that the present doesn't exist – so it cannot be now – it can only be then. Whose imagination am I a figment of? There's more I need to ask – things that have not been explained. But there's no time left. It is gone!'

Those were more of Vincent's words, spoken to me early in our life together, just after Maria Wilhelmina and I came to live with him. I still did not understand.

I was thirty and life was not getting any easier. My mother had thrown me and Maria Wilhelmina out on the street because of my drinking and I had to solicit customers with my young daughter in tow. It was difficult, as it put men off – they wanted a fantasy woman, not a real woman and Maria Wilhelmina reminded them that I was mortal. I was lucky to be able to make enough money for us to eat from day to day and, in the winter of 1880, I had to find somewhere permanent for us to live, out of the cold. I met a man in a taverne who said he knew a family called Visser that was looking for a knecht.

'What about my daughter?'

'You can bring her with you.'

We were taken to a loft at the top of a frowning house, up a very steep and narrow flight of steps. Our room was tiny and looked like it had not been used for a long time. There was a sloping roof and bare dusty floorboards and a small wooden bed with a thin straw mattress. A small stool and some faded flowers in a vase stood in one of the corners and dark cobwebs hung from the ceiling. Maria Wilhelmina was frightened – everything about this room was dark and dismal. The steep stairs were eerie, the cobwebs wraith-like, the faded flowers were ghoulish. How could we escape if someone or something came after us up here in this devil-trap?

It took me a long time to get to sleep that night. Grotesque shadows came through the small bare window in the moonlight and made the stems and petals of the flowers look like the legs and bodies of giant spiders. They seemed to be getting closer and closer to our bed. They were not flowers any more, they were fiends. I tried to pray –

> 'Ik geloof in God, de almachtige vader,
> schepper van hemel en aarde, en in Jezus
> Christus, zijn enige zoon … '

But I couldn't focus my mind on the words. I was surrounded by an undulating sea of anxiety and the bed was a shrinking island – getting smaller and smaller. I eventually fell asleep through sheer exhaustion but, after what seemed like only five minutes, I heard a voice calling loudly.

'Knecht!'

I climbed out of the thin bed and went to the door. It was a man, summoning me from downstairs.

'Get up!'

Leaving Maria Wilhelmina sleeping, I got dressed and made my way down to a kitchen, trying not to stumble and fall down the narrow steps. It was five in the morning and I was so tired I just wanted to go back to sleep. The man told me to light the fire, but there was no thin kindling like I used at home. He told me to pour some kind of oil on the wood and then stand back and throw a lighted fizz at it to set it ablaze. I thought this was very dangerous and I didn't want to do it, which irritated him greatly and he snatched the box of fizzes from my hand and did it himself, but said I would have to do it from then on.

After that, I had to go outside and feed the animals. The Vissers had a small farm at the back of their big house. They kept some cows and a hog and about ten chickens on their plot of land, along with a few feral goats that came in from the Meijendel. I had to get feed from a small barn and distribute it round to the livestock, then get water from a well that had to be drawn up by hand in a bucket. This was very difficult for me to do and it took me a long time. But I kept going, thinking about the breakfast that would be waiting for me when I finished. The work was very tiring and I'd had nothing to eat yet.

It was almost nine o'clock when I finished up and got back to Maria Wilhelmina. The rest of the Visser family were up by then and preparing breakfast of coffee and ham and fried eggs and homemade bread. I was starving and approached the table. The man pushed me away.

'You do not eat with us!'

By the time the family was finished, all that was left for me and Maria Wilhelmina was some black coffee and two slices of bread. I sat on the stairs and cried. Tears rolled down my face and dripped from my chin into my coffee. Maria Wilhelmina tried to comfort me with a hug and I knew I had to be stronger for her.

The matron of the house came and asked me why I was weeping. I didn't want to tell her the truth, that I was disappointed and disillusioned – she might call me ungrateful and throw me and my young daughter back out onto the street. It was winter and it would snow soon. So I lied.

'I'm homesick.'

'You've only been here a day.'

That made me sob even more, thinking about all the days that stretched ahead.

'Shut up! Don't be such a meisje!'

It wasn't long before the man and the rest of the household came to see what the commotion was about. All of them were shouting at me to shut up, then someone slapped me across the face. They dragged me out into the yard and left me there, like a scurvy dog. I wanted to scream at them and maybe even strike them, but I knew it would only upset Maria Wilhelmina even more than she was already. I felt sick and would have thrown up, had there been anything in my stomach.

Later, the matron came out and fetched us back inside. She told my daughter to go to the loft and stay there. She didn't want to leave me because she was frightened, but I told her I'd come to her soon. The matron beckoned.

'Come with me.'

'Where?'

'I'll show you how to clean the house.'

I followed and she explained what my work would be. As well as feeding and watering the animals twice a day, I would have to clean the whole house, wash-up, weed the orchard, bring in firewood and water the plants in the vegetable garden.

By the time I was finished, I was completely exhausted. They had dinner in the evening and, again, Maria Wilhelmina and I were not allowed near the table. We were given two plates of bony fish and potatoes, which we had to eat outside in the cold. I was afraid my daughter might choke, so I had to take what little meat there was off the bones for her to eat. After dinner, I had to do the washing-up, which I finished late. Then I went to bed. I decided that, whatever about myself, I could not subject Maria Wilhelmina to this slavery and I decided to beseech my mother to take her back in and I would provide money for her upkeep.

I was woken at five again on the following morning and my body ached bone-deep from the work of the previous day. That second day was very much like the first and, as soon as I could, I took my daughter back to Noordstraat. My mother was reluctant to take her at first, but she relented when I explained the conditions in which we were living. I promised I would go to Poeldijkstraat during my time off from work and earn enough money to keep my mother happy and stop her from constantly complaining.

During the days that followed, the Vissers increased my workload. I was expected to clean out the cow barn and the hog sty and collect eggs from the chickens. I struggled for a lot of that first week – I was miserable and tired and hungry and I missed my daughter so much. Before I took the job, it was agreed that I'd have every other weekend off, from Saturday afternoon to Sunday afternoon. I thought I would have at least one day to go to Poeldijkstraat, but the matron didn't work on Sunday and I had to do her chores as well as my own. So, on the days I thought I was going to be able to earn money for my mother, I had to stay on the farm and work even harder. They also began feeding me leftovers, like their hog. They would scrape the food onto a plate and it would all be mixed in together – potatoes and fish soup and kruidnoot and half-eaten poffertjes.

Because I was so busy all the time, the hours and days went quickly and I was beginning to get used to the heavy workload. On the second week, the thought of seeing my daughter filled me with longing and I told them I was taking Sunday off, whether they liked it or not. I jumped rather than crawled out of bed that morning and quickly completed the list of jobs they had given me. When the man got up, he was angry rather than pleased that I'd done the work so fast.

'Why did it take you twice as long to do the same jobs yesterday?'

'I don't know … '

'You're nothing but a luie hoer!'

I thought he was going to beat me or leave me without food. But, instead, he said I couldn't go to see Maria Wilhelmina. If he had cut my fingers off, it wouldn't have hurt so much.

The weeks melted into months – flowed into each other and became each other. And I wondered why I had to be born as me – Clasina Maria Hoornik. Why could I not have been someone else – a bourgeoise, or a woman from another country, or someone who could play the piano? But then I heard the tone in my head, the musical note, and I felt there was more to it – life. I felt there was some kind of destiny – some future that was linked to a bigger horizon – some associated destiny that was and would be connected to happiness.

I continued to work a lot and eat very little and I missed my daughter more and more. Whenever it was my day off, they found a reason not to let me go. Minkukel became my nickname, which means a stupid person or an idiot. The shadows of the faded flowers at night became more oppressive – I began having nightmares and I would wake up and the shadows would be there, lowering over me, threatening me, staring down at me and saying "you will never leave here, ha ha ha ha". The lack of food and sleep made me ill, but I still had to carry on working, no matter how I felt.

Whenever they all went out and I was left alone in the house, I cowered in a corner and did nothing, because I was always afraid someone like Jacobus was hiding in one of the rooms and he'd jump out and devour me. I hated being in that sinister and surly house, but I needed the few stuivers they paid me and which a boy delivered to Noordstraat, to keep my mother happy and prevent her from sending Maria Wilhelmina back to this hell.

Six months passed and it came to the point when I couldn't take it any longer – I'd gone over the limit of my endurance. My mother was complaining that the money I promised from working on the Poeldijkstraat was not forthcoming. So, one day when they all went out, I packed my bag and left. It was a long way home and I had no money, but I just had to get away. Staying was worse than going.

I wasn't far down the street when I was grabbed by a politieagent who asked me where I was coming from. When I told him, he dragged me back to the house and said if I ran away again, he'd put me and my whole family in jail for life. He was related to the Vissers and he said if I told anyone about this conversation, he would shoot me in the feet, so I'd never be able to walk again. From then on, my life became worse than ever.

It was always a struggle to pull the water bucket up from the well and once, when I was really tired and not feeling too good, it felt much heavier than usual and I let the handle slip. It spun round so fast and hit me on the head, just over my eye. I was thrown backwards onto the ground and, when I managed to get up again, I was cut so badly the bone above my right eyebrow was exposed and I was covered in blood. I didn't scream or cry, I just felt relieved because I thought they would let me rest. But when I went to tell them about the accident, they just got angry.

'You're useless, Minkukel.'

They did not get a doctor or dress the wound with a bandage or anything. It was very sore and the bone was exposed for a long time, but luckily it didn't get infected.

One weekend, the Vissers decided to go to Amsterdam and that meant I could go home. When I got to Noordstraat I ran to our house as fast as my thin legs would move. But there was nobody at home. I panicked. All sorts of bewildered thoughts came into my head. Had they been killed? Maybe that politieagent had put them in prison? Maybe my mother couldn't pay the rent and they'd been evicted? Then my brother Pieter came up behind me and made me jump. He said my mother was cleaning a house down by Bakkersstraat and she'd taken Maria Wilhelmina with her. I felt so relieved.

When my mother saw me, she couldn't believe her eyes. A rare look of concern immediately spread across her face.

'What has happened to you, Clasina?'

'I'm alright.'

'Your head … you look so thin.'

I was thin before I went to the Vissers, but now I was nothing more than skin and bone. My mother made a herb paste and put it on the gash over my eyebrow, but it was too late to prevent the scar that I carry to this day. But none of that mattered to me. I was just happy to be with Maria Wilhelmina again. The day passed quickly and I was hoping my mother would tell me not to go back. But she didn't. I probably would have gone back anyway, as I was afraid the politieagent would come and put us all in prison – and if he thought I'd told anyone about what he threatened, he would shoot me in the feet as well. So, I went back to my life of slavery as a knecht.

Before I realised it, a year had gone past.

By now I looked and felt like a fifty-year-old woman. I was so thin and my bosoms were drooping already. My teeth were going bad and my skin was hard and weathered and I always wore a sad expression on my face – a hopeless frown – a gloomy gaze that allowed no sign of laughter or lightness to displace it. The whole time I was there, I only saw my family twice. The second time I came home, my mother was doing her sewing and she didn't even recognise me.

'Clasina?'

'It's me, moeder.'

'You look like a ghost.'

I was so happy to see my daughter I couldn't find words to speak. My voice was stuck in my throat and tears clouded my eyes. There were so many things I wanted to say to her but, instead, I walked away in silence before she could hug me. Maria Wilhelmina followed me to the canal where some children were collecting water in pails, as I used to do. I watched and held my daughter's hand and thought about jumping in, pulling her with me. The children were laughing, even though it was very cold. I'd forgotten what laughter sounded like, what to be young felt like – what it was to be free and plan for a future that would never happen, just as Brechtje and I did. The feeling of belonging somewhere, of being part of a wider landscape, had been driven out of me and all I could see was sorrow.

The ill-treatment continued for the entire year I was with the Vissers and I eventually became seriously ill. I really needed a doctor or a hospital if I was going to survive. But the Vissers did not want the bother or expense of having me treated, so they took me back to Noordstraat and dumped me in the street. It was dark and I lay there for a long time until someone found me. They didn't recognise me, but I was able to tell them who I was. They carried me to our house and my mother took me in. I was so light I was like a doll. She put me in one of the beds and waited.

To see if I would live or die.

While I was recovering, Vincent spent a hard and lonely winter in Brussels, apart from the company of an artist he called Rappard. But he wanted to be reconciled with his family, so he went back to Etten to rid himself of what he called the sufferings and shame of the past. On the way there, through the train window, he saw a man sowing seed in a field and he made a drawing of the sower, in the style of Millet, the French artist Vincent admired greatly for his portrayal of peasants.

Vincent began trekking round Brabant in a cattleman's blouse, with a felt hat pulled down over his forehead and a big easel strapped to his back. What made him decide to be a painter? Was it his experiences with the miners? He sometimes said it was, but I think the need to express himself was always inside him. He tried to release it through various means, art dealing, tutoring, preaching, but it wouldn't emerge. When he sketched the miners he felt a release of that overwhelming emotion which was trying to manifest itself. He finally realised this was his true vocation – his spiritual calling.

He set up a studio in an abandoned outbuilding at the parsonage but, to achieve his artistic ambitions, he needed more than anything else to draw from models. Models were expensive to hire, so he barged into farmhouses to draw women at their work and he tried to persuade men to stand still with a shovel or a plough. He forced people to pose for him and the villagers became afraid, viewing him as mad. They began to avoid him when they saw him coming down the road and complained to his father when the parson made his ministerial rounds.

Vincent mocked the ones he was able to persuade to come to his studio for insisting on posing in their stiff Sunday clothes, without a knee, elbow or shoulder blade showing, nor any other part of the body with its dents and bumps. What a joy it was for him when he met me, who would pose in any way he wanted, with or without clothing.

Rappard came to visit that summer and it was a rare happy time for Vincent, despite the inhabitants of Brabant not exactly embracing his newfound purpose in life with open arms. Friends of the family complained about him to his father, that he was twenty-seven and not supporting himself, costing the family money they could ill afford – spent on models and drawing materials for pictures they didn't even like.

Theo, meanwhile, had become gérant of Goupil's three Paris establishments. In his elegant suits and Paris manners, he served as a vivid reminder of what Vincent could have achieved, had he been more amenable and compliant. But it wouldn't be long before Vincent saw what he believed was an opportunity to retrieve some of what he'd lost and put an end to his years of loneliness.

# CHAPTER 9

# STREETWALKING

**B**ack on the street, I was even less attractive to men than I had been before I became a knecht for the Vissers. I was very thin, my bosoms drooped like those of an old woman, I had a scar on my forehead and my skin was coarse and veined. Consequently, I was consigned to the lowest rung of the straatmadelief ladder, having to provide hand baan for the vilest and poorest customers, who could barely afford to eat, never mind pay for a hoer. Most were dirty and smelly, with rotting teeth and calloused hands. But beggars could not be choosers and I had to provide for my daughter. Sometimes, as in the past, I had to bring Maria Wilhelmina with me, when my mother was working or when she was in an ill humour and refused to take care of my daughter. But I hated doing it and tried to avoid it whenever possible.

It was about this time, in the summer of the year 1881, that I met a man called Kwame. He was a negro and, while ordinarily the white hoers stayed clear of black men for fear of reprisals from the sanctimonious and self-righteous, he was clean and smelled nice and his large teeth gleamed white in the moonlight. He paid me more than the other customers so I took a chance that I wouldn't be singled out to be beaten by the bigots. Kwame worked in a factory that made nails, close to the Poeldijkstraat district. We would normally use a room in one of the tavernes but, after a few meetings, he asked me to come to where he lived.

I left the district with Kwame when he finished his night shift at the factory and he took me to an area that was being made ready for the building of small, close-grouped houses, where the destitute could erect their own makeshift shacks. The shacks were all crowded together, made from tin and wood and other bits and pieces – they looked like rows of dishevelled drunks, propping each other up. The abode where he lived was made mostly of pasteboard and the rain came in. He shared it with four other black men and two women, all between the ages of about seventeen and twenty-five.

Unlike him, the house and people in it were very dirty and there were flies and fleas everywhere. The two women did not go on the rag when they had their menses and there was stale blood all over their bed, which the rain had spread to the floor. The kitchen was the worst place I had ever seen. The homemade wooden table had gaps and cracks in it, where bits of food had got lodged and remained, rotting and rancid. What fell on the floor was never cleaned up and the stove was just covered in sticky grease and dirt. The privy was outside – it had no roof and it stank, with slugs and maggots crawling around. But I suppose it was better than living on the streets.

I asked Kwame why he wanted to take me back there – the rooms in the tavernes were not palatial, but they were better than this. He said he wanted to marry me and he required me to see where we would be living after the wedding. There was method in his madness. Kwame was from Bovenkust in West Africa. He was brought to Holland by the Dutch West India Company to work and, to remain here, he had to have proper legal papers under the terms of the nationality law of 1850, which he could only get by marrying a Dutchwoman.

I refused to accommodate Kwame in that place and asked him to take me back to Poeldijkstraat. I also told him I could not marry him.

'Why not? Because I am a negro?'

'No, because I don't love you.'

'Love? What is that? You are a hoer.'

'Even hoers are entitled to love, Kwame.'

He shrugged his shoulders and we were leaving the house when the two women approached. They looked angry and hostile and one of them started screaming at me.

'You are fornicating with my husband!'

'What?'

'Don't listen to her, I'm not her husband.'

'Liar!'

Kwame tried to protest, but she would not be calmed. Both women began to pick up stones and hurl them at me. I tried to protect my head, but the stones were getting bigger and they were striking my body. Kwame ran away and left me to the mercy of the women. One large stone struck the side of my face and nearly knocked me over. I tried to run from them, but they followed me, still hurling stones. Blood was streaming down from my cheek and dripping off my chin and I believed that I would surely be killed.

I managed to get out of the area and, by then, the two women had stopped following me. But I was dazed and disorientated and didn't know how to get home. I was on a dark, deserted street, hoping not to be accosted by heidens or zigeuners or arrested by the maréchaussée for being in the state I was in. Then I saw a shadowy figure coming towards me and I looked around for somewhere to hide, but there was none. As it came closer, I saw that the figure was an elderly woman and I wondered why someone like that would be out alone at this time of night. When she came close enough, she noticed that I was bleeding.

'My dear child, what happened to you?'

'I was attacked.'

'Where do you live?'

'Noordstraat.'

'That's a long way from here. Come with me.'

I was reluctant to do so – there were too many strange people in this city, many of them I had already met. But I was feeling faint and didn't want to collapse on the street. She called herself Countess Carola. She was over seventy and had a face that would frighten small children, but a good sense of humour to go with it. In the course of our conversation on the way to her house, it came out that she was looking for a companion to live with her, because she was afraid of being alone.

'That's why I walk late at night, I don't like being in the house on my own.'

She was not rich, but she was financially independent and she had a nice place in an area called Buitenhof. She cleaned and disinfected my face and placed a dressing on the wound.

'You can have your own room and privy if you become my companion, Clasina.'

'But I work at night, Countess. I wouldn't be here until morning.'

'What do you do?'

I thought of Kwame.

'Late shift in the nail factory.'

'Pity.'

'I do have a daughter, she could keep you company while I'm away?'

'How old?'

'Almost five.'

'A little young, but it might work.'

And so Maria Wilhelmina and me moved in with Countess Carola. We had our own room and use of the privy and no rent to pay. She would always have eaten by the time I got in from work, but she'd have my breakfast ready for me on a plate and my daughter got on very well with her, better than she did with my mother. It was ideal – my luck had changed. Countess Carola was a very kind woman. She'd been married three times but had no children of her own – it was as if she'd adopted myself and Maria Wilhelmina. She had a fine library and I was allowed to read as many books as I liked and she also began to teach my daughter how to read while I was out at night. But she was afraid of ghosts and she kept asking me to find another job.

Streetwalking on the Poeldijkstraat was becoming difficult and dangerous for me and, when Countess Carola introduced me to one of her friends, who was a Calvinist and who was looking for a knecht, I decided to take the job. It would allow me to be back at nights and this suited the Countess and also Maria Wilhelmina. Everybody was happy.

The friend's name was Dirkje de Vries and she was a middle-aged woman with a ten-year-old son. Her husband had died in a cholera outbreak in the year of 1876 and she'd run their language school on her own since then. Her last maid left to get married and now she needed a replacement. Dirkje taught mainly French, but also English and Italian. My job was to look after her son and do the cooking and cleaning. I told her I had experience of working as a knecht for a year and she seemed happy with that and didn't ask for a reference. I would not be living with her, as I had with the Vissers, and that suited me.

The school was located in a big old building not far from Countess Carola's house in Buitenhof. Dirkje and her son, Luuk, lived on the top floor and the other two floors were used as classrooms. I was allowed to take my daughter with me to work and Maria Wilhelmina could take lessons in French and English for free. Dirkje and I got on well from the start – she liked me and I liked her. Although she was a Calvinist and I was a Catholic, neither of us went to church, so no conflict of creed arose.

Despite the school being exclusive, Dirkje was finding it hard to manage financially, because costs were so high in that area. The housework wasn't too taxing and Luuk was at school during the day, so she asked me to help out with some administration. It was something I'd never done before, but I was eager and a quick learner and I found that I could be very versatile. To begin with, I stood in for people who were away with sickness and, gradually, Dirkje taught me other things. She saw I could improvise and that I was well organised, so she showed me how to understand the practice of commerce and to keep accounts. I was fascinated. This was an entirely new world opening up before me. I became so efficient around the school she was able to cut back on costs and save on time. She was very pleased.

Every Friday, Dirkje sent Luuk back with me and Maria Wilhelmina to Countess Carola's house for the weekend. I wanted to learn French too, so I could converse with my daughter in that language and, so, increase our understanding of it. And I did – along with a little English, when Dirkje could spare me from all my other work. Dirkje was well travelled and she had many stories to tell – about the places she had been to and the books she'd read and the people she'd met. We would sit at a little table and talk. She told me to question things, to always ask why. She said I should never accept anything without knowing its true meaning. She opened little windows inside my head and let some light in. And I soared into the omniscient sky and began to know what I was – what I could be.

One Friday, Dirkje sent Luuk and Maria Wilhelmina back to Countess Carola's and asked me to stay behind with her.

'Do you think you're mature enough, Clasina?'

'Mature enough for what?'

'To learn a bit more about life.'

I was always curious and wanted to know what it was I was going to learn – maybe more about business practices or the world outside The Hague?

'Be patient, Clasina.'

I was eager and looking forward to knowing whatever it was.

In the evening, a couple of about the same age as Dirkje arrived. They were quite average, nothing exceptional about them, and I wondered who they were. Dirkje served them wine and, shortly after, a younger couple arrived, along with two girls of about eighteen. The girls looked poor, with cheap clothes and sad eyes, just like me when I was younger and working as a straatmadelief. Dirkje gave everyone a glass of wine, including myself. One of the men looked at me.

'I see we have a new participant tonight.'

Dirkje smiled at him.

'She's a beginner.'

After a few glasses of wine, they started to get very friendly with each other – hugging and kissing and touching. I stood some distance back, not wanting to get too close. I wasn't scandalised or anything like that – I was a hoer by profession after all. But this was different to anything I'd experienced before. Dirkje suggested we all go upstairs to her bedroom. I was a bit uncertain about what was going on, but curious about what I was supposed to learn. So I went with them.

Very soon, they were all naked and writhing around on the bed, all entwined with each other like a ball of worms. I kept looking, fascinated, as you can be by something that is grotesque to look at, yet you cannot turn away. They did not ask me to join in and I stayed well back against the wall. But I couldn't leave either, because Dirkje had locked the door. They stayed on the bed for about an hour, doing all sorts of things to each other. And I watched them for that hour, feeling a mixture of disbelief and disgust – fascination and fearfulness. When it was all over, they got dressed and drank some more wine and laughed and joked as if it was a respectable and polite social gathering.

When they all left, Dirkje poured me another drink. She came and sat close to me and smiled in an unsettling way. I was a woman of the streets and not much unsettled me, but I wasn't sure of my ground in this new environment.

'Are you sexually adventurous, Clasina?'

'What do you mean?'

'Did you like what you just witnessed?'

'Not really.'

I'd heard about orgies, but I had never taken part in one.

'Do not reject it until you try it.'

One drink led to another and then we danced together and she kissed me. I expected it to be disgusting, but it wasn't – much better than being kissed by a man with stinking breath or a rancid beard. It was a strange experience for me. I had never been this close to a woman before and, although it wasn't totally abhorrent, it didn't seem right either. Dirkje moved quickly and kissed me again, this time with more force. It was an awkward moment. I pushed her away gently and she complied without complaint.

'Would you like another drink, Clasina?'

'Maybe not.'

Dirkje had taken me by surprise on this night. It felt like I had been lured into a spider's web because we'd been getting on so well together. She'd given me no indication of what would be happening and I should have been warned. It made me angry to think I had been taken for granted in that way. Dirkje put the glass to her lips and drank the wine down in one gulp. Then she moved close again and removed the clip from her hair. Complete silence held the room in a vice-grip. Was I a complete fool, not to have realised what Dirkje was before now? I wrestled with the realisation of what was happening and my instinct was to go, leave the house and get back to Maria Wilhelmina at Countess Carola's. This was a complete stranger – not the woman I'd been working with for several months. But my feet were rooted to the floor.

Dirkje tried to placate me, moving closer and beginning to undress me. I did not resist, even though I knew I should. What kind of fool was I, allowing myself to be manipulated? But then, I had been manipulated and used all my life, so how was this any different? Dirkje's voice was cajoling as she removed her own clothes and lay down on the bed. Her arms went around my neck and she kissed my face and eyes as she pulled me down with her.

'What do you think of me, Clasina?'

'I don't know what to think of you.'

'Why don't you know?'

There was no answer to that question. This was not going at all well. I just wanted to get out of there, but I didn't want to lose my job and my lodgings with Countess Carola. I winced as Dirkje pushed her fingers inside me, not because it hurt, but because it felt unnatural to me. She could sense I didn't want her and she became rough and I could feel her anger being applied to my body. Even though we were supposed to be making love, Dirkje was really attacking me. Brutalising me. Trying to damage me. Trying to give me back the hurt thing I had just given to her by my rejection.

She rolled over and lit a cigarette which she smoked in silence. I knew I should leave but, for some reason, I did not. We both dressed again, after the failure of the encounter.

'I have to go now, Dirkje.'

'Is that all you have to say?'

'That's all. I'm sorry.'

'For what?'

'For not being like you, Dirkje.'

I put on my coat and made my way towards the door. Before I could reach it, the wine bottle came flying past my head, missing me by a matter of inches. I turned to see Dirkje standing by the window looking out at the street below and laughing. She spun round to face me, still laughing.

'If I'd known you were going to turn out like this, Clasina, I would never have … '

'Turn out like what, Dirkje?'

'A whimpering meisje!'

'I don't deserve this from you.'

'You deserve a blow in the face, Clasina … that's what you deserve.'

Dirkje came at me from across the room and tried to hit me. I defended myself and struck back. She toppled backwards, onto the bed. I turned towards the door again, but Dirkje grabbed me from behind, pulling at my hair and scratching at my face. She threw me over her shoulder and I sailed across the room and struck the wall. This was madness, but I couldn't stop it. I snatched up the wine bottle from the floor as she lunged again and I struck her on the side of the head with it. She slumped to the floor – eyes wide open and staring. I bent over her.

'Dirkje … '

I brushed back her hair with the palm of her hand and lifted her onto the bed. She was heavy and I struggled with her limp body. I never would have believed, looking at her lying there, that she had such virulence inside her. Such vindictiveness.

'Dirkje … '

I lay there, propped up on one elbow, looking down at her strange face and her unconscious eyes – eyes that stared back at me. All the energy was gone from her. All the determination and ferocity. She was quiet now – like a lamb. And I felt an overwhelming sense of sorrow for her that was almost unbearable.

After a while, I rose from the bed and left the house. I collected Maria Wilhelmina from Countess Carola and we trudged off into the dark night.

# CHAPTER 10

# LOVE

While Vincent was living and drawing at Etten in the year of 1881, his cousin Cornelia Vos-Stricker and her eight-year-old son came to stay with the van Goghs. Her husband Christoffel had died and Vincent felt a sympathy for her that developed into a deep passion – a feeling that had been smouldering inside him since his unrequited love affair with Eugénie Loyer in London. Cornelia appealed to his combination of carnal need and human compassion. But, when he declared his love and proposed marriage, she too rejected him.

'Never, no never!'

Those were the words she said and she left immediately for Amsterdam.

She was seven years older than Vincent and four years older than me and her rejection was a deep humiliation for the van Gogh family. Despite that, Vincent bombarded her with letters which she refused to read. Theo even gave him money to go to Amsterdam to see her, but she refused to meet him. She left the house by the back door as soon as he arrived at the front door. In the parlour, Vincent held his hand above the flame of an oil lamp, insisting he would keep it there until he could see Kee. But her father, Pastor Stricker, blew the lamp out and told him to leave the house. Vincent's persistence threatened to drive a wedge between the van Goghs and the Strickers, particularly between Vincent's mother and her older sister Mina, Kee's mother.

As I've said, Cornelia was married to Christoffel – the same Christoffel who had tried to abuse me when I was young. He became sick and died in 1878, just before Vincent went to the Borinage and when I was living and drinking with my brother Hendrik in the barn on the outskirts of The Hague. Christoffel's family had moved back to Amsterdam a few years after Brechtje died and it was there he met and married Vincent's cousin, Cornelia Stricker. What a small world it was turning out to be, here in Holland.

Even though Christoffel had been dead for three years, Cornelia was still locked into mourning. She was a severe, unsmiling woman, always dressed in high-buttoned black satin, forever joined to her dead husband by grief. Vincent's family believed marriage would anchor him and help him find his place in life, but Cornelia wasn't the right woman for them. Neither was I. When I look back now on the disparaging remarks made against me by Vincent's family and so-called friends, that I was "repulsive" and "unbearable", I know that I was infinitely less repulsive than the ugly, large-headed Eugénie Loyer and infinitely less unbearable than the hard-faced, self-pitying Cornelia Stricker. They were both unendearing women, almost masculine in appearance. I was not – I was delicate and accessible. Compared to those women, I was open and warm to Vincent and in me he finally found what they denied him – love.

After months of letter writing to Kee, none of which she read, Vincent received a warning from her Bible-thumping father, Johannes.

'Her "no" is quite decisive.'

But Vincent refused to stop.

'A lark can't help singing in the spring.'

He saw himself as a martyr for love and vowed to commit himself totally and with all his heart utterly and forever to his idea of what love was. It would rescue him from a life that had been withered, blighted and stricken with all kinds of great misery.

'A woman must breathe on me, for me to become a man.'

95

To him, of all the emotions and states of mind, love was the most powerful and he vowed to sing no other song than amour éternal.

Vincent was in love with love itself, not with Cornelia Vos-Stricker. In the thousands of words he wrote, he never even mentioned her name. The volcano of emotion trapped inside him had nothing to do with Kee, or Eugénie for that matter, it was a maelstrom of yearning to belong somewhere – to find a little corner of the world where he could be warm and welcomed. He was surrounded by cold sanctimony and just needed a little entente cordiale in his life. He was fighting for his right to exist, just as I was fighting the same battle, but on a different front.

Vincent couldn't stand it any longer and he left Etten for The Hague in November of 1881. He stayed at a small boarding house in Uileboomen, on the city's east side, and walked to the studio of his cousin, Anton Mauve, to whom he confessed that he was wrong to pursue Cornelia, with her silly notion of mystical love.

'I need to find a real woman, Anton.'

That's when he found me – for the first time.

When the gember man found me the second time, when Maria Wilhelmina and I were exhausted and starving, I didn't remember him – but he remembered me. He spoke about it on a number of occasions during our time together and the encounter came back to me, especially when I found myself carrying Willem.

Maria Wilhelmina was with me, as she mostly was after we left Countess Carola, which infuriated my mother. On that occasion, Vincent and I used a small room in a taverne called De Druif, which had an iron bed, while Maria Wilhelmina stayed downstairs. He thought I was the same age as Cornelia Vos-Stricker and I probably looked it, but I was four years younger. I was stronger than when he found me again that winter and, although he had been with straatmadeliefjes before, he was awkward and self-conscious when it came to lovemaking.

The room was bare and dusty, with little furniture apart from the iron bed. Yellow curtains hung on the small window that looked out onto Snoekstraat, at least they looked yellow – they may have been white but discoloured by time and neglect. A single candle perched in a pewter candlestick on a ledge, above a water basin, which was empty. Noises of the night floated in from outside through cracks in the window which also let in the cold. I shivered. The gember man took off his coat and put it round my shoulders.

'We should take our clothes off, not put more on.'

He laughed at my words – more a smile than a laugh. A smile that made its own sound.

'We don't have much time.'

He looked puzzled.

'My daughter … downstairs.'

'Of course.'

In the absence of any movement from him, I led him across to the bed and removed his coat from my shoulders. He stood watching me, as if he'd never seen a woman before in his life.

'What do you want?'

'Pardon?'

'To do?'

The question seemed to confuse him for a moment or two and I thought maybe he was drunk or had taken opium or some other remedy. Then he made that smile again.

'Oh, yes … what can I have?'

'With the hand, with the mouth, with the kutje but no kissing.'

'What about with the kutje and kissing also?'

'Extra.'

'How much?'

'A guilder.'

I was sure he would say it was too much, because I wasn't the girl I once was and my body was coarse, though not common. Life had left its mark on me, but it had also given me a greater insight into its realities than most bourgeoise would ever have. He didn't argue, just took the money from his pocket and gave it to me.

I did not have any contraception that night and I was initially afraid to take a chance. I didn't want gonorrhoea or to be pregnant again. But I had been told that I would never be able to conceive after Maria Wilhelmina and I was prepared to risk the clap for a guilder. We were about to do it when he hesitated.

'Wait … '

'Yes?'

'What do you think of me?'

It was the same question Dirkje had asked, before.

'I think you're very handsome.'

I always told men what they wanted to hear, whether it was the truth or not.

'But do you like me?'

'I don't know you … but if I did, I'm sure I would like you very much.'

He seemed pleased with that and we continued to the bed. It was too cold in the room to get completely naked, but we removed enough to ensure that he got his guilder's worth. He lowered me down and my arms hung around his neck and I kissed his face and eyes. I made the required moaning sound to his motion and he kissed me on the lips and inside my ear. The bed was uncomfortable and made a lot of noise, which had the effect of prolonging the moment of ejection for him. When it was over, it seemed as if he was left unsatisfied – let down – disappointed. It wasn't anything to worry about for me, it was what I felt with all men, but somehow I wanted him to be pleased with my performance. There was something different about him – something tragic. He was not like anyone I had ever encountered.

'Was everything to your satisfaction?'

'Yes, it was,'

'Are you sure?'

'I'm sure.'

I didn't want to leave Maria Wilhelmina downstairs on her own for too long. Although it wasn't the roughest part of the city, it was still a dangerous place for a young girl to be left alone. Normally, I would ask the bartender or the landlord to keep an eye on her, if I knew them well enough, but I was a stranger in this particular taverne.

We dressed and I assumed I would not see him again, so there was no point in being sentimental. I just wanted to get back to my daughter, but he clung to me as I went towards the door.

'I must go down … '

'We need more.'

'What do you mean?'

'You and I, we need more time together.'

I doubted if that would ever happen.

'Do you live in The Hague?'

'I do now.'

'Then perhaps we will meet again.'

'What's your name?'

'Clasina.'

'I'm a man with passions, Christien. I must come to you again, otherwise I'll freeze or turn to stone.'

What a strange thing to say – and did he call me Christien? I wasn't sure.

'There are many hoers in this city.'

'But not like you.'

He released my arm and we made our way downstairs. Maria Wilhelmina was just where I left her, drinking some sugar water. I put my arms around her and kissed her on the top of her head. She was such a good girl, having to do what she did and traipse around the streets with me. I hated my mother for making us do that, she had no pity, just a lead guilder where her heart should be. But then, she had to be as hard as she was, giving birth to eleven children and living on very little. There was nothing soft in her life and, consequently, there was nothing soft in her heart either.

As we left the taverne, I looked back and saw the gember man at a table with a bottle of absinthe. Another man was joining him, who I would later come to know as his cousin, Anton Mauve.

I gave my mother the guilder so she would allow us to stay at her house in Noordstraat. Next morning, I felt sick, with a pain in my kidneys. My mother called a nurse who knew about illnesses and she gave me a potion. She wasn't a real nurse, just someone who helped poor people who were suffering, like Vincent did in the Borinage. The following day I had a fever and was vomiting and had to spend the day in bed. I kept drinking water to flush the infection and took the potion, but it didn't seem to help. It got so bad I wanted to die. What was the point of living? Maria Wilhelmina would be better off if I died. So I stopped drinking the water. I didn't drink anything for a day and a half and I became very dried out – they say once you get over being thirsty, the rest is easy.

My mother tried to make me drink, but I wouldn't. I was very light-headed and dizzy and it was impossible for me to get out of the bed. My mother called for the nurse again and she immediately saw how dehydrated I was. The two of them held my mouth open and made me drink – foiling my plan to die by desiccation. I was still sick and vomiting, it was difficult for me to even keep the water down, so maybe my plan would work after all. Then Maria Wilhelmina was allowed to see me and she was crying.

'I don't want you to die, mammie.'

My heart almost broke. What could I do? I felt ashamed for trying to kill myself – it would leave her with my mother, who would put her into the orphanage like she did my brothers, or even give her away or sell her. How could I allow that to happen to my beautiful daughter? No, I was wrong. Staying with me was better than the alternatives.

I tried my best to get better, to get the fever under control with the nurse's potion and, despite how ill I was, I managed to get out of the bed I'd been in for a number of weeks. I eventually got the fever down, even though I felt weak and dizzy. But I was determined to get strong again – or stronger, as I never was that strong. I went outside to get some air and the world around me started to spin. It felt as if I was the only thing not moving and if I tried to, I was sure to collapse. After that I began to burn up. I was red in the face and sweating, even though the weather was cold, and I felt like I couldn't breathe. I was really thirsty again and my head was buzzing like a bee, so I took my clogs off to expose my feet, hoping that would cool me down. It worked.

While I was sick, Vincent's father came to The Hague and took him back to Etten. That Kerstmis, the gember man had another violent argument with Dorus, just because he refused to attend church.

'I told him his whole system of religion was horrible.'

The argument quickly moved on to his father's attempt to put him in the asylum at Gheel and there was a rage of recrimination and accusation. Vincent was furious.

'I don't remember ever having been in such a rage.'

He unleashed all his pent-up fury and frustration in a deluge of profane curses.

'I couldn't contain my anger any longer.'

His father ordered him to leave and never return.

'Get out of my house!'

Vincent never fully recovered from that argument. It represented the culmination of all the injuries and injustices he believed he'd suffered. He took the train back to The Hague and went straight to the house of Anton Mauve.

I was sick all over that Kerstmis, but we had no money and my mother insisted that I go back out on the street as soon as I could walk. Maria Wilhelmina and me were soon back out traipsing along Schoolstraat with the dogs barking and our clogs making soft scraping noises on the snow-covered cobbles and our breath coming in steamy jets, forming little clouds in the freezing air.

That's when I met the gember man for the second time.

# CHAPTER II

# MODEL AND MISTRESS

Anton Mauve loaned Vincent enough money to set up a small studio on the Schenkweg. It was a room with an alcove and a very large window facing south. He filled it with a few simple pieces of furniture and many prints to hang on the walls. Within a week, the last stuiver was gone, so he asked Theo for more, which his brother supplied.

His association with Mauve began amicably enough, but it could not last. In the beginning, I think I represented to Vincent the same kind of poverty and misery he tried to alleviate in the Borinage, but Mauve was somewhat of a peacock and a parvenu and he argued with Vincent for taking me and Maria Wilhelmina in off the street. To him, we were carrion.

Mauve was fifteen years older than Vincent, with a very different disposition. But they were similar in other ways – Mauve was also the estranged son of a preacher who had been an impoverished artist. But, where Mauve became successful by painting conventional images, Vincent did not. While Mauve and other artists stood together and imitated each other, Vincent stood alone in his work. Yes, he studied the paintings of Theophile de Bock, Isaac Israëls, Jean-François Millet and he admired Rembrandt van Rijn and Frans Hals and Jan van Goyen, but he never imitated any of them, always relying on his own talent and vision. He was very angry with the people who were calling him an amateur and an idler and a sponger on others.

After leaving Countess Carola and meeting Vincent for the second time during the winter at the end of 1881, I went with Maria Wilhelmina to his studio on the Schenkweg. He gave us food and shelter in return for me being his model. On the first day, I tried not to sit too close to him. I noticed that he seemed to have a tear in his eye and I thought maybe I should ask him what was wrong. But I had only just got there and it may have been too prying of me to enquire. And I was nervous – things had gone wrong for me in the past, just when I believed my fortunes were changing for the better. Fate had proved to be unpredictable and untrustworthy and it always took back more than it gave.

The gember man wanted something from me – more than just modelling, about which I knew nothing. Otherwise he would not have been sitting there drinking absinthe with me. At the same time, he seemed very vulnerable and I didn't want to upset him, in case he changed his mind and threw me and Maria Wilhelmina out. It was winter and the streets were as cold as my mother's heart.

He took a piece of cloth from his pocket and dabbed his eyes, then he went and stood by the window, through which the watery light of winter poured itself.

'Do you like the studio?'

'Yes, it's a fine place.'

'A little small for three of us … will we manage?'

'I've lived in smaller.'

He came back to his chair slowly and, hesitantly, moved it closer to mine. He seemed nervous, reluctant to speak what was on his mind. A silence ended with shaky words emerging.

'I've had my heart broken recently.'

'You can call me Clasina.'

'I've been humiliated, Christien.'

That name again. I assumed he hadn't heard me correctly, even though I had told him my name several times.

'My name is not Christien.'

He ignored my words, or perhaps he didn't hear them. I would learn that Vincent was often preoccupied with his own thoughts, thoughts which the words of others could not penetrate.

There was something in his voice, something damaged – something in the way he looked at me that was beyond sadness. I looked back and I wondered if he knew I saw him – not just the man, but him. I saw the way he held his glass, the colour of his hair, the way the light washed his profile, the smell of pipe smoke from his clothes, the blue-greenness of his eyes.

He'd moved so close that I could feel his breath on my face. His fingers touched my arm, very lightly, and his eyes looked deep inside me and saw a kindred spirit – another lost soul – a wanderer in the wilderness like himself.

'You have such a graceful figure. When can I draw you, Christien?'

'Whenever you like.'

'Now?'

'Of course.'

He directed Maria Wilhelmina and me to put our few belongings in the living space – then we went back to the studio. He gave my daughter some bread and cheese to eat and asked me to pose by sitting on the floor in a white smock. Which I did, while smoking a cigar.

Vincent had been hurt by a woman. I knew that, even though I didn't know who she was at the time, only when he told me later. It seemed to me that he really wanted to hide away somewhere from the pain in his heart, instead of drawing me. It went against the solitary man inside him, against all his self-imposed circumspection – against the wall he'd built up around himself to avoid being wounded again. I'd never felt so close to a man before, not even Mehdi or my father, and I wondered why I felt it now. Was it the man himself – the easy way I felt with him – the safeness of his presence – the fact that the few words he spoke sounded like something I'd never heard before, coming from somewhere I'd never known? Or was it just that the thought of going back to Noordstraat was less appealing than the thought of living here in this small place with the poor painter? I didn't know and, for now at least, I didn't care.

He took a break from drawing me and we drank some more absinthe. I lit up a cheap cigar and he put flame to his pipe. I pointed to the many drawings and sketches which were scattered all over the studio.

'May I look?'

'Yes.'

It was like an absurd garden, where pictures grew instead of flowers, but which were just as complex. He watched me as I glanced through them, anticipating my reaction. Pictures of trees and streets and people I didn't recognise – a young woman smiling, poor people working, cabbages and clogs, factories, rain, and much more.

'What do you think?'

'They're good.'

'How do you know?'

'I know what I like.'

My reply seemed to satisfy him and the ghost of a smile broke across his lips. I would come to know that Vincent didn't care what people thought of his art – except for his younger brother Theo. He was not a man to conform to shallow, transient fashions and he saw his subjects in a different light to other artists. Later, when he came to paint in oils, people would ridicule him – only because they didn't understand what he was trying to do. He was trying to paint what he saw inside his soul. Which was impossible. For now though, he used pen and pencil and chalk and watercolour and he hadn't yet formed his true style, a style which would drive him insane – or what lesser people defined as insane. To me it was not insanity, but frustration at being mortal.

He resumed the drawing and I resumed my pose. To most people, the interior of the studio would be sparse, but to me it was ornate, baroque even. It was rococo and chinoiserie and filigreed and champlené, without being presumptuous. A small fire burned in the grate, yet the interior was cool – not cool exactly – tranquille, reposante, even spiritual. It was a milieu I'd never experienced before and I was a little overawed by it, though I tried not to show it in case I alarmed him. It seemed to me as if he was a nervous deer and any unfamiliar sound or movement would make him flee. It was one thing for him to hire me to pose as his model, that was business – and even then he was apprehensive. This was different – it was personal and even esoteric. He would have to expose himself to me if we were living together and I would know him.

Was he afraid of that?

The light in the studio was strange, it came through a window that looked out over a laundry and danced with the red shadows from the fire. There was a scent of witch hazel in the air and the sound of gentle music coming from somewhere in the streets outside – I thought it might be "geef mij de liefde" or "het is een nacht" – or something I'd never heard before. I couldn't be sure. Although he was drawing, Vincent was uneasy – on guard. I don't think it was what he expected, I mean me and Maria Wilhelmina actually living here. It was one thing for someone to visit, but entirely another thing for them to remain. And Vincent wasn't a sociable man, he preferred his own company. So I really didn't know on that first day why he had invited us to stay with him. What did he expect me to be – a peasant woman – ill-educated? Which I was, of course, but I'd read a great deal and I had my own opinions. Maybe he didn't expect that.

I don't think he knew what to expect and his invitation was instinctual and spontaneous and not something he would normally have done. Maybe it was just pity – an extemporaneous attack of sorrow at the lamentable sight of myself and Maria Wilhelmina starving on the street that night. Or perhaps it was some subliminal voice, the same unconscious calling which forced him to draw and paint, despite all the setbacks he had suffered in that undertaking. The voice that expected something from him was waiting for him to appease it. But, at that time and perhaps never, he didn't know what that expectation was.

Or maybe he did.

During that winter on the Schenkweg, the emanation was coming from me. I was his muse, his talisman, his geluksbrenger. I was what he was looking for, in the distant, vague, ethereal remoteness inside his head. Now I was close, not calling from some misty shoreline in his soul. I was personal, and he didn't know if I was something to do with his earlier definition of God, or if I was a completely different entity, outside the scope of his experience – outside the preaching of his father, outside his own preaching when he decided to become a pastor. I could tell he was wondering how that could be. How could it be? But there was no time for him to think about it now, there was a drawing to be made. Vincent had that boyishness about him, something endearing that brought out a kind of maternal instinct in me, as if I had two children in that little place – Maria Wilhelmina and Vincent Willem. It felt natural and perfectly right and so easy to sustain.

Later, when we went to bed, I watched the man – he was still nervous, like the first time we lay together. He was unsure of himself in a situation where I had the most control. It was my element, not his, and he felt uncomfortable to be relinquishing control to a woman. When he spoke, his voice seemed to be coming, not from his mouth, but from the sketches littered about – as if they were speaking for him, the words he couldn't formulate for himself.

'Are you alright?'

'You may call me Vincent.'

'May I?'

'Yes.'

'And you may call me Christien.'

'Is that not your name?'

'Yes.'

As we lay together and our bodies entwined and became as one, it seemed to me that I had always known this man

– I had always known the way he looked at me, the way he caressed my skin, the way he kissed my back. I always had a knowledge of his colour, of his shape, of his teeth and his ears and his nostrils. It came from somewhere before I was born and I carried it inside me to this moment. And now it was here and it lived in the rainbow mist of latent knowledge in which truth revels. It was something that could not be measured by the conscious working will, but people were, within themselves, gifted with infinite power and the ability to know all things.

I didn't say all that to Vincent, because neither of us were ready to understand it at that time. He would come to understand it after I was gone and he would search for me. I would come back and go again and come back and go again – until it ended, as it was always destined to do. For now it was enough that he was inside me, with shadows from the red fireglow dancing to his passion, to the chinoiserie, to the scent of witch hazel, to the remote sound of the pierement.

To the straatmadelief beneath him.

It was as if time was standing still and our souls ceased to exist – our individual souls – and were replaced by a cloud of sensations that could easily be mistaken for souls. There had been so much on Vincent's mind before I came to his studio that day with Maria Wilhelmina, so much he had to do and the hurry he was in to do it. He had been thinking way ahead, three or four drawings ahead. But now all that stopped. Now it didn't matter, none of it – what was to be done, what was ahead, what was outside – in the future. Now, only now meant anything. And time ceased to exist.

Suddenly, I was filled with fear. It gripped my heart and held it fast. All my senses were alive – alert. What was I doing here? It would end in, at best, disappointment and, at worst, death. The blood rushing through my veins grew cold and my heart started to pound and short hairs stood on the back of my neck. I knew how dangerous it was – this thing I was doing, not just for me, but for Maria Wilhelmina as well. Life-threatening. I felt what the ancient holbewoners felt as they moved through their dark world at the beginning of time. I was no longer myself and could no longer explain myself – what I was doing – why I was doing it. There was no logic in the primitive night. I forgot who I was – what I was. And every moment became its own little lifetime. Birth and life and death. Birth and life and death.

And again.

And again.

Later, Vincent stood at the window, looking out. Naked. He seemed mesmerised by something. Spellbound. Watching and waiting at the window. There were a million noises outside in the streets of The Hague – wild and savage noises – they filled my ears and deafened me. My head was bursting with the sound and my heart was on fire. Then the silver moon came out from behind a cloud and shone directly through the window, illuminating Vincent and showing him to the world. And to me. I saw him.

And smiled.

Next morning I was up first and found some bread and eggs in the cupboard, along with ground berries, chicory and burnt sugar – so I was able to make a breakfast of uitsmijter and coffee, which seemed to surprise Vincent when I woke him. Afterwards, he wanted to go to the Koekamp, across from the station, so Maria Wilhelmina and I went with him. He began to draw a little bench with crooked legs and a leafless tree behind it. He used a pencil and a pen, with brown ink on paper for the drawing, which looked quite realistic. But the tree behind it looked strange in his drawing – its roots seemed to have a life of their own, roots that weren't even visible, apart from in Vincent's imagination. Maria Wilhelmina and I sat on the bench while he drew us in another sketch. This time the tree looked more normal and he sketched in other figures sitting – four altogether, along with people strolling past.

Eventually, it got too cold for my daughter and she wanted to leave, so we went back to the studio on the Schenkweg. There we had some more uitsmijter and coffee and Vincent began another sketch of me – this time sewing his shirt. Later, he went out on his own to draw – I don't know where he went and he didn't tell me. When he came back, he had a sketch of some people sitting in the waiting room of the Rijnspoor railway station. Then he sat and began to write a letter.

'Who are you writing to?'

'Theo.'

'Who is Theo?'

'My brother.'

'What do you write about?'

'Art. He wants me to be more saleable.'

I would learn that Theo was the singular most important person in Vincent's life. Although he always worked alone, he discussed every picture with his brother. And Theo offered him advice in his capacity as an art dealer with Goupil and Cie – he knew what the buyers wanted. And therein lay the problem. Vincent would not conform to popular demand, even though Theo just wanted him to be able to make a living. He wanted Vincent to paint one or two saleable pictures, for enough money to live on, then he could indulge his visions in the rest of his work. Vincent tried to comply a couple of times, but it was difficult for him to suppress the cosmic chaos inside his soul.

You see, Vincent wasn't yet fully developed as an artist and this time in The Hague with me and Maria Wilhelmina was a period which helped to grow his style and begin the emergence of his artistic process. The house on the Schenkweg was behind the railway station and surrounded by factories. Vincent could look out the window on the city, with its towers and roofs and smoking chimneys – it stood out as a dark, sombre silhouette against a horizon of light. Other artists went to the countryside to capture the changing moods of the rural landscape, but Vincent, at this time, was an artist of the poor, choosing the city, the working people and the expanding industry as his subjects.

'I'd rather draw in the filthiest neighbourhood than at a tea party with nice ladies.'

At one time, he got permission to draw in the Rijnspoor yards where they stockpiled the coal, which wasn't a public area, and he had to climb a high bank to get there. But he had to get quickly out of the way of a skittish horse and broke his painting box when he jumped from the bank. I didn't understand what attracted him to the railway yard, but he said it was beautiful there. Then, Vincent could see beauty where others only saw ugliness – I was an example of that.

We drank some jenever that night while Maria Wilhelmina slept. And we talked about many things – but mostly about ourselves. He wanted to know about me and I wanted to know about him. You must understand, I was very ill when Vincent took me in off the street and I would undoubtedly have died otherwise. So I was indebted to him for my life. He was indebted to me for nothing – unless you call being given the opportunity to have the kind of family life that he'd idealised for himself as being indebted. Of course, that kind of quiet domesticity was doomed to failure from the start.

We conversed till late and I told him everything – I held nothing back. It didn't bother him, the kind of life I'd led, the men I'd lain beneath.

'Now I don't even think about what I did before, Vincent.'

'You'll always be good in my eyes, Christien.'

Vincent said it wasn't my fault, the circumstances of my birth. I didn't choose to be Clasina Maria Hoornik, no more than he chose to be Vincent Willem van Gogh. We were not responsible for who we were, we could only try to do our best with what fate had given us. Although I'd read many books, I'd never looked at life in that way before. I'd always believed that I was who I was because that was what I deserved – and even though I knew there was something better, what I had was my lot. Listening to Vincent, I could see that it was just a game of chance – that the random roll of a biological dice determined who I was, not some great divine plan.

And it made me think even more.

# CHAPTER 12

# HOSTILITY AND THE CLAP

**W**inter slowly moved on and Vincent drew me many times during those long dark nights. As he drew me on the paper, so too did he draw me closer to him. But other people were not as happy about our being together as we were. One of them was Anton Mauve, the cousin and artist who considered himself to be Vincent's teacher and exemplar. Vincent did not see their relationship in the same way.

Mauve insisted that Vincent should use plaster casts to learn how to draw figures, not a model, especially one like me. He said Vincent was wasting his time and his brother's money on play-acting with street people. The gember man smashed the plaster cast Mauve brought to the studio by hurling it into the coal bin and said his erstwhile friend was narrow-minded. Mauve also wanted him to work entirely in watercolour, but Vincent found it to be exasperating and hopeless and he gave up trying it. He defended me to Mauve, who wanted him to throw Maria Wilhelmina and me back out onto the street.

'I will not. I will continue with her!'

In retaliation, Mauve mocked Vincent's nervous way of speaking and his habit of grimacing. He banished Vincent from his studio and vowed not to have anything more to do with him.

After that, it was Tersteeg's turn. Vincent borrowed twenty-five guilders from him, which was a very large amount of money. When he couldn't pay it back, Tersteeg said his drawings of me were charmless and unsaleable. He disparaged me and called me a faded, ill-tempered creature, a worthless rag, illiterate and consumptive – none of which was true. He said I was a sinner and a temptress, full of female lust and scheming – but how could I be all of those things at the same time? He told Vincent to stop drawing me and go back to watercolour landscapes. When Vincent did that, just to please him, Tersteeg shook his head and accused the gember man of taking opium to dull the pain he felt for being a failure. Vincent was angry and went back to drawing me.

'My drawings of her are full of character, not lust and scheming.'

'They're a waste of time, Vincent.'

'You're being thoughtless and superficial, Hermanus. I think they're very good.'

'Rubbish, like your model.'

'My model is capable of expressing deeper truths than your insipid watercolours.'

'You won't sell them, Vincent.'

But Vincent refused to listen. Of course, Tersteeg held the key to the gember man being able to sell his art – and he was refusing to open the door. Vincent would not relent.

'What I want is to be true to myself, and that means drawing Sien.'

He had come to calling me Sien instead of Christien – I didn't ask why.

'I fear you do more than draw her.'

I didn't want to hold the gember man back and I offered to leave and take Maria Wilhelmina with me. If my presence was causing so much trouble for Vincent, then he would be better off without me. But he wouldn't hear of me leaving.

'When I wake up in the morning and find you beside me, Sien, it makes the world a happier place than it's ever been.'

'But what about the dealers?'

'I won't run after art dealers. They must come to me.'

Instead, Tersteeg went to Theo in Paris and tried to poison Vincent's relationship with his brother. He prevented Theo from sending us some money he'd promised. When Vincent found out, he marched round to Goupil on the Plaats and demanded ten guilders from Tersteeg as compensation. In response, Tersteeg insulted him and called him a lazy fraud.

'You should get a job and stop taking money from your brother.'

'And you should mind your own business.'

'Believe me, you'll never be an artist, Vincent.'

That comment pierced Vincent's heart and grieved him to his very soul. I tried to console him when he returned from the confrontation, but he was distraught.

'He thinks I'm good for nothing. But I am an artist, Sien, it's in my bones.'

'I know it is, Vincent.'

'He's nothing but a dandy parvenu. I'd prefer to have no food for half a year than ten guilders from Tersteeg. The man should be sent to the guillotine.'

'Yes, let's send him there.'

We sang La Carmagnole and danced wildly around the room, knocking over tables and easels. Maria Wilhelmina joined us and Vincent soon forgot about the vindictive Tersteeg and his pretentious art gallery.

Vincent was truly a painter of the people at that time. He painted the potato market that was situated between the Breedstraat and Noordstraat in watercolour and, while sketching it, someone spat a wad of tobacco onto his paper. Instead of starting again, as a snub to Mauve and Tersteeg and their preaching about pastels, he used the brown of the tobacco spit to complete the picture. All the people from Geest came there and Vincent said painting the poor gave him peace of mind. He also painted the gasworks, the poor Jewish quarter, sand diggers, women mending nets, potato grubbers, the fish-drying barns and a bony old horse. He drew the throng outside Mooiman's Lottery office on Spuistraat, waiting for a miracle to happen, and the soup kitchen at Sint

Vincentus courtyard, where he saw so many downtrodden people it made him doubt the truth of what the bourgeoisie called progress.

'Civilisation should be based on a love of people, Sien.'

I had to agree.

It was about this time, January or February of the year 1882, that I discovered I was pregnant again. I didn't think it would be possible, after Maria Wilhelmina, but there it was. My menses had stopped a month or two since and I began to feel sick in the mornings. I told Vincent immediately.

'Is it mine?'

'Yes. You're the only man I've been with since last year.'

It was true. I slept with the gember man in November of 1881 and I used no protection, as I believed I could not become pregnant again. After that, I was sick with the fever through the rest of November and December and stopped drinking water to kill myself. I did not lie with anyone until Vincent found me again after Kerstmis and fed me and Maria Wilhelmina. So, I conceived in November and the child would be due the following August.

'Do you want me to be rid of it, Vincent?'

'Of course not! He'll be my child and I'll love him as myself.'

'What if it's a she, not a he?'

'Then I'll love her as I love myself … as I love you, as I love Maria there.'

Theo finally wrote, urging Vincent to stay on good terms with Tersteeg – after all, they both worked for Goupil and Theo considered Tersteeg as family. This enraged Vincent and he compared Tersteeg to Satan. The art dealer had become Vincent's implacable nemesis, generating fits of rage and rancour in the gember man. But Anton Mauve and Hermanus Tersteeg were not the only ones. Vincent fought with everyone – Jules Bakhuyzen, Bernard Blommers, Piet van der Velden, Marinus Boks and many others. He said he didn't need friends as long as he had me and dismissed fellow artists as being tedious and stupid and having no backbone.

He even argued with the man he called Rappard, telling him he had more serious things to do than write letters. It was just as well Rappard was in Amsterdam, otherwise he and Vincent would have fallen out completely.

But that's how it was with the gember man. He had a quick temper and arguments could materialise out of nothing. He admitted it himself – he could meet someone and, within minutes, he would be arguing with them. A word, a look, a gesture, anything could set off a storm of heated words which seemed to pour out from some fierce internal turmoil. Disagreements quickly escalated into a frenzy of argument that knew neither reason nor restraint.

I also had a short temper, having had to live and fight on the streets up to that point in time. So, you can imagine how things in the studio got broken when we argued, which was not very often. But when we did, it was tempestuous. We fought mostly over money. Like everyone else, I didn't believe that Vincent should be relying on handouts from Theo. I told him I should be contributing money and I could do so by going back on the streets. Vincent would not hear of that – he flew into a rage every time I mentioned it.

'How can I allow my wife to be a strumpet? I wouldn't be a man!'

'I'm not your wife, Vincent.'

'But you will be, when I can afford to marry you.'

'You'll never be able to afford to marry me if I don't earn some money.'

'But you're pregnant. You'd die if you had to walk the streets again.'

'I was pregnant before, and worked at the same time.'

He always retreated into his art at that stage. He'd grab his brushes and easel and storm out of the studio. I wouldn't see him again until dark, when he'd come home and it would be as if nothing had been said. He'd be cheerful and talking about what he drew or painted that day and the argument would be forgotten about – until the next time.

Vincent's Uncle Cor visited the studio in March and Vincent asked me to take Maria Wilhelmina and stay out of the way, as he wasn't looking forward to the visit and expected further hostility, just as he'd encountered from Mauve and Tersteeg. He was right.

'You must earn your own bread, Vincent.'

'Earn bread? How do you mean?'

'You must know.'

'Do you mean earn bread or deserve bread? Every honest man deserves bread, uncle, but some aren't able to earn it. If you're saying I don't deserve bread, then you insult me.'

But Cor wasn't there to fight, he was there to cajole. He passed over the drawings of me without a single comment but, when he came to a street, the corner of the Prinsessegracht and the Herengracht, he smiled.

'Could you make more of these?'

Vincent, of course, was thrilled with what he believed to be his first genuine commission and agreed to make twelve views of the city for two and a half guilders each.

I was glad that the gember man had at last managed to make some money of his own, but I knew that Cor commissioned the work to stop Vincent drawing me and, if he had no further use for me as a model, he might get rid of me. However, payment did not arrive when Vincent sent the sketches and my suspicions turned out to be true. He received a second order for six more drawings in April, but he now questioned his uncle's motives. He decided to stop work on the street scenes, but Theo convinced him to finish them. In the end, Cor paid him less than was agreed and sent the money without a single word of thanks or even appraisal. Vincent was angry – again.

'Artistic value is more important than commercial value, Sien. But I can't give my art away for nothing, we need food and a roof over our heads.'

Vincent had told Theo about his first meeting with me and Maria Wilhelmina in a letter he wrote on 23rd December 1881. He later said he was negotiating with me to do some modelling for him, but he did not mention that we were lovers. Up to now, he also hadn't mentioned that I had moved in with him and was living as his mistress and model, along with my daughter. I'm sure Theo was told about me by Mauve and Tersteeg and others, and their gossiping finally became intolerable to Vincent. In April, he wrote to Theo confirming our relationship and saying how people suspected him of something:

> *People are whispering. It's in the air, I must be*
> *hiding something. I'm keeping something back*
> *that may not be spoken about. These people*
> *pride themselves on their manners and culture*
> *… but what's more cultured, more manly, to*
> *forsake a woman or to take on a forsaken one?*

He told Theo that I was pregnant when he met me – and I was, the second time he met me. I was not pregnant on the occasion of our first meeting in November. He said I'd been deserted by the man whose child I was carrying – and I was, the gember man left The Hague after our encounter and didn't come back for a month. He said he found me walking the streets in winter – and he did. He said I had my bread to earn and he took me on as a model and had worked with me ever since. It was all true. However, he was under so much pressure from the likes of Mauve and Tersteeg and some members of his family, that he didn't want to admit to Theo that the child was his. He knew it had been conceived in November, when we lay together and I didn't use any protection, and he knew I had not been with another man since then, because of my illness during November and December. But he was worried that if he told Theo a straatmadelief had become pregnant from him, his brother would have stopped supporting us.

At this early time in his career as an artist, Vincent wanted to prove that his black and white images could achieve a better tonality and a deeper mood than the daubs of watery colour everyone was pushing him to do. He worked over the drawings again and again, shading, rubbing, erasing – using big carpenter's pencils, reed pens, charcoal, brushes, chalk and crayon.

'This little drawing of you, Sien, has caused me more work than any watercolour.'

The paper often became torn as he erased and scraped and the images grew darker as he reworked them and the drawings showed the strain of his struggle. I tried to encourage him as best I could when he attempted to produce at least one good drawing out of twenty.

'When you draw, Vincent, you are an artist.'

In April, he drew me naked, seen from the side, my legs drawn up to my bosoms and my head buried in my crossed arms. My image filled the small picture, as if I was trapped inside it. It was his first nude and he said it was the best thing he'd ever drawn. He wanted to express the struggle for life in that pale, slender image of me.

He called it "Sorrow".

Among his many sketches of that time, he'd already drawn me sitting on the floor in the white smock and continued to draw me in various poses – sewing, in a white bonnet, peeling potatoes, me and Maria Wilhelmina, two drawings of my mother's house in Noordstraat, and two more from the courtyard when she moved to the Slijkeinde in Geest because they were demolishing some of the houses in Noordstraat to lay sewerage pipes.

'I prefer to draw Geest or any backstreet than a mansion. Mansions bore me.'

He drew me with my head in my hands, standing with a kettle, and many others. Posing for Vincent was more difficult than anything else. When the light or the pose or the pencil defied him, he would fly into a rage and leap from his chair shouting.

'Damn it! It's all wrong!'

But working without a model was something he hated. He said it would be his ruin and that trying to draw a figure from memory was fraught with problems. He said I gave him the courage he needed to succeed and, because of me, he feared nothing. He swore that he would sacrifice everything, from food to pencils and paper, in order to keep me.

Many years later, when Vincent was dead, someone wrote that the work he did with me was the grittiest and most honest he ever achieved. They said his development in The Hague from the years 1881 to 1883 could be seen as the central foundation of his art.

The personal relationship between myself and Vincent van Gogh was one thing, but the professional relationship was another altogether. Vincent believed he was the master in his studio. He wanted to exert total control over his models and he insisted on getting his own way. He compared himself to a doctor and me to his patient, trying to control me in the way a doctor controls someone under his care.

'I need to get a firm hold on you, Sien. You must do as I say.'

I was not one to obey commands and, if I needed a rest or to break my pose for a smoke or a glass of jenever, then I did it. My independence led to more arguments and things being thrown about but, if he threw a pencil at me, I threw a pot back at him. He came to know how far he could go with me and lamented that his life with me was as in Shakespeare's *The Taming of the Shrew*. I retaliated that life with him was as in Gogol's *Diary of a Madman*. Then we would both laugh and sometimes sing, maybe "Alouette", the song the French fur traders took with them to Canada, while Maria Wilhelmina danced round us.

Maria Wilhelmina swept the studio and helped me to keep the living quarters clean, while I mended clothes and cooked, which made life worth living for Vincent. My daughter was almost six years old and already used to hardship in her little life. The house where we lived, on the second floor of Schenkweg 138, wasn't much, but it was better than Noordstraat, or even Slijkeinde. It was in a new area which was being developed on the outskirts of The Hague – an area of vegetable plots and cinder paths and the belch and hiss of trains a few metres from the door. It was a no man's land between city and country, where bourgeois people never came. We had a simple room with a pot-bellied stove, flued into a fake fireplace. There was an alcove for the bed and a curtained partition where Maria Wilhelmina slept. A window looked out on a carpenter's yard and the laundry lines of those living nearby.

From his earlier friendship with Anton Mauve, Vincent became an associate member of the Pulchri Studio, an art society and institution founded by the painter Lambertus Hardenberg. The gember man tried to mount a showing of all his drawings and prints in the Pulchri exhibition hall, but he was met with opposition and even ridicule, obviously instigated by Mauve and Tersteeg. The Pulchri's members dismissed the drawings as superficial and sentimental. Vincent spat on their opinions and told them they should learn how to draw themselves before they criticised anyone else.

'Go to hell! You're standing in my light.'

The more attacks he fended off, the more attacks came – one after the other. They criticised the way he dressed, the way he spoke, the way he walked, his manner, me and Maria Wilhelmina, everything. They treated me like a badly behaved dog and Vincent believed that, if they could not get him to desert me, they would try to drive him out of The Hague altogether.

'They begrudge me the very light of my eyes, Sien.'

They did whatever they could, whatever was in their power to do, against us, with not one person to take our side – except for Theo. No matter how much they denigrated us, the brother held firm.

It was about April or May when Vincent met George Breitner, a young artist who believed in gritty naturalism and the city itself was his model. He and Vincent visited and drew soup kitchens, train stations, peat markets, pawn banks and went at night into the red-light area of the Geest. But Vincent's only artistic fascination at that time was the solitary figure – mostly me. In the spring of the year 1882, Breitner had to go into hospital with the clap and Vincent was hospitalised with the same thing two months later. People like Mauve and Tersteeg delighted in saying he'd caught gonorrhoea from me, but it was, in fact, from a hoer he went to with Breitner in the Geest.

By this time, I was getting heavy with our baby and not being intimate, so Vincent kept his ailment from me. But, when he said he needed to go to the hospital to be checked, I wanted to know why.

'Just routine, Sien.'

'Routine what?'

'Nothing. It's nothing.'

'It must be something.'

I would not stop until he admitted his guilt. I was angry to begin with and we had the inevitable argument and inevitable throwing of things, along with the equally inevitable packing-up of his drawing equipment and the storming out the door, only to return six hours later with a sketch of the beach at Scheveningen and a bent-head effort at contrition.

'It was Breitner's fault, Sien.'

'What, he pushed your pénis into that hoer?'

'Of course not.'

'Well, then … '

As always, our bouts of friction could be fierce and fiery, but they never lasted long. I could see Vincent's point of view and he could see mine and we calmed as well as crossed each other. He told Theo when he wrote.

*She knows how to quiet me, which is something*
*I'm not able to do for myself. I always feel calm*
*and bright and cheerful at the thought of her.*

Despite our tempestuous arguments, we had a deep regard for each other. It was a regard neither of us had ever experienced before.

# CHAPTER 13

# WILLEM

Vincent bought medicine for me and clothes for the baby. He paid for a doctor with the rent money Theo sent, which led to the landlord threatening to evict us. Had he not, I would probably have died in childbirth. He encouraged me to take many baths and to go for walks and he gave me restoratives. He ensured I had enough food to eat and got plenty of rest. He continued to write to Theo about me.

> *I've given her all the love, tenderness*
> *and care that's in me.*

He came with me to register at the free maternity hospital in Leiden. He represented me in discussions with the medical staff and acted in every way as my husband. What man would do all that for another man's unborn child? He knew well the baby was his, despite people trying to convince him otherwise.

Although he tried to ignore it at first, Vincent's bout of the clap became worse and he had to go into the Burger Gasthuis in the Zuidwal in June. He was on a common ward with ten beds, overflowing chamber pots and unkind male nurses, yet he didn't complain. He said it was no less interesting than a third-class waiting room and he wanted to make sketches of it. His gonorrhoea was a mild case that would require a few weeks treatment of quinine pills and sulphate irrigations and he brought some novels of Charles Dickens with him to pass the time. The gember man was in bed number nine and Maria Wilhelmina and I went to visit him regularly, almost every day, and I brought him smoked beef and bread and sugar.

On one occasion, I encountered a short, white-haired preacher striding along the corridor. I didn't know it at the time, but it was Vincent's father, the man called Dorus. He walked straight past me without any sign of recognition – not knowing, I imagine, that I was carrying his grandchild. Had he known, I'm sure he would have been mortified. He asked Vincent to go home to Etten for a while after he left hospital, so he could regain his strength. So, perhaps he did know about me and this was another ploy to get Vincent to desert me. Vincent declined the invitation, saying he wanted to get back to work. The gember man never mentioned his name to me again.

I was sleeping badly and I kept dreaming I wasn't pregnant anymore. At the end of June, I felt tired and not very well. I went to the privy and noticed that I was bleeding. Vincent was still in hospital and I didn't know what to do, so I decided to go and see the doctor he'd paid with the rent money. On the way to his house on Von Geusaustraat, I felt very dizzy and I fainted. I don't know how long I was on the ground, but, when I revived, I was lying in a pool of blood and Maria Wilhelmina was crying beside me. Nobody came to help me, so I got up and made my way to the doctor. I was sure the baby was gone, that it was left on the street in that pool of blood – but it was not. It was still there, and alive. I had mixed feelings about it – on the one hand, I thought it might have been better if I had lost the baby, considering how we lived. On the other hand, I was relieved. Sometimes you can take control of your life but, occasionally, things are meant to be and there is nothing you can do to alter the outcome.

Due to my state of health and complications with previous pregnancies, the doctor predicted that the delivery of our baby would be difficult and dangerous. It was going to be premature and, at the end of June, with still over a month to go, I was sent, with Maria Wilhelmina, to the free maternity hospital early. That meant I could not visit Vincent at the clap clinic. Up to then, he was recovering well but, as soon as I stopped coming, he suffered a relapse and blamed his worsening condition on our separation. He was moved to a different ward for more intensive treatment, which included draining the bladder and irrigating the inflamed canal. They inserted catheters of increasing size into his pénis, which was extremely difficult and painful and it left him lame for days afterwards. But he did not complain.

'What's the suffering of us men, Sien, compared to the pain of childbirth.'

At the University Hospital in Leiden, I did not deliver and the waiting overwhelmed Vincent. It went on and on and I worried that I might die. Vincent decided to come to me, even though I didn't ask him to. He was still faint and feeble from his own treatment, but he left his sickbed and came to Leiden. It was now July and I was still confined, so Vincent wasn't allowed to talk to me for very long. He was dismayed with the orderlies when they told him to leave, as he envisaged that he might never see me again.

The old maternity ward of the Leiden hospital was a bleak place – it shared a lightless, airless courtyard with the autopsy room. Every so often, an autopsy worker would empty a bucket of dark, foul-smelling waste into the courtyard drain. Where it went, I do not know. The whole place was gloomy, even in daylight, with a high ceiling and heavy drapes. In summer, as it was then, the tall windows were opened, but no refreshing breeze blew through. Beds lined the walls on both sides, with two patients to a bed – a pregnant woman and a new mother. A crib for dirty linen hung beside each bed, with another crib for the baby on the floor.

It was not a good place for a newborn to experience the world for the first time. The nurses were rough and indifferent, having probably known a lot of hardship themselves. They only helped if they were paid and they held back medication and food for just such tips. The food itself was slop and the bad conditions kept so-called good women at home with midwives, leaving maternity wards like the University

Hospital for the unmarried, the ignorant and the shamed, and those exhausted by poverty and deprivation.

By the time Vincent arrived in July, the baby had finally appeared in the birth canal after a long labour, complicated by nervous exhaustion and an infection of the uterus. I didn't know what a uterus was until the doctor who Vincent paid explained that it was my womb. He drew me a little picture with a pencil so I could better understand my own reproductive innards. When I saw Vincent, I sat up in the bed and tried to be as cheerful as possible. I was grateful for his presence, even though it had put his own health in danger. But the baby was stuck fast for the next five hours, as the doctor tried to dislodge it with forceps. It was very painful, probably the most painful of all the births I had experienced. The doctor gave me chloroform, but not enough for me to lose consciousness.

Vincent was trying to comfort me and my head was on his shoulder and I was telling him I was dead and there would be no baby and no more me. Then I was back in the pain again and I believed I would have this agony for eternity because of all the sins I had committed. Finally, the baby emerged – it was a boy, shrivelled and jaundiced. Half a day after the delivery, I was still muddled, wracked with pain and mortally weak. The doctor said the shock to my system was so great, it could take years for me to recover my health – and he wasn't sure if the baby would live.

Vincent was delighted. He didn't see the grim autopsy courtyard – to him it was a garden full of sunshine and greenery – and my pain, to him, was a drowsy state between sleeping and waking. He was holding the baby in his arms, but I was so sick I couldn't take it from him. They were trying to make me bosomfeed but I could not, I was so thin and had hardly any milk. I was shaking and had no feeling in any part of my body. The doctor told me I had to hold the baby because he needed contact with his mother. I held him on my chest and fell asleep. When I woke, the pain was back. This time it was caused by another infection after the birth. Vincent said my suffering had refined me, given me more spirit and sensitivity and our sick, jaundiced son had a worldly-wise air about him that enchanted the gember man.

'What I'm most astonished at is the child. Although he's been taken with forceps, he's not injured at all. He's lying in his cradle with a smile on his face.'

In his eyes everything – the bleak room, the pale me, the yellow child, the hellish night, the rest of the world – were all transformed into the perfect expression of love. The events of that day made him so happy that he wept.

Vincent was in a rapture. He had a household which now included a son of his own. Nothing in all his years rivalled this and he went back to The Hague to create a home for us, while I recovered in Leiden.

'You deserve a warm place to return to, Sien, after the pain you endured.'

There was a terrible storm while I was in the hospital and the window of the studio was broken and his pictures blown about. He had to nail a blanket over it until he could arrange to move to a larger apartment, with a studio downstairs and living quarters upstairs, next door to the one we lived in on the Schenkweg and decorate it with his studies and prints. He bought more furniture, including a wicker chair for me and an iron cradle for the baby. He bought clothes for Maria Wilhelmina, cutlery for the kitchen and flowers for the window. He bought a new mattress for our bed and stuffed it himself with cloth and feathers. Vincent's simple wish was to sit next to the woman he loved with our baby in the cradle beside us. He got that wish when I finally returned from the hospital, needing an extended period of recovery after the difficult and premature birth.

I called the baby Willem, after Vincent Willem van Gogh, although he would never carry the name of van Gogh, due to the hatred that surrounded us.

The first week back in the new apartment at Schenkweg 136 was the most difficult. I couldn't eat or sleep properly. Vincent wasn't experienced in how to be a family man and he tried his best to learn. He loved Maria Wilhelmina dearly and told her the story of a mother by Hans Christian Andersen. He played games with her and sang to her, but baby Willem was his pride – his joy – his life force. He was experiencing the kind of love he'd never felt before and it was something he was trying to understand. He and Maria Wilhelmina did all the normal housekeeping tasks like cooking and cleaning and washing that I should have been doing and, during this after-birth illness, Vincent did not expect me to model for him, neither did he expect us to be lovers.

'My poor, weak, ill-used little wife. You're so sublime to me.'

Vincent was still painting and he didn't know what else to do to support me. I blamed him for not being there all the time to help me, but it wasn't really his fault – he had to paint. It seemed to me as if I was in some kind of perpetual bad dream. The Schenkweg was a rough area and I unconsciously heard every sound from the streets outside our window – fights and shouts and screams and glass breaking. I would hear everything in an unreal way – half awake and half asleep – in a twilight state, not knowing whether it was imagined or not. I had the taste of blood in my mouth for a month and I sobbed quite a lot, thinking I was going to die. I do not know why.

I also had lapses of memory – or part of my memory. I used to forget things – I would make coffee and forget about it and realise I made it six hours later. I would forget about food cooking and burn it. Sometimes I'd even forget where I was. When I went to sleep, I believed I was dying – for months I believed I was going to die at any moment. I was having anxiety seizures and shaking and my heart would beat abnormally fast. I felt so guilty – my dream to be part of a real family, with a man I loved, had come true and I believed I was destroying it. I should be so happy and not behaving like an unsound, insane person. It must have been impossible for the gember man, trying to cope with me – and he did his best – no man could have done more.

My mother visited her grandson from Slijkeinde and I tried to hide my despondency as much as I could. Nobody really knew the extent of my distress. Vincent did his best to understand but, despite the fact that we were so close, he knew very little about me – I mean the small things, like my favourite colour and my dislike of spiders, my woman's humours. I was desperate to talk to him – really talk to him from my soul – to try to explain what was wrong with me, even though I myself did not know what was wrong with me. But he was a patient man, at least he was with me, if not with others – even though he was tired when he came in on the days he went painting.

Vincent was caring and considerate and I loved him, but it seemed to me at that difficult time that he was keeping some of himself back. Keeping a part of himself to himself and not wanting or being capable of committing to the very intimate knowing of each other that real togetherness means – being able to tell what I was thinking and feeling. He tried to solve problems he didn't understand with love. I could have as much love as I wanted. He seemed to substitute love for that special kind of attention only a few men know how to provide. Or maybe it was me and I was being unreasonable because of what I was going through.

I knew I was very difficult to live with while I was sick. And Vincent had other problems, from both his family and his so-called colleagues, that I didn't know about. So, he dealt with the difficulties in the only way he knew how, by ignoring them. We had little money and were often hungry. I tried to show him money didn't matter to me, even though it did – not money for money's sake, but just enough to exist on. For a while after the baby was born, I was too unwell for carnal relations. That was an added difficulty for Vincent to deal with – it would have been for any man. I do not know how he dealt with it and I didn't ask or care. All I knew was, he didn't complain, he gradually nursed me back to health and I found my strength again.

Vincent sketched little Willem in his cradle at the end of July in the year 1882 and he couldn't look at the baby without being overcome with emotion. He saw his son as a light in the darkness of his life – a brightness in the middle of a black night and he explained that, while he endeavoured to go deeper as an artist, he was also looking to do so as a man. He bought a yellow blanket to replace the green one on the baby's cradle and he said it was his favourite colour.

'Yellow is the colour of life, Sien. It was the colour of my son when he was born and now it's the colour of our life here together, the colour of our little family. I'll always love yellow.'

Vincent wondered if he should invite his father to come see Willem. The man was a strict minister in the Dutch Reformed Church and I was Catholic, as well as a straatmadelief. He would probably rather have poked out his own eyes. But Vincent was optimistic.

'How could he find cold fault?'

I disagreed. I knew he would find cold fault, as would all the other members of his family, with the possible exception of Theo. And even him I wasn't sure about, especially as Vincent told him he wanted to marry me and Theo suggested he should pay me off and give me up. Vincent said he would not deceive or forsake us and marrying me was the only way to stop the world talking. He worried that the illicitness of our relationship was giving people cause to keep on trying to separate us.

He knew if he left me I'd have no other choice but to walk the streets again. I hadn't fully recovered from the birth of Willem and it would surely kill me. But there would be nothing else for me to do to feed my two children. By marrying me, he could save my life and prevent me from falling back into the horrible state in which he found me after Kerstmis. My health during that summer was very delicate and the doctor said there was the risk of a collapse of my womb that would be incurable. He told Vincent what I needed most was a home of my own and to refuse me that would be murder. The gember man agreed and said we could live together like bohemians once we were married and he was even becoming a better artist because of me.

Theo was worried that Vincent's father might again try to have him committed to an asylum if he told Dorus about wanting to marry me. Vincent reacted angrily, saying if his father did try something like that, he would disgrace the family publicly in the courts. He knew of a man who'd bashed someone's brains in with a poker over exactly the same situation and the courts acquitted him when he claimed self-defence.

Despite everything, Theo continued to support us financially, but he was against us marrying, probably in case of reprisals against himself from Mauve and Tersteeg and the uncles. I'm not sure if Vincent realised just how much he owed to Theo, but I did. Eventually, he conceded to Theo's pleas for him to paint something saleable, by going back to watercolour and landscapes, even though he really didn't want to. He was appeasing his brother in the hope that he would change his mind and support our marriage.

Theo had long wanted a reconciliation between Vincent and the family in Etten, so the gember man told him he'd invited their father to come see his new living quarters – although he never mentioned me or the baby. But, instead of Dorus, Tersteeg came to visit. He was outraged when he saw me with little Willem at my bosom.

'What's the meaning of this, Vincent?'

'This is my model, as you know.'

'Your model … or something else?'

'She'll also soon be my wife.'

'Have you gone mad, Vincent?

'Certainly not!'

'It's ridiculous … the product of an unsound mind.'

He threatened to write to Vincent's parents and tell them about this new humiliation their son was bringing upon the family and he compared Vincent to a man trying to drown himself. On the way out he looked at me and shouted to the gember man.

'This woman will destroy you!'

As soon as Tersteeg left, Vincent wrote to Theo, complaining that the gérant was meddling in his intimate affairs. He compared Tersteeg to a politieagent and said the man would happily look on if I was drowning. I wonder, if Tersteeg was standing here with me now, on the side of the canal, would he be smiling, waiting for Vincent's prophecy to come true? He began to spread the rumour that Vincent was insane, but the gember man paid no heed. It hurt him that his pictures were scorned by the art dealer and he couldn't sell any of them. Despite that, his art carried him on eagle's wings, above the pettiness of Tersteeg and the others. His convictions kept fighting to overcome the hard obstacles through love for himself, for me and our children, and for his work.

At night he'd study books on colour and perspective, during the day he visited museums, copied French cartoons and continued to draw me many times. He worked from early till late at night and, when I recovered, I posed for him again. He drew me nursing the baby, with an umbrella and prayer book, wearing a headscarf – he drew Willem in his cot many times and Maria Wilhelmina with Willem.

Vincent suffered with those who suffered and tried to relieve them as best he could. He had nothing to give, but he gave everything he had. We were living hand to mouth and it was hard, being hungry all the time. But I was used to hardship and so was Vincent. Why did we stay together? We learned to ask for only what was needed, not what was wanted. We learned to identify need, even though we both knew what it was. It took discipline – control – to control want – distinguish it from need.

And love – love! Say the word. Love!

We said it often and it meant different things to both of us at different times. How else could we clear our clouded perceptions – blow away the fog of confusion – break the chains of language – destroy the ladder of our past lives. If we did not, we might have climbed back down again. Could we be something we were never meant to be? Only if we found the still landscape with no dramas and no symbols. We listened, and heard nothing but the single note of our merging souls.

It was beautiful and appalling at the same time.

## CHAPTER 14

# THE SOUND OF SWEELINCK

Somewhere in the back of my mind was the sound of Jan Sweelinck – a chanson or a madrigal – both saintly and sinister all at once. And shadows moving in the room where only one dim lamp glowed, far away in the distance – many kilometres, it seemed, from the bed. My head felt light from the mixture of absinthe and jenever, floating on the paint-smell of the child-man beside me and the texture of his hair and the hoarse sound of his voice and the sparkle of lamplight in his eyes and the stimulating intangibility of the situation. His skin was rough and felt like stretched canvas – warm and wispy in the low lightglow. His fingers finding their way around me and his body moving to my rhythm – the tempo rubato within me. He was in harmony with my woman's cadence – moving in syncopation to my changing positions on the bed. My voice purred like a cat's and my words made no sense to either of us.

Nor were they meant to.

He made his own sounds in the crepuscule of our satyric lair – perhaps some pagan prayer, in the hope that his father would arrange for his salvation and for his eventual entry into Elysium, even after all his transgressions.

I couldn't remember how long we lay on the bed, or if I'd slept or been awake all of the time. I didn't know what day it was, or what month or year. Just something about dawn, which was now breaking over the Zoetermeer to the east. I could see faint fingers of light creeping up the windowpanes and I left the bed to make some breakfast. There wasn't much food in the house, but then there never was.

I watched the gember man as he slept on and smiled to myself as I thought of how my father would be so happy, yet extremely apprehensive, if he could see me now – being in a place where I truly belonged for the first time in so many years. And with someone I didn't really know, even though I believed I did – someone who could hurt me so badly. I didn't believe he would, even though I had no way of knowing that for sure, or how our liaison would work out in the end. But it was sufficient for me to feel the way I did.

For now.

My father would have liked Vincent – they were both dreamers, both boy-men who had wild thoughts in their heads that were unknown to the civilised and the circumspect. Vincent was a different man – not what I expected on that winter morning when he first asked me to model for him. He was stronger than me in some ways, but weaker in others. I needed someone to mend my life for me and he needed someone to mend his. We did it for each other and now we depended on each other. The world was a hostile place for us and we each had to find some close physical support from somewhere. It was almost as if we'd met by kismet.

I was thirty-two in the year of 1882 and the gember man was twenty-nine. We were not children anymore, as we once were, and the three years between us had shrunk to an insignificance. Vincent saw my face everywhere he looked, in the paintings of Eugéne Delacroix and Ary Scheffer and in the heroines of the books he read, as a modern Mary Magdalene to his personal suffering Christ. He didn't just see images, he inhabited them. He wove them into his consciousness and they blended with all the other images of his life.

'I see people as drawings, except for you, Sien … you're a masterpiece.'

And that's how he regarded me, as a kind of icon, the epitome of a motherhood which he'd longed for but never encountered in his own mother. Just as the bourgeoisie didn't expect women to think, Vincent was sometimes surprised when I did. He may even have resented it, his inability to fully control me. He believed that bourgeois women should be cultured, but not intellectual – and lower-class women should be neither. I was not cultured, at least not in the sense of the women he'd known before me, but I absorbed everything. That may not be a definition of intellectual, but it was something Vincent had never known in a woman – not in his mother or his sisters or Eugénie Loyer or Cornelia Stricker or any hoer he lay with. I think he sometimes felt threatened by it because I believe he suffered from a denied sense of inferiority, despite his artistic intransigence. He once described himself as a poor painter with an ugly face and a shabby coat, but that self-denigration was meant for the ears of others, not his own.

I made a breakfast of bread dipped in dripping and fried, then I woke Vincent and Maria Wilhelmina. Baby Willem had been awake during the night and was sleeping peacefully now, so I didn't disturb him. After breakfast, Vincent suggested that we should all accompany him to Koninginnegracht, where he intended to paint some city scenes. He carried his equipment and I pushed Willem in his carriage, with Maria Wilhelmina walking by my side and holding onto the handle. As we came into this particular street, I thought I recognised the place, although I could not remember how or why or from when. Up ahead, an old man with a walking stick was being helped down some steps by a nurse. As we approached, he turned his head and he seemed familiar. When I saw his hands, I instantly knew who it was – those large hands that had stolen my virginity.

I wasn't sure what to do. At first I wanted to turn round and walk the other way, but Vincent insisted on continuing in the direction we were going. Then I thought, why should I try to avoid this man? I had done nothing wrong. He was the guilty party! Then we were alongside and, before I knew it, the words came from my mouth.

'Hallo Jacobus.'

He gave me a puzzled look.

'Don't you remember me? I came looking for seamstress work when I was fourteen and you ravished me.'

He looked towards his nurse, while waving his stick.

'Who is this person?'

'I don't know, Mr Jacobus.'

'My name is Clasina Maria Hoornik, don't you remember? You kept me prisoner and violated me many times before I escaped. You should have went to prison.'

Jacobus began to scream – it wasn't a scream exactly, more of a high-pitched whine. His nurse called out to people in the street to go fetch the maréchaussée, but I didn't care. Everybody needed to know what this man did to me when I was but a girl and how his actions led to me being forced on to the streets as a straatmadelief. Vincent, on the other hand, did care and I could see that Maria Wilhelmina was becoming anxious. More people in the street were now calling for the maréchaussée and Jacobus' screeches were getting louder. Vincent was glancing about in panic.

'What should we do, Sien?'

'Run, I think.'

And so we did, Vincent struggling with his canvas and easel and brushes and me with Willem's carriage and Maria Wilhelmina hanging onto the handle for dear life.

Eventually, we managed to distance ourselves from the screeches and shrieks and shouts and we all collapsed onto a bench by the water, close to the corner of Prinsessegracht and Herengracht. We were breathing heavily and I had a coughing fit – then Vincent began to laugh. I didn't think it was a laughing matter, but he continued and Maria Wilhelmina joined him. Their laughter was contagious and soon the three of us were hooting loudly, to the curious looks of passers-by. When we were sufficiently recovered, Vincent set up his equipment and began to paint. I stayed with him for a while, but Maria Wilhelmina was getting distracted, so we left him to it and returned to the studio.

For a while after the encounter, I was worried that the maréchaussée would come looking for me. Jacobus was obviously a rich man and rich men always got what they wanted. Would he have me thrown into prison? Would my children be taken away from me? Would Vincent abandon me? These thoughts worried me for several weeks, but nothing happened. There were no repercussions. Perhaps Jacobus didn't want a scandal, even though I couldn't possibly prove the accusation I had made in front of his nurse and other people in that street. In the end, I put it behind me and resolved not to visit the Koninginnegracht area again.

In August, Vincent's family moved to Nuenen, a town sixty-five kilometres east of Etten, where Dorus had accepted a new position. Vincent wrote to them, but they didn't answer. August was also when Theo decided to pay us a visit, probably to see how his money was being spent. He brought presents, as well as drawing paper and crayons, and Vincent was so happy to see him. He told Theo how content he was with me and the children.

'Sien and the baby are getting stronger and I love them both.'

He showed Theo the drawing of Willem in his cradle.

'I'll draw that little cradle another hundred times, Theo.'

The gember man was full of his new family and how, at one time, he would come home to a house that wasn't a real home and had none of the emotions connected with it now. It was a place where two great voids stared at him night and day. There was no wife. There was no child. Now, when he was with us, he knew everything was right.

'The child comforts me, Theo. He plays quietly with a bit of paper, a bit of string, or an old brush and he's always happy. If he keeps on like this, he'll be cleverer than all of us.'

But none of that seemed to make any impression on Theo. I'm sure it wasn't his own feelings he was expressing, as I later came to know him as a fair and generous man. He was expressing the words of others and he rarely smiled through his whole visit. I kept the children out of their way as much as possible but I could hear them arguing downstairs in the studio. Theo was insisting that Vincent should turn away from black and white figure sketches and concentrate on landscape and colour – in other words, he should stop drawing me. He promised to continue his support for another year, if Vincent promised to end his relationship with me and I could hear his words, spoken very loudly.

'Do not marry her!'

It wasn't just family, fellow artists, art dealers and mentors who were against us – now it was his brother too.

After Theo's visit, Vincent began to go to the beach at Scheveningen to paint. Even when the wind blew strong he went there and he looked like Robinson Crusoe, stranded on his desert island, looking out to sea for salvation. He began to paint in oils that he bought in tin tubes and carried so much equipment with him that he couldn't fit on the tram and had to walk. He said he had to become a real painter, not just a drawer and sketcher. He spread the paint thick – so thick it took a long time to dry and the picture seemed to be trying to escape from the canvas. The wind often covered his work with a layer of sand and leaves and bits of twigs and he'd have to scrape it all off when he got back and repaint from memory.

'The sea came close to the dunes, Sien. The wind was so strong I could barely stay on my feet and barely see through the clouds of sand.'

On one occasion, he painted Maria Wilhelmina in a white dress, clinging to a tree, surrounded by a sea of mud. He made her look older than her six years because he didn't want the painting to look like it was of a little girl who had been abandoned – even though that was what would happen, just a short year from then.

Oil paint and canvases were far more expensive than paper and pencils, and all the money Theo sent began to be spent on them, leaving very little for food or rent – or anything else. Theo asked for one of the oil paintings, to see if he could sell it, so Vincent sent him a picture of tree roots – not the best subject for an art dealer to try to sell to his affluent customers in Paris.

Vincent's father, Dorus, paid a surprise visit to the studio in September. He made it clear that he was ashamed of me and the children and ashamed of Vincent for being with us. He did not stay long. After that, no one came and Vincent became an outcast in the art community. When they saw him on the street with me they jeered at us. The gember man blamed his own appearance, his lack of social skills, his erratic behaviour, his volatile personality – but I knew it was me. I was the hated one – a hoer, a strumpet, a straatmadelief. I was pretending to be something I was not and could never be. Their bourgeois sensibilities were appalled at the thought that I might actually be just as good as they were – and probably better in many ways.

You have to understand, there was no country in Europe more class-conscious than Holland at that time. It was impossible to break out of the class to which you were consigned by the accident of birth. Vincent came from a religious bourgeois family who were deeply scandalised by his association with me. They could not allow it to continue. There was an insurmountable gap between the social classes to which Vincent and I belonged – but the gember man didn't care about such pompous prejudice and that made his family and friends believe he was mad – because only a madman would do what he was doing and flout convention so furiously.

Full recovery after my fourth and final pregnancy had been slow, but Vincent had cared for me and nursed me back to good health through it all. I kept improving and by the end of September I had fully recovered and was back modelling for him all the time. He drew many more pictures of me besides what he'd already sketched, depicting me as a mother and wife. He painted me knitting, in watercolour, and told Theo it was a Scheveningen women in an attempt to sell it. Theo wouldn't even try if he knew the woman in the picture was me

– Vincent had no models in Scheveningen. He continuously told Theo that he loved me, but never called me Clasina in his letters, always "the woman", then "Christien", then "Sien". And I wondered if it was myself that was here with the gember man, or if some kabouter had taken my identity away and given it to another being – a woman with my face and my hair and my mouth and my feet and my hands.

Vincent was always indifferent to his own appearance. He dressed in a blue blouse, the garb of the Flemish peasant, with his gember hair cropped close and his straggly gember beard and his eyes inflamed from staring at his subjects in the sun. He had little contact with his family, except for Theo. He ate his meals seated in a corner of the room, his plate on his lap, absorbed in some newly drawn picture that would stand facing him on a chair. He'd shade his half-closed eyes with one hand, while eating with the other. He cut his own bread in thick, heavy slices, which he preferred to eat dry. He also preferred to pour his own coffee, for a reason I never knew and he never said. In fact, he was barely conscious of what he ate or drank, those necessities were considered to be trivial to him, more important was how to contrast one colour with another or how to balance them.

Vincent did not mix well with the dandified company of Hague artists and dealers. He didn't want the underlying beauty of his art to be attributed to the materials he used, as the superficial did, or even the subjects he chose, as the supercilious did – but to what was within himself. That truth, that honesty, was love. Not just any love, but a love for humanity and I, as a woman of the people, which is what he called me, personified that artistic ideal. I understood what he wanted – I gave him what he wanted, what no one else would give him – love and respect. His drawing improved after I moved in with him, but still they did not sell – not because they weren't good enough, but because bourgeois people didn't like how they came about and the difficult truth behind them.

He drew me in even more poses – fifty or a hundred – sewing again, with Willem, sweeping, saying grace, carrying a kettle, going to market, and many more. These pencil and charcoal sketches represented Vincent's intense efforts at portraiture and they revealed more about him than they did about me. He spent long hours gazing through the window, observing the ebb and flow outside the studio. He made a frame with ten intersecting wires which created a grid of little squares that helped him with what he called the witchcraft of perspective. He called the thing his little window and he used it outside, drawing the patchwork of yards, each fenced off from the other. He used it in the studio, where he peered through it at me – drawing me faithfully and always with good intention.

He'd talk to me about the books he read and compare living authors with the great masters of the past – his favourites were Emile Zola, Charles Dickens, Jan van Beers and the proverbs of Solomon. He particularly liked Zola's *La Faute de l'Abbé Mouret*, where Jeanbernat chops off the ear of the Friar, who he blames for Abine's suicide.

'I would chop off the ear of anyone who hurt you, Sien.'

I listened, because he always seemed to know what he was talking about – or, at least, I believed he did. Just as I believed he'd stay with me forever. We had no friends, no acquaintances, no social life as such. There was the art, the poverty, the love and the children. It was enough – for now.

Was he the right man for me? I knew he was, otherwise I would not have been there with him. It felt so right to me, even though I knew he couldn't be depended upon to support me and the children – yet I didn't care. It was as if I was possessed by a power that was stronger than myself, stronger than both of us – an obscure power that was trying to tell me something I couldn't understand. It was enough for me to know that the dream had come into the sunlight of waking life. Sometimes I'd look at him and want to speak, but words would not come. My mouth would open to say something, then close again without saying it. My soundless words would disperse into the ether inside the illusive space of the studio.

One night, as we lay together, the door flew open and we both jumped startled from the bed. Vincent was pale and trepidatious and thought it was some intruder, while I took a pallet knife and looked about. I laughed at his nervousness when I realised it was only the wind. Or maybe it was the consequence of my disregard for the lines of life and the circle of Venus and the fickleness of lotbestemming, which afterwards made me wonder about the consequences of my situation.

Of the price to be paid.

## CHAPTER 15

# ETERNITY IN AN HOUR

Before he met me, I think Vincent had some idea in his head of family life being one of quiet domesticity – an idealised fantasy. Instead, life with me could sometimes be turbulent and passionate. Nevertheless, it was the only domestic relationship he was to experience in his short life and many of his drawings of me portrayed me in domestic roles. Despite the turbulence of our life together, he derived intense happiness from living with me and the two young children – they were his progeny and I was his wife, in love and longing, if not in legal terms. But it was in bed where we really became as one.

At night I would watch him as he undressed. He was beautiful, slight but muscular, with pale skin that was tinted with the redness of his body hair. I don't know why, but something in the way he moved reminded me of Mehdi, but that was the only similarity. Mehdi was more handsome, but not in such a poetic way – Vincent was aesthetic, lyrical even. There was something elusive about the gember man, something enigmatic that made me want to run away somewhere with him – away from The Hague, away from Holland, away from Europe – across the wild world to some isolated island where we could live uninterrupted by the preaching and psalm-singing of the sanctimonious. But I knew that was something we would never do.

Our lovemaking became more and more audacious – far from the tenuousness of that first night we spent together. At times, bloodred light leaked from the embers inside the pot-bellied stove, turning the ambience of the studio almost demonic – vampyrish and surreal in the glow of red coals. My legs astride him and my body undulating – up and down – making my bosoms nutate while the gember man held them in his gember hands. He'd whisper things in French to me – softly – like "l'amour c'est la vie" or "du néant à l'éternité" as his fingers combed through my hair and little bubbles of perspiration appeared on the skin above his cheekbones. He would grasp my shoulders in his moment of crisis, blood draining from his face and his muscles tense under an arching back. His excitement would heighten my own and I would tighten my vulvic grip. Breath would come to us in short spasms, with me leaning my head back until my long black hair touched his legs. Savage animals howled in the streets outside, trying to get in – to join our union of Abhean and Vihansa, the synthesis of light and dark, as we came together in a rebirth of soft insubstantiality. Hearts beating. Lungs snatching at the blood-red air. Then we'd lie together in the giaour fireglow.

He smelled of chalk and woodsmoke and coal and I wanted to confide in him – tell him who I was. I had already told him about my life, right from when I was young in Noordstraat and later on the streets of Poeldijkstraat and Geleenstraat. He never asked me about Jacobus after we had to run away that time and he seemed indifferent to my life as a straatmadelief. He obviously knew what I was, as he picked me up at the Uileboomen taverne that first time in November, then again at the end of December, and it didn't seem to bother him that I'd lain with other men – many other men. I wanted it to bother him – I wanted him to know what I believed in and what I hoped for and what made me what I really was – the woman I really was.

And what hurt me.

I wanted independence for us, from the horrible world around us – to have the amenities and necessities of that world, but to be apart from it – aloof from it – uncontaminated by it. I was sure that's what Vincent wanted to, even though he was locked in combat with his art and his anger. And, somehow, at the back of my mind, I felt that this man already knew just who I was. And what I wanted. We had a unanimity between us – a eurhythmic equilibrium. It was something I'd never felt before with anyone, even my father. I wanted to stay with him forever, whether it was here in the Schenkweg, or in France or England or Africa or anywhere else in the world that he might desire to go.

I wondered if bron en herkomst made a woman truly what she was – if her fate was sealed at birth, or if she changed with each new place and each new experience. And in the end she became the sum of her life to that particular moment in time. She was no longer the woman of the past, she was the woman of the present – waiting to become the woman of the future. And who would have believed, only a short time ago, that I would be here, living in this place with the gember man and wondering how long it would be before it crumbled to sand in my hands.

It became as if we could read each other's minds. We knew what each other was thinking, without the necessity of words. I knew when he was sad and when he was happy – he knew when I was troubled and when I was content. We knew because of the dreamers within us, the one I inherited from my father and the one he took back into the world with him from the first time he died. We knew from glances – half glances – hints of smiles – something in the eyes. And from the children, who we both loved dearly. Maria Wilhelmina adored Vincent and, although Willem was just a baby, he knew his father and laughed with him in the evenings of humming and singing and dancing. And he would grow to be beautiful and intelligent and humorous and he'd love his mother and take care of her when she grew old. Vincent said he'd be famous for something – maybe music or art or literature or politics or religion. It didn't matter which. And we'd both accompany him to all the best places and be introduced to all the best people and, if he was lucky, he would find love like ours.

Once I was back in good health and modelling again, Vincent bought me a present. He had scarce money to spend, yet he bought it with what little he had. I told him it was wasteful and he should be using his guilders to provide food for the children. He replied that he believed I was sent to him by the grace of God and divine providence because, to believe anything else would be admitting there were other gods than God. And how could that be true? He said it with irony in his voice, as we both knew there were many gods. The sun was once god – and still is!

It was evening and we smoked and drank cheap jenever. Although I believed we could read each other's minds and I could see most of the man, the curtain within him opened and closed spontaneously and I could never see everything. The interior of the studio was, as ever, cool and I kissed his face and neck and we fell across the bed, lost in our mutual desire. Although we understood that the world was characterised more by bad than good, at that particular moment in time everything was right.

Even if it would be wrong again at some time in the future.

When it was over, we lay back and drank some more. I smoked a cigar and he lit his pipe. Then he gave me the gift he'd bought. It was a silver ring with the symbol of a silver yodi and he slipped it onto the middle finger of my left hand. I saw it as a sign of his good intentions and I relaxed and tried to forget for a while about the subtle, strange premonition that troubled and tantalised me.

I didn't sleep well that night. Dawn was breaking over The Hague, from the east – over the hinterland beyond the city and the factories and mills within. Even though the sun had not yet looked over the horizon, hazy light spread upwards to an imperfect sky and the birds in the trees near the railway were hysterical in their frenzy of feeding on early morning insects. It was at times like this when I could see my soul as a separate entity, existing within my body but higher in its sentient and cognitive appreciation. I'd never adhered to the teachings of my mother's Catholic religion and, at times like this, I knew there was another dimension to eternal truth – another viewpoint, other than the basic needs of the flesh and the blood and the ordinary soul.

And I was warmed by something other than the sun.

But where was it? What was it? Who was it? Who was I, Clasina Maria Hoornik? Cut off my hands and I was still Clasina? Cut off my legs. Cut out my heart and liver and kidneys – still Clasina. Take away bits of my brain – still –.

So where was it? Where was that essential thing that was me? The thought fused with the morning and the essence of the man lying asleep beside me and the wakening world.

Vincent finished his breakfast and left the studio, dragging his equipment behind him. I watched him go and hoped he would come back. He'd been a wanderer throughout his life – from Brabant to Zevenbergen, then The Hague, Brussels, Paris and London – Amsterdam, Belgium, Etten and back to The Hague. Where would he go next? And would he want me and the children to go with him? I knew it was only a matter of time, because he wouldn't be happy here in the Schenkweg forever. He was driven by something on the horizon, a light that shone for brief intervals and then dipped out of sight. It was a sorcerer's call that would forever be on the verge of being discovered, but always just beyond the next hill. He paused to look back and smile before closing the door behind him.

I watched him through the window as he strode along the street. I watched for a long time, long after he'd disappeared from view. I felt sorry for Vincent – so confused – such a lost child. I wondered if compassion for him made me a better person, or was I just feeling sorry for myself? Just assuaging my own ego with the deception of sympathy? I couldn't be sure. It made me feel good to feel sorry for Vincent, knowing that he carried the terrible burden of vision – the ability to see that the seed sprouting from the ground was as strange a truth as all the hosts of heaven – the power to talk to changelings, to raise from his grave the master musician of song who had laid a curse on all who would dig his dust.

The children woke, taking me out of my reverie, and the day moved on. We ate what little food there was, then went out for a stroll through the Koekamp. As we walked, the thoughts intruded again – doubts returned – questions. Was it right for me to be such a burden on Vincent? He had so little, yet he shared everything. Or was it wrong? What was right and what was wrong? Did anyone really know, even the evangelicals? Or was it all just a matter of conscience? Was one man's right another man's wrong – or was I just trying to justify the unjustifiable? In the end I decided that conscience was fine for those who could afford it and switched my train of thought to how we would find food for dinner.

I didn't know that Vincent was also restless in his mind, uncertain about where he was going. If it would all end in tragedy or in some fairy-tale way that doesn't ever happen. Never. Not for Clasina Maria Hoornik, at least.

In the autumn, we began going to places where Vincent could draw groups of figures – back to the soup kitchen, the station waiting room, the hospital, the pawnshop, the alms-house and even the streets. He began sketching number 199, a deaf man from the old people's home who wore a long coat and a top hat. Vincent called him Weesman, but I'm sure that wasn't his real name. He might have been one of the orphan men the gember man drew, war veterans living on charity. He came to the studio often and posed with me and Maria Wilhelmina, who had to have her hair shorn off because of lice.

As winter approached, Vincent's hospitalisation in June began to have a bad effect on him. He was often weak and despondent and he tired easily and was prey to chills. He slept fitfully and suffered from toothache that was so bad it hurt his eyes, to an extent that looking for long periods at his art subjects became impossible. Too little food and too much cheap alcohol took a toll on both of us, contributing to sunken cheeks and bloodshot eyes. Life was losing its light-heartedness and we both tried to fight off bouts of melancholy.

'Why do you stay with me, Sien?'

'Because I love you, Vincent.'

'Nearness to me brings nothing but sorrow.'

'No … nearness to you brings life.'

'I'm a leper, Sien.'

'Then I'm a leper too. Let the world stay away from us.'

Kerstmis was coming and we decided to make a fresh effort for the sake of the children. Vincent sketched myself and Willem numerous times, saying he saw something deep, infinite and eternal in our little son's eyes. So we laughed again, for a while – and sang – and danced. We drank jenever and smoked pipe and cigar and tried to ignore the world that was snarling outside our door like a rabid dog.

I never knew much about Kerstmis when I was a child, how it began on the second Saturday in November, when Sinterklaas was known to arrive in Holland from his home in Spain. He came with his servant, Zwarte Piet and, when he came ashore, all the local church bells would ring out in celebration. Sinterklaas, dressed in his red robes, led a procession through the harbour town where he alighted, riding a white horse. The children were told that Zwarte Piet kept a record of everything they did during the year in a big book. Good children got presents and bad children were put in a sack and taken to Spain. I wondered why I hadn't been taken to Spain many years ago.

December 5th was the most important day, it was when Sinterklaas brought presents. That evening was called Pakjesavond and Vincent and I entered into the spirit of the season. We played treasure hunt games with Maria Wilhelmina and Willem and we left out shoes by the stove for the presents. We put carrots in the shoes for Sinterklaas's horse and we left the window open for Zwarte Piet to climb through with the gifts. Of course, Willem was far too young to understand, but Maria Wilhelmina was very excited and it was difficult for her to sleep that night. I was excited myself, as I'd never experienced this ritual when I was young. We ate banketletter and pepernoot and everyone was happy for a change.

That night, the gember man and I lay on the soft bed with the wild smell of the sea coming through the cracks in the window. But there was still a monster in my head and its claws were sinking deeper into my conscience. I didn't want to be the cause of anguish for Vincent and a wave of regret washed over me, with the gember man's sinewy body beside me and his sadness vibrating the strings of my soul. I didn't want him to suffer because of me, to be estranged from his friends and family and to lose his means of survival. I remembered when his kindness healed up the hunger inside me and he sang to me of things I didn't understand. The blunt knife of remorse cut into my heart when I saw the pain sometimes in his fragile face. But there was nothing that could be said in our haven of hallucination without inflicting hurt on one or the other of us, after I'd accepted his outstretched hand. I needed him back then and I couldn't now give back what I'd taken.

Why did I feel so sad when I was with this man, with the guilt in my eyes reflected in the lamplight glinting on our bodies? How easy would it have been for me to submit – to concede to the detractors – to give in to their rules and pompous rationale? Why could I not do it? I never wanted to be the cause of grief to Vincent, but it would have meant cutting the tenuous thread that was holding me to life. As I lay beside him on that night, I didn't want to have to move again, just to be always there – and I hoped Sinterklaas would bring me the gift of an eternal present.

We made physical love again, as we had many times and I felt his lips on my eyes again and my head filled with Kerstmis angels and the fire in the stove turned to a rainbow. He caressed my small bosoms and whispered something soundless in my ear, then moved his body over mine. I could hear the dogs growling outside on the Schenkweg, while Vincent and I lay there, at the centre of our little universe.

The silent noise of passion became deafening and his breath evaporated into the ambience of the room, taking my doubts away with them, like sand spilling through an hourglass. Our faces pressed together and our tongues met. The dogs howled outside the window. Birds screeched in the dark trees.

The climax came quickly for him and then we relaxed. Calmness came creeping upon us and sanity slipped back slowly. We lay together in the emberlit gloom.

'Pass me a cigar please.'

'And a kiss … for kindness.'

We smoked and I could see his passion had been replaced with pensiveness.

'Thinking about Theo?'

A little startled look flickered across his face. Then he turned away to re-light his pipe. When he turned back he was smiling and the lamplight danced in his glowing eyes.

'Thinking about you, Sien.'

I lay back and allowed the smoke from my cigar to curl up around the sadness hanging over him that would not be discussed. And I wanted to take out my heart and throw it through the window for the dogs to devour. Someone told me once, it may have been Mehdi, that the union of male and female in every human being achieved a new level of knowing and symbolised the union of opposites in the cosmos. It unlocked the secret power of nature. So, the bliss of carnal coming together became the bliss of enlightenment.

But I knew, when I slept, I would dream of familiar fiends and wake all cold and shivering in the morning.

# CHAPTER 16

# DESTITUTION

Some say music is the purest form of art, that it takes us above all earthly things – all mundane matters. It's like being on the opium pipe, they say. And, yes, sometimes I heard the musical tone and I knew I'd never understand that sound as I understood it then, in the studio on the Schenkweg. Sometimes it began quietly, like a ghost tiptoeing through a forest. Then it became louder. And darker. Louder. Darker. Huge. Overpowering and intimidating. So loud it almost blew my mind apart. Then it quietened again – became slow and sad, occupying my complete concentration. And I could lie down like a tired child and weep away the life of care I'd borne and yet must bear till death, like sleep, might steal upon me.

And I asked myself, would I hear that music after I was dead?

Softwhisper.

As time went on, extreme poverty put a lot of pressure on our relationship. It became more volatile. Vincent was destitute and spent most of the money he received from Theo on painting materials. There was only one solution – the old one.

'I must go back to the streets, Vincent.'

'No, Sien … certainly not!'

'How else will we survive?'

'We'll survive … we've survived up to now, haven't we?'

'Barely.'

You have to understand, I always had to do whatever was necessary to survive. It was a fact of my life which I was used to. Vincent, on the other hand, was totally blind to everyday needs. He required nothing except the barest of essentials to exist, as long as he could draw and paint. I myself could exist on very little, but the children could not.

I wanted Maria Wilhelmina to go to school and be educated – she had already learned to read and write from Countess Carola and some French and English with Dirkje de Vries. I considered an education no burden to carry, even if she got married and didn't use it. I'd been educated to an extent in the orphanage and by my own efforts, but I wanted more for my daughter. Schools, however, were expensive and we could barely afford to eat.

'I need you here, Sien, to model for me.'

'I've already sat for over fifty sketches, Vincent.'

'I know, my art is developing … my style. I need to find my own unique style and I need you for that.'

'Why? You never listen to what I say about your art.'

'I do! I do!'

'It doesn't seem like it, Vincent.'

'That's because I'm the artist and you're the model. But I do listen, even if it doesn't seem like it.'

Vincent sent all his work to Theo, but Goupil and Cie wouldn't exhibit any of it, probably because of the way Vincent was dismissed from their employment seven years earlier, but mostly because of Tersteeg's influence. He'd sometimes rage about it, in our little studio, throwing things about and banging his head with his fists. It was always better to keep out of his way when he was in such a mood.

'They're philistines, Sien, the lot of them.'

He would shout at the top of his voice and cry out in frustration.

'My fate is being determined by fashion. Fashion is responsible for our poverty. Fashion is starving our children.'

And he refused to become a slave to what he called fashion, to pay homage to it, to kneel at its feet. Vincent never had any need for convention, he was a stranger to its laws and emulations. He despised good taste, hated public opinion and would willingly destroy all that was considered to be fashionable.

But it wasn't just fashion, it was because Vincent was living with me. I knew that and considered leaving many times – but where would I go? Where would my children go? I know I was modelling for Vincent without being paid – but I was living in his apartment and eating his food and drinking his absinthe, when he could afford it, and his jenever when he could not. I wanted to pull my weight and the only way I could do that was to go back on the streets.

Theo continued to meet Vincent's expenses, but little else. I'm not complaining about that – I have to say here that I was eternally grateful to Theo, without him, our small family would surely have starved and he had my gratitude for his kindness. But it wasn't enough for a family of four to live on.

'Will you marry me, Sien?'

The question took me by surprise, even though Vincent had been talking about it and writing about it in his letters to his brother.

'Marry you?'

'Yes, you know … marry me.'

I didn't know how to answer. Of course I'd marry him, but I didn't know if he really knew what he was doing, going against everyone's advice. Vincent could put himself in jeopardy at times and not be aware of it, or even care. But I wanted to marry this man more than I had ever wanted anything in my life.

'Are you sure?'

'Of course I'm sure, Sien.'

'I mean, are you sure you're doing the right thing?'

'Maybe not the right thing by other people, but the right thing by us.'

'Then … yes, of course I'll marry you.'

'Good. So now I can keep you off the streets.'

That was his plan – marry me so that, as his wife, he could prevent me from going back to being a straatmadelief. I was upset and disappointed at first, thinking his offer of marriage was no more than an attempt to control me. I left the studio, taking Maria Wilhelmina with me and leaving Willem with Vincent. I went to a taverne near the railway station, where the patrons bought me absinthe and jenever and I stayed there until late. The house was dark when I returned. I listened. Quiet. Maria Wilhelmina was tired and went immediately to her bed.

The door to the bedroom was open and I stepped silently inside. No sound. I could see Vincent – make out the shape of him, sitting on the bed, looking out through the window. He must have known I was in liquor.

'Did you drink absinthe?'

'Yes.'

'And jenever?'

'Yes.'

'Did you fornicate for it?'

'No.'

He lit a cigar and handed it to me. Situations like this were perilous. We'd fought before and those conflicts were full of fury and passion, but over quickly. This time was different – there was a silent menace in the room with us. The danger was palpable – like a heartbeat. My brain was full of sound and I was afraid he would tell me to go, there and then, to take the children and go.

His features were obscure in the semi-darkness, except for his eyes. Wild eyes. Dangerous eyes. He poured something into two glasses and handed one to me. I drank from the glass and grimaced, then drank some more.

'What is it?'

'Cognac.'

Something I'd rarely tasted before. I wondered why he was still awake, but didn't ask. Was he waiting for me? Did he know I'd come back – I'd have to come back? Of course he did. His eyes reflected my own face, my own eyes. Did I see guilt in them? Perhaps not. Perhaps everything was acceptable within the context of the night.

He touched me, but I didn't react, just sipped from the glass. He poured more cognac, then lifted my face to his and I kissed him softly on the lips, noticing for the first time that he was naked. I touched his neck and he made a sound – a hollow sound, almost distant. He held my shoulders and steadied me, then gently lowered me onto the bed. His hands moved across my body. Searching. He kissed me as he eased my legs apart, trying to say something that just wouldn't be said – or maybe it was said but just not heard. Cognac from his lips wet my mouth and the sound inside my brain began to blow me apart.

I couldn't remember much of what followed, because whatever it was stole the night away from me like a thief. The experience was hazy, translucent, dreamlike. Soft sounds of pleasure. Strange words. Heat. Blood. Another cigar. When I finally woke the next morning, the children had been fed and Vincent was gone. He'd prepared bread and herring for me and I ate it slowly, nursing the headache that was hurting my eyes. I'd drunk far too much the night before and I was sorry for doing it. Vincent didn't deserve that kind of behaviour, that was the behaviour of a hoer and I was no longer one of those. Later, I noticed a red stain on the bedsheet that looked like blood, but I wasn't injured. I scrubbed it off, so that Vincent wouldn't see it when he came home.

If he came home.

He did, late into the evening. He'd drawn an old woman lifting potatoes and also a portrait of a man called Jozef Blok, a Jewish bookseller from whom Vincent bought prints, and the entrance to the pawn shop in the Korte Lombardstraat. I'd waited apprehensively for him all day, not knowing what to expect when he did come back. Thoughts came to me out of the blue – strange thoughts, not thought before. Was life a fatal disease? Was it actually something other than it seemed? Questions that had no answers.

Vincent hesitated when he came through the door, and he rarely hesitated. I knew his vulnerability made the situation dangerous, so I waited for him to speak, to gauge the mood and how I should react. I'd cooked what was left in the cupboard – some potatoes and a little rookworst. Neither myself nor the children had eaten since breakfast because there wasn't enough for all of us. He stood still, halfway through the door – half in and half out, as if he was surprised to see me, as if he thought I'd be gone. I noticed several scratches on his face where the blood had dried.

He stared hard at me and I was afraid of his face for a while. Then his expression softened and he pulled off his hat and stowed his equipment and sketches away. He looked at the food on the table.

'I've eaten, have you?'

'Yes.'

I lied.

'And the children?'

'You made them breakfast, remember?'

'So I did. Let them have that food too. I don't need it.'

Maria Wilhelmina didn't need to be told twice, and I mixed some potato with a little karn melk for Willem. There was even a slice of rookworst left for me, which I ate with the herring I couldn't stomach for breakfast. Vincent had brought back a bottle of homemade kruìde baggâh that someone had given him and we sat by the fire and drank it in the evening, when the children were asleep.

The gember man was silent, smoking his pipe and contemplating the flames of the fire inside the stove. I puffed on half a leftover cigar and waited for him to speak. When he didn't, I decided to take the initiative.

'What happened to your face?'

'Do you not remember?'

'I'm sorry for coming back like that last night.'

'Why did you, Sien?'

'Because you asked me to marry you.'

Vincent puffed vigorously on his pipe without response, then he burst out laughing. He coughed up pipe smoke and almost had a fit before he could stop.

'I didn't realise a proposal of marriage would elicit such a response.'

'It was because of your motives.'

'My motives?'

'To control me.'

'I don't think I could ever control you, Sien.'

Vincent explained that he was only thinking of my welfare when he said I shouldn't go back on the streets. I was at death's door when he found me and he hadn't forgotten that. It had taken a long time for me to recover after Willem and he didn't want me descending into that state again. If we were married, then his family and friends would have to accept me – it would be a fait accompli and there would be nothing they could do about it but accept me into that society which, in turn, would lead to further commissions for Vincent and an end to our beggared situation. It made sense to him – but I wasn't so sure of such acceptance, under any circumstances.

'And what about love?'

'Of course I love you, Sien. Do you not know?'

I knew.

'And your face?'

Apparently, I came in intoxicated and we began to make love, in the middle of which I screamed "Jacobus!" and scratched his face. My scream woke the children but I was too drunk to attend to them, so Vincent settled them and, by the time he came back to bed, I was asleep.

'I'm so sorry.'

'No matter … I've heard the name Jacobus before.'

'Have you?'

'That day in Koninginnegracht … the old man.'

'Yes.'

'Then it's me who should be sorry, if I remind you of him.'

'No, no, no, no … '

I flung my arms around him, kissing his cheek and neck and knocking the pipe from his grip. Vincent was the complete opposite of Jacobus, the other side of the moon compared to that monster. I told him so and explained that of course he didn't remind me of Jacobus. It was just that I experienced a recurring nightmare where his big hands came at me like giant spiders. It was a combination of his assault and the eerie room where I slept when I worked as a knecht for the Visser family. My inebriated state must have conjured it up during our lovemaking and I was so sorry.

I couldn't express my regret enough and Vincent just kept laughing. It amused him greatly. I washed the wound on his face and put some lotion on it to prevent infection. I came and sat on his lap and put my arms around his neck.

'So, what's your answer?'

'Answer?'

'Will you marry me?'

'Of course I will.'

We made love again that night, only this time properly, with no nightmares and no screeching or scratching. Afterwards, he brushed my hair with the palm of his hand and lifted me from the bed. He said I felt like a little rag doll – nobody would have believed I had such determination, such resilience. Vincent carried me to the window and we looked out across the city, then up into the night sky. It was clear and a full moon shone its silvery light onto us. It was the most perfect moment of my life, with the gember man holding me in his strong arms and the stars smiling back at me from the vastness of the cosmos.

'We're part of it, Sien, the starry night.'

'I know, Vincent.'

'When I die, look up and you'll see me.'

'You'll never die, Vincent.'

After a while, he carried me back to the bed and lay me down. I looked up into the bright eyes that smiled back at me. We were quiet now, like lambs.

Until sleep came.
Softwhispering.

# CHAPTER 17

# LOSING LOVE

On New Year's Day in the year 1883, Vincent received a letter from Theo in Paris, informing him that the younger brother had taken a mistress. Vincent was delighted. Now both van Goghs were in similar situations and Theo would know how Vincent felt about me and he'd understand the bond between us. He would retract his threat to stop supporting Vincent if he didn't end his relationship with me. Except that Theo's mistress was gentille and Theo was dismayed that Vincent could compare me to his woman. His lover was not stupid or indelicate of manners or narrow-minded or lacking in appreciation of books and art, as they said I was.

Women had always been Theo's weakness, in a life otherwise composed of duty and compliance. Paris was full of women from rural France – educated, cultivated, the daughters of provincial tradesmen and storeowners. They were as bourgeois as Theo himself. This particular woman was Marie Caron. She was middle class and young and found herself out of her depth in Paris and needed Theo's help to survive, just as she'd always needed the support of her social group – unlike me. So, it was alright for Theo to have a lover because she was gentille and cultured – an innocent maiden from a Jules Breton painting – but not for Vincent to have me, a product of the streets, of the unfairness of society, the moral brutality of the very people who criticised me.

Theo did everything for her and wanted to marry her as soon as he met her – yet he advised Vincent against marrying me. Vincent urged his brother to marry Marie and to have a child with her, as he'd had with me. Theo might have done so if Dorus hadn't objected, saying it was immoral to have a relationship with a woman from a lower station in life. That comment was obviously directed at Vincent and me, rather than at Theo, but Theo didn't marry her or have a child with her. He did, however, set her up financially and he continued to see her. It was just another example of the hypocrisy of the van Gogh family and their legion of spies in The Hague.

The bourgeois attacks on me resumed – the fatuous, the impotent and the cynical scoffers – how could Vincent see anything in me, a woman who was less than human in the eyes of the poisoned epistle writers. They called Maria Wilhelmina an urchin and a creature in their conceited belief that they were somehow superior in intellect and ethics to street animals like us. In their opinion, we were born ignorant and wretched and it was our lot to remain so. No amount of refinement could redeem us in their eyes. It massaged their haughty egos to think of us in that way, to believe that they were somehow deserving of respect, simply because they were born into better circumstances.

It was eroding the bond between myself and Vincent. This constant, never-ending disparagement of our closeness was wearing us down, as a grindstone wears down even the strongest metal. The gember man began to lose faith in himself because of the ceaseless criticism. He began to see himself as a sick painter, worthless rubbish, and he descended into self-loathing. We fought over small things – things that had never bothered us before.

'Neuken, neuken! You're such a bastaard, Vincent van Gogh!'

'I knew my father, did you?'

'Why say such a thing to me? There's no reason to say such a thing.'

'Perhaps we've gone as far as this histoire d'amour will take us, Sien. I mean, when we start calling each other names …'

'You're just a selfish bastaard!.'

Vincent walked to the door.

'That's your answer to everything, Vincent, run away.'

He frowned, and I could tell he was stung by that remark.

'I'm not running away. I never ran away from anything in my life.'

'You ran away from everything in your life and now you're running away from me.'

He tried to re-establish his righteousness.

'No I'm not. I'm just saying that when two people start calling each other names, it's time to reassess the situation.'

'You're a klootzak bastaard!'

I was sure he'd been called many worse things in his life, but not in the same context. I was calling him a coward and he knew it.

'We're both getting what we want here, are we not Sien? Or, at least, I thought we were, until this name calling started.'

'I'm not getting what I want, Vincent. What about your friends and family, they want you to get rid of me.'

'I depend on them.'

'What have they done for you? Nothing. Except Theo, he's the only one who's helped us.'

'You don't understand, Sien …'

'What don't I understand?'

He just shook his head and opened the door.

'And what about the children? What about our son?'

He left the studio. I shouted curses after him.

'You're a schele, paardereet bastaard, Vincent van Gogh!'

And I threw his canvases out the door.

Arguments like that became more frequent and we both knew we were heading for disaster, unless we did something about it. It would be a shame to lose what we had together – something that was beyond carnality and love and all that sentimentality. Understanding. A kind of understanding.

More than understanding. Like comfortable silences. Easiness. More than that even. It was difficult to explain – put a name to – describe in detail. Neither of us wanted to lose that elusive thing, whatever it was, and both of us were prepared to compromise to keep it. Within reason. Within the acceptable levels of our extraordinary awareness of each other.

There was always a breaking point, of course.

March 1883 was Vincent's 30th birthday – mine had come and gone in ignominy three years earlier. Maria Wilhelmina and I baked a cake and we sang "lang zal hij leven" to him and, for another while, we were a little family again, at home and content in the place that was a refuge – a harbour from hostility. But it was only for a day.

To avoid being jeered at, Vincent walked the streets only at night. In the empty Plaats, he would stop at Goupil's gaslit window and stare at the art displayed there. The buyers wanted pleasant and attractive, the nouveau riche didn't want to see the ugly truth of the consequences of their wealth and greed. They wanted to pretend that the world was a charming landscape like their lives and the images they hung on their walls. Poor people like me were to be ignored, as well as anyone who painted us – particularly an artist who came from a bourgeois family and who should know better.

Vincent continued to sketch and draw working people – potato diggers, coal carriers, peat cutters and more. I helped him with suggestions, with redrawing, with insights into the poverty-stricken essential being of the people he drew, so that his pictures would be more representative of them. In so doing, Vincent's sense of perspective improved, as did his mastery of the human form and the raison d'être of his art. In that respect, at least, the gember man shared his inner self with nobody – except me.

But debts continued to mount and there was never enough to eat. By the end of July, bailiffs were pounding on the door. One of them pushed his way into the studio and, when Vincent tried to get him out, he grabbed the gember man by the throat. I hit him with a stick and Maria

Wilhelmina kicked his shins and we eventually managed to get the brute back through the door, but not before he threw me against the wall and Vincent to the floor. Tax assessors also sent summonses, but Vincent rebuked them when they called.

'I lit my pipe with your summonses.'

They threatened to seize our meagre possessions, but Vincent told them everything belonged to Theo. They threatened to serve writs and to have him put into prison, but he said they would have to catch him first.

We fought increasingly about me going back on the street to help out. He accused me of having a bad temper and I accused him of blinkered intransigence. He accused my mother of trying to draw me away from him and back to my former life to suit her own purposes and he ordered me to break off all contact with members of my family. At the same time, members of his family continued to attack and slander me and my children. Willem was the only thing holding us together at times. When Vincent was at home, he would not leave his father alone for a moment. If Vincent tried to work, he'd come crawling to him across the floor, gurgling and crowing.

'Look at our little man, Sien, a year old and already the most cheerful child imaginable.'

He'd pull at his father's coat or climb up against his leg and insist upon being taken up onto his lap. Vincent would let the infant look at his pictures, which the little boy seemed to love and his cries of joy delighted the gember man.

'At least somebody appreciates my art.'

Theo came again in mid-August. Vincent met him at the station and they walked to the studio. On the way, Theo told him that business at Goupil had fallen off due to the long depression and his finances were strained to breaking point. He asked Vincent to take on a paying job somewhere and only to paint on a part-time basis. Vincent refused. At the studio, the brothers argued loudly and Vincent accused Theo of not doing enough to sell his work and of colluding with Mauve and Tersteeg to keep him poor and unknown. This accusation hurt Theo, after all he'd done for us. He told Vincent that it was I who had driven away Mauve and Tersteeg, and he should never have fathered a child with me. In a rage, Vincent picked up his equipment and stormed out of the house, as was his custom whenever he found himself in a losing argument.

When he was gone, I poured some of the wine Theo brought with him and we sat together in silence, as in the quiet aftermath of a storm. Theo spoke first.

'Why does Vincent call you Sien? I know your name is Clasina.'

'It's short for Christien, which he's always called me.'

'Christien is a boy's name.'

'Perhaps that's why he shortened it to Sien?'

The conversation, which was nothing more than small talk, paused. The brother's face grew serious and a frown replaced his pleasant visage.

'I must talk to you, Sien. You're the only one who can save him now.'

Theo told me that he was under orders from the family to stop financially supporting Vincent as long as he was with me. Tersteeg, who was very influential at Goupil, was also putting professional pressure on him and his position as gérant in Paris was under threat.

'What do you think will happen to him if I lose my job and have to stop sending money? If he can no longer paint?'

'I can work. I have offered.'

'Do you think, Sien, that you can earn enough at your age to keep four people and also pay for Vincent's art supplies?'

I didn't reply, but my silence said more than any words could.

'I addition, Sien, Uncle Cor has agreed to commission another set of pictures.'

'That's good news.'

'But only on condition … that he leaves you.'

I poured some more wine, but Theo had finished speaking. He stood up and put on his coat. He had made his position clear enough.

'That's the situation, Sien. Vincent's future is in your hands.'

'But what about our son, Theo? He loves Willem.'

'You must tell him the child isn't his, that you were carrying before you met him.'

'I can't do that. It would break his heart.'

'If you don't, it will end his life.'

'And mine, Theo. I know I've been a hoer, but this is bound to end up with me jumping into the water.'

'I'm sorry you feel like that, Sien, but you must do it.'

Theo did not seem too concerned about me jumping into the water.

'Make him believe it's his decision and that it's best for both of you … and the children, of course.'

He left and I drank the rest of the wine, trying to decide what I should do. I was already wracked with guilt, knowing I'd brought so much trouble upon the gember man.

When Vincent returned later that evening, we spoke little. I knew what Theo said was true – if he stopped sending money Vincent would be unable to paint. If he was unable to paint, he would die. But first he would resent me and Willem for being the cause of his death. Still I clung on to hope, that something would happen to change the situation – but it didn't.

It was over.

When he returned, I sat the gember man down in the Schenkweg apartment and spoke to him in hard, cold terms.

'It's impossible for us to remain together, Vincent.'

'Why, Sien?'

'We're making each other unhappy.'

'No! I don't want you to be abandoned and alone again. I love you and the children.'

'I know you do, but … '

'We can leave the city, go to some little village, away from everybody … somewhere we can live a more normal life.'

'No, Vincent, we cannot.'

'And I can't desert my son, he dotes on me.'

I took in a deep breath and held it for as long as I could.

'Willem is not your son.'

There was silence in the room. Then Vincent laughed.

'Why say such a thing?'

'Because it's true.'

'But … he was conceived in November, when I first lay with you. You told me … '

'I was already pregnant.'

Vincent stood up and paced around the room, rubbing his forehead. I'd hurt him deeply and I could feel the pain I had inflicted.

'No! It's a lie! Theo put you up to this, didn't he?'

I did not reply.

'Or Mauve! Or Tersteeg! It's not true! I refuse to believe it!'

I waited until the squall had subsided and the gember man sat back down, sobbing. I don't know if he believed me or not, but we both knew we had to part – it was the only way.

Vincent picked Willem up and hugged him. Maria Wilhelmina clung to his leg, she hated to see us arguing. Tears were running down Vincent's face as he hugged Willem.

It was heartbreaking – the gember man was crying, the children were crying, I was crying.

'But what will you do, Sien? You mustn't go back … '

'I'll get a job.'

'Where will you live?'

'With my mother.'

'No!'

'Yes … I must.'

'What will be the fate of my poor little boy?'

Once we managed to subdue ourselves, we talked long into the night and agreed that Theo's support had to be maintained. Vincent would leave The Hague for Drenthe, to get away from the bailiffs, and accept his uncle Cor's commission.

I would go to Slijkeinde and, when things improved, we would come back together again.

On Sunday 11th September in the year of 1883, I went with Vincent to the train station. Even when he was already in the carriage, he still held on to Willem. It was a parting of inexpressible sadness.

Both our hearts broke.

# CHAPTER 18

# THE HEKS

All around me was the static of sorrow. My time was spent in sorrow, listening to the sound of it. Sometimes the sky was like velvet. Rippled. And I felt alone underneath it. Not alone – solitary, but not alone. The air around me was firelike – and I felt the glow. I felt the force that Vincent had inside him – the longing to lose everything – every feeling. Hate and happiness and frustration and fear and life and love and hope and the human thing. The human thing. Whatever it was. All the things that it was. I wanted to go away from the solitude, into the knowing. To find something. What it was all about. The end result. The absolute absolute. To find the answer to the only question left.

Why?

My mother was surprised to see me and the children. She believed I had finally been able to make something for myself – a life that might mean something, even if I was still destitute. But now I was home again, with my head down and my back bent.

'What happened this time?'

'I can't tell you.'

'Why not?'

'I just can't.'

She didn't ask me any more questions, just resigned herself to the fact that I'd not made a life for myself, as she thought when Vincent painted her and the house in Noordstraat. My mother was a very stoical woman and took everything life threw at her in her stride. Worse things had happened to her, so me being home was a minor disappointment that was added to all the other disappointments that made up the sum total of her misfortune.

Industrialisation had reached the Geest and it brought many factories, so work was becoming more available and wages were gradually improving, even if working conditions were not. My brother Pieter was still at my mother's house in Slijkeinde, as well as my sister Maria, who was eleven. Now there was also me and my two children. My mother said I should get a job in one of the factories, but I didn't think I was strong enough – the work, even for women, was heavy. I knew it could kill me. Perhaps that might have been a good thing, if not for Willem and Maria Wilhelmina.

I tried – I went to the bier brewery that employed hundreds of people, also a factory that turned beet into sugar, an ironworks, and even a textile mill, but they took one look at me and shook their heads. I finally got a job digging weeds from a huge beet field. Working eight hours a day, it would take me three weeks to complete the job and I would not get paid until I finished. I thought about going back on the streets, as I'd wanted to do when I was with Vincent in Schenkweg, but then I remembered how I was when the gember man found me and saved my life. I thought I would try the weeding first and only go on the streets as a last resort.

It was a one hour walk to the farm and it was late October and cold for the end of autumn. Rain began to fall, sleeting into my face like splinters of glass on a howling wind. I was wearing a long hessian dress, covered over with a light cassock coat, open at the front, with laced-up ankle-length boots on my feet, and it wasn't long until I was wet through. The farmer met me at the entrance to the field, which was about twenty acres in size. The weeds were knee-high and he gave me a weeding hoe called a scuffle to dig them out with and then pile them by the side of the field to rot. I was to return the hoe to him each evening and collect it from him again every morning.

The field itself was on high ground, with a stagnant pond down at the lower part, close to a hedge of laurel. It was a desolate place, a mostly featureless landscape, with little shelter from the wind and freezing rain. The sky was composed of varying shades of grey and it lowered over me like a heavy damp blanket. I was left totally alone in the field and I moved over it like a dark, crawling beetle. The hours passed slowly and I worked with a mechanical rhythm, a forlorn figure on the bleak landscape. Late in the day, the rain stopped, not that it mattered much to me as I couldn't possibly have been any wetter or more miserable. My back and shoulders ached, as well as my legs and hips, and my hair was plastered to my face, but I worked on until the light faded and it was time for me to trudge homeward again.

Day merged into day and the field seemed as if it was growing in size and I'd never be finished weeding it. One day I felt very hot and clammy, as if I was going to faint. So I made my way down to the pond and drank some water and washed my face and neck. When I stood up to go back to work, my legs would not respond properly. There was no one else about and I staggered back up the hill, holding on to the scuffle for support. I collapsed among the weeds and lay there out of sight of anyone who might be passing. At the end of the day, the farmer came to look for me as I hadn't returned the hoe. He couldn't see me at first and I could hear him calling.

'Vrouw! Vrouw!'

By then I had started to see visions. A red rash had appeared all over my body and my stomach felt like it was on fire. I heard the farmer's voice, but did not know if it was real, or if I was imagining it. I tried to call back.

'Meneer … meneer … '

He came and found me. A look of shock came over his face when he saw the state I was in.

'What happened? Were you bitten by a viper?'

'No … '

'What did you do?'

'I drank the water … '

174

I pointed towards the pond.

'That water is stagnant and contaminated with acid from the laurel leaves.'

The farmer left me lying in the beet field. I raised my arms to him – for him to take me with him. I thought he was leaving me there to die because I hadn't finished my work and was such a disappointment.

Everything was starting to grow dim and I thought night was falling. Then the farmer reappeared, leading a horse. He helped me up onto its back and I clung on for the hour-long trudge home.

When we got there, my mother tried to make me better with camomile and fennel flowers. She even rubbed sugar into my legs like she used to do to stop the worms coming up and out of my mouth when I was a child. But nothing worked. I just got sicker and sicker. Everyone believed I was going to die. I was in constant excruciating pain and it felt like there was a steel band round my stomach and it was getting tighter and tighter. I vomited anything I tried to eat and my organs were beginning to stop functioning. Death was not far away. My mother couldn't afford a doctor, there was no municipal medical relief and we had no sickness fund insurance.

Then a man called Bram came and told my brother Pieter that he knew of a woman who could cure anything. But I would have to be taken to her and she lived in the middle of the Rijswijk Forest. My brother asked the farmer if he could borrow his horse – and this time I had to be tied on to its back to prevent me from falling off because I was too weak to hold on. Pieter set off across the farmland and fields with me, until we came to the edge of the forest. There was no track or trail to follow and my brother only had a vague idea of where the woman lived. So we trekked through the trees, making very slow progress for several hours. Finally, after what seemed like eternity, we emerged into a clearing with an old ramshackle house and beautiful wildflowers growing all around it. I was only half aware of what was happening, but I could see Pieter going up to the door while the horse stood still. A very old woman with long white hair came out. She had dark skin and she looked very fragile – almost as fragile as me. Pieter spoke to her for a short while, but I couldn't hear what they were saying.

The old woman came over and told Pieter to take me from the horse and carry me into the house. I had lost so much weight I was no heavier than a little doll and could easily be lifted. The house was bare inside, with no furniture, except for a single wooden table. It had an earth floor and a big brick fireplace. Many jars hung from nails in the walls, containing all sorts of potions. There was a hammock where she slept and an old lute which she played for her own pleasure and no one else's. She said her name was Merga and she was a heks, who had the gift of healing called brauche – she could cure with natural remedies and by using the mysterious forces of spirits and ghosts.

Pieter put me on the table and the heks looked inside my mouth, then she pressed hard on my stomach. It hurt very much and made me moan.

'Poison.'

My brother was amazed how she knew straight away what was wrong with me.

'How can you tell?'

'By her mouth.'

Then she went out and was gone for a long time – maybe half an hour. I thought she wasn't coming back. Maybe she knew she couldn't cure me – that it was no use and I was going to die. So she went away. But she did come back, carrying a big jar with a lot of green plants inside. She put fire to the mixture and a big flame shot out of it. She blew the smoke into my face and began walking round me, chanting over me and clicking her fingers. I couldn't understand the words she was reciting, they sounded German but could have been any language. When she was finished, she gave Pieter one of her jars, with a dark green liquid and leaves inside it.

'She must take it all, leaves as well.'

My brother thanked her and offered her some money which she refused to accept. Then Pieter carried me outside and put me back on the horse.

As soon as we got home, I began to take the green medicine. It was horrible. Very bitter, and the taste stayed in my mouth for hours. But I didn't throw it back up, it stayed down. I took the potion every morning until it was all gone. It lasted about a week and the bitter taste remained on my tongue the whole time. But I was already feeling better by the time I'd finished it and my brother made some snert for me and I managed to eat it. It was the first food I had taken in several weeks, without being sick. Next day, I managed to go outside without help and no one could believe it was me. They thought I had died and it was my ghost leaving my body. They ran away and hid in their houses and I smiled with one side of my face and scowled with the other.

But I owed my life to the heks called Merga and I wanted to thank her personally. I knew she wouldn't accept any kind of reward, so I took her a poem I'd written for Vincent, but never gave to him.

I travelled into the forest and tried to retrace the way we came when I was tied to the back of the horse and so sick. Dying. I couldn't remember. I seemed to be going round in circles for hours. Then I heard a sound, unlike any of the forest noises. I listened – and heard it again. It was the musical note, now played on a lute string. As before, not a melody or a tune of any sort, just a single note. It sounded again and I followed it, trying to fathom its symmetry – its meaning. It seemed to be calling me – luring me – to its strange, enchanted essence. I emerged into the clearing with the old house surrounded by wildflowers. Everything was still and quiet. Otherworldly. Eternal. Time seemed to be standing still, there in the clearing.

I approached the house and called the heks' name.

'Merga.'

No reply. The door was unlocked. I opened it and looked inside.

'Merga … '

There was nobody at home. But the old lute was there, close to the hammock. I went back outside and sat down and waited. After about an hour, Merga returned. She was carrying a bag full of leaves and berries and herbs and flowers. She did not seem surprised to see me.

'Ah, the poisoned vrouw. How did you get here?'

'I heard you playing.'

'Playing?'

'The lute.'

'Ahh … '

She smiled wryly and put down her sack. Then she sat beside me on the ground.

'I've come to thank you.'

'For what?'

'For saving my life.'

'I did not save your life.'

'But … '

'You were not meant to die.'

She took a bottle from her pocket and offered it to me. I hesitated, looking carefully at the clear liquid inside. She laughed.

'It's water, from the spring.'

I drank the water and gave her my poem.

'What is this?'

'A poem. I wrote it for you … to thank you.'

'I cannot read.'

So I read it for her.

> *The wind blows hard, the sky is scarred.*
> *My soul stands still, upon the hill.*
> *It looks away, its dead eyes stray*
> *To floating clouds, like ghostly shrouds.*
> *I watch it there, wind blows my hair.*
> *I hear my name, called through a flame.*
> *I turn around, drink the compound.*
> *Merga's smile ends my harsh trial.*
> *I walk towards her and leave the brim*
> *Of the dark hill. We meet, stand still.*

*She turns the tide of tears I cried*
*And lets me live, my thanks I give.*
*The wind has gone and I walk on.*
*The clouds have blown away and flown.*
*The sky is blue, the world is new.*
*My soul and I, our hopes soar high.*

It was just a simple verse, and I lied about writing it for her. But I changed Vincent's name to Merga's and re-wrote some of the words to make it fit the situation.

When I finished reading, she took the poem from me and placed the paper to her forehead. She held it there for a long time, with her eyes closed. Then she spoke in a voice that seemed to be coming, not from her mouth, but from the forest all around us.

'Sien … '

It was the name Vincent called me. I was surprised she knew it.

'My name is Clasina.'

'You do not belong here, Sien.'

'Where do I belong?'

'In your own world. In your own time.'

'How do I get there?'

'Listen … and you will know.'

Then she went inside the house, taking the poem with her, and closed the door.

I waited for a while to see if she would come back out. When she didn't, I left and made my way back through the forest. I heard the note again, the musical note, away in the distance. Saying goodbye. And I knew what I had to do.

When I got a bit stronger, I went back to finish the job on the farm. I felt renewed when it was done and I stood in the middle of the beet field that was finally free of weeds. I was ready to revisit the world again. I knew I could do it. The heks told me I could. When I went to see the farmer to be paid, he said he didn't have all my money – farmers were like that, always complaining they had no money.

'I can give you half now and half in three weeks time.'

179

'I want it all.'

'It's the best I can do.'

So I had to settle for half, because I knew I couldn't stay in The Hague for three weeks to collect the rest. I had to go now, or I wouldn't go at all. I told him to give the rest to my mother.

In early December, before I left, Vincent arrived unexpectedly at my mother's house in Slijkeinde. He looked gaunt and unwell and very weak and I asked him where he'd been, but he just shook his head and didn't answer. We gave him some food and allowed him to rest and he told me he'd made a great mistake in leaving me. I told him what I said about Willem wasn't true – the boy was his son and I only told him he wasn't to appease Theo.

Vincent reassured me that he didn't believe what I'd said and was aware of why I'd said it. He told me he still loved me, as I still loved him, and he would make good on his promise to marry me, once he'd been to see his parents in Nuenen.

'I've been longing to see you again, Sien.'

'And I you, Vincent.'

'You're a brave woman and a good mother, but I can't call myself a man.'

'Why not?'

'I wasn't able to take care of you.'

'It wasn't your fault, Vincent.'

'You have to know, I was never ashamed of you and I never will be.'

'I know.'

He left on Sinterklaas Day, saying he'd be back. I waited, but he didn't return. What did come was a letter from Theo, saying I should not rely on Vincent's promise. He would never be allowed to marry me and I would be wasting my life if I believed him. He said I should leave The Hague because, as long as I was there, Vincent would keep trying to come back. If I did, he promised to meet me in a town of my choosing and help me to get settled.

All my hopes died on that day. Again, I felt I was a failure. Good for only one thing.

I had tried several times to make a better life for myself, but each time fate had intervened and drove me back to what I was born for – the street. For that's where I would have to go. I couldn't subject Maria Wilhelmina to that life again and Willem was too young to be taken with me. So I gave both my children away – Maria Wilhelmina to my mother, who promised to take care of her, as long as I sent money regularly. Pieter was still making furniture and was getting married and moving away. He agreed to take Willem and to bring him up as his own son. I didn't want to leave my little boy with my brother and, while I was still in The Hague, I visited him to see how he was settling and I brought him liquorice. Afterwards, I would stand some distance away from Pieter's house and watch the comings and goings of my son for hours, not wanting to go, not wanting to break the last bond I had with him and his father.

But it was all just prolonging the inevitable.

And so I left again, head down, back bent. It was my destiny to be a straatmadelief for the rest of my life – to walk the streets and be abused by vagabonds and vigilantes. At thirty-four, I'd be a hoer that was past her prime, too old and skinny to be worth much to the vagrants of Poeldijkstraat, who would try to beat me when they got drunk and blame me for all their misfortunes. I'd be lucky if any man would want me and I'd probably end up old and alone, stealing from my neighbours to stay alive and accepting the poverty that was going to be part of the rest of my life. I would never see the places Vincent told me about – never read the books – never meet the people – never understand the meaning of this life, apart from the endless treadmill of trying to survive.

I did what Merga the heks told me to do and I left The Hague. Vincent had already gone and I travelled to Delft, which was a big town about sixteen kilometres from The Hague, accepting a ride on a cart from a trader in leather who was going that way. While I was travelling, I fell asleep on the back of the cart and dreamed about what I would do when I got to wherever I was going – wherever I was meant to go. I woke when I felt the trader shaking me.

'We're in Delft, miss.'

It was already 1884 and I didn't know what I was going to do. I put my hand into my pocket and pulled out the money I had left, to check how much. A small piece of paper came out with it – an address. I tried to think whose it was. Then I remembered. Mehdi had given it to me before we parted company – before I had Fleur. He talked about going to Delft, away from The Hague and he asked me if I wanted to come with him. I didn't at that time, but now I was here. It must have been in my unconscious – Delft. And I had travelled here without knowing why.

# CHAPTER 19
# THE BROTHELS

The address Mehdi gave me was a taverne on Van der Helmstraat in Delft. It was closed so early in the morning and the street itself was deserted. A cold north wind blew down off the Markermeer, at this early this time of year, so I sat down above a ventilation grid where warm air was emerging from a bakery down below. I could hear the voices of the bakers and smell the wonderful aroma of the bread. It made me realise that I hadn't eaten anything at all during the previous day. The smell of baking and the warmth of the emerging draught lulled me into a false sense of security. My eyes began to close from the tiredness that was upon me.

Nights were long and days were longer, with the sky slate-grey above. My mind craved some kind of mooring – it was adrift on a rapid river of uncertainty, rushing headlong to hell. Faces flashed past me – male – female – young – old. Familiar feelings returned – not felt for some time, but back now. Despair. Disgust. Anxiety. Apathy. Regret. Resignation. All came close in the dark-light. And I knew I would dream the end of the dream I began all that ancient time ago – all through the long minutes and days and years. And I pretended for a while to be somebody else, until it all fell away and I was still me. I knew the nightmare would be re-dreamed, over and over again – until it became reality. My mouth opened and closed, but no words emerged. I was drowning in dissolution and a face kept coming back into my head with the eyes pleading and the soft soul crying its little heart out.

Then I woke up. I'd fallen asleep on the street, which was still deserted, apart from a road sweeper. He looked at me, said nothing, and moved on. I felt ashamed. Once the town woke up, people started milling everywhere. I waited for the taverne to open. It was a big place called Het Kasteel – it was shaped like a castle as well, with a pointed roof and a huge black and white sign. I paid for a kleintje of beer and sat in a secluded corner, waiting to see if Mehdi made an appearance. The taverne was quiet at that time of the day, but it wasn't long before a woman on her own attracted attention. A young man approached me and said his name was Tammo. He wore a bright waistcoat and had a bourgeois accent. He bought me a drink and, as we talked, it became obvious to me that he was looking for a hoer, but didn't know how or where to find one or what to do when he did. It was an opportunity and I could look for Mehdi later.

'Are you looking for company, Tammo?'

'Yes … I am.'

'Does this taverne have rooms?'

'I don't know.'

It didn't.

Tammo said we could go back to his house, which was close by. He did not say that his mother would be there – perhaps he thought she'd be out somewhere and he was as surprised to see her as I was. I sat with him and his mother, who taught piano, in their conservatory. She was very haughty and did not like me at all. When Tammo went to the kitchen to get us coffee, she asked me to leave him alone. I had very little money, so I had to be mercenary.

'How much is it worth?'

'I beg your pardon?'

'How much for me to leave your boy alone?'

'How much do you want?'

I thought about it.

'Five guilders.'

She didn't hesitate. I could have asked for ten.

'Alright, but you must go away.'

'I promise. You'll never see me again.'

She gave me the money and when Tammo returned from the kitchen I was gone.

I went back to the Het Kasteel and bought a half bottle of absinthe and smoked a cigar. I asked the barman if he knew Mehdi.

'Mehdi who? Or who Mehdi?'

I didn't know – I only knew him as Mehdi. I gave the man a description, but he still didn't know – or maybe he did, but did not want to give me any information.

'Are you a hoer?'

'No!'

'You look like a hoer. If you want work, you should try Het Jeneverhuis on Mouterpad.'

Het Jeneverhuis was a brothel situated down a narrow street in the town centre. There were some worn leather chairs in the reception area and a tall woman with bleached hair looked me up and down when I entered.

'What do you want?'

'I'm looking for work.'

She came out from behind her counter and circled me, feeling my bosoms and my kont and my legs.

'How old are you?'

I lied.

'Twenty-eight.'

'You look older, and you're very skinny. Then, some customers like skinny women with no tits and some like them older. There's no accounting for taste, is there?'

'Not when it comes to men.'

'Experience?'

'I worked in the Geleenstraat area of The Hague.'

She looked impressed. I didn't mention Poeldijkstraat.

'Have you ever had the clap?'

'No.'

'Are you clean now?'

'Yes.'

All the rooms in Het Jeneverhuis had fancy names – like the Gold Room and the Amber Room and the Rose Room. But that was the only fancy thing about the place. Each room had a washbasin and a double bed, nothing else. When a woman went into a room with a customer, it would be written down on a sheet: "Sophie in the Amber Room for 1 hour". I was given a price list as if it was a menu; hand baan, one guilder; oral, two guilders; missionary position with no kissing, three guilders. Extras and alternatives could be negotiated in the room between the woman and the customer. I had to give half of what I earned to the receptionist at the end of each shift. The shifts were 2:00pm till 10:00pm and 10:00pm till 6:00am, and the busiest times were Sundays, holy holidays and Kerstmis. The place was very regimented – if you missed a shift, you had to pay a fine of two guilders and, if you missed more than three, you were thrown out and there was no way back in.

When a client came to Het Jeneverhuise, we had no idea what he was going to want. The receptionist called out, 'Klant', and all the women started fussing about, getting their hair straight and pushing up their bosoms, slapping on rouge and sprinkling perfume. Then they strutted out as if they were on a promenade, while the customer sat there with a glass of jenever and decided which one to pick. Although I'd been a straatmadelief in The Hague, I thought this was very demeaning and it took me some time to get used to parading myself like an animal. But I learned how to hide my feelings and not to show emotion and it became very mechanical after a while.

We all had working names – mine was Pandora, who was the first human woman and who opened the jar and released evil into the world. I don't know why they gave me that name, maybe because I looked like a woman who would do that kind of thing. There would normally be about six to nine straatmadeliefies to a shift, and no two looked alike – some fat, some thin, blonde, brunette, tall, short. Het Jeneverhuis catered for all tastes, with the ages of the women ranging from eighteen to sixty. The oldest woman there was a grandmother, but she was very elegant and always very busy. Also different nationalities – French, German, Dutch, Danish, Belgian, one Chinese and two African negro. I'd say most of the women were in their twenties – they didn't employ many very young girls because they wanted hoers who were mature about the work and who would not cause any problems for them – women who were reliable and able to deal with it. They also catered for all different tastes in body size – most of the hoers were curvy with big bosoms and big konts. I was one of the leanest women there, although I didn't have a good body anymore, like I did when I first worked for Mehdi on the Geleenstraat.

We came in and went out the side entrance, into a dirty alley, not on to Mouterpad. There was no smoking inside and the beds had to be stripped and made ready for the next woman after use. Stockings only were to be worn – no bare legs unless specifically asked for – and no fraternising outside work. I found the other women I worked with to be very detached, and reticent. They did not speak about their personal lives and it was almost impossible to strike up a meaningful conversation with any of them. I didn't know if that was because of Het Jeneverhuis' stringent rules or if it was just them. They were all experienced street women, so I suppose that impassiveness came with time, as we became hardened to what we were doing.

The women at Het Jeneverhuis were checked for disease every six weeks. They were all well dressed and I was expected to be so as well, as the brothel regarded itself as a high-class establishment, or so the receptionist kept saying, even though it clearly was not. The five guilders I extorted from Tammo's mother bought me what I needed, and the money I made on my first shift paid rent for a small room above a cobbler shop on Westlandseweg.

I never saw the owners of the brothel and the day-to-day running of Het Jeneverhuis was left to the receptionist. On one occasion I had a heavy menses and didn't want to work, but she told me I had to. She gave me a sponge and told me to boil it until it was sterile, then squat and push it as far up inside me as possible – it would absorb the blood and nothing would show while I was working. On another occasion she told me she had been a straatmadelief herself once – she had used the money she made wisely and bought a house and now she didn't have to work on her back anymore.

The customers at Het Jeneverhuis were mostly workers or soldiers and they didn't have to be members to gain access. Neither did they have a lot of money to spend, so we weren't often asked to perform deviant services, just straightforward hand baan or straight neuken. I thought, these men must be able to get that kind of satisfaction from their wives, so why come here and have to pay for it? It was a mystery to me. Then again, it was probably safer coming to the brothel than picking up a streetwalker.

I was making enough money at Het Jeneverhuis to send some to my mother for the upkeep of Maria Wilhelmina, but there wasn't enough for my son Willem. I wrote to Pieter and explained and he said not to worry, Willem was his son now and he would take care of him. After paying my rent and buying food, I had nothing left over and I was working more than fifty hours a week. Even if I wasn't with a customer, I still had to be present in the brothel in case I was required. I got very sore and tired. I had a urinary infection and fever blisters from being run down. I was also changing as a person and becoming insensitive to things around me – I could feel the hardness coming on me like a protective covering.

Another thing I did not like was being told what to do – the receptionist was always chiding me about cleaning. If things were quiet, I was expected to clean the floors and washbowls and it really annoyed me. I wasn't there to be dusting stair bannisters and sluicing out privies and not getting paid for it. There had to be other brothels around, so I started looking. In actual fact, there was quite a number, all in the vicinity of the Westlandseweg. But I didn't know if they would employ a woman like me, in poor health and not very appealing to men. In the end I took a chance on an establishment called De Plezierkoepel on Tingieterpad. It was just opening and everything was new. The brothel had a reception like Het Jeneverhuis, with a small kitchen/laundry at the back. It was situated at the edge of the marketplace – ideal for the customers to discreetly come in the back way. Upstairs, there were only three rooms – the master room, the double room and the single room. It wasn't nearly as big as Het Jeneverhuis, but it didn't have as many rules and regulations either.

The owners were Swedish and women who wanted to work there had to be interviewed. I put on my best clothes that I'd bought from the Saturday flea market close to Nieuwstraat, and went along. There were two men and a woman, all older than me – maybe in their late forties. I could see them looking me up and down and frowning when I came in front of them. I knew I would have to sell myself and prove that, despite my appearance, I could still make money for them.

'What is your name?'

'Clasina Maria Hoornik.'

'Experience?'

'I work at Het Jeneverhuis.'

'Why do you want to leave there?'

'Too many rules.'

The woman came across and appraised my body, just as the receptionist did at Het Jeneverhuis. She did not look impressed.

'You are older than we want, and you are quite thin. Are you popular at Het Jeneverhuis?'

'As popular as any other. Men look for all kinds.'

She smiled.

'Indeed they do.'

She returned to the men and they whispered together.

'You need to go upstairs with Arvid.'

It looked like I was going to have to perform to get hired. I went upstairs with the man. He lay on the bed and I remember how grotesque it all seemed, with me climbing on top of him and moving up and down, up and down, up and down. After a lot of grunting and groaning, it was over. I got off the bed.

'That will be three guilders, please.'

He looked at me in surprise, then laughed.

Back downstairs, the other two were eating meatballs with potato. They looked at Arvid and he nodded his head.

'Would you like something to eat, Clasina?'

'Yes, please.'

I was starving – I ate with them and they hired me. So I left Het Jeneverhuis and my shifts at De Plezierkoepel started immediately afterwards, with the working name of Salome, who danced the seven veils and was rewarded with the head of John the Baptist.

The receptionist was a negro woman who looked as strong as a man and who had a vibrancy about her and a carefree attitude. The other women ranged from nineteen to middle-thirties and they were a lot friendlier than the hoers at Het Jeneverhuis. The establishment had a much more relaxed atmosphere and it was open every day and every night, even on Sundays.

I could fit in as many customers as I was able – the more I serviced, the more money I made. I could smoke inside as well and I lived on potatoes, herring pie, bottles of beer and cheap cigars. If I wanted to be protected, I had to buy my own male shields, but a nurse from the infirmary came round every month giving health advice about diaphragms and spermicidal douches, as well as free rubber goods. I was always first in the queue. If a woman did get the clap or any other disease, word would go around the other brothels and it would be very difficult for her to get re-hired anywhere. The rumour of disease in a brothel was the kiss of death for that establishment. The customers would go elsewhere and the place would go dark.

One Sunday night at the end of February, when it was cold and snowing, none of the women turned up for the shift except me. The receptionist shook her head …

'Let's just close up, Salome.'

'No, I can work on my own.'

'I don't think so.'

'I can. If they want me, they'll just have to wait until I'm ready. I need to earn money.'

But there were no customers either, the weather was too bad, even for fornication. The receptionist was about to close, when a big man came through the door.

'We're closing.'

'Do you know who I am?'

'I don't care who you are.'

I was happy to accommodate him, it would be some money for an otherwise wasted shift.

'What are you looking for?'

He eyed me up and down.

'Not a scrawny bitch like you.'

'I'm the only one here tonight.'

'Very well, but I'm not paying.'

The receptionist threatened to call for the maréchaussée. He laughed.

'You'll be lucky. There's nobody out tonight.'

He brandished a knife. I tried to push past him to get out of the brothel, but he grabbed me and held my arm really tight. I tried to prise myself away from him, but he would not let go. He started to leave, pulling me with him, whispering in my ear.

'You make a fuss, I'll slit your throat.'

He pushed me up the steps and outside into the night. We moved towards a hooded gig and he threw me inside, then he jumped into the driver's seat and we took off. I tried to get out, but he held me back, whipping the horse and moving faster and faster. He never said a word, just looked straight ahead at the road. I was banging the sides of the carriage, hoping he'd be stopped by the maréchaussée, but he wasn't.

After about ten minutes he came to a halt in a dark, deserted street and climbed out of the chaise. He put a finger to his lips to indicate that I shouldn't make a noise. Then he dragged me into a dark house and pushed me up the stairs and into a bedroom.

'Ik moet pissen.'

My voice was hoarse with fear. He grunted and pointed towards a door. I went into the room, which had an earth closet but no window for me to escape through, and I knew he was standing outside, waiting for me. When I emerged, he flung me up against a wall – I could taste the whisky on his breath, see the desire in his eyes, despite him saying I was a scrawny bitch. He pulled my arm up tight against my back and tried to pull my dress off with his other hand.

Suddenly there was a sound of gas igniting and a light shone through the grimy window of the house. It was a lamplighter outside in the street and it took my assailant by surprise – enough of a distraction for me to get loose from him. As soon as he let me go, I brought my knee up into his scrotum and he bent over double in pain. Before he could recover, I was gone down the stairs and out through the front door. I could hear him stumbling after me and I ran and ran and ran, even though I did not know where I was or where I was running to. Down an alley, through another alley, into some woods and out the other side, until I came to Westlandseweg, from where I was able to find my way back to my lodgings.

Next day I went to De Plezierkoepel to start my shift as usual, still shaking from the previous night's experience. The owners were there, all three of them, just like when I started at the brothel. They took me into the same room where I was interviewed.

'We cannot have you here anymore, Clasina.'

'Why not?'

They looked from one to the other.

'The man you assaulted last night, do you know who he is?'

'Assaulted? He tried to ravish and maybe murder me.'

'His name is Hannes Bakker, he is a high member of the Penoze.'

I had been around long enough to know that the Penoze was a Dutch crime gang, similar to the Cosa Nostra in Sicily. They were notorious and very dangerous. I could see that the Swedish owners were frightened.

'We have already been threatened. It is not safe for you here.'

'In fact, it is not safe for you in Delft … maybe even in Holland.'

I knew I'd have to leave.

I never found Mehdi.

# CHAPTER 20

# THE GREAT MISTAKE

When Vincent left The Hague on that September day in the year of 1883, the day I took Willem to the train station to see him off, he'd travelled to the isolated moors of Drenthe, a remote province in the northeast of Holland. It was a place of unremitting bleakness, just like the bleakness in Vincent's heart. The damp moors stretched to the horizon in every direction, where peat was harvested for fuel. The gember man carried his loneliness as he carried his artist's equipment – it weighed heavily upon him and he told Theo how much he missed me.

'The memory of her cuts right through me. I think of Sien with such regret.'

He saw us everywhere, like ghosts – in a poor woman on the heath, a mother and child on a barge, a cradle in a taverne.

'When I saw it, my heart melted and tears came to my eyes.'

He longed for our life together on the lonely moors and bitterly regretted that he hadn't married me, as he'd wanted to.

'It would have ended all my anguish, which has now been doubled.'

He wrote to me and waited each day for a reply.

'The fate of you and my poor little boy cuts my heart to shreds.'

I did not reply to his letter, as I wasn't given it by my mother and I was in the process of leaving The Hague at the time. In any event, I wouldn't have wanted to jeopardise the commission from his Uncle Cor. As it happened, Cor never did commission the work from Vincent, as was promised by Theo in return for me leaving. Vincent sent his uncle many sample drawings, but received no response. By believing Theo and putting Vincent's future before our own, we had both lost too much and gained too little. The mistake we made drove the gember man into deeper and deeper depression. He was choking on guilt and regret and he even thought about ending his life. The bleakness of the storm-ravaged peat-bog country overwhelmed him and he dearly wanted to return to The Hague and to me.

But Vincent had no money for train fares and Theo hadn't sent him anything for months. He wrote again to his brother, saying he wanted to return to The Hague to find me and Willem, but Theo invited him to Paris instead, promising a business venture that would be of benefit to Vincent. Of course, just like Cor's commission, it was just a lie to keep us apart. Vincent tried to paint, to alleviate his loneliness, but the landscape in early winter offered little to inspire him. He ran out of materials and was unable to buy more because he had no money. The townspeople of Hoogeveen, where he'd found lodgings, considered him to be strange, mad even, and they kept their distance from him. They wouldn't extend him credit and, after less than three months, he left Drenthe.

Vincent had to walk twenty-five kilometres to the train station, dressed in tattered clothes and being jeered at by the locals. It took six hours to cross the moors, carrying what he could, in a storm of freezing rain and snow. He had to stow away in a freight car when he got there. Back in The Hague, as I have already said, he found me at my mother's house and we spent those few hours together. He was ill from exposure and my mother loaned him money she could not afford so he could travel on to his parents' house in Nuenen to recover properly before returning to marry me, as he promised.

As you know, he was not allowed to come back.

Life with his father was no better than it had ever been and, in many ways, it was worse. They argued about everything, but mostly about me – about his family's rejection of me and Willem. When Vincent told Dorus that he'd been to see me in The Hague, where he renewed his vow to marry me, the father threatened again to put him into an asylum.

Living there became impossible for Vincent, yet he had to stay as he had no money and the bailiffs were still looking for him in The Hague because of the debts he owed there. The pervading problem stayed with him – nobody really understood him, except me. To them he was eccentric and ungrateful, provocative and argumentative, demanding and abusive. To me he was none of those things, but I understood why it might seem like he was to other people. They all wanted him to conform, to be bourgeois like them, to paint pretty watercolours, to accept the unacceptable. Vincent could not do or be any of those things.

Nuenen, like Drenthe, was an isolated, depressed place, with farming and weaving suffering from industrialisation. The new threat of the asylum from his father drove the wedge deeper between the two of them. Vincent called Dorus a prim, self-righteous prig and took to walking long distances into the bleak surrounding countryside in winter. The villagers, as in Drenthe, avoided him because he swore so much, dressed strangely, smoked his pipe like a chimney and drank cognac and absinthe from the bottle. They called him schilderonzin and he called them ignorant kluiten.

He wrote again to Slijkeinde, a letter asking me to wait for him, but I'd already left The Hague when it arrived and I didn't see it until I returned, seven years later.

Isolated from the company of understanding adults in Nuenen, Vincent sought the company of country boys, who accompanied him on his excursions and found birds' nests for him. He allowed them to watch him paint and he conversed with them as if they were his peers. I think it may have brought him back to happier days of his youth in Zundert and he identified as one of them, carefree in the bosom of nature as he was back then, with his water insects and beetles and things with spindly legs and compound eyes and shiny metal colours.

Vincent decided to draw the weavers of Nuenen, as he'd always wanted to draw poor working people, as he considered them to be artists in their own right. He was criticised for wanting to do this by everyone – they said he shouldn't mix with these poor people. But Vincent did not listen.

'I paint what I feel and feel what I paint.'

So he took his equipment into the dark rooms where few shafts of dusty light cut through the gloom during the day and, by night, the work was lit by low fires and yellow gas lamps. To Vincent, the monstrous black looms in the tumbledown cottages were full of strange poetry. They stood on hard-beaten clay, blackened like the choir stalls of an old church. The dirty grey figures of the weavers were as pale as the ghosts that haunted him in his remorse and could be seen through the swirl of yarn dust, with their white, nervous, never-resting fingers working to the constant click-clack lament of the looms.

The work continued ceaselessly and the loom stood like a huge insect, trapped inside a cell, its posts and beams stretched out like big spider legs. Two skeins of warp moved like breathing lungs at its centre, up and down, merging and unmerging, as the shuttle flew between them, trailing its web of weft. The men worked the black looms, while the women and children wound the bobbins. They used the same looms as their great-grandfathers had, the beams greasy with the grime of generations. The work was badly paid and Vincent spent hour after hour in the soot-stained rooms, leaning against the wall, only inches from the relentless clattering of the machines.

The weavers were regarded as the disciples of the devil by the Protestant bourgeoisie and drawing them was an act of rebellion on Vincent's part, against his preacher father.

'Vincent, why are you still working with those dreadful weavers?'

'I'll consort with who I like.'

He did it to escape the torment of the mistake we'd both made in separating. We knew we should have married and to hell with the consequences – if we'd only had the courage to do that, there would have been nothing anyone could have done about it. It would have been a fait accompli. But we didn't and now we both regretted it bitterly.

'I've lived with Sien's warmth, now everything is grim and cold and dreary around me.'

Vincent, trapped in Nuenen, was engulfed by darkness and melancholy.

He would bring his sketches into the parsonage dining room and set them up on chairs, by doing that he invited the weavers to his father's table. This outraged Dorus, who chided Vincent for refusing to paint colourful landscapes like other, successful, artists. The only thing that stopped this antagonism was when his mother had a fall and broke her hip. Vincent stayed by her bedside for months, tending to her every need, until she was well again. Even then, he carried her into the garden and read to her, rekindling the lost days they had together when he was a small boy in Zundert.

At this time, Vincent's relationship with Theo was at an all-time low. He blamed his brother for our separation and for the decline in my fortunes when he came to see me before Kerstmis. He promised to continue supporting me and Willem, even though he hadn't the means to do so and I had, by then, left The Hague. Theo responded by demanding that he renounce me once and for all. But Vincent wrote back that nobody would ever be able to make him do that. He described Theo's betrayal in The Hague as depriving him of his wife, his child and his home and he vowed to return. He called Theo narrow-minded and high-and-mighty and conceited and self-righteous and many other disparaging names.

Dorus was aware of this correspondence between his two sons and he kept a close eye on the gember man, repeating the asylum threat every time Vincent mentioned my name.

Margot Begemann was the spinster daughter of Nuenen's richest Protestant family. She was forty-three and lived next door to the parsonage – a simple woman who knew nothing of the world outside her village. She was fragile, highly strung, theatrical and lacking emotional attachment. She came to see Vincent's mother after the accident and returned again and again over the following months. She admired Vincent's attention to his mother and took a naive interest in the art of the man who was twelve years younger than her.

'Why do you never sell your work? Strange you don't do business with your brother or Goupil? Why do others sell and you don't?'

These questions irritated the gember man. Still, Margot got up at dawn every morning to watch Vincent setting out on his painting trips – in his loneliness, he must have seemed like a kindred spirit to her.

Margot began to visit his studio and to join him on walks. She was part owner of the Begemann family business and Vincent gave her gifts of his art, desperate for appreciation from somewhere – anywhere. The van Goghs were struggling with medical bills and dowries for the daughters. And Vincent's youngest brother, Cornelius, had to leave school and take a job at a factory owned by the Begemanns. I'm sure Vincent may have seen in her a solution to his family's financial problems.

Margot inevitably fell in love with the gember man and, in September of 1884, she declared that love. Being still in love with me, Vincent was unsettled by this and fearful that she had developed brain fever. However, a Begemann niece saw them together and told the family that Vincent had compromised her maidenhood and sullied the good name of Begemann.

Vincent denied the charges against him, but the family believed that Margot was pregnant, which she was not, and they planned to send her away. Before that could be done, she escaped and followed Vincent to a field on the outskirts of town where he was painting. Coming upon him, she fell to the ground in a spasm. She lost the power of speech and jerked in convulsion. She had taken strychnine. Vincent realised she'd swallowed something, but not what that was. He forced her to vomit, then carried her to a doctor in Eindhoven, eight kilometres away. The doctor gave her an antidote and she recovered, but she was immediately sent to the Willem Arntz asylum in Utrecht and everyone was told she'd gone abroad.

Vincent believed he'd done Margot a favour by rescuing her from the melancholy of a loveless life, but he blamed himself for foolishly misinterpreting her feelings.

After this incident, as the year went on, Vincent grew more gaunt and pale. He wasn't sleeping or eating properly and he complained of weakness, melancholy and anguish.

'There are many days when I am almost paralysed.'

He was drinking too much, as was I, and behaving violently in a dark mood of guilt and self-reproach. This culminated with him threatening his father with a carving knife. Dorus's health was not good at the time and he became too weak to argue with Vincent. The gember man, seeing the effect his presence was having on the father, talked about leaving Nuenen for Antwerp in Belgium to try to find buyers for his work, which had been suggested to him by Rappard. Up to that point in his life, Vincent considered the pictures he made in The Hague to be his best work, especially the nude portrait of me called "Sorrow". I know that because he told me when I saw him in Antwerp the following year.

Throughout the winter, Dorus's health continued to deteriorate and he died in March of the year 1885 with a stroke or a heart attack, I'm not sure which. He was buried on Vincent's 32nd birthday – the gember man was unmoved.

'Dying is hard, but living is harder still.'

Vincent found a model called Gordina De Groot to pose for him – he didn't call her by her true name, but by "Sien". The following month, he finished a painting he'd been working on for some time, called "the potato eaters". People said it was modelled by Gordina De Groot's family and perhaps it began like that, but the finished picture was of the Hoornick family. It had me on the left, Maria Wilhelmina with her back to the painter, my mother to the right, and my brothers Pieter and Carolus, all seated in a room at the Noordstraat – I could tell because the clock on the wall was the one my father bought at market. Vincent used portrait sketches he had drawn during our time together in The Hague and he painted it by heart.

Nobody liked it.

After Dorus's death, Vincent's sister Anna took over the parsonage and she threw the gember man out. She accused him of killing their father and of trying to kill their mother. Vincent packed up his belongings and moved into a small studio which was given to him by a man called Schafrath, the caretaker of the Catholic church in Nuenen. The gember man filled it with bird's nests and plants to paint and he lived there on dry bread and cheese. He dressed only in long woollen drawers with a straw hat on his head and his pipe dangling from his mouth. When Gordina De Groot became pregnant, the Catholic priest blamed Vincent because he was easy to blame – a wild, unmanageable man who mixed with people below his class and roamed the countryside in dirty clothes. Vincent believed the father of the unborn child was Gordina's cousin and a member of the priest's congregation, and the reverend father was protecting the man by accusing Vincent. The gember man was evicted from the studio by the Catholic sexton. When he left, Schafrath burned all the paintings and sketches he left behind.

I wrote to Theo van Gogh after I started working at De Plezierkoerel in Delft. He came to see me there some time later, as he had promised in his letter. He took me to a restaurant and ordered waterzooi with carrots and potatoes and a bottle of very good wine.

'How are you Christien?'

'My name is Clasina.'

'Sorry, I'm used to Vincent always calling you Christien in his letters.'

'I know.'

'And Sien.'

He poured some wine and took a sip. He didn't look well, thin and pale and careworn.

'In answer to your question, Theo, I'm as well as can be expected. How are you?'

'Not so well. Vincent is being troublesome in Nuenen.'

'You should have left him with me.'

'Perhaps.'

He related what had happened to Vincent since leaving The Hague while we ate. Theo's voice seemed to indicate that he, like myself and Vincent, realised it had been a great mistake to separate us. He told me about the trouble at the parsonage and how Vincent's presence affected his father's health and was probably responsible for his death. He paused and took another sip from his glass.

'Could you both go back to The Hague and live together again, Sien?'

'That wouldn't be possible at the present time.'

'Why not?'

'I'm in some trouble, Theo. I have to get lost for a while.'

'What kind of trouble?'

'With the Penoze. I don't want to bring them to my family's door.'

A look of fear spread across his face. Even Theo knew that the Penoze were not to be entangled with.

'What will you do, Sien?'

'Try to disappear, at least for a while … until they've forgotten about me.'

He took an envelope from his pocket and gave it to me. I opened it to see some banknotes inside. I counted them – two hundred French francs.

'The money I promised in my letter.'

'Thank you.'

By now we had finished the food and wine, so I stood up to leave.

'You could come to Paris, Sien.'

'Paris? I know nobody in Paris.'

'You know me.'

His voice sounded apologetic, as if he was trying to atone for what he'd done to me.

'You mean … live with you?'

'Why not?'

'Would Vincent be there too?'

'No.'

I sat back down on the chair, trying to understand what he had just offered and why he would even want to. Was it remorse? Was it guilt?

'I was told you had a mistress called Marie, Theo. What would she say?'

'Marie and I no longer see each other.'

Ah, it was neither remorse nor guilt – it was lust. But I was far from at my best, surely he could have found another, younger, much prettier mistress in Paris? It was a puzzle to me.

'What about the Penoze?'

'They have no jurisdiction in France, Sien.'

I have to admit, at that moment, I was tempted, no matter what his reason for offering. Theo was no Vincent, but he was clean and educated and he had money. He could support me and, once I was there, I might be able to get Willem and Maria Wilhelmina back and bring them there too. But what about Vincent? It would be the cruellest of betrayals for me to live with his brother – the brother who had split us apart and broke both our hearts.

'Thank you for the offer, Theo, but I couldn't do that.'

He scribbled an address on a piece of paper and handed it to me.

'If you ever change your mind.'

# CHAPTER 21

# OUTCAST

I started to drift around, from Delft to Rotterdam, Dordrecht, Antwerp – all over the country. I sent some of Theo's money to my mother and, when the rest was gone, I learned how to be resourceful, stealing from traders and markets, pickpocketing, searching through rubbish tips for food, scavenging cigar butts from the street, sleeping in barns and doorways. It was cold that winter and all I had to keep me warm was a hooded coat Vincent's mother sent in her one act of kindness towards me. I had long hair at the time and I used to wrap it around my neck like a scarf.

Sometimes people would throw a few coins at me, other times I would go up to drunken men in tavernes and dupe them – get them to spend money on me with the promise of cheap sex, but they never got what they paid for – I'd always find a way out before it came to the point of accompanying them into the privy or outside to an alley. When I could, I'd steal their purses and get out before they noticed.

This duping and homeless lifestyle went on for about a year. I have to say I'm not proud of this time in my life, which might seem ludicrous under such circumstances, but I was alone and getting older and I had to survive in any way I could. I also had to be very careful – the tavernes I frequented were rough and populated with all kinds of vagabonds and ne'er-do-wells. What I mean by that is they were used by people who worked for the Penoze – small-time villains, burglars, robbers, opium dealers, enforcers, bailiffs, that kind of ruffian. It was very dangerous, but they were the only places where I could blend in unnoticed. If any of them caught me trying to dupe them, I would end up badly beaten – or dead. That's why I kept moving from place to place, so nobody ever knew who I was or could pin me down.

But I was getting tired of the constant trekking around and I missed my children.

I found some cheap lodgings in an armenhuis in Rotterdam. It was very dilapidated and there was no washroom or kitchen – it was just a basic room for sleeping in. The first night there I went along to a taverne on Calandstraat where I heard a shylock frequented. They said he would loan money to anybody, even a hoer from a brothel. I wore the best clothes I had, which were clean but not very stylish and I hoped the dim light of the taverne would conceal my worn-down boots. My face was pale enough, so I didn't need powder, but I applied charcoal to my eyelashes and some beetle blood to my lips. My hair was put up in a braid, revealing my slender neck and my fingernails were clean and cropped short.

The shylock was seated in a shadowy corner, doing business with many people who were lined up by his table. I waited until it was quiet and he was just about to leave.

'Excuse me, meneer … '

'Yes?'

'I would like to ask for a loan.'

He looked me up and down, then sat back in his chair.

'How much of a loan?'

'Twenty guilders.'

'That's a lot of money.'

It was to me, but not to him. He asked what I needed it for and I told him to renovate my lodgings. I didn't have a husband to do that and the work would be too hard for me, so I needed to hire a builder.

'And how will you pay it back?'

'Do you want me to be honest?'

'Of course.'

I told him I was a straatmadelief and I worked in a local brothel. I earned seven guilders a week, so I could pay the loan back in ten weeks.

'What about interest?'

'How much is that?'

'Three guilders a week.'

I feigned shock and put my hand up to my mouth.

'So, I will have to pay back more interest than the sum I borrow?'

'That's how it works … otherwise you could go to a bank.'

He laughed loudly. I pretended to think about it.

'Very well, I have no choice.'

He asked where I lived and I told him on Calandstraat. The park side of Calandstraat bordered a respectable area, but the dock side was rough and down-at-heel.

'The park side or the dock side?'

I lied.

'The park side.'

I thought he would tell me to come back after he'd made sure I was telling the truth, but he began counting out the coins there and then.

'Five guilders, here, every week. Do not miss a payment.'

'What if I do?'

'Well then, we will have to consider some other form of satisfaction … ?'

He waited for my name.

'Salome.'

I was about to leave. He grabbed my arm.

'Do you think I'm stupid?'

'No, meneer … '

'You could just run off with my money.'

'I won't.'

He pulled me up a stairs and into a small room, furnished only with a bed. I'd been in many such rooms before and I knew what was expected. I lay back on the bed and lifted my skirt. What was the point in resisting? He dropped his britches and grunted on top of me for about five minutes. Then it was over. I knew men had to have this kind of relief, but I didn't know why. Mehdi told me that carnality was the second greatest instinct in men. When I asked him what was the first, he said self-preservation. So I suppose, as long as it wasn't life-threatening, men were unable to resist this instinct which was in them since they walked on four legs as animals. He pulled up his britches and walked to the door.

'Don't try to run with my money. I'll find you.'

I bought a bottle of absinthe and a tin of cigars on the way back to my lodgings. I drank and smoked until the early hours and I tried to sleep, but could not. What was I doing? I knew I would not be able to pay back the loan and, if I ran, he would surely find me and kill me – or have someone else kill me. When I looked through the window, I thought I could see a dark figure out on the street, watching – had they followed me back from the taverne on the shylock's orders? Or was it just my imagination?

Before it got light, I packed my few belongings and left Rotterdam. I travelled on foot to the outskirts of the city, where I managed to get a lift from an old farmer on the back of a cart full of onions, turnips and rhubarb. He was travelling southeast, away from danger and across the river Lek, to some remote village – but I didn't care where. He gave me some leek soup and bread to eat and I slept in his barn that night. Next morning I paid him ten stuivers, for which he was most grateful, and I was on my way. I walked south, intending to make my way to Dordrecht, which I believed would be far enough away so the shylock wouldn't be able to find me. When I came to the next town, I was able to buy a ticket on a public coach for two guilders that took me the rest of the way.

The shylock asked if I thought he was stupid – that's exactly what I thought. If he was stupid enough to fall for the dupe, then he deserved to lose his money – money he would easily recoup with his extortionate interest. He had a nice comfortable life, while I was existing on the edge of oblivion. I just did what I thought I had to do, that's all. When I got to

Dordrecht, I sent seven guilders to my mother for the upkeep of Maria Wilhelmina.

I did not need to work for a while after arriving in Dordrecht, thanks to the shylock's money. However, I knew it would not last forever, so I observed the brothel situation in that town, not knowing at the time that Vincent had worked in the bookshop there when he was a young man. I found an amenable establishment called Het Rode Licht that was smaller than Het Jeneverhuis and not as busy as De Plezierkoepel. The brothel was grim and full of a kind of latent despair, but I did not see it that way – to me it was an opportunity. I was getting past the point where any establishment would hire me, so Het Rode Licht would be better than nothing.

The brothel looked in great disrepair from the outside and it was just as bad on the inside. The floorings and furniture were worn and threadbare. The chairs were broken and the rickety stairs had no bannister. The rooms looked like the inside of a poorhouse and the beds dipped in the middle from overuse. The washroom had no water, the curtains were crying and the bedcoverings looked as if they could get up and walk out on their own. But beggars could not be choosers.

The owner's name was Belle. She was tall and blonde and in her early fifties. She said everything would be getting fixed, people had let her down, stuff was on order. The straatmadeliefies were very rough also, so I fitted in perfectly. Some were from outside the city – from Antwerp and Rotterdam, others were German and French – all had addiction problems with alcohol and opium. Some were loud and foul-mouthed and some were reclusive, morose, almost misanthropic. Some had been abused and some were still being abused. None of them were there to make friends, they were there to make money – just like me. The brothel itself was different to what I had been used to. There was no receptionist, no security, and the women did everything for themselves. It was bizarre rather than disorganised, but fascinating in a strange way that appealed to my self-destructive nature. When I arrived for my first shift, the hoers were drinking alcohol openly. This was unheard of for me – the other brothels had strict no-drinking rules, as we had to be at our best for the customers. Here it just looked like a group of half-naked women in conversation, having a drink, rather than a professional establishment.

The customers were as rough as the place itself because Belle didn't care who came through the doors, as long as they could pay. There was no dress code and they could be drunk or drugged – if they had a pulse, Belle let them in. For her it was a matter of quantity, not quality. I kept a low profile on that first shift, as some of the women had regulars and I did not want to tread on their toes. The routine with the cash was fairly slipshod, like the rest of the place. Belle took her half of whatever I earned, but it was difficult for her to know how much that was, because nobody kept a check, like the receptionists did in the other bordeels I had worked.

After a couple of weeks, I noticed there was an increasing level of opium and alcohol being taken by the working women at Het Rode Licht. I went to see Belle.

'If the maréchaussée raid us, Belle, I'll be arrested and so will you.'

I was thinking about the shylock and the Penoze, who were undoubtedly still looking for me and who were probably bribing the politie. I could not afford to be found. What I didn't know was, it was Belle who was supplying the hoers with opium and jenever, for which they were paying from their earnings. The next thing I knew, this wild German woman who they called Brunhilde came at me, screeching and calling me an informant.

'I will tear your hair out, you hündin!'

I was used to taking care of myself, but she was much bigger than me and I tried to stay calm. Belle intervened before I had to fight her and probably get hurt, but things were not working out as I expected at Het Rode Licht.

The final act in that sordid drama came a couple of nights later. A customer came in and asked for a kind of perverted performance which I will not describe here. He chose me because I was relatively new and he wanted to try me out. I did not want to do what he was asking. Belle intervened again.

'You have to do it, Clasina.'

'It's perverted.'

'If you don't, you'll have to leave.'

I was about to refuse again, even if it meant losing my job, when there was a commotion at the front door. The shylock from Rotterdam had turned up with some ruffians and they were going from brothel to brothel, looking for me. When Belle confronted them, she was punched in the face and knocked unconscious to the floor. The other women were all clucking around like constipated chickens and the customers were running out the back way like fleas off a dead dog. I ran out with them.

Het Rode Licht was closed down by the authorities after that.

It was time for me to move on – again.

I was an outcast. Alone. But that worked in my favour for once because I did not want anyone to know who I had become – a bad women – an outlaw. I began calling myself Christien, as Vincent called me, and used my mother's maiden name also. So I became Christien Pellers and, after walking for so many kilometres from Dordrecht into the countryside, I finally got a job with a family called Mansouri near the small hamlet of Ossendrecht. The wife was called Anke and she was pregnant. The husband's name was Hakim and he was Algerian, just like Mehdi, though not as handsome. I asked him if he knew Mehdi, but he did not. A mother-in-law called Fenna lived with them as well, they had a pig farm and a little shop. My job was to work with the pigs and as a seamstress and help out in the shop. I told them I was twenty-five, even though I was ten years older than that and looked ten years older again. I'm sure they didn't believe me, but I wanted them to think I was young enough to do the work.

So, here I was, with no background for anyone to investigate and no story to tell. I didn't want Anke to know about my past, how I was promiscuous and loose and worked on the street and in brothels as a hoer – maybe she'd be afraid I would tempt her husband and she would tell me to leave. They liked the idea of me being anonymous because, if I had no family, there would be nowhere for me to go and I wouldn't need any time off. They didn't pay me wages, just gave me food and castoff clothes.

They lived in a very old farmhouse and I slept in the loft. I wasn't allowed to use the family washroom and I had to clean myself outside with a makeshift shower that only had cold water. The privy was a hole in the ground and that and the slurry I had to make up for the pigs attracted rats. The Mansouris were in their twenties – she came from a wealthy family in Breda, who were grain merchants. But her brother got involved in crime and killed someone and most of their money went to paying his legal costs. The family of the man he killed was connected to the Penoze, who set fire to the grain stores and burned them down. So Anke had to marry Hakim the pig farmer. When I heard about the Penoze, I wanted to run away immediately. But I had nowhere else to go, so I stayed. I believed, if I remained vigilant, I could get out before anyone came looking for me.

I ate whatever the family ate, but I had to sit separate from them. The mother-in-law was the hardest on me. She complained that I was a disgusting, ignorant woman, which she herself was – it was a trait of the Dutch, if they had more than you, they thought they were better than you and they let you know it. Maybe it was the same elsewhere, but it seemed to me to be embedded in the Dutch national character and stemmed from a flawed code of etiquette and a national derangement about success, along with an illusive and mistaken notion of what success really was. I'm reviving Vincent's words here, but it was true, nonetheless.

There were three good things about the job – the first was the good food, the second was a really pretty stream that ran past the end of a big field at the edge of the pig farm. I used to walk there and dream like my father, even though I didn't get too close to the water because of what happened to me in the beet field. The third was books. Anke was a teacher in the small local school and she kept a lot of books in the house. I was allowed to read them when I had time and I took full advantage of that privilege and used every spare minute to do so. I'd read many of them before, but it refreshed my love of literature and it was no burden to read them again. Some were schoolbooks with tests in them and I interpreted them my own way and let my mind fly away over the rivers and hills.

The husband hardly spoke to me, except to give me orders, and I think he saw me more as a beast of burden than an actual human being. But, as long as I completed my work, I could do whatever I liked – read the books or stroll by the magical stream and dream.

I stayed with the Mansouri's for almost a year, until I was approaching thirty-six. During that time I missed my children greatly, as well as missing Vincent and the time we lived together. The longer I stayed away, the more I thought about Maria Wilhelmina – I wasn't sending any money to my mother and I was worried that she would put my daughter into the orphanage. The more I thought about it, the more I worried. I finally wrote a letter to my brother Pieter, asking how he and my son Willem were and if my mother was still taking good care of my daughter. I received a letter some time later, saying everything was as it was when I left The Hague, but little else. Despite the brevity of the letter, it eased my mind. I also wrote a letter to Vincent's brother, Theo, asking how Vincent was. I didn't know if he would reply, but I hoped he would. Theo was basically a good man and I never blamed him for what happened. He always said he would like to see Vincent settled and, had it been up to him alone, we would still be together. It was the rest of the prudes who were steeped in their own false sense of importance and over-inflated pride.

I could not talk to anybody about my feelings, of course, because the Mansouris believed I had no family. I was the woman from nowhere. And that's how I felt, like I did not belong anywhere in this world. I longed for someone to love – to love me like Vincent did. If someone had, I would have loved them back unconditionally. I would have given them my love for theirs – forever – for as long as they wanted it. And, even after they stopped wanting it, I would still have continued to give it. Just as I did with Vincent. I saw myself as a tiny irrelevant speck in the huge maelstrom of humanity, spinning round and being blown about like a feather in a gale – not knowing where I would eventually end up.

There was a church close to the pig farm, where I had to go every Sunday with the family, and a dirt road going past it. I always wondered what was down that road and, one day after I'd finished my work, I decided to take a look. I walked and walked, as if in a trance, past houses and fields and farms – losing track of time and distance – thinking about Vincent and my children and not seeing the time slipping by. Then I noticed that night had come upon me. I had walked a great distance from the Mansouris pig farm and I would never be able to get back there before it became so dark I wouldn't be able to see.

'Christien, what are you doing here?'

I whirled round, startled. A woman called Claudette, who I knew from going to the church, had come up behind me.

'Claudette, it's you.'

'Of course it's me. Why are you here in the dark?'

'I went for a walk … but it got too late.'

'You can stay at my house.'

She was on her way home and she took me with her. I stayed the night and, as soon as it got light, I made my way quickly back to the Mansouris. They were very angry. They had been out looking everywhere for me – in the fields and the trees behind the farm and the stream where I used to walk. How inconsiderate of me to stay out all night! They considered that they owned me – like their pigs. They told me

I would have to leave because I was too irresponsible. They couldn't trust me anymore. All I'd done was go for a walk – a long walk but, in doing that, I had shown independence and what would I do next? I was dangerous because I thought for myself, even if it was in a very limited way.

The Mansouris were not bad people. They believed I had no family and they were doing a charitable thing by helping me. I was a good worker, but that was all I would ever be to them. They couldn't think of me as anything else, certainly not as their equal, and they would never see the seething, swirling firmament in the background behind them – just themselves, standing smugly in the foreground.

In a way, I was pleased to have to leave. I'd been there too long and it was time for a change. I'd had enough of working for nothing and I believed the shylock and the Penoze had stopped looking for me now.

It was time to move on.

In the meantime, Vincent found himself alone and unwanted in Nuenen. So, at the end of November in the year of 1885, he left Holland for the last time and took the train to Antwerp. He was completely destitute and had to leave all his drawings and paintings behind.

# CHAPTER 22

# ANTWERP

The harbour area of Antwerp was chaos – carts and wagons choked the narrow streets, cattle snorted and steamships whistled – sailors staggered from taverne to taverne and dockers wrested with heavy goods from all over the world. There were fights and bottles broken and cursing and crying, while the ships bobbed and creaked in their slips and a forest of masts reeled back and forth like drunken trees. Built on the estuary of the Rhine river, the city was one of Europe's busiest ports and full of all nationalities from every corner of the world. The brothels advertised hoers from many nations who catered for every carnal desire. They stood next to tavernes and saloons and English public houses and French café-concerts.

When Vincent arrived, he rented a room over a paint shop on the Rue des Images, between the station and the city centre, away from all that hustle and bustle. With Theo's money, he fitted it out with canvases and brushes and paints – all the things he had to leave behind in Nuenen. In the first few weeks of his stay, he studied the pictures in the churches and galleries, especially those of Peter Paul Rubens, and tried to paint the tourists he encountered at the city's medieval landmarks, like the cathedral and castle. He believed he could sell those pictures to the foreigners who might be looking for souvenirs of their visit. They did not buy his work, so he decided that painting naked females might have a better market. Away from the puritanical vicinity of Nuenen, he was sure he would be able to find a model to pose nude for him. He took to roaming through the streets and alleyways of the harbour area, in search of someone who would consent, but models were expensive and he had no money to pay for a straatmadelief's time – he needed a woman who would pose for free.

In the meantime, I arrived in Antwerp from Ossendrecht, which was only thirty kilometres away. Antwerp had a large population of straatmadeliefies and I couldn't get work in any of the brothels, there was a surplus of younger, better looking women to populate them. So I used the few guilders I had left to rent a small room on Brasiliëstraat. From there I plied my trade as best I could on the harbour streets at night and rested during the day. It was dark and dangerous, but at least, to some extent, I was the master of my own fate and not that of a bordeel madam or a greedy souteneur. The work and good food on the pig farm had made me strong and I was relatively healthy, given my circumstances. I hoped to make enough money in this sinful city to be able to return home to The Hague to see my children.

Vincent, on the other hand, was not very well. He became even sicker from traipsing the harbour streets of Antwerp in the cold, wet winter and, when we came upon each other by pure chance on Amsterdamstraat, it was like a mirror image of the time he saved me and Maria Wilhelmina in The Hague. I saw a man carrying painter's equipment late at night, having emerged from the Scala café-concert. I was curious because of the equipment, which I'd seen Vincent carry many times. I came close and saw the gember beard and I knew it was him.

'Vincent?'

He looked, but he did not see me.

'Who are you?'

'Do you not remember?'

He looked closer.

'Sien? Is it you? What are you doing here?'

'What are you doing here, Vincent?'

'Trying to sell my paintings.'

'And have you … sold any?'

'No.'

With that he staggered against the wall and I could see he was very weak and possibly going to faint. I supported him as best I could and managed to get him to my room on Brasiliëstraat, which wasn't very far away. Once there, I made him some soup and laid him down on the bed.

That night, he told me about what had happened to him since the last time we met and I told him as much about me as I thought he needed to know. I didn't want to upset him in his frail condition, so I left out a lot of my story, as well as my meeting with Theo. It seemed that life had treated him roughly, more roughly than it had treated me, but we were together again as before and that's all that mattered. We were an odd couple, both struggling to survive in our different ways. Both being who we were. I think Vincent appreciated the fact that right then I was prepared to accept who he was on the surface and did not need to look for anything underneath. The man I saw in front of me was enough, and I told him so. It was better like that – no sentimentality and no false colours.

My room was warm, with a dark wooden floor and several small, framed pictures on the wall that Vincent said were lithograph prints of Johannes Vermeer's lacemaker and girl with a red hat. I didn't know that. We both felt easy here – it didn't bother us that the area had a reputation for violence and depravity. It was a little oasis in an insane world. We could be ourselves here and forget about the things that had hurt us – the things that had disfigured us and made us ugly. Vincent could hold himself together and I could find a kind of sanctuary.

We sat on the bed together with our backs against the wall and watched the dancing flames in the little fireplace. Vincent seemed mesmerised by the movement and we were still and silent for a long time. I could hear him breathing, smell the paint and perfume of the street from him – that artist smell

I'd missed so much. I kissed his face and neck and undid the buttons of his shirt. The room grew starbright for a moment, then darkened to deathness. Vincent's face twisted and his body went rigid and began to convulse in short spasms. I held his shoulders. Holding on. Holding on. When it stopped, we relaxed again – two bodies on the bed, like one strange animal, male and female, frail and more frail. I heard the note played on a lute string and the voice of Merga the heks.

'You do not belong here.'

But I did. I did belong here.

We lay still again, for a long time. For all time. Then he put his arm around me and kissed my forehead. I kissed him back – my lips on his thin features, making the pain go away. I pressed my face into his chest and ran my hands through his hair. Then I moved my body across him so lightly it was as if I was weightless. A clock began to tick somewhere in the room – it was probably ticking all the time, but I didn't notice it until now – and, once I did, it sounded like a hammer striking an anvil. Every strike was an exploding second in my life – running away from me.

Vincent's face began to twitch again. His body began to shake – grotesquely, abnormally, convulsively, insanely. I was no longer near him. He floated away and I tried to call him back. The paintings on the wall were shouting something, but I couldn't hear them with the noise of the clock. I began to hum a tune – the English "Greensleeves" that Vincent had sung to me in The Hague. The sound seemed to touch his soul and assure him there was nothing to be frightened of. Nothing existed except the moment we were in. The cosmos had exploded and we were what was left. Us. Just us. Me and the bed that was floating in the aftermath and the gember man who was so close he was part of both – the three were one – me and the bed and him. A trinity of touch. Eternal in that eternal hour of night.

Our bodies were sealed together – everything was understood and our minds fused into the unified roundness of man and woman.

The circle was complete. The half made whole.

A moon shone its silverness through the window, filling the room with ghostly light. I looked down at Vincent and saw that his eyes were closed and his body moved only to the rhythm of the breath that escaped from him. I wanted to place a pillow gently over his face and peacefully extinguish the life from him, so he would never be disappointed again. But my hands wouldn't move. I felt something hot on my face and was surprised when I realised it was a tear.

The moonlight crawled around the room and spread to the walls and ceiling. The clock had stopped ticking and the paintings ceased shouting. But the sound of the lute remained, floating on the silverness, then decaying and turning into a ball of squirming maggots that fell on the bed. I brushed them off and they slithered away across the wooden floor and disappeared into a mousehole. The silver moonlight was cold, even though the room was warm. I closed my eyes and tried to sleep, but the darkness behind my eyelids was overpowering, so I opened them again to the sickly smell of the maggots, crawling closer to the bed and squirming away again as soon as I looked in their direction.

Vincent stirred beside me, but didn't wake. He whimpered softly like a small animal that was hurt in some way. I wanted to shake him, to stop the nightmare, but decided not to. Instead, I lit a cigar and watched the blue smoke curl upwards through the silver room. It moved very slowly and enveloped everything. It took on a life of its own and made patterns that had some significance, even though I didn't know what. I watched it for hours and days and months and years – for all time.

There was a glossy texture to the night and I slipped off the bed and stood naked at the window. Outside, the sky had turned to fire and I could feel the fundamental forces of nature all around. They came and went into me. Filled me. Became me. I was part of all things, yet I still felt alone in the vast cosmos as I stood there naked. Vincent stirred again on the bed behind me. I turned back into the dark room and forgot what I was thinking about. The silverness gradually grew more gilded as the milky winter sun came up.

Dawn broke and I fell asleep.

It was a restless sleep, with many demons in the room with us. Vincent cried and tears rolled down his protruding cheekbones and stained the bedsheet a transparent colour. If I'd been awake I would have comforted him, but I slept the sleep of the dead and woke to a blustery afternoon in Antwerp. I made coffee with some bread and sliced gouda which was ready when Vincent finally woke. We ate in silence and the room acquired a strange aroma for a while. At first I thought it was the coffee, but then it seemed to be something else – a colour I couldn't identify. Violet maybe. Not warm, but not cold either. A Vincent colour. It belonged to him – the gember man. It overpowered my own turquoise smell, but I didn't mind and, after a while, the violet and turquoise mixed to make a vivid terre-verde.

Vincent was the first to interrupt the silence. He told me he was overstrained and was having problems with his digestion. I could see he was very thin and undernourished, his gums looked sore and some of his teeth were loose. He coughed for a length of time when he lit his pipe after eating, so long that I thought he might choke.

'You need to see a physician, Vincent.'

'I'll be alright.'

'I don't think so.'

That day, I went with him to see a doctor called Amadeus Cavenaille on the Rue de Holland and he told Vincent that he had syphilis.

'That can't be, doctor.'

'Why not?'

'I haven't been with any hoers.'

He looked at me with a wry smile when he said that. I knew it wasn't me – we had slept without carnal contact that night and whatever was ailing him had been doing so for some time.

Now, I don't know if it was syphilis that was wrong with Vincent, but the doctor told him there were more ways of getting the disease than through lying with a hoer. He asked Vincent if there was any madness in his family. The gember man said his sister Wil had shown signs of dementia and had been considered for an asylum – one of his aunts was epileptic and there were several cases of mental disturbance on his mother's side – the Carbentus family. The doctor told him that syphilis could be passed on from mother to child and maybe Vincent's mother Anna had inherited it as a carrier and had passed it on to him. It may have lain dormant in him during his younger years and his lack of proper food and exposure to the weather had brought it on now.

'Can it be cured, doctor?'

'I think it's too late for that, but it can be treated.'

Vincent was sent to Stuyvenberg Hospital at the end of the Rue des Images for alum and sitz baths and mercury – he could not pay, so he painted the doctor's portrait instead. With mercury, the cure was worse than the disease because it caused cramps, diarrhoea, melancholy and salivation – not just drooling, but lots of mucus from the affliction that caused further infection to the mouth and gums. As a result, Vincent couldn't chew food very well and he became too weak to paint. His loose teeth began to rot and break off, so I paid fifty francs to a tandarts to have them removed with some kind of a wrench, while Vincent numbed himself with absinthe.

I nursed the gember man through the Kerstmis of 1885 and into the year of 1886, while he was feverish and saw visions of his dead father at the bottom of the bed. He cursed the world – the art dealers and the critics and all the people who had spurned him, including his own family. He was not himself and at times he didn't even know who I was. He wrote to Theo about his fantasies of painting naked women, which he now considered to be the most important thing he could do for his art. But it was all an illusion – a troubled body contributing to a troubled mind. Theo wrote back that

Vincent should leave Antwerp for the sake of his health, but the gember man refused and told his brother not to interfere with his obsession.

'I no longer care what people say about me, Sien, or about my work.'

'You never did, Vincent.'

Theo again threatened to stop his money and Vincent called him a blockhead.

By the end of January, his health had improved somewhat and he said he no longer needed the services of Doctor Cavenaille.

'I want to enrol in art school, Sien.'

'Will that cost money?'

'Theo will pay.'

He wanted to study Rubens again and learn to brighten his palette. But his professor thought his drawings inadequate and put him back to a preparatory class. Vincent did not get on well with his teachers and there were constant arguments and altercations and he was thrown out of the school. As a result, his health began to deteriorate again, whether from physical causes or from frustration and anxiety it was difficult to know and, in February, he collapsed. Death seemed to hover about him and he became afraid of going mad and dying before his talent was recognised. He even painted himself as a skeleton smoking a cheap cigarillo.

There were times when I thought I might have been better off if I'd never met the gember man – if I'd stayed as a young ignorant girl, with an undisturbed mind and a blind acceptance of everything.

While I was stronger than Vincent at that time, looking after him was beginning to take its toll on me and I knew I could not go on doing it forever, especially when he raged against the world. So I wrote to Theo and told him that, if he didn't get Vincent out of Antwerp, his brother would certainly die. Theo was surprised to find that I was with Vincent. He was disappointed that I'd gone to Antwerp instead of to Paris with him, even though I hadn't come to Belgium with

Vincent and it was purely by chance that we'd come upon each other. Nevertheless, Theo was angry and said Vincent could not come to Paris. But I didn't care, Vincent had saved my life once, and now I had to save his. I put him on the night train and sent him to Theo. Again, as he did in The Hague, he left behind all his debts.

And me.

# CHAPTER 23

# PARIS

I was still in Antwerp when I received another letter from Theo, included with it was a train ticket to Paris. He wrote that Vincent had arrived at his small bachelor apartment on the Rue Laval, just off the Boulevard de Clichy. It was perfectly suitable for Theo alone, but unsuitable for both of them and also as a studio for Vincent. So, the gember man had found a bigger place on the Rue Lepic in Montmartre, where all the artists gathered. It was a wild area, but becoming bourgeois when the middle-classes began moving in. It was a large apartment on the 4th floor, high enough to avoid the smells of the street – Vincent had the smallest of three bedrooms, with Theo occupying the second and the third being used as the gember man's studio.

The brothers van Gogh moved in there together in June of 1886. However, things were not going well. Vincent had enrolled in the atelier of Fernand Piestre, an artist known as Cormon, but he was fighting and arguing with everyone there. They were all searching for a new, modern art formula, but Cormon was not open-minded about this and the initiation rituals at the atelier were designed to humiliate artists like Vincent, who were different. Cormon himself rarely attended the atelier and the place was run by a bully called Louis Anquetin and a deformed inbred aristocrat called Toulouse-Lautrec. Needless to say, Vincent did not get on with them and he was mocked, scorned and ignored. So he left after only three months.

The gember man also tried to get a model to pose privately for him at his studio, but none of the women he asked would do it. None would come to the Rue Lepic, as I had come to the Schenkweg. This also annoyed him greatly because he was reduced to painting the little nude statuettes that Theo collected. In short, things were not working out for Vincent in Paris – or for Theo, who was growing increasingly angry with his older brother. Through the summer of 1886 Vincent took over the whole of the Rue Lepic apartment, with paint and brushes and pictures everywhere. His disorder spread to every room – discarded clothes, wet canvases, and he even used Theo's socks to clean his brushes. He didn't wash and always looked dirty, which offended Theo's bourgeois friends.

The gember man insisted on coming with Theo to receptions and nights out at the theatre or the opera, but Theo didn't trust his brother's behaviour enough to introduce him any further into his circle and, in the end, Theo stopped being invited to social events because of Vincent. Neither did people want to visit Rue Lepic, because it always ended in arguments with the gember man. Theo's best friend in Paris was Andries Bonger and he resented Vincent being in the city.

'The man has no manners, Theo, he's always quarrelling with everyone.'

In fact, all Theo's friends found Vincent impossible to get along with and many considered him to be mad.

And so, Theo sent me a train ticket, asking me to come to Paris for two reasons – the pretence was that I would pose for Vincent, as I had always done, but the real reason was for me to try to control him, to accompany him and keep him happy, so that Theo could get his own life back. In his letters, Theo always referred to me as simply S – not Sien. It was at my request, as I didn't want Vincent to know his brother was communicating with me. After all, he was the main cause of our break-up in The Hague and, for Vincent to find out he was writing to me, would be a betrayal, especially in the wake of Theo's proposition to me in Delft, that he now seemed to have forgotten about. I think Theo let people believe that S was a French woman, a mistress who had succeeded Maria and who he was sharing with Vincent. And it suited me for those hypocrites to think that.

Theo always felt guilty for his part in tearing the gember man and me apart, even though I didn't blame him – although Vincent did. It wasn't entirely his fault. He was essentially a kind man who I believed bore no animosity to me. He was just the messenger of the rest – the pious father, the vindictive mother, the haughty uncles, the holier-than-thou friends, all full of prudishness and puffed-up priggery.

If there is one unforgivable sin in the world, it is the sin of sanctimony.

When I arrived at the Rue Lepic, a concierge greeted me at the heavy oak front door and led me into a cool passageway with a view of the garden to the back. Vincent was out and Theo came down and escorted me up to the 4th floor apartment, where he kept all Vincent's pictures which he could not sell. They covered the walls and were stored on top of furniture and under the beds and the whole apartment looked like an untidy art gallery and an unruly paint shop, with pots of colours left lying around that people could easily step into if they weren't careful.

'I'm glad you came, Sien.'

'I wouldn't have, had Vincent not been here. Where is he?'

'Out painting.'

'Does he know I'm arriving today?'

'No … I didn't tell him.'

'Why not?'

'I want it to be a surprise.'

Of course, that wasn't the reason Theo hadn't told Vincent of my arrival – the truth was, he didn't know how Vincent would react.

All Theo wanted to talk about, after he gave me some coffee and a croissant, was how Vincent had turned the Rue Lepic apartment into a hell of argument and recrimination. They fought about everything, from money to family to art.

'His behaviour is unbearable, Sien. He's destroying my life.'

'It's my fault, for sending him here.'

'Yes it is, so now you must correct it.'

'He would have died had he stayed in Antwerp, Theo.'

Theo poured some cognac into his coffee and offered me some, which I accepted.

'He shows me nothing but contempt, Sien, in private and public. He blames me for all kinds of things, of which I'm innocent.'

'I'm sorry about that.'

'Are you … are you, Sien?'

I didn't know if I was or not. I mean, I should have been gloating that Theo had been proven wrong for breaking us up, but I wasn't. I felt sorry for this nervous man who was trying to deal with the complicated extremes of his erratic brother and didn't know how.

'He's selfish and heartless and I don't know how to reason with him, Sien.'

'So you want me to do it for you.'

'Precisely.'

There was another reason, which I did not know about on the day I arrived. Theo's best friend, Andries Bonger, had a twenty-four-year-old sister called Johanna, who lived in Amsterdam. Theo was in love with Johanna, who he called Jo, and was intending to propose to her. He wanted to bring her to Paris and marry her, but that was impossible with Vincent in the apartment. He believed he was on the threshold of a new life which was threatened by the gember man's presence in Paris. It was also a source of anguish for Vincent, because Johanna didn't like him. She said he was impetuous and violent and, if Theo married her, Vincent believed his source of income would come to an end. The younger brother could hardly support Jo and Vincent, who even threatened suicide if his brother married her. Theo was desperate for help.

'He even tells me that he despises me and that I'm repugnant to him.'

'Don't expect too much from me, Theo.'

'Just do what you can … please.'

Apart from me, Theo was Vincent's greatest advocate and it was unfair of the gember man to treat his brother as he did. Theo knew about art, as a dealer, and he tried to get Vincent to conform, to paint what the public wanted. He explained about accepted ideas of line and colour, spontaneous form and the different aspects of shape. He said Vincent could be a good artist some day – if he lived long enough and took advice from people. We both agreed he had talent and that his gift originally sprang from the first impressions nature had made on him, back in Zundert, when he went to the stream with his bottle and net, when he lay in the fields and watched the high birds singing to him. Since then, he had experienced life at the other end of the spectrum and it had also left its mark on his art.

But the gember man was spontaneous and completely discarded artistic convention. Even though he changed his style of painting in Paris to brighter colours and very short brush strokes, he still considered the art market as commercialising something that was essentially beyond the value of money.

Vincent came in late that evening and it was obvious that he had been drinking. He began to argue with Theo straight away because he had been banned by the gendarmes from painting on the streets.

'They said I was being disruptive.'

'And were you, Vincent?'

'Of course not, I merely lined up my wet canvases against a wall and asked passers-by what they thought of them.'

'And you argued with them?'

'Only if they said they didn't like them.'

It was at that point I emerged from Theo's room. Vincent looked at me, looked away, then looked back again, as if he didn't believe his eyes.

'Sien … is it you?'

'Yes, it's me, Vincent.'

'What are you doing in Theo's bedroom?'

'Waiting for you, of course.'

Vincent hesitated, as if he was sizing up the situation. I could see a look of doubt and puzzlement on his face. Maybe I should have waited for him somewhere else, and not in his brother's room. I could see Vincent's mind working, asking questions – was I being carnal with Theo? Was I his new mistress? Then his eyes lightened and he dropped everything and rushed to me. We hugged and he swung me around in his arms.

'I'm sorry for being ill in Antwerp, Sien.'

'Don't be, it wasn't your fault.'

'I barely remember leaving … it's all a blur.'

'The medicine affected your mind. I hope you're better now.'

'I certainly am!'

But he was not – both he and Theo were receiving treatment for the supposed hereditary syphilis. They attended two doctors, Louis Rivet and David Gruby, who prescribed iodine of potassium to purify the blood, and they were told to get as much air as possible and to go to bed early and to eat plenty of fresh vegetables and no alcohol, which neither of them did. Theo's illness didn't seem to register with Vincent. They were both suffering from bouts of nervous depression but, during my time in Paris, Theo seemed to be much worse than Vincent.

The gember man lifted me from the floor and I wrapped my legs around him, while he carried me to his room. He fell across the bed, bringing me with him, but I was apprehensive because of the syphilis. Vincent was blasé about it.

'Once you've had it, you can't get it again.'

'I've never had it, Vincent, and I don't want it.'

'But I'm cured, Sien.'

It was a lie, so much believed by him that it had become the truth. The truth was irrelevant. The lie had superseded the truth. But he was who he was and his face was child-pure, even if the rest of him wasn't. I could not refuse him, we were who we were – an unholy union, both existing in the consequences of lives that were half fact and half illusion.

When we lay together that night, Vincent spoke to me about leaving.

'Let's get out of Paris, Sien. Let's escape to the south of France.'

Which is what Theo wanted. So I agreed.

'Of course. I'll go wherever you want.'

'But first, Sien, we have to go back to Holland and retrieve our little boy, and Maria Wilhelmina too, of course.'

'That would be wonderful.'

It would have been wonderful indeed, had it happened.

We drank some cognac and he manoeuvred himself into position over me and our bodies writhed on the bed for about ten minutes before he gave up. When the fruitless effort was over, we lay together and just held hands. It was enough. After a while, he lit his pipe and I lit a cigar and we were silent while the smoke swirled around us. My mind drifted, there on the bed with the gember man. It seemed to me, although it hadn't been said, that to him, I was not like other women. They always wanted him to play a part, something he could never do. I don't think he even knew what that part was and I suspect neither did they – some elusive, abstract role that probably didn't even exist in reality.

I never wanted the impossible from him, yet I knew there was something else – not a dimension that wasn't there, not even the charisma and passion I loved him for in The Hague – there was something else, some essence not easily defined. He never exposed himself enough for me to define it properly. Oh, I knew he expressed a great overwhelming love for Cornelia Vos-Stricker and others, but that wasn't really exposing himself, that was just mimicking the romance in the novels he read. Or maybe it was just an illusion and there was nothing more for him to give – nothing of him to give. I think what I felt inside was a kind of persuasiveness. A cynosure. A wanting to be with him because there was nowhere else worth being. And that was me – not him.

'Shall we get married, Sien, before we go to the south of France?'

'Do you still want to?'

'Of course.'

'Will your family allow it?'

'My father is dead.'

'Will Theo allow it?'

He did not answer.

I felt suddenly strange, light-headed. I thought it might be the cigar, or the journey from Antwerp. More than light-headed – a peculiar feeling. It was as if something was touching my body, something cold that gave me gooseflesh. I looked across at Vincent – he was engrossed in his own thoughts. The feeling made me uneasy. I got off the bed and left the room.

Shortly after I arrived, Theo resolved to travel to Nuenen to visit his family and, from there, to go to Amsterdam to propose to Johanna Bonger. He moved Andries Bonger into the apartment to keep an eye on Vincent while he was away. The man took an immediate dislike to me, writing to Theo that I was highly strung, mentally unstable and physically unattractive. He also called me S in his correspondence, although I don't know why. Maybe because Theo did. Vincent just ignored Dries, as he called him, and we did whatever we liked. The gember man humoured him by giving him a self-portrait in a grey hat – it was actually Theo's hat, but Vincent wore it for the picture. He used to wear all his brother's clothes and discard them wherever he took them off. In the end, Theo had hardly any shirts left, Vincent wore them all and just left them lying about covered in paint.

He took me to a café called Le Tambourin on the Boulevard de Clichy, where he introduced me to a woman called Agostina Segatori. She was middle-aged and sultry looking and she hung Vincent's painting on the walls, which he gave her in return for food and drink. She asked me if I wanted work.

'What kind of work?'

'You know … pierreuse, lorette, gigolette … '

This made Vincent angry.

'She's my model. She's not a hoer!'

A man at the next table shouted over.

'She looks like one.'

Vincent jumped up and there was a fight. A bottle got smashed and the gember man's face was cut. He punched the man and I kicked him. Then Segatori smashed one of Vincent's own paintings over his head. The café was in turmoil and I decided it was better to get Vincent out before he came to any worse harm than a cut face and dented pride.

In Amsterdam, Theo didn't have the courage to ask Jo Bonger to marry him and move to Paris so, instead of escaping to the south of France, or going back to Holland to collect Willem and Maria Wilhelmina, Vincent stayed in Paris for another year and a half – and I stayed with him. He painted me there and gave the picture to Theo, who hung it in the living room of the apartment. It can be seen in Vincent's portrait of a Scotsman called Alexander Reid, which he painted when Reid visited the Rue Lepic.

That Kerstmis, Theo's malady became worse – his joints stiffened until he could hardly move, his face swelled up until his features were barely distinguishable, he lost weight from his already thin body and he was weak all the time. I did my best to keep Vincent away from him, insisting we go for long walks where he could paint on the banks of the Seine without being harassed by the gendarmes. Contrary to what some people thought, Vincent did have a sense of humour and he'd try to mimic the people we met along the way, who thought he was a madman.

The gember man's absences from the apartment were good for Theo and, with the assistance of his doctors, he began to recover. Vincent himself was suffering from paralysing nightmares and he painted two more skeleton skulls, as if in anticipation of dying.

It was my job to keep Vincent away from Theo and allow the younger brother to get his life back. As the year

1887 wore on, we frequented the cafés and bistros of Paris, even going back to Le Tambourin, where Vincent painted Segatori looking rather bored at one of her tables. After that initial mêlée, I got on well with the woman. She'd had a life similar to my own before coming to run Le Tambourin and we exchanged tales of our exploits as straatmadeliefies and laughed together at the pathetic antics of some of the men who had paid for our services. But then the Italian Cosa Nostra began to frequent Le Tambourin and I was afraid they might have connections to the Penoze, so we stopped going there.

Instead, we went to the bohemian tavernes which the artists frequented. We drank with Toulouse-Lautrec, who painted Vincent sitting in a booth, and with others who Vincent knew – Camille Pissarro and Armand Guillaumin and Émile Bernard. But Vincent would argue with them and tear off his clothes and fall to his knees to make a point about art and, when we came home late at night, he would keep Theo awake by also arguing with him about what had gone on in the tavernes. The gember man rarely saw anyone else's point of view and, when he was arguing, he'd pour out his words in a wild mixture of Dutch, French and English, hissing through his teeth.

We were drinking too much, from the cheap cafés of Montmartre to the risqué Moulin de la Galette – absinthe in the afternoon, wine with dinner, beer at the erotic cabarets such as Le Chahut, and cognac at any time. Vincent began to paint withering sunflowers and attempted to bring them back to life with thick layers that he called an impasto technique, as if he was trying to revive the unique creative atmosphere of The Hague, which had withered like the flowers.

None of this was advancing Vincent's reputation as an artist, which I hoped would happen when I put him on the train for Paris. He continued to argue with Theo because everyone was getting their work displayed on the middle floor at Goupil in an initiative for new artists – except Vincent. He had to settle for an exhibition in the Restaurant du Chalet but nobody came – apart from a man called Paul Gauguin who had recently returned from a long voyage to the Caribbean. Vincent was painting interesting pictures that nobody wanted. It was painful for both of us to see lesser artists become successful, while he languished in oblivion.

In the summer of 1887, Theo journeyed to Amsterdam again. This time he did ask Johanna Bonger to marry him, but she turned him down. He felt spurned and humiliated and, when he returned to Paris, he decided to compensate for the rejection by throwing himself into the bohemian lifestyle which Vincent and I were living. Of course, Theo's frailty meant he was unable to sustain this demi-monde mode de vie and his health soon began to deteriorate again – frozen joints, swelling, exhaustion. Vincent called it a maladie de cœur, just as the gember man had suffered after me, and perhaps it was – but it was also caused by Theo trying to follow the example of his brother's disordered behaviour.

In December, Émile Bernard, Louis Anquetin, Toulouse-Lautrec and Vincent organised an exhibition at the Grand-Bouillon Restaurant du Chalet. Bernard and Anquetin sold paintings – Vincent did not.

It all came to an end at the beginning of 1888. Vincent was out painting and, this time, I did not go with him because it was too cold and I was tired. As I lay on the bed, I heard someone come to the apartment – a man, who spoke loudly to Theo. When he left, I went out of the room to see who it was.

'Someone from Le Tambourin.'

'Was he looking for Vincent?'

'And you, Sien.'

A cold chill ran through me. Theo could see I was frightened.

'When we met in Delft, Sien, you mentioned the Penoze …'

'Was it them?'

'I don't know. But you shouldn't worry, we can go to the gendarmes.'

Theo meant well, but he was not in good health and I didn't want to bring trouble to his door after his generous hospitality. We went to his room and he poured some cognac. We talked – me saying I should leave immediately, as soon as Vincent returned, and he asking me not to. He still hoped for the hand of Jo Bonger and I knew how his heart was broken by her rejection. I sympathised, stroked his hair, as I would a sad brother. He mistook my gesture and kissed me. When we looked around, Vincent was standing at the door. He threw his canvas and equipment to the floor and stormed back out.

I tried to find him, even going to Le Tambourin, where I was accosted by a rough-looking Mediterranean man.

'You! We have been looking for you.'

I bit his hand and broke away from him and ran from the place – and I kept on running. I didn't go back to the Rue Lepic to collect my few belongings, just walked and walked until I was on the outskirts of Paris. I kept looking back to see if anyone was following, until an elderly couple in a carriage stopped and allowed me to ride with them as far as a village called Bacouël. I thought I was going south, as Vincent said we would, and I needed to keep out of sight – if the Penoze could find me in Paris, they could find me anywhere.

I didn't realise it but, in fact, I was going north.

# CHAPTER 24
# ZIGEUNERS

I travelled on, keeping away from large towns and staying in the countryside. On the way, I told fortunes in the hamlets I passed through – I wasn't really a waarzegster, but I'd seen my mother do it when I was young and I knew enough to convince the country folk, who were very superstitious. The farmers' wives loved to hear that good fortune would come their way and they paid money for my lies and gave me food and cognac.

After skirting a village called Toufflers, I finally realised where I was – not the south of France, but on the Belgian border. My heart sank and I did not know what to do. Just then, I came across a zigeuner encampment in a field. I was very tired from walking, so I thought I would take some rest there.

It was bright in the field. A spring sun was shining and birds were chirping and early flowers bloomed along the hedgerows and the grass was high and sweet-smelling. The encampment comprised of small makeshift huts and some tents and carts and a lot of people milling around. Horses grazed and fire-smoke rose into a scudding sky. The women had reddish-black hair, long over their shoulders, and wore beads round their necks and foreheads. The men wore hats with feathers in them and leather leggings and some had silver earrings in their ears. Dirty-faced children played between the horses' hooves and dogs barked at me as I approached. It looked like a scene from some past time, not the year of 1888.

I had always been afraid of the swarthy zigeuners and I wasn't sure why I'd now stopped here – apart from the tiredness that had crept over me. Just then, a young girl approached me and silently took my hand and we made our way through the low spread of huts and tents and carts with bright yellow-spoked wheels and woven baskets of wildflowers hanging from the shafts. The people stopped what they were doing to stare at me as I followed the girl. Faces peered and the air was full of strange words and I remembered some of the stories my mother used to tell when I was little – about far-off times that were gone and would never come back, except to a few, who'd see them on bright spring days in remote fields, for an instant – a moment – a brief second. Before they disappeared again.

The girl brought me to where a group of women were gathered round a little pot, over a small fire. I stretched out my hand in greeting for them to shake, but they stepped back as if I was threatening them. Then one of them offered me some liquid that was brewing in the pot. It tasted like tea, but it wasn't – it was something else, something I'd never drank before, and I'd drank a lot of different brews over the years. It was hot and, even though it tasted strange, it sent a sense of warmth throughout my whole body, which took the great tiredness away. This gesture seemed to spark up the others and they came close and touched my clothes and hair and conversed together in their secret sing-song language.

Suddenly, a tall man with hair like jet and deep-blue eyes came from behind one of the tents, leading a coloured horse. He came close to the group of women and spoke to them and they bowed their heads to him, as if he was their king. He then swung himself up onto the coloured stallion and rode it off at speed, coming back at the gallop and stopping just inches short of me. I'd always been a bit afraid of horses because they're such big animals, but on this occasion I was not afraid and I didn't jump out of the way. Somehow I knew he would not allow the horse to trample me, he was just showing everybody what he could do, even if they knew already. People in the field were chanting 'Zoni! Zoni! Zoni!' and I knew it was his name – the horseman's.

The group of women began to drift away and I joined a crowd following Zoni up along a sloping hill, away from the encampment, to a stretch of level ground about a kilometre long. I was feeling a little light-headed by then and somewhat mercurial, as if I was becoming part of something again, something I once was and had forgotten how to be. I thought it might be the effect of the liquid I'd drunk from the pot over the fire – maybe it had some mushroom or herb or alcohol in it. And I thought it might be better to be in the bright field with these strangers than out on the lonely road again.

Zoni rode away to a starting point where a group of horsemen were lined up for a race. By now the field was teeming with people and I did not know where they all came from – men and women and children. I could hear the high-pitched sound of their voices as I approached, bargaining and bantering and wagering on their favourite horse and rider. They made bets with trinkets of gold and silver, and beads and bracelets of teeth and claws. Children and dogs ran in and out of the crowd with honey-balls and corn-cakes in their hands. And I knew who they were, even though there was no way I could have known.

Zoni lined up with the others – about ten altogether, the excited steeds rearing and bucking and the crowd calling out. I had a guilder in my pocket and I tried to place a wager on Zoni, but the bet-takers looked at it and laughed, as if they had no use for that kind of currency.

Then the race was off.

The horsemen seemed to be keeping up with each other for a while, maybe half a kilometre, and Zoni was there with them. It was difficult to see, with the crowd so excited and the noise in my ears. Those riders who hadn't slipped off their saddle-less steeds turned at a given point and began to race back towards the starting point, where I was standing. I could see them approaching, hooves flying and nostrils flaring and the horsemen trying to force each other off the level track.

Zoni was at the front and I could hear my own voice shouting with the crowd.

'Zoni! Zoni! Zoni!'

About two hundred metres out, I saw him lean over the horse's neck and whisper something in the animal's ear. And the two seemed to me to be one – horse and rider. Zoni became the horse and the horse became Zoni, blended together like one creature. The people around me cleared back out of the way, to allow the racers to fly across the finish line and they passed me in such a flash I couldn't see who had won. Then Zoni was taken from his steed and carried shoulder-high by the crowd. The bet-takers paid out medallions and amulets and some of the wagerers were happy and some were not.

Suddenly, there was a distressed call from the edge of the crowd. It was the young girl who'd taken my hand when I entered the field and guided me into the encampment. Everybody turned to look. I could see dozens of maréchaussée entering the area, brandishing weapons. The zigeuners began to panic and run in all directions. Horses reared and dogs barked and there was chaos all around me. I was confused and alarmed and I didn't know what to do – all alone in a swirling maelstrom of turbulence and commotion and fear. One woman drove her wagon past me, moving very fast, and I was just able to jump into the back of it. I hid under some blankets, hoping nobody would see me and I stayed there as the wagon rocked and rolled over the uneven ground.

When it finally came to a halt, I could hear someone speaking. I emerged from under the blankets to see a woman of about my age giving the horse a drink of water from a bucket and talking to it. She was startled at my sudden appearance and stepped back defensively. I identified her as one of the women round the small fire, the one who gave me a drink from the pot.

'Who are you?'

'Do you not remember? You gave me a drink … '

'The Gorgio woman.'

'Yes. My name is Christien.'

Hers was Settela. She said her family were Cerhara tent dwellers, or maybe Chlara carpet traders, she wasn't sure. They'd travelled south from Romania and camped by the shores of the Van Gölü, near the border between Turkey and Persia. At least, that's what she was told.

I camped that night with her and her horse and her bow-top wagon that she called a vardo, in the small forest of Spaubekerbos, close to the river Keutelbeek, from which Settela drew water. She gave me coffee and potatoes cooked over an open campfire, and continued her story about how her people crossed the Mediterranean Sea and lived with the Gitana Espagñola for a while, before moving up to Holland. She played a musical instrument called a zurna and we sang songs that neither of us knew and laughed together and it was as if we had been together forever. Which, of course, we had.

'Do you have a man, Settela?'

'I did.'

'What happened to him?'

'He was killed in a knife fight in Amsterdam.'

'I'm sorry to hear that.'

'Do you have a man, Christien?'

So I told her about Vincent. How we lived together and were lovers and how I had a son for him and how he wanted to marry me, but people would not allow it. I told her how he smoked his pipe, how he ate his food, how he spoke about many things and how I listened and learned. How I sometimes felt so sad when I was with him and other times felt so glad. How we lay on our summer bed, with only the gaslight from the street shining on our skins and the window open to let in the sounds and smells of our little world, which I remembered was still spinning – even though Vincent was gone. I told her I would always love the man who moved me and whose painter hands made such patterns on my mind and whose gember body knew my own so well. I told her how I was an onwetend young woman then and didn't fully understand him. But the more I thought about his words, the more they made sense to me – especially after he was gone.

For the rest of the year of 1888, Settela and I travelled up through Belgium and into south-east Holland. We told fortunes and I mended clothes and she played the zurna. We kept to the back roads and the farms, doing seasonal work when we could and begging when we couldn't. We moved from place to place and that suited me well. As time went by, the wandering and chaotic poetry and dark longing within me were making me unsettled. I wanted to go to The Hague to see my children, but Settela wanted to get camped down somewhere for the winter, which was fast approaching. We had a little money from working through the autumn and there was fuel and water and plenty of good grazing for the horse in the deep mysterious woods of Liesboscht, where we came to settle. It was close to the village of Heike, which was home to many zigeuners and had strange swampland called the Passievaart to the west. It was ideal for Settela, but not for me. I didn't want to leave her alone, but she said she would be fine. She'd survived several winters on her own and this would be no different.

The village of Nuenen, where Vincent's family moved before his father died, wasn't far away and I wondered if the gember man might be there. Perhaps he hadn't gone south after all, but went back home. My heart was longing to see him again, just to look at him and try to explain what had happened in Paris. But Settela didn't want to get too close to towns or cities – her man had been murdered in Amsterdam and places with too many people frightened her. Unfortunately, I stayed too long and snow was falling when I left the campsite and set out on my own to walk towards Nuenen.

After a few kilometres, the snow was thick on the ground and the sky was as white as the land. I didn't see the steep side of an embankment in front of me and I tumbled down. Down and down. Over and over. Until I hit my head on a boulder at the bottom and was rendered unconscious. When I opened my eyes again, I could see nothing, just whiteness all around. I could move one of my arms, so I wiped the thick covering of snow from my face. It was day, with a blizzard falling hard and I could not see further than a couple of feet. I didn't know how long I'd lain there – maybe an hour, maybe a day. I felt a pain in my head and put a hand up to find congealed blood on my right temple. My clothes had been torn in the fall and the bag with my belongings was nowhere to be seen.

I tried to stand, which I was only able to do after several unsteady attempts, but I was relieved to find that, as far as I could tell, no bones were broken. I was disorientated, not knowing how far I was from a pathway or which direction Nuenen was in. The incline I'd fallen down was too steep for me to climb back up and I knew I might freeze to death if I didn't get to the town before nightfall. I stumbled along in the direction I thought was right. My feet and hands were cold and my head was hurting and I swallowed some snow to slake my dried-up mouth. I could only move very slowly, as the going was rough and the snow was deep and visibility was very poor. I was also treading carefully, as I did not want to fall down again.

Darkness began to envelop me. I decided it was no use to keep stumbling about in the night and was trying to find some shelter when I saw, through a break in the blizzard, what seemed to be a column of smoke rising up into the grey-black sky. I struggled on and came upon a hunter, cooking a rabbit over a fire. He was startled when I stumbled into his camp.

'Who are you?'

'I'm lost.'

'And half frozen by the look of you. Come to the fire.'

He wrapped me in a heavy coat and gave me hot coffee to drink. Gradually, I began to warm up.

'Are you hungry?'

'Very hungry.'

He pulled a leg from the roasted rabbit and I ate it furiously, almost making myself sick.

'Are we close to Nuenen?'

'Yes, not far … about a kilometre or so. Are you going there?'

'Yes.'

'I'll take you, when it gets light.'

I was thirty-eight now and it was unlikely that I'd be able to survive this kind of life for much longer. I had achieved nothing since I left Noordstraat five years earlier – the musical note of the old heks had been wrong. I didn't find my destiny. Every time I thought things were getting better, they just got worse again. So what was the point in even trying? I had again sunk down to the level at which I belonged. Over the time I'd been away from The Hague, my motivation was to merely survive and to avoid being killed by the Penoze or imprisoned by the maréchaussée. Those were negative and short-term objectives and I had lost my motivation to find happiness and my dream of making my children proud had evaporated in the oppressive climate of hopelessness that constantly surrounded me.

That's not to say I never laughed – I did. With Settela. The way only free people can – excited about small things that would seem insignificant to others. Talking about tonight, or last night. Living as only free people can live – lightly. Carrying nothing. There were times when life seemed so ridiculous, when I traversed the countryside with the zigeuner and watched the tide of humanity ebbing and flowing. All going somewhere – all with somewhere to go – somewhere that seemed so important to them, pushing and crushing to get there. While we watched from our futureless vantage point and laughed at them in a nervous, wishful-thinking way. And I felt a small sadness inside – an uneasy restlessness, like the world was closing in on me and it would never open up again.

I still didn't know if Maria Wilhelmina was with my mother and I resolved to put my fear of the Penoze to one side and get a job in Rotterdam on my way to The Hague and send some money. But I needed to rest and recover first. The hunter took me into Nuenen early next morning. I had nothing but the clothes I was wearing. I had lost my few belongings in the fall and my money was also in my bag. I wanted to go back and search for it, but the hunter told me it would be useless, I'd never find it in the snow and only get lost again. Maybe he wanted to go find it himself, after he took me into the town? If he did, he never brought it to me.

'Do you know anyone here in Nuenen?'

'The van Goghs.'

'They're not here, they moved to Breda.'

Breda was a small parish about seven kilometres from the Belgian border, in the province of North Brabant.

'Can you take me there?'

'I cannot. It's sixty-five kilometres away.'

I don't know why, maybe it was folly, maybe it was fate, but after a short rest, I set out again, travelling west, stopping to sleep in barns along the way and taking water from the troughs of animals and what little I could forage in food from the winter fields. I wrapped myself in sacking and, when I finally arrived in Breda, two weeks later, I was close to exhaustion. I was struggling along Graaf Engelbertlaan when I was struck by a passing carriage. The driver shouted at me.

'Get out of the way, you dirty zwerver!'

I fell to the cold ground and was unable to get back up. I could see the feet of people passing and hear their grumbles.

'Filthy zigeuner.'

'Should be thrown in the river.'

'Shall I kick her, moeder?'

'Better not, you might catch cholera.'

I don't know how long I lay there, being stepped on and spat on and dogs urinating on me and children poking me with sticks. Then a face bent down and appeared close to mine. I could not put a name to the face, even though I knew it from somewhere. It came closer, with a hand up to its mouth – I didn't know if this was in surprise, or in an effort to avoid contagion.

'Sien? Is that you, Sien?'

I didn't answer. It could be a spy for the shylock – but he only knew me as Salome, not Sien. Maybe the Penoze – the Mediterranean man?

'It's me … Theo.'

Theo? That name was familiar. He caught my arm and lifted me to my feet. I held on to him tightly .

'Why are you here, Sien?'

I had to think.

'Looking for Vincent.'

'He's not here.'

He took me to a nearby café. The owner didn't want to let me in and we had to sit at a table in the courtyard. Theo bought me stamppot and coffee, and a glass of cognac after I finished eating – and I knew I wouldn't die that day.

'I tried to find you after you left Paris, Sien … in The Hague.'

'Why?'

'To make sure you were alright.'

'Why?'

'You know why.'

But I did not.

He told me Johanna Bonger had finally accepted his proposal of marriage and he was in Breda to inform his family and make preparations for the wedding. But his words went over my head and floated off across the town square.

Until he bought me another glass of cognac.

# CHAPTER 25

# ARLES

Theo told me that Vincent had left Paris on the same day I did. He travelled south to a town called Arles, in Provence, where he rented a room above a restaurant. It was snowing when he arrived and the wind blew through a broken window. Through the early months of the year of 1888, he froze in his little room, sick and suffering, waiting for spring to warm his heart again. When colour finally came back to the Arles landscape, it came in a wave of blooming orchards and daisies and buttercups and roses and irises. It was like nothing Vincent had ever seen, even in Zundert and, every day, he carried his equipment down a tree-lined road to the countryside to paint.

He was still suffering from stomach disorders and fevers and tiredness, his teeth ached and he found it hard to digest food. He was also impotent and unable to get an erection. He blamed these afflictions on the bad wine he drank in Paris, even though they were more likely caused by the so-called syphilis diagnosed by the doctors. He stopped smoking and drinking for a while, but that only made him think more, which he didn't want to do.

'Did he mention me, Theo?'

'Not at first, Sien.'

'What about Paris?'

'Nothing. He did say the light was yellow in Arles.'

That made me smile and I remembered the yellow blanket he bought for baby Willem back in The Hague and how he said yellow was the colour of our life together.

But the loneliness that had dogged Vincent all his life returned in Arles. He held the local people in contempt for their boorishness and they resented his strangeness. They sensed his disdain and returned it, calling him ugly and mad. According to Theo, whole days passed without him speaking to a single person.

'He said he kept thinking of Holland and The Hague.'

'And his son, Theo, did he mention Willem?'

'Only that he was suffering inwardly with a disordered heart.'

Apparently, Vincent believed everyone was against him in Arles and it was far from the idyll he imagined when he asked me to go south with him when we were in Paris. He complained about it to Theo in his letters, but there was little the brother could do.

'I'd fallen ill again, Sien, and couldn't cope with his discontent.'

On one of his painting excursions, Vincent saw an uninhabited house which was painted yellow, like the light all around him. It was dilapidated, but he was having problems with his landlord at the restaurant and was seeking a place of his own. This house seemed to be just what he wanted. It was in a dangerous part of the town, with drunks and vagabonds frequenting the all-night cafés and tavernes and the brothel district was on the other side of a nearby park and the train station only twenty metres away. But, to Vincent, it was his castle in the air.

The summer landscape of Provence turned hot and harsh, with the mistral wind scouring it with dust. Flies and mosquitoes bothered Vincent when he went out to paint and the colour drained away from the countryside. So he trawled the brothels and back-alleys of Arles in search of a model to pose for him in his studio, just as he did in Antwerp. But he couldn't find anyone willing to do it.

The gember man also had dreams of establishing a community of painters at the yellow house who could pool their resources and live and work together under the same roof. All his life he was looking for a place where companionship formed a barrier against the indifference of the world. He wanted other artists to join him in the yellow house but none would come – except for Paul Gauguin.

Vincent's Uncle Cent died that summer and left nothing to Vincent or Willem. He made it clear in his will that neither Vincent nor our son would have any share of his estate, even though he left large sums of money to servants and distant relatives. Theo also benefited and he used some of that inheritance to pay off Gaugin's debts and expenses so the artist could go to Arles and be Vincent's friend and relieve his brother's loneliness. Paul Gauguin, a Frenchman with Creole blood, was a brash, outspoken opportunist and he thought Vincent had money. Vincent was the opposite – intense, introverted and had difficulty expressing himself verbally.

The gember man painted the sunflowers again while he waited for Gauguin to arrive in Arles. It was a yellow picture – yellow flowers, yellow background, yellow vase and yellow table. He also painted the dark sky, with candles fixed to his hat for light, because he always said that the night was more alive and richly coloured than the day. He called that painting "starry night". Also the interior of the Café de la Gare, a place, according to Vincent, where you might go mad or commit a crime. When he painted in the street, as he did with the café in the Place du Forum, he was treated with hostility and ridicule by the locals, just as he was everywhere else he went. On one occasion, he was even attacked by a gang of louts, with his tubes of paint being squeezed out and his canvas kicked away. He believed all that would change once Gauguin got there.

Paul Gauguin didn't arrive at the yellow house until late October. Although Vincent was impotent, Gauguin was not – he was virile and robust and more interested in the tavernes and brothels than the Arles countryside. Back in Paris, Theo even sold five of his paintings, something he was never able to do for his brother. It hurt Vincent deeply. So, right from the start, things did not go well between the two artists, certainly not as Vincent expected. Gauguin had no trouble attracting models to pose for him. Gauguin said Arles was a filthy place and everything was better in the north. Vincent liked to paint outside, Gauguin preferred the studio. Vincent was spontaneous, Gauguin worked slowly and methodically – Vincent could paint a dozen pictures while Gauguin painted one. Gauguin ridiculed Vincent's art and his way of painting and every day brought a new conflict between them.

As Gauguin's success in Paris continued, so too did Vincent's sense of demoralisation. In December, Gauguin said he'd had enough of Arles and he was leaving. Vincent was distraught – even though they weren't getting on, he didn't want Gauguin to leave and to be left with his loneliness again. He began to see apparitions and he wrote on the wall of the studio in yellow chalk, "I am the holy spirit". He was tortured by Gauguin's success and his own continuing failure.

Celebrations for Kerstmis were under way in Arles, with everyone rehearsing the miraculous birth with clay santons and pastorals being staged at the Folies Arlésiennes. Vincent became obsessed with the image in his head of baby Willem in his cradle – an image he had drawn many times. Theo told me it caused his eyes to grow moist and his heart to melt. The gember man had described me and newborn Willem in The Hague as that eternal poetry of Kerstmis with the infant in the stable, a light in the darkness, a brightness in the middle of a black night. He painted my face on a portrait of the local postman's wife, holding not her own infant, but baby Willem.

In this reverie, Vincent saw some value in his life – only to have it sullied on December 23rd, the Sunday before Kerstmis. Gauguin was leaving and they argued again, with Gauguin screaming at him –

'Everything is yellow. Yellow! I hate yellow.'

Then he stormed out of the yellow house. To Vincent, yellow symbolised Willem, his son, and Gauguin had insulted him. By insulting the gember man's memory of Willem, he had also insulted me and our family life in The Hague and this angered Vincent greatly. He ran into the Place Lamartine after Gauguin, who was crossing the square when he heard someone behind him. He turned to see the gember man, who called him a murderer, then ran back to the yellow house. It had been raining for days, a cold winter rain, and Vincent was overcome by remorse and regret – for The Hague, for Antwerp, for Paris.

Theo's proposal of marriage had been accepted by Jo Bonger, Gauguin had a wife and children – he had nothing. Nobody. Delirious and disorientated, he stumbled to his bedroom, to the corner with the washstand. He looked in the mirror and saw a stranger looking back, someone he did not recognise. He picked up his razor and cut off his left ear. It must have taken some force to slice through the gristle and he must have been soaked in blood. He covered the wound with a bandage and wrapped the severed ear in a piece of newspaper and left the yellow house. He went to a brothel on the Rue du Bout d'Arles and asked for Sien. The brothel receptionist, a woman called Rachel, would not let him in because of the blood.

'There's no Sien here.'

Vincent handed the ear to her.

'Tell her to remember me.'

He returned to the yellow house, collapsed on his bed and waited for death. Gendarmes were called, who went to the house and found Vincent unconscious.

Theo told me that he'd arrived in Arles on Kerstmis Day. By then, Vincent had been moved to the hospital and Theo went there and lay beside him on the bed. They talked about their childhood in Zundert and Theo wished his brother had found someone to whom he could have poured out his heart – if so, it might not have come to this. Of course, he had found someone like that – but I wasn't there.

Both Theo and Gauguin left Vincent and returned to Paris that evening. The younger brother had other things on his mind, he had to come here to Breda to announce his forthcoming wedding to his family and make all the arrangements.

'Could you go to him, Sien?'

'I was on my way to The Hague, to see my children.'

'Please … he has no one else. I'll pay, of course.'

And I agreed, if I could rest for a while first to regain my strength. Theo told me to meet with a man called Joseph Roulin when I got to Arles. He would organise everything for me.

I arrived in Arles and was met at the station by the postman, who didn't introduce himself but I assumed he was Joseph Roulin. He took me to the yellow house and left me there, with directions to the hospital.

The cleaner who Vincent and Gaugin employed, a woman called Thérèse Barbezier, fled when the gember man cut his ear off and the house was in a chaotic state, with Vincent's bedroom covered in blood and the pictures which Gauguin didn't steal strewn all over the place. Food rotted in the kitchen and mice scurried across the floor. I put my bag in what must have been Gauguin's room and made my way to the hospital. It was next to a Catholic church and it looked like a prison, with high stone walls and small narrow windows. The name over the main door read "Hôtel Dieu" and the paraphernalia of religion filled the corridors.

I found a reception and the nurse there asked if I was related to the patient. When I said I was his lover, she frowned and sent for a doctor called Rey. Rey was a young man, a junior member of the hospital staff. He told me Vincent could not have visits, except from close family.

'I'm the mother of his son. Is that close enough?'

He thought about it for a moment, then beckoned for me to follow him. As we walked along the corridors, I asked him what was wrong with Vincent.

'He has the fièvre chaude.'

I didn't know what that was, but I stayed silent while the doctor elaborated.

'He's been behaving very strangely.'

'What do you mean?'

'Climbing into bed with other patients, chasing nurses in his nightshirt, washing himself in the coal bin … '

I smiled to myself, even though it wasn't funny – it sounded like Vincent alright.

'We have had to put him in a private room.'

By that he meant they had to lock him up in an isolation ward.

When Rey opened the door, Vincent was completely covered by the bedclothes and I could hear him sobbing. Rey gave me a concerned look.

'Will you be alright … by yourself, I mean?'

'Of course.'

When Vincent heard my voice, he uncovered himself and stopped sobbing.

'Mama … '

I went to him. Rey left the room and locked the door from the outside.

'No Vincent, it's me, Christien … Sien.'

'Sien?'

'Yes.'

'They want to put me in an asylum, Sien.'

'Who does?'

'The doctors … and the postman … and a priest called Salles. They're writing to Theo. Don't let them do it, Sien.'

Vincent couldn't remember cutting his ear off – all he could remember about the incident was darkness. It descended on him without warning and it was as if he had suddenly disappeared from the world. He was lost in a wave of anguish. Since then, in his confinement, he was haunted by shadows. He believed them to be real because they spoke to him, accusing him of doing terrible things.

'I called out your name, Sien, but you didn't come.'

'I'm here now.'

The doctors believed him to be mad and they issued a certificate of mental alienation and proposed committing him to an asylum in Marseilles. They had already written to Theo and were only waiting for his reply.

'I'm not mad, Sien.'

'Then stop acting as if you are.'

I explained that he had to show them he was sane – convince them.

'I'll write to Theo, Vincent, and ask him not to agree.'

'Will you stay with me?'

'I'll stay in Arles and visit you.'

Afterwards, I went back to the yellow house and wrote to Theo, begging him not to have Vincent committed. Theo had other things on his mind – Jo Bonger, so he hadn't even replied to the doctors. After that, I set about cleaning up the yellow house, which included removing the bloody bedsheets and scrubbing everything in Vincent's room, to make sure the house was a fit place for him to return to. I visited him every day and made sure he was making the right impression. He began by convincing Rey in their consultations. He and Vincent walked together round the hospital courtyard and the gember man promised to paint him when he got out. Rey agreed to come to the yellow house to see it for himself and to ensure there would be someone to take care of Vincent if they released him. I showed him the paintings and persuaded him that Vincent was a peaceful, loving artist and that his ear-cutting episode was an isolated incident.

Rey told me that Vincent had mental fits, preceded by difficulty breathing which required rest. These enforced periods of rest drove him mad, he just wanted to be out painting. He also suffered from melancholy, which nothing could dispel – an aching in his soul for what was lost, what he longed for, but what could never again be. While he was lying in the hospital ward after one of his attacks, an old man was brought in and laid close by. He had the strange appearance of a wild animal rather than a man and Vincent was told he was a herdsman – nobody knew how old, but certainly over eighty. He looked after his sheep since being a boy, along the southern plains. He lived out in the open, wearing only the skins of animals, sleeping in the heather, eating fruits and drinking the milk of his herd. He lived a life of even tenor, clear as a starlit night. He was found dying, having been overcome by the cold of a severe frost and carried to the hospital by village people. He survived and, when he recovered, he told Vincent the story of his life, which left such a deep impression that Vincent painted his face. I expect that picture is lost now, like many of the others.

Perhaps some day the world will come to appreciate the métier of the gember man who I loved and who loved me in return.

In the end, Rey signed the release papers and Vincent came back to the yellow house on 7th January in the year 1889. He was true to his word and painted Rey after he was released – and later he also painted the quadrangle in the hospital. When his ear healed, he began to work feverishly and his sense of the universal rhythm of nature seemed to have returned. He would get on his knees, shielding his eyes from the sun with his hands. Then he swayed from side to side, tilting his head. People passing would look at him and think he was having a seizure. He would walk this way and that, looking at his subject from many angles, or he'd sit staring at the picture for a long time, then jump up and attack the canvas, paint two or three strokes quickly, then move away again, narrow his eyes, wipe his forehead and rub his hands. He even painted another starry night, this time with a view over the Rhône. If you look closely, you can see a pair of lovers in the foreground – it is Vincent in his straw hat and me in my long coat.

But he was still suffering from nightmares and visions. He saw representations of little Willem everywhere – in a pastoral at the Folies Arlésiennes that moved him to tears – a tableau of the mystic crib and a peasant woman singing to her child. He imagined painting a lullaby of colours. However, no money came from Theo in January and the rent on the yellow house didn't get paid. The landlord issued an eviction order, but both Vincent and I were drinking too much to take any notice of this. As the days passed, our behaviour became erratic and the townspeople began to throw stones at us when they came upon us in the street. Vincent believed they were going to poison him.

Then, in February, the gendarmes came and dragged the gember man away to the hospital, where they shackled him to a bed in the isolation cell. I tried to stop them, but they just pushed me aside, so I ran to Salles the priest for help. Salles had always frowned on my presence in Arles and referred to me as the cleaning woman, even though the cleaning woman was gone and would not return. Despite his dislike of me, I believe he spoke cordially about me in his letters to Theo – probably because he was receiving money from Theo and didn't want to jeopardise that contribution to his church. He said Vincent should be in an asylum because he was mad and I was incapable of taking care of him. The postman had moved with his family to Marseilles and there was no one else to help.

They kept Vincent in isolation at the hospital for over a week without allowing me to see him, before letting him return to the yellow house when they decided his condition had improved. Five days later, the gendarmes came again and dragged Vincent away again. We had been drinking, so we were unable to resist. This time, they threw me out of the yellow house, closed the shutters and locked the doors. A complaint had been made to the authorities by local people, calling Vincent le fou roux and saying they lived in fear of us and our scandalous behaviour. Thirty people had signed a petition – peasants who still believed in demons and, in their ignorance, that we were the spawn of Satan.

With nowhere to live, I decided to use the rest of the money Theo had given to me in Breda to travel to Marseilles. I could not return to my mother's house in The Hague with Vincent locked up and nobody to help him. I'd promised I would not let them put him into an asylum and I believed I could get some work in Marseilles and earn enough to pay an advocat.

In isolation, the more Vincent complained about his treatment, the more they called him a dangerous madman. He forgot what I told him on my first visit – to stop acting like a lunatic and convince them of his sanity. They took everything away from him, even his pipe – he was allowed nothing, not a book or a glimpse of the sky. The priest wrote to Theo, begging him to put Vincent into an asylum. I could not stand it anymore, they wouldn't let me see him and I was in danger on the streets, so I had to leave, for the time being at least. I told Doctor Rey to let Vincent know that I would come back with help.

When I could.

# CHAPTER 26

# MARSEILLES

Back in Holland, there was a movement called the Midsummer Night Association and a debate about prostitution ignited. Hundreds of books and pamphlets were written by people defending public health and those who considered the medical checking of prostitutes a licence for visiting brothels. The proponents for ending prostitution called themselves abolitionists, just like the man in the black hat who had attacked me almost ten years earlier. They chose that name because of its meaning in the fight against abolishing slavery and they protested in front of the brothels. After so many centuries of condoning it, criticism against prostitution was leading to new morality laws called zedelijkheidwet. This caused fights in the streets and a dangerous atmosphere for someone like me, a reine des trottoirs. I did not need such aggravation at that time, another reason why I decided to go south instead of north, as well as to help get Vincent released.

I heard they paid good money in the Marseilles brothels. If I could get a job there, I could send some to my mother so she would keep taking care of Maria Wilhelmina, who was now about thirteen years old, and use the rest for an advocat. Willem was about six and I hadn't seen him for so long. But I knew my brother Pieter would take care of him, so I wasn't as worried as I was about Maria Wilhelmina. My mother could be a hard woman and, if money was scarce, I was afraid she might send my daughter on to the streets as she did me. So I made my way to Marseilles, which was only ninety kilometres from Arles. I had a little money left and I rented a small room in a taverne on Rue de Ruffi. Over the next few days, I tried and tried, but none of the brothels would hire me because I was too ugly – that's what they said.

I fell into melancholia.

Vincent and I suffered from this melancholia at the same time – it was almost as if we were transmitting it to each other over the distance between us. My depression was difficult for me to define – to quantify. Everybody feels a bit dejected now and then – a bit sad and sick at heart. But what I felt was different, more severe. It didn't just come for a little while and then leave, it stayed for more than a month. My melancholia made me feel hopeless and lose interest in everything, including myself. I was constantly tired and waves of suicidal thoughts would wash over me. Life was no longer worth living and I was plagued with feelings of guilt and lowliness. It was there constantly, lurking in the shadows of my mind. I can't say if the melancholia Vincent felt was exactly the same, but I imagine it was somewhat similar.

It became worse as time went on. It wrapped itself around me like a blanket and kept me warm. It became my friend and comforted me in a friendless world. It kept me company in my loneliness. I embraced it like a lover and grew to depend on it. With the melancholia came tiredness and lethargy. Most days I wished I hadn't woken up. Even things like walking and talking became difficult. I crawled from one day to the next. I sat in dark taverns in the evenings with one glass in front of me, rather than go upstairs to my room and face the emptiness. The dark shawl of depression closed itself around me and there seemed to be no way out of it.

Then I stopped eating. On the first day I ate and drank nothing except jenever. Next day, the lack of energy filled me with foreboding – what was the point of living – I was ugly – I would only disappoint myself again. Demons came and lay with me in the night, many demons. I was alone and would always be so – nothing was real except the impenetrable melancholia. I ate and drank nothing but absinthe on the second day, or the third, or the fourth. By the end of that week I had almost ceased to exist. I felt sick and could hardly get off the bed, but I had no yearning for food. During the second week, I had a few sips of water, but not much, because I believed it would burn my intestines. By the end of that week I had lost almost all of the little weight I carried and I was nothing but a bag of bones. I was unable to walk without holding on to the walls, my hands were shaking and it felt like every organ in my body was convulsing with cold. I was also seeing visions – demons during the night and angels in the day. It was becoming more and more difficult to determine what was real and what was unreal and I wondered if I, myself, was real, or just a figment of someone else's imagination.

I knew I was going to die – but I couldn't help myself. Suicide came and sat on my shoulder, whispered in my ear. I managed to resist it for a while, but the impulse grew stronger and stronger. Starving myself to death seemed like a dramatic option – a grand gesture – an impressive exit. In my delusional state, I thought people would finally see me. If I died in theatrical circumstances, people would talk about me and I would have their attention – if only for a while. And, if they gave me attention, they must also give Vincent attention. My disordered mind could see the headlines;

*"Imprisoned Artist's Amoureuse Kills Herself For Love"*

Until it came to actually finishing it, then it grew sordid and ugly and tragic, in the worst possible way. To die ignominiously in my little room would not have the desired effect. It would be no glorious exit, nobody would even know who I was. No, I had to live. Suicide could come at some more convenient time.

I tried to get downstairs, to the taverne, to eat some food, but I was so weak I collapsed and fell down the steps. When the innkeeper saw me, he hardly recognised me. He helped me to a table and brought me some soup and asked one of his girls to feed it to me. I could only take a little at a time, without throwing it back up. I was severely malnourished and had developed anaemia. I knew I was sick and would die if

I didn't eat, but I had to recover slowly. I had taught myself how to go without food and now it was difficult to learn how to eat again. While I was recovering, I didn't drink any alcohol and this also affected me greatly. I developed the sweats and the shivers and the visions whirled around me day and night for a full week. To be kind to the innkeeper, he made his girl stay with me and look after me until I was through the worst of it. I have not met many men with such a sense of decency and I owe him a debt.

But I had very little money left and I had to find work. The innkeeper's girl took me to a house on the quays, where a Russian woman called Galina lived with six very noisy children between the ages of four and twelve. The house was a slum, dark and dismal with no lighting or heating. There was no furniture either, the washroom was falling down and smelled horrible, and the kitchen was dirty and greasy. It looked like a kind of almshouse, where people might only stay for a short while, before moving on to somewhere else. The building was crawling with rats – if anything dropped on the floor, the rodents would run out and eat it. The children were unwashed and slept on bare mattresses, they did not go to school and they were constantly shouting and swearing and fighting.

My job was to look after the children while Galina went out to work. My room was small and smelled of mould and urine. It had a single bed and a shelf, nothing else, and a grimy window that looked out over a garden full of high weeds. I'd lived in many disgusting and frightening places, so it was nothing new to me, but it was difficult to sleep with the noise of the children and the rats scurrying round under my bed. I had arrived on Sunday and I got up early the following morning, expecting Galina to go to work, but she just hung round the house drinking and smoking all day. I tried to communicate with the children as best I could, but they could only speak Russian and I could not. I didn't have any specific duties, Galina just seemed to want someone to be there with the children when she went out – and she went out a lot. I was not happy with the situation, but I told myself I was here now, so the best thing I could do was get on with it. There was no food in the house and I had to go buy milk and bread with some francs I found in a tin. As soon as I got back, the children mobbed me like starving cats and anything that dropped on the floor was devoured in seconds by the rats.

Galina had a French beau who looked like Oude Rode Ogen, with hair like a horse's mane and gold teeth. She would disappear for days at a time with him and I would be left alone with the children. The agreement was that I would be paid one hundred francs each week, but I never received any money while I was there. When I asked Galina for my wages, she made the excuse that her payment was late. I do not know what kind of payment she meant, but it never came and I never got paid. One day, after a couple of weeks, Galina went out and left me with the children, as usual. I thought she was with her beau, but he came round on his own with a bag of caramels for the children. He spoke to me in French and made gestures, indicating that he wanted me to go somewhere with him. I worked out that he was saying I had to go with him to get potatoes. I tried to speak French in a broken accent.

'What … about … children?'

'Ne vous en faites pas. Nous ne serons pas long.'

I didn't understand.

We walked through many backstreets, until we came to a house where a group of people were drinking wine and smoking opium pipes. Galina's beau tried to get me to smoke a pipe and I was really tempted, but I refused. I tried to tell him I wanted to leave and, eventually, he took me back the way we came, without getting any potatoes. As we passed a narrow alley, he pulled me in there and started touching me. I knew he carried a knife and that I was in danger, so I smiled at him and made a drinking sign – he smiled back. We went to a taverne called Le Syndicat and he bought two drinks. We sat at a table and I indicated that I had to go to the privy. As soon as I was away from him, I ran out of the taverne and back to Galina's house. He came after me and was banging on the door, but I would not let him in.

'Ouvre la porte, salope!'

'Gendarmes! Gendarmes!'

I was shouting through the window and attracting the attention of people in the street. The gendarmes did not come, but it was enough to make him go away.

The following day, Galina left the house and took all the children with her. She said something to me before she went, but I couldn't understand what it was. She wrote an address in Russian on a piece of paper, but I didn't understand what that was either. I thought she was just going out somewhere for the day, but evening came and she did not come back. It got dark and there was no light or heat and the rats were scurrying around and squeaking. She didn't come back the next day either. I was freezing and the only way to keep warm was to stay in bed, fully clothed and pile the coverings from the other beds on top of me.

On the Friday, I went out and tried to find the address written on the piece of paper by Galina. It took a long time, but I finally knocked on the door of a house on Rue Bonneterie.

'Hallo.'

'Hallo … '

'Who is it?'

'Do you speak Dutch?'

'I am Dutch.'

Was this coincidence or was it fate? She was about thirty and she told me her name was Tess. She had only been in Marseilles a week and she was looking after children for a very poor family in this house and had not been paid. We spoke for a while and I told her I was supposed to be doing the same thing, but the family had left and didn't come back. We agreed to meet on Sunday at a taverne called La Caravelle and I bought some food on the way back to the cold house. I ate it before going inside, because the rats would swarm round me if they smelled it and climb all over me and sit on my shoulders like squirrels. It was hard staying in that cold dark house with only the rodents for company.

Nobody came by and I never saw Galina or her children again.

When Sunday arrived, I went to the taverne to meet Tess, but she did not arrive. I waited all day, but she didn't come. When I went back to the address on the piece of paper and knocked on the door, nobody answered. I had no money left for food or lodgings, so I went back to the cold, rat-house and stayed there for the next two days. Late on Tuesday evening a man came. He was big and swarthy and he was surprised to see me.

'Who are you?'

'Christien.'

'What are you doing here?'

'Waiting to be paid.'

I told him Galina didn't pay me and she owed me three hundred francs for three weeks' work. I'm not sure if he believed me or not, but why would anyone with money be living in a place like this?

'Galina should have paid you.'

'She did not.'

'That's not my fault.'

'Mine neither.'

He said I had to leave the house, as it was going to be torn down for development. I said I would not leave until I was paid. He became agitated and it was clear that he needed me to go immediately. I decided to push my luck.

'I'll go and get the gendarmes and they can sort it out.'

'Wait, I'll give you two hundred francs.'

'Three hundred.'

'Take it or leave it.'

I decided to take it.

Vincent was released from the Hôtel Dieu for the third time while I was away in Marseilles. It was in March of the year 1889 and Doctor Rey rented him two rooms in his private house, in return for a promise that Theo would introduce the young doctor into Paris society the next time he was in that city. The doctor made Vincent take potassium bromide, which was a remedy given to dogs that had fits. It muddled the gember man's mind and things became unclear to him. He didn't remember that I'd been to the yellow house or that I'd promised to come back to Arles – or maybe Rey didn't tell him. Vincent also continued to drink absinthe, to control the lights in his head.

After a few days of freedom, the gember man realised that he was unable to live on his own outside the hospital and he asked Salles the priest if he could be taken to a small church-run asylum in Saint-Rémy, a town in the hills, about twenty-five kilometres northeast of Arles. In Paris, Theo was consumed with his new status as a married man and with his new wife, Johanna Bonger. He wrote to Vincent about how wonderful the wedding was and about the joy he had found with Jo. He failed to realise how callous and insensitive his words were to Vincent, who had been denied the same chance of marital happiness with me.

Much of Vincent's work that remained in the yellow house during his confinement at the Hôtel Dieu was ruined by dampness and mould. The ones he could save, like the sunflowers and the starry nights, he packed up and sent to Paris. Sadness and remorse still haunted him and he wrote back to Theo about killing himself – it was either that or the French foreign legion for five years. He arrived at the asylum of Saint-Paul-De-Mausole in May of 1889 and, despite his misgivings, Vincent found peace at the asylum, untroubled by hostile neighbours or gendarmes or creditors or landlords or mocking children or stone-throwing inbreds. He was given therapies, which included being able to paint, and he seemed to discard the awful sense of worthlessness that always stalked him. The bright sun, the intense colours of the sky, the green fields, the riots of flowers and corn and vines and twisting olive leaves and sombre cypress trees inspired his paintings which harked back to what he called times long past.

Strange as it may seem, in the beginning, Vincent felt part of something in the asylum, just as he had with the miners in the Borinage years earlier – part of a community. He found friendship there and was content for a time. But the letters from Paris put an end to that. Jo Bonger wrote to him, telling him she was carrying a baby – a boy, who she was going to call Vincent. The gember man was reading an Ernest Renan play at the time, about doomed lovers and the sanctity of motherhood and how being lonely was worse than being dead. It all deranged him again and he believed that the place he was in was a sane place and it was the rest of the world which was mad.

Perhaps he was right.

In this state, Vincent painted the starry night again, which he had originally done just before Gauguin's visit. This time he saw beyond the sky, beyond the infinite number of stars up there, beyond what was visible to everyone else. He saw something which was truer to himself – to his own visionary strangeness. He painted in violet and ochre, in swirls of fantastic imagination, in spirals of cypresses. It was a night sky that had never been seen before with human eyes – whirlpools of stars, streams of vapour, rising thermals and a moon which was more than just a moon. It was a maelstrom of light and dark and movement and energy and ecstasy and terror and mystery and clarity which was visible only in the gember man's eyes.

When I returned to Arles from Marseilles in June, Vincent was gone and no one would tell me where. The yellow house was unlocked and some furniture of Vincent's still remained. So I moved in and kept quiet so as not to attract the hostility of the neighbours. And I waited to see if Vincent would come back. By that time, he was being allowed out and into the town of Saint-Rémy, along with an escort from the asylum. And, in July, he asked a doctor called Peyron if he could take a trip to Arles to bring back his furniture. Salles the priest was gone and so was Doctor Rey, so Vincent came to the yellow house alone, apart from the asylum warder, a simple young man who was more interested in going to a brothel than in watching Vincent.

He didn't recognise me at first because of all he'd been through and he thought I was the postman's wife who he'd painted.

'Augustine, have you come for your portrait?'

'It's not Augustine, Vincent. It's me, Sien.'

'Sien?'

'Yes, did they not tell you I promised to come back?'

'No, they did not.'

We went to a taverne to drink, while the warder from the asylum went to a brothel. Vincent told me what he could remember about his experiences since he was dragged away from me back in February.

'Must you go back to Saint-Rémy, Vincent?'

'I must. Otherwise they may put me in a worse place, the municipal asylum in Marseille, or the one in Aix-en-Provence.'

'I'm so sorry.'

'Come with me, Sien … we can be together again.'

'I can't, Vincent. I must go to my children.'

'Our son, how is he?'

'He's well, with my brother Pieter.'

I lied to him. I didn't know how Willem was and I was ashamed to tell him so. I also did not want to upset him any more than he already was, in his fragile state.

Later that night, the warder from the asylum came back and took Vincent away.

Back in Saint-Rémy, he made a pietà, copied from a work by Eugène Delacroix, with his own features as Christ and mine as the Virgin Mary's. I know some people said the Virgin's features were those of someone called Sister Epiphany, but look at the eyes – they are mine! Vincent also painted a mountain view with a dark hut at the bottom. It was a scene from *Le Sens de la Vie* – the little mountain cabin called the "enchanted asylum" where the hero of the book found happiness with his wife and child. It conjured up the image of Theo and Jo and their baby son to haunt him – along with the ghost of what could have been, and was for a short while in The Hague – until it was taken from us.

I decided it was time to go home, to see Willem and Maria Wilhelmina.

# CHAPTER 27

# MARIA WILHELMINA

She was being strapped in again, yet she did not complain – it was a nightly ritual for the little girl, compelled by her troubled spine to sleep in that big ugly bed. It was frightening for the other children to see this drama every night – the stuff nightmares were made of. They could turn over and bring their knees up to their chins if they wanted, she couldn't. The bed was made to fit her body shape while lying flat on her back, out of some kind of hard material that felt like gypsum plaster, moulded to fit her exact shape, like a body splint.

'Bless her, she's such a good little lamb.'

Maria Wilhelmina felt sorry for her.

'Still, it must be doing her good.'

It was standard treatment for children with consumption of the bones and, just as the other children had to watch the ritual night after night, the girl took it as normal to be strapped in by the matrons. They were not encouraged to ask questions and experience taught them not to bother, because answers were very few and mostly negative. They were just glad it wasn't them who had to sleep every night in that hard straitjacket.

The Catholic orphanage where Maria Wilhelmina worked as an apprentice was the same one myself and my brothers lived in for varying periods of time when we were young. My daughter was fourteen and training to be a keeper, so she could pay her way in my mother's house. My mother had moved again while I was away, this time to Bagijnestraat, close to the rood licht district, which made me fear for Maria Wilhelmina. But she was alright, she had a good head on her shoulders and was strong in her determination. She got the job because she could read and write and could speak French and English, taught to her by Countess Carola and Dirkje de Vries. As a junior trainee, she had to accept everything as being normal, even if her instincts told her otherwise – Maria Wilhelmina always had a habit of being curious about things, just like me. This girl seemed perfectly happy with the situation when I asked her about it on visiting my daughter at the orphanage and wanting to see if my old teacher, Lotte, was still there.

'My bed was made especially for me.'

She said this with a certain amount of pride, because it set her apart from the rest of the urchins. Her bed was special, so that made her special.

One day the bed would no longer be there and neither would the girl. Consumption was a killer and there was no reprieve. I told Maria Wilhelmina not to ask too many questions of the House Father or House Mother. Young people who were prone to be inquisitive like her were usually marked out as troublemakers. "You have got to watch that one" was a remark I'd often heard about myself when I was there, because my questions annoyed them – especially the awkward ones they didn't want to answer.

It wasn't as if I was being deliberately difficult. I just wanted to know. For instance, children who wet their beds sometimes got a pepernoot when they had a dry night. Every night was a dry night for me, but I never got any reward. I wondered why. I thought I should try it and find out, but the first time I wet the bed deliberately, I was rewarded with a beating instead of a biscuit. That left me trying to work out why grown people acted so unpredictably. My small world was an uneven place, with many ups and downs.

And it certainly wasn't round.

Maria Wilhelmina told me that the children who wet their beds were also the ones who cried a lot. Sometimes she felt the need for tears herself, but they were hard to come by for her. Instead, she just got angry. She said she envied the crying ones – their bibs would be soaked and she was curious to understand why they had to bawl so much, to create so many tears. Her own bouts of anger, instead of tears, convinced the House Father and Mother that she was a hard girl and, as such, would be an asset to the orphanage.

My daughter wasn't able to understand why she couldn't cry – I told her not to be concerned about it – there were worse things in the world.

'Was I born on the street, in a snowstorm?'

'Who told you that?'

'Oma.'

My mother also told her that I was a hoer, an alcoholic, and mentally unsound.

'You were not born on the street, and I'm none of those things.'

She had little recollection of her childhood days, or of being on the streets with me, which I was thankful for. She did remember Vincent and she called him 'the painter' and said she thought he was her father.

'He's Willem's father.'

'Who is my father?'

'A man called Sem Janssen.'

I lied. I didn't know who her father was.

'Was he a nice man, like the painter?'

I answered that question with another lie. It was better for her not to know that her father was just another customer and could have been any one of half a dozen men. She was unaware that the world she'd been born into was a cruel one and it was best if she remained in ignorance of it. Life with my mother had not been too bad for her, as there was only the two of them – unlike when I was her age, with ten other children coming along behind me.

She told me about sitting with my mother on Sunday afternoons, reading. One day my mother got annoyed at her for constantly talking. She held out a needle and thread and threatened to sew up my daughter's mouth, which put the fear into her. Maria Wilhelmina ran to an old grandfather clock that stood in the hall of the house in Noordstraat and was thin enough to squeeze inside. But this became a rod for her own back – the subsequent threat of locking her in the clock was enough to keep her quiet on Sunday afternoons from then on. Until she outgrew the clock and began talking incessantly again.

Maria Wilhelmina's lack of memory of most of her childhood enabled my mother to mould her to her liking – in her own image, perhaps. She was considered to be precocious and, unlike me, was encouraged to read and write and to think about her future. Maybe my mother was atoning for her treatment of me by showing more regard for her granddaughter. I tried to convince myself that was the case. My daughter was a pliant thing – she could have been taught to believe anything my mother said, mostly about how bad I was and what an unfit mother I was. Nevertheless, Maria Wilhelmina was glad to see me. And I was so happy to see her.

As my daughter advanced in her knowledge of the orphanage, she became aware that some of the children in the home had a family. A "family" – it was a word she just did not understand. But she gradually accepted the notion of it and, if these children had a family, why were they in the orphanage? All she knew was, she didn't have one and she began to wonder why that was. Who did she belong to – apart from the woman she lived with and who she called Oma? The situation was a mystery to her. Her whole life was a question to which she did not have an answer. But it didn't stop her imagining that she might be the lost offspring of a prince or a passing circus performer or a dark-skinned zigeuner who had been run off by the maréchaussée and accidentally left her behind. She believed he would come back for her some day, whoever he was – just turn up out of the blue sky on a silver horse or in a golden carriage and whisk her away before Oma could stop him.

But he didn't.

And she was disappointed.

The lack of information about who she really was left her with the feeling of not being a complete person – a genuine person. Certain credentials of a real person were missing – essential credentials. This was made all the more poignant by the questions being asked of her by other people she came into contact with and she was left having to make things up.

'My father is the king of Rumania.'

'No he isn't!'

'He is.'

'If he is, why does he not look after you?'

That's when she got defensive and angry.

'Why don't you mind your business?'

Coupled usually with a kick in the shin.

Maria Wilhelmina knew she had a mother, but not seeing me and only having a sketch of me that Vincent drew for her, left her unable to identify me in her head or even give a simple description of me. She said she just couldn't conjure up in her mind what I looked like, even after having lived with me until she was almost seven years old. Of course, she could have decided that I was the queen of Rumania, living with the king, but my mother put that notion out of her head. So, in her own mind she belonged to no one and, in reality, she was right.

Families visited their children at the orphanage from time to time and Maria Wilhelmina took notice of that. She didn't question why I never came to Noordstraat or Slijkeinde to visit her and she became immune to the disparaging remarks made by her Oma about me. Until one day the House Mother let slip that of course she had a family. She had a mother, a brother called Willem and a father called Vincent. When she found this out, she told the news to anyone who would listen. And so, I was her mother and now I was here – just an ordinary person with dark hair and, as adults went, smaller and thinner than she had imagined. Certainly not the queen of Rumania. Nevertheless, she was quite mesmerised by this mystery woman who had finally come back to her and she had a thousand questions for me.

She was at pains to point out that life with my mother wasn't bad. She was content here, even without a family, as such. There was a certain pleasure in singing hymns on Sunday and being captivated by the changing angle of the sun, shining through the stained-glass windows of the church. It was surely God's blessing being bestowed upon her, bathing her in many colours, proving that the day was, indeed, bright and beautiful. Small joys like that were her memories, little pleasures which other people might consider insignificant.

And disquiets.

She spoke solemnly about the time she saw her first funeral. She was walking back to Slijkeinde when she had to stop and stand to show respect while a horse-drawn hearse and its cortège passed by. She was amazed by the lovely flowers on the coffin – never before had she seen anything that beautiful and she was enthralled. Then she noticed the mourners and some were weeping. Confusion set in – why were they not as happy as she was, looking at the lovely flowers. A boy, standing with his cap in his hand, noticed her smile and decided to wipe it off her face.

'There's a dead man in that box.'

She became worried. Who was in the box and why? Were they sure he was dead? What if the man wanted to get out? Could they just have another look to make sure? Panic came upon her that night as she fought a battle to get out of her box, pushing, screaming and forcing her way through, until she finally escaped the sheets encasing the bottom of her bed. The feeling of suffocation played a lot on her mind after that.

When I first left Maria Wilhelmina with my mother and went on the road, Oma gave her to a farming family because, she said, she couldn't afford to feed her. I knew nothing of this, of course, until now. She had memories of being taken out on a two-wheeled, horse-drawn milk delivery cart, in which the farmer's wife did her rounds. The milk urns sat in the back of the cart and milk was ladled into jugs brought out by the customers. This became a regular thing, until they put her on the horse and she screamed because the width of its back had her legs stretched so wide it was painful.

On one occasion, the farmers took her to the top of what she saw as a mountain. A black and white goat caught her interest and she wandered off to talk to it and got left behind. A search party had to be sent back to look for her when they realised she wasn't with them. She said she wasn't worried or fretful – she was still talking to the goat when she heard a voice and saw a figure coming along the path. He picked her up and carried her down to where they were all waiting.

I noticed, in her room, she had a bunch of irises in a vase and it brought my mind back to Vincent and I wondered how he was. His painted flowers were described once by somebody as "plants radiant with life in tender, quivering form, shy as silken butterflies". But that's not how he thought of them, he preferred the words of William Wordsworth: "To me the meanest flower that blows can give thoughts that do often lie too deep for tears".

It is a poem about loss.

Vincent always said that he painted for those who didn't know the artistic aspect of a picture, like me. There were so many facets to him. But all the art world ever saw was a laughable failure. I hope, if his work is successful in future times, it will be remembered that the people who flatter him then will be the same people who scorn him now.

After a few months with the farmers, she went back to Noordstraat, in the same way as I would go back there after my sojourns in the orphanage. My mother's house became her permanent residence after that.

'Where have you been, moeder?'

It was a question constantly asked by Maria Wilhelmina and one which was very difficult for me to answer. How could I explain to her about Vincent – who he was and how much I loved him, without making her feel disappointed that he

274

wasn't her father, even though he treated her as his daughter when she was with him. It would be unfair for her to think that her own father was a ghost and Willem's father was a god.

So I made up a story.

I told her that her father was a dashing cavalry officer and he was going to marry me and take me to live in his castle in Friesland. At the time, the Dutch army was fighting a war in Aceh, which was in Sumatra, and he was killed in an attack on the Sultan's palace. His family knew nothing of our love affair and did not recognise Maria Wilhelmina as his daughter, just as Vincent's family did not recognise Willem.

'What's the matter with these people, moeder?'

'They only see their own bigotry, they're blinded by it.'

'But we know who we are, do we not?'

'Yes we do. We certainly do.'

She asked me many questions about her imagined father and I told her he was handsome and gallant and kind and generous and she thought about him and pictured him in her mind and even drew him on his imagined horse, charging the Sultan's palace. She also wanted to know about Willem's father and I told her about our time with Vincent on the Schenkweg. She had some memory of it and recalled a man with gember hair and a gember beard who played verstoppertje with her and made her laugh.

'Where is he now, moeder?'

'He's in France.'

'Why are we not with him?'

'Because he's on retreat.'

'Retreating from what?'

I wanted to say the world. But instead I explained that a retreat in this sense was a spiritual thing where a person went to reflect and to get a clearer picture of where they were in their life and where they wanted to go next.

'Will we live with him when he's finished retreating?'

'I don't think so.'

'Why not, if he's Willem's father?'

'He's very poor and can't support us.'

'Then he can come here and we'll support him.'

I smiled and hugged my daughter. I loved her so much and regretted the years I'd been without her.

'We'll see what happens Maria Wilhelmina. Nobody knows what the future will bring.'

'God does.'

My mother and the orphanage had obviously instilled much of their Catholicism into my daughter.

'I'm sure he does. But we'll wait and see.'

I hadn't yet been able to visit Willem, even though I'd been back in The Hague for some time. Pieter had moved his family to Rotterdam and, every time I said I would come to see my son, he replied with an excuse that it wasn't a good time and I should wait a bit longer. My mother was also against bringing Willem to Bagijnestraat. She said he was having a good life with Pieter and it wouldn't be wise to disrupt that. In any case, he was only a year old when I left him and he wouldn't know who I was. I took from her words that Pieter had told Willem nothing about who his mother and father were and that he didn't want the boy to find out.

I was prepared to wait until the time was right – for Willem's sake.

And so I settled into my mother's house again. I was too old now for the street life and, anyway, I'd had enough of it. I got a job as a washerwoman in a laundry. The work was hard and hot but, with my wages and Maria Wilhelmina's pay from the orphanage and my mother's sewing, we were able to support ourselves. I thought then that my travelling days were over and I would die where I was born – here in The Hague.

# CHAPTER 28

# DEATH AND DESERTION

When Vincent returned to the asylum of Saint-Paul-De-Mausole after Arles, the darkness returned with him – visions, fainting, forgetfulness, anguish. He experienced fits of despair, punctuated by periods of visionary ecstasy.

'The sadness will last forever.'

He ate dirt from the garden and paint from his tubes and drank turpentine and oil from his lamp. He assaulted his warder escort, so they took his equipment away and stopped allowing him out. His throat swelled with sores and he found it difficult to eat. He wanted to die – or, at least, to escape from the asylum. It was October of the year 1889 before he recovered enough to be allowed to paint again.

I tried to find out as much as I could about what was happening to Vincent, but it was difficult. In Paris, Theo's health was deteriorating, but he managed to get two of Vincent's paintings, the first starry night and a picture of irises, into an Indépendante show. He also secured an invitation for Vincent to exhibit his work in January with Les Vingt, an avant-garde group in Brussels. When Kerstmis came, the gember man was overcome by nostalgia again and he painted a young couple under a yellow lamp, bent over a baby in a cradle. It was us – Vincent in his hat, me sewing, and baby Willem smiling.

The latest malady left him in his cold room with his head in his hands, talking to himself about his sad and melancholy past. Meanwhile, I read a written piece about Vincent in the *Mercure de France*. It was entitled "The Isolated Ones" and it acknowledged the "truthfulness of his art and the genius of his vision". Other pieces appeared in *De Portefeuille* and *La Vogue* and *Le Moderniste Illustré* that described his sunflowers, which were on display in the window of Tanguy's paint shop in Paris, as "fantastically spirited, intense and full of sunshine". The piece in *Mercure de France* was written by an art critic and poet called Albert Aurier and it created fresh interest in the Les Vingt exhibition, which was to open in a few weeks. Nobody had heard of Vincent van Gogh and they wanted to see what Aurier was talking about.

The showing was held in the Palais des Beaux-Arts in Brussels in January of the year 1890 and I took Maria Wilhelmina there. Vincent's sunflowers and other paintings took their place beside work by successful artists like Paul Cézanne, Pierre Renoir and Henri Toulouse-Lautrec and I told her they were painted by Willem's father. Of course, the traditional critics couldn't understand Vincent's wild imagery, but new reviewers praised him. I heard that Les Vingt's founder wrote to Theo about the exhibition, but Theo was more focused on another Vincent – his newborn son. Despite the apparent success, no sales resulted from the exposure and nobody went to see Vincent at the asylum. The demons came back and stayed with him for months.

In March, Theo sent ten of Vincent's paintings to the Salon des Indépendants in the Ville de Paris. Again, many people came to see the work of the man who Aurier had written about. He was the star of the show and praised in *Art et Critique* and *Mercure de France*. One painting was actually sold. People were asking where he was and why this genius was being held prisoner. So Theo sent him a hundred and fifty francs and arranged for him to leave the asylum and go to see a doctor called Gachet, who lived in a village to the north of Paris. After he left, the Doctor Peyron's son found a box of canvases and he and his friends used them as targets for their bows and arrows and shot holes in them. I'm glad Vincent did not see that.

Theo met him on the way, in Paris, and took him to his new apartment at Cité Pigalle, where they were greeted by Jo Bonger and Vincent saw her child, named after him, who was ill with colic. He would have preferred it if Theo had named his boy after Dorus, as Vincent already had a son named after him – his own. Tears filled his eyes, thinking of Willem, who he had not seen for seven years. He didn't stay long, as it was too painful for him to see Theo's apparently perfect little family life, so he moved on to the small town of Auvers-sur-Oise. It was used by the Parisienne elite as a summer escape from the city, consisting of low thatched cottages by a placidly flowing river, with well-trodden steps linking streets at different levels, flowering chestnuts, white dusty roads and a patchwork of tilled soil.

Vincent decided to paint it all – the rolling countryside, full of glowing gardens interspersed with woodland – an ancient tower – an old sandstone church. The gember man had a brief new lease of life and took his mahlstick, his palette and his bundle of brushes and began to work again. Before the first picture was finished, he began a second, then a third – such feverish activity, like the approach of a storm.

In reality, nothing had changed for Vincent. People in Auvers were suspicious of the curious stranger, just like the people everywhere else he'd been – and he was still beggared. He took a room at the local taverne, run by a man called Ravoux and his family, who also gave him a small space to use as a studio. He went to see Doctor Gachet in a house full of cats and dogs and chickens and Vincent soon realised that this man would not be able to cure his so-called insanity.

'He's sicker than I am!'

But Vincent agreed to paint Gachet, if only to get his help in persuading Theo to come to the country for the sake of the health of his baby. You see, Vincent had begun to fantasise about having a family again, like the one he had with me on the Schenkweg, and he imagined Theo's family could be a substitute. He pestered his brother to come with Jo and the baby to live with him. But, of course, Theo's family was not his family and the whole idea was impossible. Nevertheless, they did come in June – but went back to Paris the same day.

Vincent's despair began to return and Theo feared a new lapse into dangerous melancholy. The gember man's letters were abstractly mentioning suicide and that he hadn't much time left. He had fallen out with Doctor Gachet and the Ravoux family and had no friends to alleviate his loneliness. Theo sent a young painter called Hirschig to Auvers to provide Vincent with companionship, but he found the gember man to be like a bad dream and called him a dangerous fool and he quickly disappeared. Several other artists also came and went.

In the end, Theo took his wife and child to Holland to live with Jo's family for a while, to recover their health. He stopped in The Hague on his way back to Paris in July and that's where he found me.

'There's no one left but you, Sien.'

He told me his baby was sick, continuously crying day night, Jo was sick with worry and he himself was sick. He worried about money, about feeding his family and about taking care of Vincent.

'I can't do it all, Sien. I need help. I made a dreadful mistake in parting you and only a wife and child will make a man of Vincent again.'

He told me that darkness had fallen over the gember man and he was seeing threats everywhere. He was painting troubled skies and bleak landscapes with frightened crows – pictures that were remorseless and ominous.

'He said the very roots of his life are threatened, Sien.'

Vincent had expressed horror when he thought about the future and Theo was afraid of another incident like the ear-cutting – or even worse.

I was still at my mother's house with Maria Wilhelmina, but planning to go to see my brother Pieter and my son Willem in Rotterdam. I had just begun to know my daughter again and was just about to meet my son again after all the years away from him. But what could I do? I could not abandon Vincent. I had to go.

'Can I bring him back here to The Hague with me ... it could be like it was, Theo, with Maria Wilhelmina and Willem?'

'If he'll come, Sien.'

Life had gone full circle. I was so happy. I told my mother and my daughter that I'd be back very soon.

'That's what you said the last time, moeder.'

'I know, and I'm sorry.'

'It's alright, I understand.'

'Thank you.'

I hugged Maria Wilhelmina and shook hands with my mother and took the train to Paris, where I changed at the Gare de Lyon for Auvers-sur-Oise. I arrived at about noon on July 27th and was told that Vincent had just finished lunch at the taverne and had gone back out into the country to paint. I asked for directions and they guided me towards a small hamlet called Chaponval to the west of the town. The road was lined with walled farmyards and it crossed the Rue Boucher after about eight hundred metres. I kept walking, looking for Vincent, until I came upon an old taverne that was frequented by poachers and other shady sorts. Vincent's painting equipment was outside, leaning against the wall.

I went inside and saw the gember man at a table with a group of young men. They seemed to be drinking together, but the youths also seemed to be mocking Vincent, taking his hat and laughing at his disfigured ear. I approached the table. Vincent looked round. He studied me for a moment, as if seeing one of his visions.

'Sien?'

'It's me, Vincent.'

One of the youths pulled up a chair for me and bowed in the manner of addressing an aristocrat. I immediately knew he was mocking me also. I sat and a glass of absinthe was placed in front of me. The one who had produced the chair, and who I presumed to be the leader of the group, spoke to Vincent.

'And who's this, Toto, your cantiniére?'

'She's my wife.'

'Your wife? And how good is she in bed, Toto?'

Vincent didn't answer. The dog turned to me.

'Did you know, Madam Toto, that your husband is the faithful lover of the widow wrist?'

The others all laughed loudly at this.

I tried to ignore the pig, but he was intent on humiliating Vincent as much as possible for the benefit of his hee-hawing friends. He then tried to goad me.

'Madam Toto, if indeed that's who you are, may I say you look more like a talonneuse, and a cheap one at that.'

They hee-hawed again. I looked at Vincent. He didn't say or do anything. It was time for me to teach this loud-mouthed bully a lesson.

'You know about hoers, then?'

He was surprised by my answer, unused to people standing up to him – especially women. I continued.

'Ah yes, I remember you from Paris. The girls there said you had a tiny pénis. They had to look for it with a magnifier.'

More hee-hawing. But the bully didn't like some of his own medicine. He pushed my glass closer to me.

'Drink, Madam Toto.'

'I don't want your drink, monsieur petit pénis.'

With that, he grabbed my face and tried to pour the drink into my mouth. Now, I was not as strong as him, but I'd been on rough streets long enough to know how to handle boys. I brought my knee up hard into his testicles and he fell to the floor holding his groin and groaning. The drink he tried to pour down my neck spilled on top of him and he now looked like what he really was – a grovelling cur. The others growled at me and I gave them my fierce stare, then they backed away and retreated from the taverne, dragging their leader with them.

I sat down.

'Who was that, Vincent?'

'The smoked herring boy.'

I found out his name was René Secrétan, a bourgeois youth with a rich father. He came to Auvers in summer with his older brother Gaston, who liked painting and who was a friend of Vincent's. But René was not like his brother, he was an ignorant, boorish boy who would rather annoy people than be civilised. His father's money allowed him to get away with it here in the countryside and he and his friends liked to torment Vincent. They put salt in his coffee and a snake in his paintbox and took every opportunity to mock his ear and his way of speaking. In every way, he was an obnoxious individual, who deserved to be locked away from decent people. But I wasn't here to talk about René Secrétan.

'I've spoken to Theo, Vincent. He's agreeable for you to come back to The Hague with me.'

'The Hague?'

'Yes, to our son, Willem. We can live as a family again. You can paint and I can sew and clean. The children are grown, Maria Wilhelmina is working. We'll get by until you sell some pictures.'

'You think so, Sien? How wonderful. When can we go?'

'Whenever you like.'

'I have a lot of canvases … I'll have to make plans to have them shipped.'

'Of course.'

'Ravoux will do it. He's my friend. I'll arrange it when we go back.'

We remained at the poacher's taverne celebrating our reunion and return to The Hague until late afternoon. Then it was time to go to Auvers to make arrangements. It was getting dark when we came to the intersection with the Rue Boucher. We were passing a walled farmyard when a figure jumped out in front of us. He was dressed strangely in a fringed tunic and high boots and a wide hat with the brim turned down so it was difficult to see his face. He was obviously drunk. I was startled, but Vincent seemed to recognise him.

'It's Puffalo Pill.'

'Don't you mock me!'

I recognised the voice – it was René Secrétan. He pulled out a small pistol and pointed it at us. Vincent ran into the farmyard, pulling me with him. We hid behind a dunghill. René followed us, brandishing the gun. Vincent dropped his equipment as René came round the dunghill and he tried to reason with the boy.

'René … where did you get that gun?'

'From Ravoux.'

'You've had too much to drink. Why don't you just go home.'

'I want satisfaction from Madam Toto.'

He pointed the gun directly at me. It looked like a toy and I was sure it was meant only to frighten me into apologising to him. But I'd had enough of this fool and his pranks. I marched forward towards him and his toy gun. Vincent shouted.

'Sien … no!'

When I got close, I grabbed his hand and tried to make him drop it. He was stronger than I thought for a sixteen-year-old and it took some effort for me to get him to let go of the gun. In the end I wrested it away from him but, as I turned to Vincent, the gun went off. It wasn't a toy after all. There was a loud bang, then utter silence. All three of us, me, Vincent and René, stood motionless like statues. Then I noticed that Vincent was clutching his stomach and a small amount of blood was oozing through his fingers.

'You shot him! You shot him!'

René began screaming and ran off into the darkening evening.

Vincent leaned against the dunghill. More blood was coming through his fingers.

'The gun, Sien … put it down.'

I placed the weapon carefully on the ground, then rushed to him.

'Now, take my equipment to that wall and burn it.'

'Why … '

'Just do as I say!'

I did as he said and set fire to his easel and canvases and the rest of his equipment. It all burned up quickly because of the paint.

'I'll tell them I was painting in the wheatfields. They'll look there for evidence, not here.'

I was trying to stop the wound from bleeding, but he didn't want me to.

'Now, go quickly to the train station at Pontoise … it's about six kilometres. You must get out of here.'

'I can't leave you like this, Vincent.'

'You must, Sien. René will lie to save his skin. They'll believe him over you. If I die you'll be convicted of murder and go to the guillotine. Think of our son … '

'No … '

'Please, Sien … go now! I'll tell them I shot myself. They'll believe that.'

'No … '

'Take the gun, throw it in the river. Go now!'

I picked up the gun and reluctantly left the farmyard, staggering in the direction of Pontoise, not really fully conscious of what I was doing. Tears clouded my eyes as I threw the gun into the water at a bend in the river, close to the poacher taverne. I waited for the next train at Pontoise station, then I left.

I later found out that Vincent made it back to town and told them he'd shot himself. He leaned on the billiard table at the inn and said he was wounded. Then he climbed the steps to his attic room, groaning. The innkeeper went upstairs – the door was unlocked. Vincent was lying on the narrow iron bed with his face turned to the wall.

'What's the matter, monsieur?'

'I shot myself.'

Ravoux saw the of blood coming from his stomach. The gendarmes were summoned and wanted to know where the pistol was. Vincent would not tell them.

'I'm free to do what I want with my body. Can I have my pipe and tobacco?'

The gendarmes asked if he intended to commit suicide and he said he did. When they explained that suicide was a crime, in his pain and confusion, he told them not to accuse anyone – that it was his fault, he wanted to kill himself.

René Secrétan and his brother left Auvers that night, obviously taken away by their rich father, who didn't want his son involved in a scandal.

Theo arrived at the taverne the next day and rushed upstairs to Vincent's room. The gember man was sitting up, smoking his pipe.

'They said you wounded yourself again, Vincent.'

'I have.'

'Where's Sien?'

'Sien? There's no Sien here.'

'Did she not come?'

'Do you mean Adeline, Ravoux's daughter? She's downstairs.'

'You must not die, Vincent.'

'It is easier for me to die than to live, Theo.'

Vincent left the world that night.

Émile Bernard wrote that, at his funeral, the walls of the room where his body lay were covered with his last canvases, forming something like a halo around him. Over the coffin was draped a simple white sheet and masses of flowers – the sunflowers he loved so much, yellow blossoms everywhere. It was his favourite colour, a symbol of the light in his heart and of his son, who was also in his heart. Theo sobbed ceaselessly as people carried the coffin to the hearse. Outside, the sun was scorching. They climbed the hill of Auvers talking of him, of the bold forward thrust he gave to art, of the great projects that always preoccupied him, of the good he had done. They arrived at the cemetery, a small graveyard dotted with fresh tombstones. It was on a height overlooking the fields ready for reaping, under the wide blue sky which he loved. And then he was lowered into the grave. He would not have been sad at that moment, the day was much too much to his liking.

What I have to say is this, where was Émile Bernard and the rest of them when Vincent was struggling?

Nowhere to be seen.

# CHAPTER 29

# ARNOLDÚS

Is this hell? Is this where I have finally fallen to – deserve to be? Will I die here? Or am I already dead? Now only what I can see exists. Only what I can touch and feel. There were once other things to deal with – time and strangeness and living each moment on the edge of eternity – paying the heavy price of awareness. Is there such a thing as never? Or forever? Forever never – never forever. My fractured perceptions were flawed. The past never existed – or, if it did, it ceased to exist as soon as my awareness moved beyond it – yet it haunts me, like a ghost in the gloom. Nothing matters, even the present which I am inhabiting now. Or is today no more real than yesterday? I live in my little room – crouch in my corner. I watch the dark sky through the small window, high up in the wall.

The moon is battered.

Broken.

Theo lost his reason after Vincent's death. He attacked his wife and child and was admitted to the Willem Arntz asylum in the town of Den Dolter in the province of Utrecht – the same one where Margot Begemann had been treated years before. He was suffering from dementia paralytica, a paralysis said to have been caused by overwork and great sadness. He spent his last weeks in a state of deep melancholy and total apathy. He died in the asylum on 25th January in the year 1891, less than six months after Vincent. He was thirty-three.

I myself was overcome with despair for a long time – longer than I can remember. I contemplated killing myself, but decided I couldn't do that until I had seen my son again. I took Maria Wilhelmina with me when I journeyed to my brother Pieter's house on Walenburgerweg in Rotterdam to see Willem. The weather was frightful when we arrived and we had to walk through a copse of trees. The fear of being struck by lightning turned to hysteria in Maria Wilhelmina and I had to reassure her that she was safe because lightning would not strike us or the trees. She was tensed up so tight that she couldn't open her eyes. She fumbled and felt her way along, clinging on to my coat and singing hymns.

Pieter's house was at the end of the street, painted blue and white. I had a fleeting vision of it, somewhere at the back of my mind, even though I couldn't remember being there before now. The boy was swinging his legs back and forth, his eyes quietly looking to the floor. His grey cap sat on his gember head and matched his grey suit – a suit that was old and new at the same time. Old insofar as it wasn't fashionable and was probably meant for someone more advanced in years, and new because it hadn't been worn before. His feet wore polished black lace-up boots. The room felt like a holy place in the silence between the two of us – everyone else remained outside, also silent, as if to preserve the solemnity of the reunion. It seemed as if talking or making any kind of noise would be very taboo.

I studied him before speaking. His features were strong and angular and brooding and, when he held his head at a certain angle, I could see Vincent in him.

'How are you, Willem?'

My whisper seemed to echo off the walls.

'I'm well, thank you.'

His voice was formal – polite, almost deferential.

'Do you know who I am?'

'You're my mother.'

'Did someone tell you that?'

'Yes, Uncle Pieter.'

I wondered what else Uncle Pieter had told him and made him do. I had heard stories while I was in The Hague.

'Did he make you walk for three hours to piano lessons?'

'Who told you that?'

'I heard. Is it true, Willem?'

The boy lowered his head.

'It was good for me.'

'I suppose Uncle Pieter told you that too?'

He didn't answer.

I waited for him to ask me where I'd been, as Maria Wilhelmina did – but he remained silent, looking down at the floor, swinging his legs. Outside the room, we could hear the sound of muddled conversation and the clip-clop of distant heels scuffing the wooden floor, now that the ice had been broken between us in the room. Lingering in the air was the evocative smell of carbolic soap and a pungency of wax polish from Pieter's furniture making. Willem was approaching nine years old when I came back from my wanderings. Like Maria Wilhelmina, I had not seen him for almost eight years and, although my daughter had some recollection of me, he did not.

I brought him a glass jar of liquorice as a small gift and he took it and held it tightly to his chest but didn't attempt to open it.

'Do you know my name?'

'Moeder?'

'Yes, but my name is Clasina Maria.'

'Maria … like grootmoeder and my zus.'

'Yes, and your sister is here with me. Has she been visiting you while I was away?'

'Sometimes.'

'How many times?'

'Two times … I think.'

I was disappointed that my mother had not made Maria Wilhelmina keep closer contact with Willem. They needed to be together. But I was back now and that would all change.

Pieter came into the room and broke the thread of reconnecting that was gradually forming between us. He was married now, with children of his own.

'I'm pleased you two are getting on.'

His voice betrayed a kind of hopefulness – maybe because I was back and he could relinquish the responsibility of looking after my son. Glancing from one to the other, he smiled with relief and, with a flourish, he brought his hands together in prayer fashion. By this time, Willem had opened the glass jar and was chewing on a piece of liquorice.

'How do you like your mother, Willem?'

'I like her well enough. Will my father be coming too?'

Pieter and I looked at each other. I felt sorry for my son, he was being expected to suddenly accept being transported into the centre of someone else's story, and to fit into the scene as though he knew the narrative.

'Your father is dead, Willem.'

He showed no emotion at this news.

'Who was he?'

'He was an artist we lived with many years ago in The Hague. His name was van Gogh. You're called after him, his middle name was Willem.

'I draw very well too.'

Maria Wilhelmina and me stayed at Pieter's house that night and it was good to be close to my son again – it was like being close to Vincent. I needed to make myself clear to my brother about what I wanted to do.

'I want the children to live with me, Pieter.'

'Where, Clasina, on the Bagijnestraat?'

'I don't care where.'

'What about here, in Rotterdam?'

'That would be fine too.'

Pieter obviously had a plan of his own, but he was reluctant to divulge it immediately. We had dinner and, afterwards, when we were alone, he told me what it was.

'The children need a legitimate name, Clasina, it will be easier for them later, especially Willem.'

'He has a name, it's van Gogh.'

'I mean officially. The van Goghs will never accept him and you know it.'

Pieter sighed. I was grateful to him for taking care of Willem for all these years, even if he did it in his own way. He paced the floor for a moment, then took a long drink.

'I have a friend who will marry you. Willem can take his name.'

I could not believe what he was saying.

'And who is this friend?'

'His name is Arnoldús van Wijk. He's a sailor, away at sea most of the time. You will not need to be a wife in the biblical sense, it's just an arrangement.'

'An arrangement?'

'For Willem's sake.'

Arnoldús van Wijk was eleven years younger than me and Pieter promised to pay him three hundred guilders for his part in the arrangement. My brother wanted me to meet him before I rejected the plan so, that night, I went with him to the van Wijk family house at Verlaatstraat 30, which was a waterside area of Rotterdam. The mother took an immediate dislike to me and, when Arnoldús wasn't listening, she whispered that her son could do a lot better. She was very controlling and self-opinionated, but the father was more easy-going. The man was suffering with dementia and had his highs and lows and was on potions to keep his lapses of memory under control.

After a lot of thought and conscience-searching and persuasive argument from Pieter, I reluctantly agreed to the arrangement. We couldn't live at the van Wijk house because Arnoldús had a volatile relationship with his parents, or at Pieter's – so my new husband-to-be started looking for a place of our own. We eventually found somewhere on Rochussenstraat, which was a nice enough area, where the people believed themselves to be respectable and god-fearing. The house itself had two floors – three bedrooms, a kitchen, a parlour and an inside privy. Pieter gave us furniture that he'd made and the van Wijks gave us a tin bath and some pots and pans.

And so I became a respectable married woman for the first time – Clasina Maria van Wijk. Maria Wilhelmina also took the van Wijk name and so did Willem – he became Willem van Wijk, instead of Willem van Gogh.

I had no money and no job and Arnoldús was paying for everything, which I did not like, so I took in seamstress work as in the old days in Noordstraat with my mother. My new husband didn't want to go back to sea, now that he had a family, so he took on labouring jobs on building sites when he could get the work. We got on alright together for a while, but gradually our relationship began to turn sour. He wanted to be in charge of everything, make all the decisions, go out and not come back all night and expect me to accept it and keep my mouth shut. That was never the way I was made.

After we fought, we'd go back to what was a version of normality. But, inside, I felt hurt and lost and I didn't want to be in this world. It was as if nothing had meaning any more, my beautiful dream had been shattered, so why bother to go on living. I couldn't see anything positive to live for after the illusion of the elusive love I craved had disintegrated. Of course, there was always my children to live for and that was the only thing that kept me alive.

We began arguing all the time and it wasn't like when I argued with Vincent and we were back being lovers so quickly afterwards. Arguments with Arnoldús were vindictive after the three hundred guilders Pieter paid for the arrangement were gone and he kept threatening to throw me out – the tenancy of the house was in his name. So Maria Wilhelmina went back to The Hague to resume her job at the orphanage.

I think Arnoldús would have liked to have had a child of his own – of his own blood. He was certainly young enough, but I was far too old. The having of another child, even if I could conceive one, which was unlikely even with modern new-century medicine, would kill me. So we kept on arguing. We argued about everything – money, his drinking, my frigidity, the colour of the sky, the length of the day. It all got too much at the house on Rochussenstraat when we eventually fell behind with the rent and were threatened with eviction by the landlord. He was a tattooist and he knew a lot of rough people, so Arnoldús stole some jewellery from his mother to give him, but it wasn't enough and we had to find somewhere else to live.

We walked the streets of Rotterdam until we found another house to rent. This one was on the Delfshaven Embankment, down near the docks, which was known to be a really rough area of the city. But we did not have much choice. The Embankment was a grim place. It was dark and dreary and I didn't like taking Willem there. It was populated by a mixture of many races and nationalities – French, West Indian, African, Asian and there were lots of gangs, including the Penoze – although it was doubtful if they were still looking for me after all this time. I was always afraid of being pulled into a dark alley and murdered and I walked with my head down so as not to attract attention to myself. The negro women would be standing in front of the tavernes, as I did in my youth, their hair wrapped in bandanas, chewing tobacco and speaking patois, always scowling. They knew I was an outsider and didn't fit in, so I looked at the ground and scurried from one place to another. The water in the river was coloured green and black and it was notorious for suicides. Houses were boarded up, shops were shut down, hoers roamed the streets and stabbings were commonplace.

I was happy to take in seamstress work when we were at Rochussenstraat, but nobody could afford to pay for that in this place. Money was becoming very scarce – that's when Arnoldús accused me of stealing the jewellery from his mother to pay the rent to the tattooist. The old woman had threatened to disinherit him, so he told her it was me and, to prove his innocence, he had me arrested. What a thing to do! Why would anyone do that? The politie came and took me to the guardhouse, where I was questioned in a windowless cell with bars on the door. I was afraid I would go to prison.

They questioned me for hours, but I was in shock and unable to answer them. I think they realised I was innocent because, in the end, they stopped and left me alone. I wanted to tell them that it was Arnoldús who'd stolen the jewellery, but I knew they wouldn't believe me and that it would only make matters worse.

I conjured in my head what prison would be like – would I get beaten? I would surely die there. How would I survive? In the end, they questioned the tattooist, who testified that Arnoldús gave him the jewellery. Arnoldús then signed a statement, withdrawing his accusation. I was told there would be no further action. Arnoldús should have been arrested and charged with making a false allegation but, of course, he was not.

That was the end with Arnoldús, I'd had enough and I vowed to leave him.

He was surprised when I said I was leaving. Up until then it was always him leaving me or threatening to throw me out, but now the shoe was on the other foot and he did not like it. He went to the door and wouldn't get out of my way. He persuaded me to stay because it was the easiest thing to do. I was in his city with no friends and no money and a son to look after. I suppose I could have went back to my mother, but it was a while since we'd been in contact and I probably didn't want to admit defeat – that I was a failure at marriage, just as I was a failure at everything else. After Arnoldús persuaded me to stay, we decided it was best if we left the Embankment, as it seemed to be having an adverse effect on both of us. We had just about enough money to rent a house on the outskirts of the city and Arnoldús said he would go back to sea if he couldn't find work.

When we arrived in Oude Noorden by the River Rotte, we sat in a café, sharing a meal of potatoes between the three of us. That was all we could afford and we resembled de aardappeleters Vincent had painted back in The Hague. The house we rented was an old farmhouse, right at the top of a steep hill, and there was no answer when we knocked on the big blue door that looked more like a gate. We were walking round to the back when this youth of about thirteen years sprang out from nowhere. He looked like a zigeuner, with black hair and eyes and he spoke with a lisp. We couldn't understand what he was saying for a few minutes, but once we got an ear for his words, he told us we were at the right place.

Arnoldús couldn't get work on the city outskirts, so he went back to sea, leaving Willem and me alone. The youth with the lisp turned out to be a burglar and, after we moved in, he was constantly knocking on our door, trying to sell the things he'd stolen. We had no money and could not afford to pay him, but he was kind-hearted and sometimes gave us enough to buy food with. One night we were asleep in bed when I heard a loud banging. I jumped up and, as soon as I opened the door, the youth pushed his way in carrying a sack with something moving inside it. He looked me up and down in surprise.

'You're not Mila!'

He turned around quickly and made his way back out through the door.

'Sorry, wrong house.'

But handouts from the young burglar were not enough. I felt really defeated and I feared for Willem's health. We had nothing – no heating, and winter was approaching. We were living on scraps and I had to get money from somewhere to keep us going until Arnoldús got back from his voyage. I hadn't spoken to the van Wijks for a long time, but I had to ask if they could help, even though they disliked me. I expected them to refuse, but they didn't and we were able to struggle on until Arnoldús came home. When he did, I ran to the market to buy food, as we were starving. I felt bad on the way there and vomited on the side of the road, even though there was nothing in my stomach.

I stayed with Arnoldús for as long as I could. It was not his fault that I still loved Vincent and not him. His father died and we moved in with his mother at Verlaatstraat 30, which was better for Willem. I stayed there until the children were grown – until Maria Wilhelmina was twenty-seven and left to work as a nurse in Maastricht – and Willem was twenty and training to be a draughtsman at the state water works.

Then it was time for me to go.

Love is a much-maligned word, is it not? People think carnality is love, but it isn't. You love your dog or your children – that's love. The thing between a man and a woman is not love, has nothing to do with love. It has something to do with movement and smell and taste and touch and sound and sense and light and dark and addiction and compulsion and violence and hope and despair. But it has nothing to do with love.

Carnality with Arnoldús was infrequent to begin with and then non-existent – not on his part, but on mine. I'd had enough of it in my life – I didn't want any more. Maybe it was because I never felt affection when we were doing it – with him or any man – except Vincent. It wasn't his fault.

I'd been brought to eternity's gate by the gember man and nobody would ever match that again.

# CHAPTER 30

# SORROW

The mystery of life should not be a problem to be solved, just a reality to be experienced – if there is such a thing as experience. The pendulum clock continued to tick. Sometimes I didn't hear it. Other times it sounded like a hammer striking an anvil. Every tick an exploding second – every tock a dying moment. What was there before the world began? What will come after it? What will fill the space left behind – the time still to come? Does time exist at all, or is it just something we created when we began to measure it? Maybe everything really just is. That's all.

I heard the vibration of the cosmos and I called it love and wanted to go to it – needed to go to it – needed to dissolve in it – it called me home. Nothing was lived, everything was relived – in the same way that all events are interlinked with each other – are part of each other – become each other – die and are reborn as each other. Real love is the shedding of old feelings, emotions, longings, wants, and the knowledge that there will be no more turbulence.

An exhibition of Vincent's work opened at Rotterdam's Oldenzeel Gallery, just about a kilometre from where I lived on Verlaatstraat, but I did not go. Émíle Bernard wrote sketches of the gember man's life for *La Plume*, even though he knew nothing of that life. And there were articles about Vincent by Octave Mirbeau in *L'Écho de Paris* and by others in *De Portefeuille* and *Les Hommes D'aujourd'hui*. Johanna Bonger, the widow of Theo van Gogh, had begun to find recognition for Vincent's work, beating down the high walls of convention that had always condemned his art. She financed a series of exhibitions after she moved to Bussum in the Het Gooi region with her son and married the painter Johan Gosschalk.

Vincent's letters to his brother and others were also being discovered – but sections of them from his time with me were missing and some sections were cut or obliterated or destroyed by his family. They did not want the truth to be known about Vincent's relationship with me and his son. They painted us out of the picture – the canvas of Vincent's life. And that was fine – I didn't want to be associated with the self-righteous and sanctimonious. But I did want to be known as a person in my own right and my story was Vincent's and Vincent's story was mine.

The gember man told me once that, if he ever committed suicide, it would be by drowning – that was the most artistic way to go. He did not get the choice.

$$\text{(5)}$$

Before I set out for the harbour on this freezing night in November, I have one more ritual to perform in his honour. I put the silver ring Vincent gave me on the middle finger of my left hand, so they will recognise my body when they find it. Then I take a razor and slice my right ear off. Vincent had sliced off his left ear, so I thought it appropriate that I do the opposite side – like Saint Peter asking to be crucified upside down, because he was not worthy to be killed in the same manner as Jesus.

I wrap the ear in newspaper, just as Vincent had, and put it in my pocket. I wrap a bandage round my head to staunch the bleeding, so as not to attract attention on the way.

Then I step outside.

I walk through a park to the Kerk of Sint Eduard the Martyr. It's very late and there is no one about – no priests, that I can see. I stand in the nave and look up towards the altar.

Then I pray.

I am not yet born. O fill me. With strength against those who would freeze my humanity, would dragoon me into a lethal automaton, would make me a cog in a machine, a thing with one face, a thing. And against all those who would dissipate my entirety, would blow me like thistledown hither and thither. Or hither and thither like water held in the hands would spill me.

'Hallo … '

I turn to see a young priest behind me.

'Are you alright?'

'I'm fine Father.'

'You look pale.'

'I'm alright.'

'There's blood on your clothes … '

'Just a small cut Father … you know how these things bleed.'

'You should go to the hospital. What happened?'

'I'll go there in a while. I'm just saying a prayer first Father.'

'We haven't seen you here before.'

'That's because I don't believe in heaven.'

This remark takes him by surprise. He obviously thinks I'm an insane person and he leaves me alone. I try to remember my prayer, the one I was saying to myself before he interrupted me. My concentration is broken and it takes me a while to get it back.

Let them not make me a stone and let them not spill me. Otherwise kill me.

I can see some movement towards the rear of the church – heads bobbing up and then down again. It's the priest, with some politie. I make my way slowly to a small side door and slip out, as the figures come closer in the gloom of the old kerk – hushed voices, drunk on dogma. I slide the bolt across so they can't follow, then creep along Kievitslaan. It is time to get to the water – do it there as I intended in the first place. Do it in the early hours. In the pearly hours. The diamond drops of misty morningtime. Do it with dignity. Kill myself with kindness.

I move west into Gaffeldwarsstraat and continue down through Breitnerstraat. Although I'm determined, I feel confused at the same time and want to get it over and done with. No more prevarication. No more mockery.

I move erratically to confuse anyone who might be following – sure I can see the uniforms of the politie behind me, although it's probably just my imagination. I increase the speed of my steps through the late-night streets – along Rochussenstraat and across through an open, derelict area. I come to a sudden halt on a deserted street – I can remember this place. A small dark memory at the back of my mind. Delicate. Skindeep. No – that was Delft. But the Penoze are after me, so I can't stay long enough to think about it. The alleyways around this part of the city swallow me up and I decide I must have lost whoever might be following. I look around to see if anyone is acting suspiciously. Anyone? Nothing. Nobody. I am alone.

I think I'm in The Hague again, where I'm drowning in despair. Being dragged down and drowned in a sea of slouching people and the swirl of apathy and indifference – a private world of pathos and piety. I wander around like a lost soul. Bounce about. Forget where I'm going and where I've come from.

I meander down along Gravendijkwal and find my way to a green place where I sit on a bench near a monument. It's a familiar bench, the one Vincent drew so long ago? The little bench with crooked legs and a leafless tree behind? He used a pencil and a pen, with brown ink on paper, but the tree looked strange – its roots seeming to have a life of their own, roots that were only visible in Vincent's imagination. Maria Wilhelmina and I sat on that bench twenty-two years ago, while Vincent drew us in another sketch, with other figures sitting – four altogether. I feel safe in here, behind the iron railings, looking out at the night city all around me – a motionless tableau of sight and sound and smell.

No – that was another place.

I can feel the fear. The mistrust. I can taste the turbulence, sense it. It tastes like death. I witness crimes of violence in the blood-air and hear screams in the silent street-music and smell decay in the unique perfume of purgatory. I sit on the unfamiliar bench with my head in my hands. I sob, and tears fall from my eyes onto the short winter grass.

I sit for a long time. Dawn is breaking to the east before I force myself to make a move. I know I have to get somewhere. I've been out all night and Maria Wilhelmina will be alone again. I wander back out of the park in the middle of the dockland area and look around. Which way should I go? I can't be sure. I go south along Westerlaan. It's murky here. Dark and dangerous. Strange sorts staring at me with deadly eyes. I change direction several times. The eyes still follow me. Everywhere. They know I'm a streetwalker. Hoer! Tramp! Straatmadelief!

I cower on a corner until the noise in my head abates. Then I continue to walk in the pale early-light. Morning people are out and about now, going to work or to market. I move past a school and a group of girls comes towards me. Laughing. Excited about some young-girl thing, shining in the softness du matin. One of them I know from somewhere. Once. Before. A small face holding on to my hand as the dogs along Schoolstraat bark at us as we trudge through the cold. Our clogs making soft scraping noises on the snow-covered cobbles and our breath coming in steamy jets, forming little clouds in the freezing air. Her coughing – hungry, but I have nothing to feed her with, nowhere for her to rest her head, no shelter from the cold.

'Maria Wilhelmina … ?'

The girls look at me with a mixture of fear and bemusement and step out into the street to get past. Hysterical giggling behind hands. They glance back over their shoulders. I call out after them.

'Maria Wilhelmina.'

They stop and turn to stare at me. One of them points a frightened finger. Looks at me with nervous eyes. Knowing but not wanting to know. Denying?

'How do you know my name? Who are you?'

'I'm … '

'You're a dirty hoer! Don't you come near me!'

'I'm … '

'You're disgusting … covered in filth and blood. If you come near me I'll scream. I'll call for the politie. If you come near me … I'll have you arrested.'

Denied. Like Christ. The girl turns and rejoins her friends. They continue on their way with words like beggar and tramp and mad floating after them, fading into the morning mist and disappearing from sight and sound. I feel my heart beat faster. Heart. Beat. There is no anger in me, no regret, just a deep sadness. A deep, deep, deep, deep sadness. Like black velvet. Wrapping itself around me. And I remember what it is I have to do.

I find myself at the harbourside – a canal on Provenierssingel, just north of the central station, close to an ornamental garden. A familiar voice speaks to me.

'Sien?'

'It's me Vincent. I'm home.'

'Why did you take so long?'

'I had to wait for the children to grow.'

'How is Willem?'

'He's well. They call him Willem van Wijk now.'

'Not Willem van Gogh?'

'No.'

'Why not?'

'You know why not.'

My ear begins to bleed again. I put my hand up to the side of my head. Blood seeps through my fingers. I know why I'm here and I hear the sound. I listen and hear it again. The musical note, played on a lute string. Not a melody or tune, just a single note. I understand its symmetry – its meaning. All music is inherent in that one tone – like religion. It's the sound of my soul, trying to break free and fulfil itself in an eternal present, not in a past that never was or a future that will never be. It calls to me – lures me into its strange, enchanted essence. Everything is quiet. Otherworldly. Eternal. Time is standing still, here on the side of the harbour canal. I hear the words of the old heks, speaking to me from the water.

'You belong in your own world, Sien.'

'How do I get there?'

'You are already there.'

Vincent sings to me – music fills the air and I float on its changing colours. My heart is light again as I listen to his voice in the dreamlight morning. He sings a peasant song. It reminds me of the egg dance I saw when I was young. We dance and I can feel his breath on my neck – him singing, humming, to the music in my mind. I'm weak from my life on this earth, but I do not try to resist. I allow my mind to whirl inside my head. His voice has a silver sound, humming words from another world I've known so well. He holds my hand so I won't fly away and it feels as if we are now one, together again – at last. Joined. Dark and light – or dark and darker. Midnight and crow-black. Two halves of the same whole. Part of that inevitable primal force. And I feel an ecstasy I've known before and always knew I would feel again – some day. That day is now. Birds fly around my head and make me forget the world. They sing a song of life, to accompany my soul on its journey.

The time for my final dream is now. They said I was full of evil, but I was only a dreamer – like you, Vincent.

You were like me Sien, you had a direct link to God. Those people didn't understand, none of them. The bullet set me free, Sien. The water will do the same for you. Do not ask who made God – ask who makes God. Who makes God is God. The sun was once God. And still is. You are your own creator, Sien – of God and time, and you wear both like a ball and chain – measure them and carry them with you. But they are illusions.

I need to recognise what I'm seeing, Vincent – and what I'm not seeing.

There is a rock, a kilometre high and a kilometre wide and a kilometre deep and a small bird comes every hundred years to sharpen its beak. When the rock is gone – has been worn away – then you may begin to see. When your body feels as if it is closing in on itself – growing more dense – more tightly packed – like a piece of condensed coal. Like something that can be held in the hand. And squeezed. Packed tighter and tighter. Crushed. Ground down smaller and smaller. Not human any more. Inhuman. That is you – and your God.

Now I find myself standing on the edge of the canal, trapped inside my own body – but not for much longer. I long to be out of it – to escape from it. To leave a life where nothing could be taken for granted. Where anything could occur in its turmoil – like on a battlefield – where every soldier believes death will visit the next man, not him – otherwise he would never fight. Where many die unprepared. I needed to use my time in that life more wisely. If I do nothing with today, it is because I believe I have many more days. I believe I could spare one – or two – or a hundred. I never asked – what if tomorrow were to be the final day of my life? Would I have wasted today?

There is danger around every bend in the road – behind every tree in the forest – in every man's smile – in every woman's eyes. The danger is everywhere. It is constant. It makes me lose touch with language – and love – and logic. And the wall of dreams gets higher, so high it is impossible to ever break out. The terminal isolation of delusion looks over that wall. And says – suicide.

Carve your failure in stone!

I have seen the fall from Eden. I know the real trauma of that forgotten moment, when man stepped out of the darkness and into time. The sky was full of fire. The fundamental forces of nature were all around. I was part of all things. The reality I observed was altered by the act of observation and I had to choose my own path through the forest of lightness that flowed into me. Filled me. Became me. And now I can stand naked in the cosmos and shout, 'I know that I know.'

Now. And most people do not die – they are killed. On street corners. In cardboard boxes. Scraping out waste bins. Exploited. Lied to by the callous and uncaring. Scavenging scarecrows in barren wastelands and polluted hinterlands – being robbed and ravished and reduced to dust.

The real nature of Human?

I look up at the fading stars, as I promised Vincent I would after he was dead. I see him, as he promised I would, through the holes in the sky.

I jump. The water is black and cold, yet I am warm.

The last thing Vincent painted was a gothic church in Auvers – with no door and a woman walking away with her back to him. The church is French, but the woman is Dutch.

Look at it – I am that woman.

*'A man who was dying asked to be left alone with his wife.*
*When they were alone, he embraced her and said, "I loved you."*
*Then he died.'*

Vincent van Gogh

# GLOSSARY

Abhean – god of artists
Advocat – lawyer
Amour éternal – eternal love
Akavit – alcoholic drink, similar to
vodka
Alleluja Den Blijden Toon – Dutch
ecclesiastical song
Alouette – lark (bird)
Amoureuse – lover (female)
Armenhuis – workhouse
Au Charbonnage – At The
Coalmine
Bastaard – bastard
Banketletter – Dutch pastry
Bier – beer
Bordeel – brothel
Bourgeois – middle class
Brauche – herbal healing
Bron en herkomst – source and
origin
Cantiniére – loose woman
Chanson – song
Cordon sanitaire – sanitation
De aardappeleters – the potato
eaters
De Druif – The Grape
Demi-monde – half-world
De Plezierkoepel – The Pleasure
Dome
De Portefeuille – The Portfolio
Drugsverslaafde – drug addict
Du matin – of the morning
Du néant à l'éternite – from
nothingness to eternity

L'Écho de Paris – French newspaper
Een Kindelien so Loovelick –
traditional children's song
Entente cordiale – friendly
agreement
Erwtensoep – pea soup
Fait accompli – already done
Fanchon – Dutch lady's hat
Fièvre chaude – hot fever
Fizz – match
Geef mij de liefde – give me the love
Gember – ginger
Geluksbrenger – good luck charm
Genièvre brûlé – burnt juniper (gin
cocktail)
Gentille – kind
Gérant – manager
Gevangenis – jail
Gewone – ordinary
Giaour – infidel/pagan
Grachten – canals
Grootmoeder – grandmother
Grote – great
Guilder – Dutch coin
Hand baan – masturbation
Heiden – a pagan
Heks – witch
Herberg – a hostel
Het is een nacht – it is a night
Het Jeneverhuis – The Gin House
Het Kasteel – The Castle
Het Rode Licht – The Red Light
Histoire d'amour – love affair

Hoe leit dit kindeke – how lies this little child

Hoer – whore

Hofvijer – a lake in The Hague

Holbewoners – cavemen

Hollandesche Maatschappij van Landbouw – Dutch Society of Agriculture

Hündin – bitch

Hutspot – mashed potato, carrot and onion

Ik geloof in God, de almachtige vader, schepper van hemel en aarde, en in Jezus Christus, zijn enige zoon – I believe in God, the almighty father, creator of heaven and earth, and in Jesus Christ, his only son.

Ik moet pissen – I need to piss

Jenever – Dutch gin

Jongen – boy

Kabouter – gnome

Karn melk – churn milk

Kelder – cellar

Kerk – church

Kerstbrood – Christmas bread

Kerstmis – Christmas

Kind – child

Klant – customer

Klapstuk – a kind of pot roast

Kleintje – measurement of beer

Klootzak – asshole

Kluiten – clods

Knecht – servant

Koekamp – park in The Hague

Kont – buttocks

Kroeg – a Dutch bar

Krùide baggâh – Dutch moonshine

Kruidnoot – spice nut

Kutje – vagina

L'amour c'est la vie – love is life

Lang zal hij leven – long will he live

*La Plume* [*The Feather*]– French art magazine,

Le Chahut – lewd version of the cancan

*Le Faute de l'Abbé Mouret* [*Abbé Mouret's Transgression*] by Emile Zola

Le fou roux – the red fool

Le jeune monsieur qui n'etait pas comme toutes autres – the young man who was different

*Le Sens de la Vie* [*The Meaning of Life*] by Edourad Rod (1889)

*Les Hommes D'aujourd'hui* [*The Men of Today*]– French journal

Lotbestemming – destiny

Luie – lazy

Mahlstick – artist stick

Maladie de cœur – heartache

Maréchaussée – 19th century Dutch military police

Meijendel – wild pasture (national park)

Meisje – girl

Meneer – sir

Métier – job

Mode de vie – way of life

Moeder – mother

Nationale en Internationale Tentoonstelling – National & International Exhibition

Ne vous en faites pas, nous ne serons pas long – don't worry, we won't be long

Neten – nits

Neuken – fucking

Niflheim – Norse world of darkness

Nom de guerre – war name

Ontspannen – laid back

Onwetend – ignorant

Oude Rode Ogen – Old Red Eyes

Ouvre la porte, salope! – Open the door, bitch!

Paardereet – horse's ass

Pakjesavond – Dutch "parcel evening"

Pappje – dad
Parvenu – nouveau riche
Pepernoot – gingerbread
Pierement – street organ
Pietà – religious picture
Pinksterliedje – song of the Whitsun flower
Poffertjes – Dutch pancakes
Politie – police
Politieagent – policeman
Reine des trottoirs – queen of the sidewalks
Pierreuse/lorette/gigolette – French terms for prostitute
Raison d'être – reason for existence
Reposante – restful
Riepe Garste – lively traditional Dutch dance, lots of foot stamping and hand clapping
Riveriervismarkt – a fish market in The Hague
Rood licht – red light
Rookworst – smoked sausage
Santon – nativity figure
Schele – cross-eyed
Schilderonzin – crap painter
Sepia – brown pigment
Serveerster – a waitress
Sint-Jacobskerk – St James' Church
Skotse Trije – lively traditional Dutch folksong, usually accompanied by accordions
Sinterklass – Father Christmas
Snert – pea soup
Snoep – candy
Souteneur – pimp

Straat – street
Straatmadelief – prostitute
Stamppot – stew
Stuiver – Dutch coin, one-twentieth of a guilder
Talonneuse – hooker
Tandarts – dentist
Taverne – bar/café
Teef – dog (bitch)
Tempo rubato – musical term to denote the perfomer is free from the set pace
Tranquille – peaceful
Trui – sweater
Uitsmijter – Dutch breakfast with egg
Vader – father
Verstoppertje – hide and seek
Vihansa – goddess of struggle
Vrouw – woman
Waarzegster – fortune teller
Waterzooi – Belgian stew
Winterpeen – winter vegetables, mainly carrot
Wittewijven – spirits of "white women" in Dutch mythology, who took children
Yodi – Chinese symbol for a bond between two people
Zedelijkheidwet – morality law
Zigeuner – gypsy
Zigevner – a Roma gypsy
Zus – sister
Zwarte Piet – Black Pete
Zwerver – tramp

*Als tranen een trap konden bouwen* – If tears could build a staircase
*En herinneringen een weg* – And memories a lane
*Ik zou regelrecht naar de hemel lopen* – I would walk right up to heaven
*En bring je weer terug* – And bring you home again

# LAUREN FRANCES
## Author and Artist

Lauren is an avant-garde artist whose work has been the subject of book covers, exhibitions and was even used on Paris streets during the "yellow vest" protests in 2018. Her emerging work is seen as the next "big thing" to hit the commercial art world and she has been likened in style to Andy Warhol and in originality to Banksy. She has art exhibitions scheduled in London, Paris and Tokyo.

Lauren has an extensive knowledge of the work of Vincent van Gogh and is a student and admirer of his.

*Sien* is her debut novel, planned as the first in a trilogy. The second book, *The Van Gogh Veil*, is a novel about Willem, the son of Sien and Van Gogh who was given away by his mother and never acknowledged. The third, *Maria Wilhelmina*, is a novel about the life of Sien's daughter who lived with Sien and Van Gogh.

Lauren is also working on a thriller series about **Maddy Murphy**, a hard-nosed freelance journalist who follows the stories the tabloid hacks ignore. This leads her into dark places, but she's a tough lady and able to take care of herself.

*www.instagram.com/labhrai*

Lightning Source UK Ltd.
Milton Keynes UK
UKHW011909290621
386378UK00001B/59

9 780995 751583